Hearts
of
Steel

Books by Elizabeth Camden

THE BLACKSTONE LEGACY

Carved in Stone
Written on the Wind
Hearts of Steel

HOPE AND GLORY SERIES

The Spice King
A Gilded Lady
The Prince of Spies

The Lady of Bolton Hill
The Rose of Winslow Street
Against the Tide
Into the Whirlwind
With Every Breath
Beyond All Dreams
Toward the Sunrise: An Until the Dawn *Novella*
Until the Dawn
Summer of Dreams: A From This Moment *Novella*
From This Moment
To the Farthest Shores
A Dangerous Legacy
A Daring Venture
A Desperate Hope

Hearts of Steel

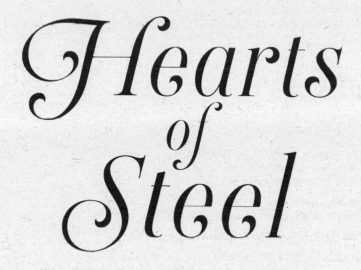

ELIZABETH CAMDEN

BETHANYHOUSE

a division of Baker Publishing Group
Minneapolis, Minnesota

© 2023 by Dorothy Mays

Published by Bethany House Publishers
Minneapolis, Minnesota
www.bethanyhouse.com

Bethany House Publishers is a division of
Baker Publishing Group, Grand Rapids, Michigan

Printed in the United States of America

Library of Congress Cataloging-in-Publication Data
Names: Camden, Elizabeth, author.
Title: Hearts of steel / Elizabeth Camden.
Description: Minneapolis, Minnesota : Bethany House, a division of Baker
    Publishing Group, [2023] | Series: The Blackstone legacy ; 3
Identifiers: LCCN 2022023118 | ISBN 9780764238451 (paperback) | ISBN
    9780764241307 (casebound) | ISBN 9781493440610 (ebook)
Subjects: LCGFT: Historical fiction. | Novels.
Classification: LCC PS3553.A429 H43 2023 | DDC 813/.54—dc23
LC record available at https://lccn.loc.gov/2022023118

This is a work of historical reconstruction; the appearances of certain historical figures are therefore inevitable. All other characters, however, are products of the author's imagination, and any resemblance to actual persons, living or dead, is coincidental.

Cover design by Jennifer Parker
Bridge photography by Thomas Lehne / lotuseaters / Alamy Stock Photo
Cover model photography by Mike Habermann Photography, LLC

Baker Publishing Group publications use paper produced from sustainable forestry practices and post-consumer waste whenever possible.

23 24 25 26 27 28 29   7 6 5 4 3 2 1

Prologue

*M*aggie Molinaro was five blocks from the safety of her uncle's garage when she noticed the gang of boys following her. Boys or young men? It was hard to tell, but they looked mangy and tough, and she shoved her ice cream pushcart faster on the crowded Manhattan sidewalk. The umbrella made wheeling the heavy cart awkward, and the boys were gaining on her.

"Hey, how about an ice cream, girlie?"

They wouldn't have called her girlie if her father were here. Maggie had been working this pushcart since leaving school last year when she was fifteen, but this was the first time she'd gone out alone. Normally she and her father worked as a team, but not today, and the last mile home went through a rough part of town. Dilapidated tenements towered over the buckled concrete walks, making it hard to move quickly.

Jeering from the boys got more aggressive, and she picked up her pace, desperate to reach her uncle's tenement. Uncle Dino sank all his money into his fledgling pushcart business, and he would scare those boys away.

She swallowed hard, regretting how she told Dino she'd be meeting her father at Washington Square, and it was okay to take the pushcart out alone. It was a lie. Everyone knew that if her father missed one more shift, Dino would fire him, and nobody wanted that. Until last year they all had shared a crowded tenement room, but she and her father had to move out because her dad complained Dino had too many rules.

Maggie didn't mind Dino's rules. Dino never had to lie or cheat to make rent. Dino never had to beg for scraps at the soup kitchen because he spent all his money at the pub. Someday Maggie wanted to buy a pushcart of her own and follow in Uncle Dino's footsteps, yet everything would go sour if he had to fire her dad.

She tried to move faster, but other pushcarts crowding the walk blocked her progress. An arm landed around her neck as the stink of dirty wool hit her nose.

"I said, how about an ice cream, girlie?"

"I don't have any left." She mashed the palm of her hand against the top drawer to protect the cashbox. The loan on the pushcart was due tomorrow, and no matter what, she had to protect the cashbox.

The arm around her neck tightened. "Check it out, Jamie."

One of the other boys opened the cart's lid and reached a dirty hand into the cold compartment. "Lookee here," he said, grabbing a few bars of ice cream and tossing them to the others. Then he reached down again and grabbed a lump of melting ice.

"Catch," he said, lobbing it at her face. She gasped and batted it away. The ringleader lunged for the cash drawer, but she got there first and slammed it shut.

"You've got what you wanted, now leave me alone," she said, her hands beginning to shake.

"You think we got what we wanted? Think again."

An old man selling pretzels from a nearby cart stepped forward. "Leave her alone, lads."

They circled in closer, and her mouth went dry. She shouldn't have tried to do this without her dad, and now the boys had circled her cart, bracing it in place. The ringleader tried for the cash drawer again.

"Get your hands off my cart," she ordered, trying to sound strong.

"Leave that girl alone," a woman scolded, but she was wheeling a baby carriage and moved along quickly. Other pedestrians looked on with disapproval, though no one helped as the jackals swarmed her cart. She pressed both hands against the cash drawer, but it didn't take them long to wrench her away. A gloating boy grabbed the cashbox, tucked it under his arm and sprinted away, but they weren't done.

"Okay, stand aside," the ringleader said and grabbed the handles of the cart. Understanding dawned.

"No!" she shouted, clutching a handlebar with both hands, holding on for dear life. The ringleader pounded on her hands. She didn't care if he broke her fingers, she wasn't letting go.

"Help! Somebody please help me!"

Nobody came forward, and the boys kept shoving the cart down the street. She hung on, trying to dig her heels into the pavement, but it didn't work and she was dragged along with the cart.

"Send for the police," the pretzel vendor called out, and the ringleader upped his game. He punched her in the jaw. While the pain made it hard to see, she held on. One of them kicked her legs, and the ringleader drew back to punch her again. She couldn't let go of the cart to defend herself and the blow knocked her down. Her face smacked the metal rim of the cart before hitting the pavement.

"Help!" she screamed. Blood streamed into her eyes, blurring her vision. By the time she scrambled to her feet, the boys were a block away with the pushcart. She ran after them but stumbled on a crack in the walk and went down sprawling. They had everything. She was never going to catch them. The pretzel vendor put an arm around her.

"There, there, it's going to be okay," he said.

No, it wasn't. Uncle Dino still owed two hundred dollars on that cart. The payment was due tomorrow, and he wouldn't be able to pay.

Everything hurt as she struggled to her feet. Grit embedded in her palms itched, but her forehead hurt the worst, pulsating like a white-hot knife across her eyebrow. Blood stung as it dribbled into her eye. A lady from a nearby shop brought her a lump of ice wrapped in a rag to hold to her forehead.

"Oh dear, I'm afraid you're going to have a scar from this," she said. "Such a pretty face you had."

Maggie didn't care about a scar. All she cared about was how to tell Uncle Dino that she'd lost everything.

Pain throbbed with every step on the long trek home. The ice in the rag melted, the cut still bleeding after walking the five blocks to the garage in a back alley, where other street vendors locked up their carts overnight.

Dino was inside, wiping down his cart and happily singing a church hymn, his Italian accent still strong. He stopped singing when he saw her face. He dropped the rag and ran to her.

"Oh, *bambina*, what happened?" He led her to a bench, and her aunt rushed to her side. Maggie would give anything if she didn't have to tell them. She couldn't do it.

"I'm sorry" was all she could choke out.

"Somebody got the cashbox?" Dino asked gently. She nodded, and he cringed a little, probably thinking he'd only lost a day's income when it was so much worse. Her stomach hurt at the thought of telling him. Her lungs seized up and she couldn't speak.

"Where's your father?" Aunt Julie asked. Maggie couldn't look at either one of them, instead staring at the concrete floor.

"He was drunk," she whispered, still not able to look up. Dino didn't deserve this. Dino had worked hard all his life and done everything right, yet he needed to know.

"They got the cart," she choked out, and Dino groaned as if he'd been shot. Then he hugged her. *He hugged her!*

"I'm so sorry," she sobbed. "I'm so very sorry."

"Shhhh," Dino soothed. "We'll figure something out."

The bank had little mercy, insisting that Dino was still responsible for the loan on the stolen cart. Her uncle asked for an extension on the loan, and the bank gave him two weeks to make up the shortfall or else their other cart would be repossessed.

Maggie and Dino worked their single pushcart all day, then moved it to Broadway to sell ice cream to theatergoers at night. They worked from sunrise until midnight each day, but with only a single cart, they couldn't make up the shortfall.

Dino sold his queen-sized bed and dining room table to make good on the loan. He and Julie had to sleep on the floor, but the sale of their furniture let them save the one remaining pushcart.

Maggie and Dino continued their fourteen-hour days to earn as much as possible from that last pushcart, and by the end of the summer they had paid off its loan.

A year later, they had saved enough to buy a second pushcart and paid for it in cash. Never again would they be at the mercy of the bank. But even with two pushcarts fully paid for, they did not ease up on their schedule. They hired a wiry, middle-aged man named Spider Mackenzie to help staff the carts. Though Spider had a terrible name, he was a tireless worker. With both pushcarts on the same fourteen-hour schedule, their fortunes began to turn, and soon they were ready to buy a third cart.

Every dime of profit was reinvested back into the business. Within five years they had a fleet of twelve pushcarts and twenty-five employees, selling ice cream all over Manhattan. They operated the carts from ten o'clock in the morning until midnight when the Theater District closed. They were earning money hand over fist, but through it all, Maggie never lost her fear of debt. She and Dino never bought anything unless they could pay for it in cash.

Their success did not come without setbacks. Her father continued to drink, even though it had been eight years since Maggie's mother died and it could no longer be used as an excuse for his drunkenness. He tried to sober up, but one night he broke into Dino's locked desk drawer and stole everything inside to buy a ticket back to Italy. She hadn't heard from him since.

It had hurt, both financially and spiritually. Maggie had been born right here in New York and would never consider leaving, but the incident taught her to always have enough cash squirreled away for emergencies. The theft meant she and Dino had to dig into their savings to pay their employees at the end of the week, and it had been a costly lesson.

The work was exhausting, but as the years passed, the sweat, toil, and long hours became a strange sort of joy. Maybe that wasn't the right word. *Pride? Accomplishment?* Whatever the word, by the time Maggie turned twenty she had learned to love her job. It was a thrill each time she sold ice cream to a child giddy with delight. Balancing the accounting ledger at the end of the month felt like a triumph. Every time she banked a little more money, it fueled her ambition to cut costs, streamline the business, and earn more. Spider taught her how to disassemble the pushcarts down to their components to clean, oil, and repair them, and the satisfaction from keeping their equipment in flawless order was also a thrill.

From Dino she learned the importance of a positive attitude. She saw it every day when customers walked past other ice cream vendors to patronize Dino's cart because he greeted everyone with booming, buoyant good cheer. People were drawn to Dino because he loved everyone and everything. He danced to celebrate a sunny day, and he also danced to welcome the rain. It simply wasn't possible to stay in a gloomy mood when Dino Molinaro was nearby.

From Aunt Julie, Maggie learned how to dream. Julie could always see beyond the sooty streets and their dank little apartment to imagine what life could be like if they kept working hard. Like a master storyteller spinning daydreams, Julie spoke of someday opening an ice cream parlor, where they could sell to customers who came to them instead of pushing carts all over the city to chase down business. Julie dreamed of creating a haven where people could relax in a spotlessly clean parlor that felt like home.

The opportunity to make it happen came when Maggie saw a storefront for lease on Gadsen Street. The four-story brick building had a bright, sunny retail space that could be turned into an ice cream parlor, but even more tempting was the dairy operation making butter and cheese in the back. If they leased the creamery, they could start making their own ice cream instead of buying it from a supplier.

Dino signed a one-year lease on the shop and the creamery. Aunt Julie began making ice cream from her own recipes in the creamery, and it was *good*. The best in the city! Julie's signature recipes made the Molinaro Ice Cream Parlor the most popular restaurant on Gadsen Street, with so many customers they bought tables for the sidewalk to accommodate the overflow.

Maggie and Spider built flower boxes to spiff up the outside of the shop, filling the planters with delphiniums, petunias, and trailing vines of ivy. The largest planter was reserved for Uncle Dino's olive tree, which he'd brought as a cutting from Tuscany, but it was as tall as Maggie now. Seeing this Tuscan olive tree flourishing among the towering buildings and worn cobblestones of Manhattan was a testament to the spirit of survival, and Maggie smiled at it each morning when she arrived for work.

The only weakness in their business was that they couldn't make ice cream fast enough to stock their fleet of pushcarts. Hand-churned ice cream was a labor-intensive product, and they didn't have the equipment to speed up operations. They still had to buy ice cream for the pushcarts from a supplier, and it ate into their profits. Maggie dreamed about what it might be like to someday own a real factory with modern equipment. While most women her age dreamed of marriage and family, Maggie fantasized about the day she could afford to buy an ice cream factory.

Dino was content with his life, but Maggie could never achieve the level of security she wanted by selling other people's ice cream. Every time she paid the ice cream bill, she thought of how much more they could earn if they bought newfangled machinery to make ice cream faster and cheaper but every bit as good because they'd still be using Aunt Julie's recipes.

Then came the morning their landlord announced he was putting the building up for sale, and Maggie spotted her chance. If they owned the building, they could invest in expensive machinery that would eventually pay for itself and make them richer than ever before.

Dino wasn't interested in buying the building because it meant taking out a loan, and he refused to go into debt, but Maggie worried about Dino, especially after his back seized up while simply leaning over to lift a bucket of ice cream. How could they ever feel safe if a simple injury could land Dino flat on his back for a week? They both feared debt, yet the advantages of owning the building were huge.

"There's a nice apartment upstairs," she said. "We can move in and save on rent. We won't have to lease the ice cream shop because *we will own it*. Then we can buy real factory equipment and supply not just the pushcarts but expand the business to supply every hotel and restaurant within miles of this building. Dino . . . we could be rich!"

Though Dino was tempted, he still worried about the burden of a loan. "Buying the building would be hard enough, but we'd still need a second loan for the factory. We already have more than enough. Look around you . . . we're happy, aren't we?"

Were they? Sometimes Maggie snapped awake in the middle of the night, fearing the world they'd built could come crashing down. In the quiet of the night, she lay awake and wondered what it would be like to live without fear. Sliding back into poverty was always one injury or one theft away, and she redoubled her efforts to persuade Dino.

"I want us all to have a big nest egg so we can finally be safe," she said, but Dino's sigh was heavy.

"Oh, Maggie, will there ever be enough to soothe the worries you've got rolling around in your head?"

Maybe not, but she didn't mind working hard to earn more. She *liked* working! She spent weeks going over their finances and calculating the costs for the equipment and interest on the loan. Long after the ice cream parlor closed for the night, she and Dino sat at a table, the lantern casting a warm glow around them as they studied their account books and a map of the city.

"There are eight hotels in walking distance," Dino said. "If we can supply ice cream to half of them, it will earn as much as the pushcarts do." Maggie studied the restaurants, theaters, and cafés marked on the map. All of them might buy their ice cream, if only she could ramp up production, but first they needed to conquer their fear of debt and build a factory.

"It's always been you and me, Dino," she said, hope beginning to bloom. "I know we can make it work, but I don't want to do it without you."

His smile was equal parts fear, hope, and anticipation, and after a week of analyzing their accounts, he finally agreed to her plan.

On her twenty-sixth birthday, Maggie put on her finest suit and bought a brand-new straw boater hat with a matching hatband. She looked as spiffy as any other person of business as she strode into the bank with Dino beside her. He twisted his cap and looked anxious, but Maggie was resolved. She walked into the bank manager's office with her shoulders back, eyes confident.

"I want to build an ice cream factory," she announced.

It was the start of their new life, and there would be no turning back.

1

*T*he prospect of apologizing to the only enemy Liam Blackstone had in the world was galling, but he'd do it to keep Fletcher's respect. Liam strode down the street alongside his mentor, listening to Fletcher's reasons he should apologize to Charles Morse, possibly the biggest scoundrel in the city.

"The point of yesterday's outing was to have a cordial afternoon sailing in the harbor so you and Charles could bury the hatchet, not to stir up new resentments," Fletcher said. "Throwing him off your yacht opened up a whole new front in the war between the two of you."

"He slapped a seventeen-year-old deckhand," Liam bit out.

"Yes, and that was regrettable, but there were better ways to handle it than letting your temper fly off the handle."

Yesterday's fight had been a doozy. The afternoon sailing excursion on Liam's private yacht had collapsed quickly after Morse struck the deckhand, a sweet kid named Caleb. While Caleb could be a little slow, once he understood a task, the kid carried it out doggedly and never tired. The problem was that Caleb couldn't adjust. Any change to his routine got Caleb flustered, which was what happened when Morse started banging out orders yesterday.

They had been a mile out at sea when Morse slapped Caleb. Liam ordered Morse to be rowed ashore, and the incident cast a pall over the rest of the afternoon. Several of the other businessmen aboard the vessel privately commended Liam for the way he protected the deckhand, but no one approved of what he'd done in throwing Morse off the yacht.

Now Fletcher was dragging Liam to Morse's home like a disobedient child to apologize. The Morse estate squatted on a large plot on the richest part of Fifth Avenue. It was where robber barons flaunted their wealth in grandiose palaces towering five stories high with molded entablatures, spires, and turrets . . . so different from the slum where Liam grew up.

"I understand you are still new in the world of Wall Street," Fletcher said. "Everyone appreciates the fresh perspective you have brought to the board of directors. You are the only one among us who has actually worked at a steel mill or made anything with your own two hands. Against all odds you persuaded the board of directors to authorize a huge pay raise for the men in the steel mills—"

"Over Morse's objections."

"Yes! Charles Morse is the shrewdest man on Wall Street, and you got the better of him. Be proud of that. You won. Why can't you simply get along with him?"

Because Charles Morse was a bully. He showed it in his brusque manner in dealing with servants and how he cheated at cards if he couldn't win honestly. If the rumors were true, even Morse's own wife disliked him, and they were newlyweds.

Fletcher continued his litany. "You are the two youngest men on the board of directors, and I'm baffled as to why the pair of you can't get along. He is only forty-six, and you're what, thirty-seven?"

"Thirty-five," Liam corrected.

"Old enough to control your temper," Fletcher said. "I've

spent the past year playing peacekeeper between the two of you, and my patience is wearing thin. You are an asset to the board, but if push comes to shove, we need Morse more than we need you. As chairman of the board, it is my job to create a strong and productive group of people dedicated to maintaining U.S. Steel's prominence in the industry. If the two of you can't manage to be in the same room without coming to blows, it won't be Morse I ask to leave."

The pronouncement landed like a fist to Liam's gut. He was the only person on the board committed to putting the welfare of the workers ahead of profits. U.S. Steel employed 160,000 frontline workers in steel mills all over the nation. They were in Pittsburgh, Scranton, Cleveland, and Chicago. Those men earned a living with their hands, their backs, and their brawn. They didn't get ahead by scheming, cheating, or smacking servants. They depended on Liam to represent their interests on the company's board of directors, and if he had to swallow his pride and kiss Morse's ring to keep his seat, he'd do it.

They marched up the flight of marble steps to the cool shade beneath the stone-arched portico of the mansion.

"This is where I leave you," Fletcher said, offering a good-natured handshake.

Liam was flabbergasted. "You're not coming inside?" This would be a disaster without Fletcher to play the peacekeeper. Morse usually pretended to be friendly in front of the chairman of the board, but when no one was watching, Morse's true colors emerged.

"You need to manage Charles Morse on your own," Fletcher said as he retreated down the steps. "Take my advice and apologize for what happened yesterday. Get the incident behind you, and we can begin this afternoon's board meeting with a clean slate."

Fletcher sauntered toward the street as though the matter were already settled, while Liam braced himself for the confrontation ahead. Maybe it was for the best. He wasn't required to like Charles Morse, he merely needed to form a workable truce.

He drew a deep breath and rang the bell. Distant chimes tolled inside the mansion, sounding like gongs of doom. Everything about going down on bended knee before Charles Morse felt wrong, and yet it had to be done.

It was still early, which probably accounted for why the door was answered by a parlor maid instead of the butler. She looked about twenty, with freckled skin and a shock of red hair.

"Can I help you, sir?" she asked in a charming Irish lilt.

"I'd like to see Mr. Morse, please."

"Do you have an . . . um, can I ask your name? I mean, who shall I say is calling?" She continued to stammer and blushed furiously, explaining that it was the butler's morning off and apologizing that she didn't recognize him.

"Relax, you're doing a good job," he assured the nervous maid. "Please let Mr. Morse know that Liam Blackstone is here. He'll understand why."

The maid led him to a parlor to wait while she delivered the message. The parlor was gussied up like the rest of the house, an opulent mess with patterned wallpaper, gilded hardware, and fussy doodads cluttering every surface. It even smelled like money with the lingering scent of expensive cigars and sandalwood oil.

He shoved a hand into a trouser pocket to toy with Darla's empty pill case. Whenever he was nervous, he rolled it in his palm, popped the lid with his thumb, then snapped it shut. Roll, pop, snap. Roll, pop, snap.

It was no surprise that Morse made him wait. Ten minutes stretched into twenty as Liam paced, too anxious to sit as he scrutinized every object in the overly decorated room. Why did rich men feel so compelled to show off their fortune? He leaned over to scrutinize a gold mantel clock surrounded by dark red enamel. A chip marred the edge of the enamel, revealing a tin frame instead of silver. The clock was probably a cheap imitation. Rumors abounded that Morse was a skinflint beneath all the frippery, which explained the imitation clock.

An ugly lump of granite looked out of place among the fancy

knickknacks on the mantel. He tilted the rock to examine the flecks of green and orange.

"Copper," Morse announced from the doorway, his voice chilly.

Liam turned, the rock still in his hand. Morse's growing dominance in the copper industry was one of the reasons Fletcher wanted to keep him on the board. Now the rock made sense. It gave Morse an opportunity to brag about his vast copper mines out west. Liam set the rock back on the mantel and faced Morse, a good-looking man with a strong build and a full head of black hair that matched his neatly groomed mustache.

"Thank you for seeing me," Liam said, striving for a polite tone.

Morse gave the slightest tip of his head but remained frosty. "Your ship's rowboat is dreadful. It doesn't have any ballast, and there were no cushions on the seats."

That's because it wasn't meant for ferry service. If Morse had simply shown remorse over slapping Caleb, Liam wouldn't have ordered him ashore.

"Charles, we are two men of business who only want the best for the company," Liam began, but Morse interrupted.

"Do we? It seems you care more about the workers in the mills."

As if those workers weren't part of the company, Liam thought before continuing as though he hadn't heard. "We don't need to be the best of friends, but I am prepared to be cordial. You couldn't have known that my deckhand struggles when he gets contradictory orders, and I shouldn't have lost my temper. I'm sorry."

He waited, hoping the older man might express remorse for striking Caleb. It didn't happen. "Perhaps you should consider hiring a better quality of staff when entertaining guests," Morse said.

Liam resisted the urge to defend Caleb. "Whatever the cause of the incident, again, I'm sorry I got angry."

"Can't you control your temper even when you're in a business gathering?" Morse asked. "Perhaps that's how they handle things in the back alleys, but you are among men of high caliber now."

Liam itched to point out that slapping a deckhand wasn't a sterling example of gentility, but a ruckus in the hall distracted him. It sounded like two women squabbling. The Irish maid's voice was easily recognizable, but there was another woman in the mix, sounding equally adamant about demanding an audience.

The frazzled maid rushed inside. "I'm sorry, sir, but she insists on seeing you."

Could this be the newlywed Mrs. Morse, whose discontent was already stirring rumors?

Liam immediately discarded the idea when a pretty woman with glossy black hair pushed her way into the room. She was smartly dressed in a trim blue jacket and a straw boater hat, but this was a woman of the middle class, not a pampered millionaire's wife. She was lovely in a fierce, strong sort of way. Even the scar splitting her left eyebrow didn't detract from her appeal.

The woman held an envelope aloft. "This bill is four months overdue," she stated. "I've sent invoice after invoice and you have ignored them all, so I have no choice but to collect in person."

Morse flushed in outrage. "How dare you. If there has been a mix-up in the payment of a legitimate expense, you should submit the bill to my secretary, not interrupt a business meeting like a fishwife."

He brushed her aside and stomped into the hallway, shouting for servants to remove the intruder, but the woman didn't back down.

"I've been hectoring your secretary for months," she said. "He's refused payment, and I won't tolerate it any longer. You owe me ninety-five dollars for the ice cream we delivered to your wedding reception at the Belmont Hotel, and it's now four months overdue."

"Then of course I refuse to pay," he retorted. "Your complaint is with the Belmont Hotel, not with me. If you haven't been paid, I suggest you take it up with the hotel."

"The Belmont told me you stiffed them too," the woman said. "Perhaps they're willing to absorb the loss, but I won't. You owe me seventy for the ice cream, a ten-dollar late fee plus three percent for interest."

"That doesn't add up to ninety-five," Morse snapped.

"I added the court fee I just paid to file a lawsuit against you."

After a momentary pause of surprise, Morse threw back his head and affected an exaggerated laugh. It had a fake ring to it, but still he carried on for several seconds before dropping the theatrics and looking at the woman with contempt. "You're suing me over a ninety-five-dollar bill?"

The woman nodded. "I hate bullies. You have succeeded in bullying the hotel and the baker who provided the wedding cake, but I'll sue you to kingdom come until I've been paid in full."

A group of servants gathered in the hallway, watching the confrontation and looking to Morse for direction, but he waved them away. This likely wasn't the sort of interaction he would be proud of. To Liam's surprise, Morse agreed to pay.

"Very well," he said tightly. "The cost of a nuisance lawsuit isn't worth my time, and it's little enough to pacify an annoying gnat." He beckoned the woman to follow him into his private study.

Liam followed. He didn't trust Morse alone with her and monitored the interaction from the open doorway of the elaborate book-lined study.

"Please address the check to Molinaro Ice Cream," the woman said primly. Morse affected an indulgent grin as he opened a desk drawer and removed a leather book of checks. The smile didn't reach his eyes as he wrote out the check, the pen scratching in the quiet of the heavily carpeted, silk-draped room.

Liam took the opportunity to study the woman. She was slim but strong. They had the same coloring, with olive complexions and dark hair. Her pretty gamine face was full of character, even with the faint white scar that bisected an eyebrow.

Odd. He had an identical scar splitting his left brow. She

must have felt his stare because her gaze flicked to him. Her eye landed on his scar, and a hint of surprise crossed her face. She noticed their matching scars too, and he flashed her a wink.

She flushed and looked back at the bank draft as Morse pulled it from the notebook, gently wafting the slip of paper to dry the ink. He rose and fanned himself with the check, drawing out the moment as he scrutinized the woman. Several seconds passed in silence. If Liam wasn't a witness, he suspected Morse would make her beg for the check.

"Give it to her," he said.

Morse continued fanning himself a few more times before flicking the check toward the woman with a twist of his fingers. "Don't spend it all in one place," he said with a smirk.

The woman snatched it from his hand, then whirled to leave the room.

"Thank you, sir," she whispered as she passed him, trailing the soft scent of vanilla as she hurried down the hall.

Morse resumed his seat and looked up at Liam. "This whole apology nonsense isn't going as swimmingly as Fletcher hoped, is it? But what a good little soldier you are to come across town and offer it."

Heat gathered beneath his collar, but he wouldn't let Morse goad him. At this very moment there were 160,000 men showing up to work in sweltering steel mills all across the nation. They had a grueling week of dangerous labor ahead of them, and Liam was their only voice. He wouldn't let Charles Morse run him off the board.

"Fletcher wants what's best for the company, and that means you and I need to get along," he said.

"Fletcher wants to make money," Morse corrected. "He needs me on the board because he knows I can make it happen. What I can't understand is why he needs *you*."

Liam raised his chin a notch. "He needs me because the unions trust me. I can keep peace in the mills."

"You were appointed to the board because of family connections," Morse said dismissively.

22

He tried not to wince, but the charge was true. If Liam weren't a Blackstone, he wouldn't have had the leverage to demand a position on the board. Everyone knew it, and Morse gloated.

"You have nothing but an eighth-grade education and a history of rabble-rousing from your days as a union boss," Morse continued. "I could go into any steel mill in America and find men who are more intelligent, more articulate, and better educated than you. You've still got calluses on your hands and a chip on your shoulder."

Liam shoved both hands in his pockets, not because he was embarrassed of his calluses but because clenching Darla's pill case helped stifle the impulse to beat the smirk off Morse's face. He longed to throw that punch but settled for skewering Morse with a look of contempt.

"I don't need your approval. Any man who would stiff a woman over a piddly bill for ice cream isn't someone whose good opinion I value."

"You'd better start valuing it," Morse said in a silky tone. "No one on the board likes you. Everyone wants you off, and I'm going to call for a vote of no confidence. I've wanted to call it since the day your family forced us to accept you on the board, and after your stunt yesterday, I've got enough men on my side to vote you off."

An ache began in the pit of his stomach. Liam knew since his first board meeting that he was in over his head. All those men had college educations and tight friendships. While his fellow board members grew up in New England boarding schools learning to play polo and speak foreign languages, Liam was in a Pittsburgh steel mill shoveling coal into furnaces.

"Hogwash," Liam said. "The only reason the unions didn't go on strike last year was because they knew I was on the board and looking out for them."

Morse shrugged. "None of those men get to vote. This afternoon the board will discuss how to recapitalize the sinking funds for our subsidiaries and whether we should renegotiate the maturity dates. Each member will be expected to offer his opinion. And yours is?"

Silence stretched in the room. Liam rarely spoke at board meetings on anything other than labor issues because he lacked the qualifications for an informed opinion. Everyone knew it. He clenched his teeth, scrambling for a way to defend himself, when Morse offered a surprisingly kind concession.

"Come, Liam. You accomplished your mission in getting the steelworkers a considerable pay raise, but now it's time for you to go back home and enjoy the fruits of your accomplishments. Your father would be proud of you."

Liam stiffened at the mention of his father. Theodore Blackstone was the chink in his armor, a great man whose memory Liam would never be able to live up to.

"Did I ever tell you that I knew your father?" Morse asked. "What a rare combination of academic brilliance and compassion. He was always so even-tempered and gentle. He founded a college, correct?"

"He did."

"You must be very proud to be descended from such a man," Morse continued. "Theodore Blackstone was a man for the ages."

Liam didn't even like hearing his father's name uttered in this gaudy house. "Look, shut up about my father, okay?"

"My apologies," Morse said. "It must be intimidating to walk in Theodore Blackstone's footsteps."

It was the first entirely true statement Liam had ever heard Morse say. Yes, it was intimidating to be such a great man's son, and Liam desperately wanted to be worthy of his father's legacy. The only way he could ensure his father's humanitarian interests would triumph over men like Charles Morse was to keep his seat on the board. Nothing and nobody was going to stop him. It didn't matter that he lacked an education and didn't have any friends on Wall Street; he had a seat on the board and would fight to keep it.

Everything else was secondary. He would force himself to get along with Charles Morse. He could get used to being lonely. For a while he'd hoped that Darla Kingston might be the answer for his loneliness, but she had let him down in that department. When Liam finally found a woman to marry, she would be a woman of valor. A woman who wouldn't be afraid to stand in the breach with him and face down dragons.

He let go of Darla's pill case and faced Charles Morse.

"Any man with a beating heart would be honored to walk in Theodore Blackstone's footsteps." He smiled a little. "Brace yourself, Charles. I intend to ensure that my father's humanitarian sentiments are well represented on the board of U.S. Steel. You will *never* succeed in voting me out."

Liam turned on his heel and left Morse fuming in his office, but secretly he feared he wouldn't be able to live up to those bold words.

2

Morse's threat to get Liam voted off the board worried him more than he cared to admit. Strike that. Morse's threat *terrified* him, which was why Liam made an appointment with his lawyer to discuss it.

Patrick O'Neill wasn't merely his lawyer, he was also Liam's brother-in-law, best friend, and only ally in the coming battle against Charles Morse. Liam invited Patrick to meet with him aboard the *Black Rose*, the 230-foot yacht that had been Liam's home for the past two years. Living aboard a yacht was an unconventional choice, but he never felt comfortable in New York, and this yacht had once belonged to his father. It felt good to live aboard the ship Theodore Blackstone loved so well.

Patrick arrived at the *Black Rose* armed with the thick pamphlet that contained the operating agreement for the board of U.S. Steel, the largest corporation in the world. Liam fidgeted while Patrick studied the document in a deck chair beside him. Wind tugged at the pages while the cry of gulls mingled with clanking chains from a cargo ship being unloaded in the neighboring berth in the busy port.

"Well?" he prodded. "Is it legal?"

"It's legal," Patrick replied in a flat voice. "According to the rules of the board, Morse has the right to call for a vote of no

26

confidence. Next week there will be a straw poll about whether to proceed to a formal vote. If a majority agrees, you get three months to gather evidence, interview witnesses, and make your case before the final vote of no confidence."

"It sounds like a trial," Liam said.

"It is. Voting you off won't be easy, but you will be entitled to mount a vigorous defense."

Liam sighed. The problem was that his qualifications were flimsy compared to the other men on the board. Serving on a corporate board only required a few days of work per month, but during the rest of their time, his fellow board members were at the helms of their own lofty corporations. They were renowned men of business and captains of industry who made America thrive, while all Liam did was tinker with new alloys of steel.

He had an even bigger problem to confide to Patrick and didn't want the deckhands currently oiling the ship's lanterns to overhear.

"Let's go below to the cardroom," he suggested. "There's something else you need to know."

They headed down the steep set of stairs leading belowdecks, then down a narrow passageway that led to the cardroom, where a row of brass portholes overlooked the harbor. Card tables were interspersed with upholstered seating covered in shades of forest green and rich leather. Patrick settled into a low-slung club chair while Liam closed the door behind him.

"I've got another problem," he began. Confessing this weakness was horrible, but Patrick needed to know. "I'm leaving town for a couple of weeks, so I'll need you to cover any steel business that comes up while I'm gone. Can you do that?"

"What?" Patrick shot up out of his chair. "You can't go on vacation in the middle of a crisis. We need to work on a battle plan to save your seat."

A deep, searing pain started to throb in Liam's gut. He reached into his pocket to start fiddling with Darla's pill case again, hating this conversation. Anything he told to Patrick would get back to Gwen. Though Patrick was an honorable man, he tended to overshare things with his wife, and since Gwen was Liam's sister . . . yeah, if Patrick knew the problem Liam was harboring, it was going to get back to Gwen because married people told each other everything.

He jerked his hand out of his pocket and met Patrick's gaze. "I'm leaving on doctor's orders," he admitted. "I'm supposed to go to the Woodlands Health Clinic for a month."

"A month!" Patrick said, his voice appalled.

"Dr. Jergins suggested three months." His doctor wanted him to quit the board of directors altogether, but that wasn't an option Liam was willing to take. It was embarrassing to let a stomachache rule his life, but he'd tried all the easy cures and none of them had worked.

The irony was that over the past two years he'd led labor rallies, survived two separate murder attempts, and learned the people he thought were his parents were, in fact, grifters who'd been lying to him his entire life. He sailed through it all with flying colors. A good fight was invigorating. Leading union crusades and slaying dragons was fun. It was serving on the board of directors that had been Liam's undoing.

"The doctor says I need to get away from the stress of business to let my ulcer have a chance to heal," he continued. "I was hoping you could be my proxy on the board while I'm gone, but I hadn't expected Morse to come after me like this."

Patrick sat back down. "Can it wait? If you leave now, it will confirm Morse's charge that you aren't fit to serve. Can you hold off until the autumn?"

Liam hadn't told Patrick any of the details of what was ahead if the ulcer got much worse. The lining of his stomach was corroding, and acid was eating holes in his gut. If those wounds broke open, it would cause internal bleeding that could kill him.

"The doctor wants me to leave right away, but I could stay for a few more weeks if it would help stave off whatever Morse has up his sleeve."

Patrick shook his head. "I don't want to sound unsympathetic, but if you leave before this issue is won, Morse is going to stir up the fight again."

Patrick's tone was heavy with warning and made Liam's belly ache worse than ever. Defeating Morse's vote of no confidence would be a temporary victory unless he could figure out a way to gain the upper hand over Morse. Corporate boards were mindful of their reputation and feared bad publicity due to ethical violations. He rubbed his hands together so hard his knuckles cracked as an idea came to the fore.

"This morning I saw Morse try to stiff a woman over a piddly bill for ice cream. It wouldn't surprise me if he stops payment on the check he wrote her." He recounted the full story for Patrick, who seemed intrigued.

"Knowingly passing a bad check is a crime," Patrick said. "It would look especially bad for Morse since he is one of the biggest bankers in the city."

A trickle of hope took root. Morse hadn't wanted to write that check and might have only done so because Liam and a bunch of servants witnessed the embarrassing confrontation with the ice cream lady. It would be monumentally stupid for Morse to risk his reputation over ninety-five dollars' worth of ice cream, but Liam hoped he would.

"I'll find out if the check cleared," Liam said, knowing if Morse stopped payment on it, he would have his first bit of ammunition in his quest to neutralize Charles Morse's power on the board.

3

On mornings as difficult as this, Maggie tried to re-member all the reasons she loved owning an ice cream factory. The culinary challenge of developing the best ice cream in New York was a joy. Keeping the machinery hum-ming along at full capacity was a challenge, but a satisfying one. She learned how to change pulley belts, repair the motor boxes, and keep the refrigerated rooms cold by getting trained in basic electrical wiring. Best of all, she loved watching little kids as they approached the counter in the ice cream parlor, their faces a perfect blend of anticipation and torment as they wrestled with the age-old challenge of choosing the perfect flavor.

But the one thing Maggie loathed was conflict with her em-ployees, and they were coming at her hard this morning.

"We ought to get paid more when the weather is this hot," Gary Johnson said, his scowling face in stark contrast with the cheerful blue-and-white pinstripes of the Molinaro uniform. They were at the back of the factory, loading carts for another day of business. Half a dozen other pushcart vendors were lined up behind Gary, all of them looking annoyed.

"You *do* get paid more," Maggie pointed out as she held a clipboard to her chest. "You get paid on commission, and sales are always sky-high when it's hot."

At least it was cool inside the factory. The cavernous production room was two stories tall to accommodate the maze of rotating pulley belts overhead. The high ceiling kept the factory cool, as did the brick walls and hundred-gallon vats of ice water circulating around the tubs of churning cream.

Antonio Gabelli, the man who'd been delivering their ice ever since they purchased the building, glared at the complaining vendors as he wheeled another hand truck filled with slabs of ice toward the cold rooms. Why couldn't all the people she dealt with be as sensible as Antonio? The double doors at the back of the factory were open for Antonio to roll his cart in and out as he delivered two tons of ice, and she methodically ticked off each batch on her delivery chart. Careful attention to finances was the reason she finally had a stable home and business, and she wouldn't put it at risk by letting the vendors intimidate her.

"Where's your uncle?" Gary asked. "Dino understands simple math and the burden of putting food on the table."

Dino was shopping for his wife's fiftieth birthday present. He'd been diligently saving to buy Julie a nice pearl brooch, but the real reason Gary wanted to talk to Dino was because her uncle could be a pushover. Maggie, however, was thrifty to a fault.

"I understand math," she pointed out. "I also understand you're likely to earn twenty percent more in commissions because sales will be brisk today."

"One of these days we're all going to quit, and then you'll be sorry," Gary said, which was met by vigorous nods from others on the pushcart crew.

Antonio wheeled his empty cart back to the ice truck parked in the alley, which was when she noticed the tall, handsome stranger loitering in the doorway at the back of the factory, watching everything.

The stranger's black hair and chiseled jaw made him darkly attractive, and he looked familiar. He wore an ordinary white shirt with black trousers held up by a pair of red suspenders, but there was something about the fine cut of his clothes that made him appear like a man of consequence.

Then he flashed her a wink, and she instantly recognized him as the man she'd seen at Charles Morse's house last week. What was he doing here?

"I'll be right with you," she said, then turned her attention back to Gary and the other vendors, who still wanted to belly-ache about their pay.

"You could afford to pay us a lot more if you weren't such a skinflint," Gary said.

Antonio was wheeling in another cartload of ice when he abruptly parked it to glare at Gary. "Knock it off, all of you," he warned. "If you don't like working here, go out and find someone who'll pay you better, but don't shoot off your mouth to a nice lady like Miss Molinaro. Got it?"

She set a hand on his shoulder. "Antonio, it's all right."

"It's not all right," he groused. "You and your uncle run a decent business, and they shouldn't mouth off at you like that."

He jerked the cart back into motion, and she stared in surprise at Antonio's retreating form. What had gotten into her mild-mannered iceman? Complaining from the pushcart crew was nothing new, but maybe they realized the truth of what Antonio said because they quickly finished loading their carts and left the factory without more grumbling.

She glanced at the stranger in the doorway, who'd witnessed everything. It was embarrassing to have her company's dirty laundry aired before a stranger.

She gave a carefree shrug. "Please don't think badly of them. They think I'm rich because of all this," she said, gesturing to the factory. She was still in debt for the building and the factory equipment. That debt was why she watched every penny, but that wasn't a matter to discuss with a stranger. She managed a smile and stepped forward to offer a handshake. "I'm Maggie Molinaro. Thanks for sticking up for me last week at Mr. Morse's house."

"You were a tough cookie," he said with a nod of admiration. "I'm Liam Blackstone. The lady working the counter in the parlor said I might find you back here." His curious gaze scanned the production floor, and she smiled, trying to imagine it through his eyes. Some people might look at this factory and only see hulking galvanized steel machines, a concrete floor, and a dozen pulleys with rotating belts overhead, but Maggie saw productivity and security. The factory was her proudest accomplishment.

"It smells really good in here," he said.

"It's the vanilla. We use gallons of it because vanilla has always been our best-selling ice cream."

"Really? I've always thought vanilla to be the most boring of flavors."

She shook her head. "Restaurants add a scoop of vanilla ice cream to each slice of pie and cake they serve, so it accounts for a third of our business. What can I do for you, Liam?"

For the first time, he looked a bit uncomfortable as he glanced at a few of her employees boxing up ice cream at the worktables. "Is there anywhere we can go to speak privately?"

She pointed to a rubber belt at the base of the mixing machine filled with a batch of half-mixed peach ice cream. "I need to swap out this belt to get the mixer back in action. We can talk over there."

He blinked in surprise. "You service the machines yourself?"

"I don't like paying maintenance costs for something I can do on my own." This morning's job was easy: just removing a belt that had lost tension and putting a new one on the pulley. She hunkered down beside the pulley and used a tension bar to begin wiggling the old belt free. "Well?" she asked him.

"I came to see if the check Morse gave you has cleared."

Just thinking about that bad check made her annoyed, and she glanced up at him. "No, it didn't. My bank didn't give me a reason either; they simply said the check couldn't be honored."

A quick flash of elation lit Mr. Blackstone's face, but maybe she imagined it because it vanished quickly. "What are you going to do about it?" he asked politely.

"I'll proceed with the lawsuit," she said. She laid the old belt on the floor and stood to look him in the eye. "I've never had to sue anyone, and I don't really know what I'm doing, but I can learn."

"My lawyer's office is only a few streets over," he said. "Patrick is famous for standing up to scoundrels like Charles Morse. Would you like me to introduce you?"

She hadn't even considered getting a lawyer. Was it naïve to believe a jury of her peers would have a sense of fair play and do the right thing? He was kind to offer the introduction, but she wasn't the sort of person who could afford a lawyer.

"You say 'my lawyer' like most people would say my hat or my dog," she teased.

He looked a little embarrassed but then returned her teasing tone. "Yes, I'm a very powerful man," he said, the flush on his face growing deeper.

"Modest too."

He let out a burst of laughter. "That's one thing no one has ever accused me of. *You*, on the other hand, have a good deal to be proud about. I love Molinaro Ice Cream. I used to buy it all the time."

"Used to?" she asked pointedly.

"Yeah. You had a cart parked at Pier 19 every day. I used to grab something each time I passed, but I haven't seen that pushcart in months. What happened to it?"

She knelt to clean the grit off the pulley and prepare it for a new belt. "Pier 19 wasn't profitable enough. When we moved to Pier 15, our sales went up twelve percent. Can you hand me the new belt right behind you?"

He quickly spotted the coiled canvas belt and brought her one end. He patiently handed her more sections hand over hand until she had it mounted on all three pulleys surrounding the mixing machine. "How can I convince you to move that cart back to Pier 19? Name it and I'll do it."

"Why the urgency to get it back to Pier 19?" she asked.

"Because that's where I live. My ship is permanently docked

at Pier 19, and I used to buy something from that pushcart every night on my way home from work. Sometimes I'd buy ice cream for my entire crew."

She loved the note of paternal pride in his voice. Still, she wasn't about to back down. "If you'd bought twelve percent more, we might still be there. Are you a ship captain?"

"Nope. Just a man who likes living at the harbor."

"But you don't actually *live* on Pier 19, do you?"

"I live on my ship, and that's where it's docked. Right now there's a pretzel vendor and a lady who sells foul-smelling sausages at the base of the pier. We'd much rather have a Molinaro pushcart."

She reached for a ratchet to twist the bolt into the pulley bearing. "And I'd rather have the extra twelve percent I get at Pier 15."

"Would it help if I said that my doctor ordered me to eat more dairy? I drink milk by the gallon and eat enough cheddar cheese to risk turning yellow, but I'd rather have ice cream. Miss Molinaro, you can help a sick man on his road back to health and wellness."

"Call me Maggie," she said as she dropped the hand tools into an old crate, then looked at him with concern in her eyes. "Is it an ulcer?"

"Yeah, and it hurts like the dickens."

She nodded. "My dad had them, so I know how miserable they can be. I'm sorry about that."

"Sorry enough to move a pushcart back to Pier 19?" It looked like he was struggling not to laugh, and she smiled in return.

"Twelve percent is twelve percent," she said, enjoying this harmless bit of unexpected flirtation, but Antonio was heading her way again, his cart empty. She needed to sign off on the delivery and arrange for payment. He parked the empty delivery cart, still a little winded from hefting tons of ice.

"That's the last of it, Maggie," he said. "And I've got some bad news. I'm afraid this is my last day delivering ice for you."

"Oh, Antonio! We're going to miss you. What's next for you?"

Antonio wiped the sweat off his forehead. "I'm not really sure. My grandfather announced that he's closing the business, and I didn't hear anything about it until yesterday. He's going to sell what he can and abandon the rest. Then he's moving upstate."

She gaped at him because this made no sense. Gabelli Ice was a thriving company, so why were they pulling out of the business with no warning? Something was wrong. Antonio looked regretful, embarrassed . . . and something else she couldn't quite put her finger on. Worried, almost as if he was afraid of something.

She couldn't operate an ice cream factory without massive deliveries of ice every three days. Without ice, the electrical motors that kept their refrigeration rooms cold wouldn't be up to the task, nor could they keep their churns cold enough to make ice cream.

Her mouth went dry, and she tried to sound calm. "Is someone else going to deliver our ice on Wednesday?"

"I tried to line something up for you with Manhattan Ice," he said. "You'll have to go to their office in Midtown to sign the papers if you want the deal."

She turned away to brace both hands on the worktable, her mind awhirl. Liam put a hand on her shoulder.

"Is there anything I can do to help?" he asked.

Not unless he had access to twelve tons of ice per week. She tried to hold her panic at bay and sound lighthearted. "I'm sorry about Pier 19, but I need to go lock down a deal for ice."

And it needed to be done *today* or the factory would grind to a halt.

Maggie caught a streetcar to Midtown and spoke with the manager at the Manhattan Ice Company. The news wasn't good. She stared at the proposed contract in dismay.

"That's twice what I pay for Gabelli Ice," she told the cigar-smoking manager.

He merely shrugged at her from behind the tiny desk in his crowded office. "It's been a hot summer, and price adjustments are fair game when it gets this hot."

The exorbitant price increase would force her to recalibrate her entire budget. Surely she could find someone else to deliver ice to the factory at not so high a cost. The problem was that she didn't have much time.

"Look, do you want ice or not?" the man asked with the cigar still clamped between his teeth.

"I'll let you know," she said, then set off in search of cheaper ice.

It resulted in a frustrating afternoon as she consulted with three other ice vendors, all telling her the same thing. They blamed their shockingly high ice quotes on the extremely hot summer, but she noticed a curious detail. All of them used the same phrase: "price adjustments are fair game." There was nothing particularly odd about the comment other than the fact that all four vendors used the exact same phrase.

In the end she returned to Manhattan Ice to sign a one-month contract for twelve tons of ice per week. The limited contract gave her breathing room to line up a better deal somewhere else, but at least she would have ice on Wednesday.

⁂

The only good thing about Maggie's frustrating trip in search of ice was that it let her check up on Philip with her making a quick stop on 28th Street. It was an annual ritual, her monitoring how her old sweetheart was progressing in his dream.

She held her breath as she arrived at Tin Pan Alley, the nickname given to these few blocks of music stores. Plenty of people who worked in the music industry lived above the shops too. Not Philip, of course. He couldn't afford to live among the well-heeled people who managed to thrive in this competitive industry.

A bell above the door dinged as she entered the sheet music store, the familiar scent of old paper surrounding her. Bins of music were categorized by type. Maggie walked past the prominent displays of operettas and piano solos to reach the selection of popular songs.

Hundreds of popular songs were grouped by songwriter, but the only one by Philip was a single copy of "The First Rose of Spring." She bought the sheet music for this song three years ago when it first came out, and judging by its tatty condition, this copy had been sitting on the rack for a long time.

A gangly clerk behind the counter who had been tuning a banjo set it down to come to her side.

"Can I help you find something?"

"Do you have anything written by Philip Altman?"

The clerk gestured to the page she held. "That's the only one that sells. We moved everything else he wrote to the back."

"Could I see them?"

The clerk nodded and went to the back room, but Maggie's heart sank. Philip would never sell anything if his music was stored in a back room. He once had such high hopes. Both of them did. They'd spent countless evenings huddled together on a bench overlooking the Hudson River, sharing dreams about someday striking it rich, she in ice cream and he on Broadway. The difference was that while Maggie had achieved her dream, Philip lived in a shabby apartment without running water.

He was married now and had a child. His wife mended costumes for vaudeville dancers, and given where they lived, she probably didn't earn much either. It had been five years since Maggie and Philip parted ways, yet she still worried about him.

The clerk emerged with a stack of pages. "This is what we've got. He puts out eight or ten new songs a year, but no one ever buys them. We only get the songs because they come bundled with everything else the publisher sends. We don't even bother setting them out anymore."

Maggie paged through the selection, choosing one of each song. With a new baby, it was more important than ever for Philip to earn something from his music.

"How much do I owe you?" Only a fraction of it would trickle down to Philip, but how could she simply do nothing? She would add these songs to the others she'd bought over the years and stored in a box beneath her bed.

The sun had set by the time she arrived back at Gadsen Street and trudged up the flights of stairs leading to the fourth-floor apartment she shared with Dino and Julie. It was a finer place than any of them ever imagined they could afford. The large main room had built-in bookshelves and big windows overlooking the restaurants of Gadsen Street, even though her bedroom window had a view of a brick wall across the alley. That was okay. Someday when she was genuinely rich, she'd have a view of something pretty, but for now this apartment was fine.

She knelt beside her bed to pull out the box of Philip memorabilia. There were programs from vaudeville shows they used to see every Friday. A photograph of her and Philip sharing a horse on a merry-go-round, and a ticket stub from a baseball game they attended long ago. And of course, Philip's telegram congratulating her on the day the Molinaro Ice Cream Parlor opened for business. Wasting money on a telegram was typical of Philip's impracticality. He had been at her side for the grand opening party, so there'd been no need to send a telegram earlier in the day, but that was Philip.

Had she done the right thing in walking away from him? She probably wouldn't have had the courage to invest in the factory if her future had been linked with Philip. At first her loneliness after they parted hadn't been too bad, but as the years passed, her longing for a partner had grown and intensified. As other women her age got married and started households of their own, Maggie got up each morning to turn on the electricity and get the factory machines running.

It was a good life. She and Dino had forty employees and sold eighteen flavors of ice cream. Maybe someday she could find a man to welcome into her world, but she would *never* go back to poverty. Her dream of running a successful business was now a reality. That wasn't the case for Philip, whose hope of becoming a songwriter seemed to be growing bleaker with each passing season.

"Hang in there, Philip," she whispered as she set the new sheet music in the box and slid it under her bed. Sometimes, no matter how desperately hard a person worked, there were no happy endings, and she feared this was going to be Philip Altman's fate.

4

*L*iam needed to capitalize on Charles Morse's blun-
der in bouncing that check, and luckily his cousin
Natalia grew up in the banking world and could
help. Natalia was one of the few people he could trust in the
Blackstone family, even though her father was the infamous
Oscar Blackstone.

The Blackstone family once had two brothers at the helm.
The kindly and wise younger brother was Liam's father. The
scary and scheming brother was Natalia's father. Any doubt
about Oscar Blackstone's ruthless nature had been put to rest
last year when he fired his own daughter from the family bank.

Being ousted from the job she loved had devastated Natalia,
but she had since been slowly rebuilding her life with her new
husband, a Russian count with whom she had adopted two
children. They spent most of their time in their country house,
but while in town they stayed at the Dakota, a grand apartment
building overlooking Central Park.

Natalia welcomed him into her home, looking more relaxed
than the uptight woman who once worked at her father's bank.
Today she wore a loose gown with her dark hair braided over
one shoulder. The mournful sound of a violin dirge was playing
somewhere in the back of the apartment.

"Dimitri is trying to master a Tchaikovsky solo," she explained. "Please forgive him, he's doing his best."

Liam met her eyes in sympathy. "How can you stand that racket? It sounds like a dying cat."

"He loves dabbling in music, so I don't mind," she said as she led him to the parlor with a view of the park. Personally, the wailing of a violin would drive him batty, but maybe enduring stuff like that was the nature of true love. Liam wouldn't know. He thought he'd been in love with Darla, but it had been only an illusion.

Natalia set a tray with cool drinks on the tea table. "Tell me what's worrying you."

"Charles Morse. What is his reputation in the banking industry?"

The corners of Natalia's mouth turned down as she used tongs to drop ice cubes into the glasses. She poured him some lemonade but still hadn't answered.

"Well?" he prompted.

"There's a reason we never let Morse get any sort of stake in the Blackstone Bank," she finally said. "He's a brilliant financier, but he can't be trusted."

Liam leaned forward. "How do you mean?"

"He is a master at leveraged investments and inflated valuations. He pumps up share prices by watering the stock and printing cheap paper, but it's all a house of cards."

Liam shifted in discomfort. "I have no idea what you just said. Can you say it again but in plain English?"

"He's a cheat," Natalia said bluntly. "Don't trust him. Don't buy anything he sells. And don't join any sort of business alliance he cobbles together. I once reviewed a proposal he wrote to build a railroad in Canada. At first it looked like an attractive investment, but the fine print was all slanted in his favor. It was designed at the outset to double-cross both his partners and his customers while he skimmed a profit from every share he sold."

It was Charles Morse's influence in the banking industry that had earned him his seat on the board. Morse had a substantial stake in at least half the banks operating in the city, but according to Natalia, his fortune had been built on shell games and banking schemes few people understood. Despite his shady reputation, no one had been able to pin a specific crime on him.

But writing a check for a legitimate expense and then revoking it out of spite? Such an act was so straightforward that any schoolchild could understand it. Liam explained how Morse wrote a bad check for ninety-five dollars to Maggie Molinaro, the ice cream lady.

"Maggie wants to take him to court over the bad check," he told Natalia. "Is that the best way to handle it?"

Natalia shook her head. "Morse could drag out a court case for years. It would be better if she filed a complaint with the New York State Banking Department that regulates the industry. Trust me, that will get Mr. Morse's attention far more quickly."

"Can the state revoke his license to operate a bank?" Liam asked.

"They won't do so over such a small check," Natalia replied. "Instead, they'll suggest he make good on the check or else face a formal reprimand for an ethical violation."

Liam smiled. Men serving on the board of a major corporation needed to be of sterling character. Getting slapped with an ethical violation would cripple Morse in the eyes of the board of directors. It was the perfect opportunity for Liam to turn the tables on Charles Morse.

But first he had to persuade Maggie to withdraw her lawsuit in favor of a formal complaint to the state's banking authority. It would give her satisfaction, but more importantly, it would give Liam a silver bullet to take Morse down.

Liam headed straight to Gadsen Street in hopes of getting Maggie to drop her court case. It was evening, and the street-lamps cast a warm glow over the people dining at the outdoor cafés. Gadsen Street was renowned for its restaurants, cafés, and bakeries. Piano music from an Irish pub mingled with laughter as he navigated past diners chattering at outdoor tables. Outside a high-end Italian restaurant, the waiters balanced trays and delivered platters of fragrant pasta in garlic cream sauce. The scent of warm bread and hot coffee lingered outside a bakery. Then came a cheese shop, an oyster and seafood restaurant, and a bistro where the mandolin player serenaded the diners.

To his surprise, he spotted Maggie sitting with a companion outside a Jewish deli. She must have already spotted him, for she was whispering to her friend with corkscrew blond curls as they both looked directly at him. Maggie was blushing, and she flashed him a wink as he drew near.

That wink. It sent a flash of anticipation through him as he approached her table. "Hello, tough cookie. Can I join you?"

"I'm not a tough cookie, but yes, please join us," she said, gesturing to the remaining chair. Light from the streetlamp sparkled in her eyes as she introduced her friend named Frieda, who worked at an Italian deli down the street.

Frieda opened a cigarette case and offered him one. Cigarettes were a vice he'd given up on doctor's orders, but it had been two weeks since he'd indulged, and the ulcer had been behaving itself today.

"Thanks," he said, accepting a cigarette, then lighting both his own and Frieda's. "Do you get in trouble for eating at a competing deli?"

"My boss will have to find out first," Frieda said.

Maggie didn't smoke but had plenty to say about the fierce competition on Gadsen Street.

"The Irish pub and Alfonso's Deli have been at war with each other for years," she said. "Last year, Mr. Alfonso bought all the corned beef from the local meat-packer so there wasn't any for the Irish pub on Saint Patrick's Day."

"Don't forget the backbiting right here," Frieda said with a nod to the steakhouse next door. She went on to explain how the Porterhouse was too highfalutin to set tables outside, but whenever a table from the Jewish deli encroached an inch onto their sidewalk, the Porterhouse threatened to sue.

"Mr. Prescott from the Porterhouse speaks with a British accent even though he was born and raised in Brooklyn," Maggie added. That prompted Frieda to perform a brilliant impersonation of the fusty Mr. Prescott, and Liam relaxed and enjoyed the banter. He'd forgotten how much fun it was to shoot the breeze with ordinary people who were like him.

Soon Frieda's break was over and she stood. "Back to the salt mines," she joked, then headed down the street toward Alfonso's Deli, leaving him and Maggie alone at the table.

It was finally time to talk about Morse. Even thinking about Charles Morse made his cigarette taste bitter. He crushed it out and leaned back in the chair.

"About that lawsuit you want to file against Morse," he began, "I've got a cousin who says you'll get more satisfaction if you take your complaint to the state agency that regulates banks."

He explained the process to her, which would only require filling out a few forms. At the very least it would prompt Morse to pay what he owed, but it might even put his bank into a probationary status for ethical violations. To his surprise, Maggie seemed to shrink before his eyes.

"Over ninety-five dollars? You want me to threaten a millionaire's banking empire over ninety-five dollars?"

"You were willing to take him to court over that amount. What's the difference?"

"A jury of my peers!" she said. "Normal people on a jury have a sense of fair play, but what you described sounds like it will punish Morse's entire bank. That's not a fight I want. I'm *not* a tough cookie. All I want is to get paid for my ice cream."

"If he's cheating you, he's cheating others," Liam pointed out. "Filing a complaint will force him to treat everyone fairly whether they're rich or poor. Maybe you're not a tough cookie, but I am, and I'd be alongside you the entire time. And I'm very strong," he added for good measure.

"There's your modesty showing again," she said, and he grinned.

"I know how to get things done. If I see someone getting stomped on, I'm not going to look away. Morse tried to stomp on you, just like he stiffed the baker and the hotel. There are bound to be others out there. How about you and I team up and make sure the state of New York knows what sort of banker they've granted a license to? I'll take you to my cousin's apartment, and she can help us fill out the forms."

Maggie bit her lip as she mulled the suggestion. "Will I still get paid for my ice cream?"

"He'll be *begging* to pay for your ice cream," Liam affirmed. "I expect he'll pay the cake baker and the hotel too. Charles Morse needs to clean up his act, and this is the best way to get him in line. Deal?"

"Deal!" she said, thrusting her hand out, and they shook on the plan. The way she beamed at him made him feel ten feet tall as heat crept up his face. He always blushed when a woman got to him. It was like shouting to the world that he had a crush on someone, but he didn't care. He really liked her and—

"Do you need this chair, Maggie?" a waiter asked with a hand on the back of the empty chair.

Maggie instantly stood. "Sorry, David. We're finished and will be on our way." She sent Liam an apologetic glance, prompting him to stand. "A table should turn over every twenty minutes, and we've been costing them money by hogging it."

He understood but didn't want the evening to end. "Show me the rest of Gadsen Street," he said, and she happily obliged, pointing out the various fancy restaurants interspersed with cafés and delis. The cobblestones were kept clean, and flower boxes bloomed before every restaurant. Liam searched the crowded street in vain for an outdoor table he could commandeer without interruption, but only the cheese shop had tables open.

Liam escorted Maggie to the front bow window filled with imported cheeses from all over the world. The display featured pale wedges of French Gouda, blocks of Gorgonzola from Italy, and rounds of cheese from Holland coated in red paraffin wax. Liam didn't know much about cheese, but Maggie was taking dreadfully long debating whether to order a wedge of Asiago from Italy or a bit of smoked Gouda from France.

"Let's try one from every country in Europe," he suggested.

Her eyes grew round. "Are you paying?"

"I'm paying," he said, and ten minutes later they had a nice outdoor table filled with exotic cheeses. The waiter rattled off their names as he pointed to each selection, and Liam chose a pungent Pecorino as his first foray into Italian cheese. Maggie looked at him across the table in speculation, the lamplight casting a glow across her gamine features. Then she asked the question he'd been dreading.

"I can't resist any longer . . . are you *that* Liam Blackstone?"

The question was bound to come up sooner or later, yet he wished it could have been later. It had been nice not having the barrier of a fortune standing between them. Would she treat him differently once she knew? Plenty of women did after they learned he was filthy rich, but he still hoped Maggie might be different.

"Yeah, I'm *that* Liam Blackstone," he reluctantly admitted. "You've heard about me, have you?"

"Anyone who reads the newspaper has heard about you."

Liam's story had been tailor-made for tabloid headlines. He came from one of the richest families in America, but at the age of three he'd been kidnapped and held for ransom. Though Theodore Blackstone had paid the ransom, his son was never returned. After a few years, Liam was presumed dead, but his father never stopped looking into the faces of children who played in parks or poured out of schoolhouses, unwilling to surrender hope that his son might still be alive. Years passed, then decades . . . but Theodore Blackstone never saw a trace of his son.

That was because Liam didn't play in parks or go to school. He'd been sent to Pittsburgh, where he was raised by a brutal man who took twisted satisfaction in subjecting Liam to the same level of poverty all the other workers who toiled in the steel mills endured. Over time, Liam forgot where he came from and grew up believing he was the son of a steelworker until a series of events led him to the truth.

It caused a sensation when Liam returned to the Blackstone fold two years ago with indisputable proof of his identity, especially given that Liam had spent most of his life denouncing the robber barons who ruled Wall Street. The newspapers were covered with his story—how he'd been yanked out of school in the eighth grade to shovel coal into steel mill furnaces and how he could barely read, had a temper, and had a long, colorful history of arrests for back-alley brawls and stirring up the unions to attack the owners of the steel mills.

It wasn't surprising that the men on the board of directors hated him, but Liam would rather discuss anything besides his past. He glanced at the thin white scar splitting Maggie's eyebrow. It was the only thing that marred her beauty, but in an odd sort of way, it made her look strong. Like a survivor.

"We have matching scars," he said. "How did you get yours?"

"When I was sixteen, I got mugged," she said, immediately rousing every one of his protective instincts.

"What happened?"

"My dad and I used to sell ice cream from a pushcart. One day, I went out on my own without him. That was a mistake. A gang of tough kids surrounded me and got it all. I put up a fight, but as you can see . . ." She gestured to her scar and shrugged a little, as though she'd long gotten over the incident.

"Did they catch who did it?"

"No, but life went on. How did you get yours?"

The sharp cheese soured in his mouth. He reached for a glass of water to rinse it back, wishing he didn't have to answer, but he could hardly clam up since he was the one to start this conversation. Besides, it was time to quit being ashamed of it.

"My dad was a brute," he said. "Crocket Malone, that is. Crocket was the guy who raised me after I got snatched from my real family. He believed in pounding a kid into manhood with his fists. One time he caught me reading something he didn't like and used the book to smack me across the face. It split my eyebrow."

She looked appalled. "What on earth were you reading?"

"Just a book," he said with a shrug. He didn't want to revisit his idiotic childhood dreams and switched the topic to the one thing in his life of which he was truly proud. "My real dad wasn't a brute like Crocket. Theodore Blackstone was good down to the marrow of his bones. He built a college and spent the rest of his life trying to cure disease among the poor. The day I learned that Theodore Blackstone was my real father, I felt both hopeful and terrified at the same time."

The greatest tragedy of Liam's life was in never having a chance to see his real parents again. His real mother died decades ago, but Theodore lived until just a few years ago. Theodore never got over the loss of his son and worked himself into an early grave trying to make up for the sins of his rich family. He never learned his son had survived.

Liam inherited Theodore's looks, his fortune, and his yacht, but not his temperament. Liam's nature was hot and impulsive like Crocket Malone's, but he intended to rise above it.

His darkest fear was that he'd follow in Crocket's footsteps instead of Theodore's, which was why he needed to do everything by the book. Follow the rules, go to church, control his temper, and still fight for the better world envisioned by Theodore Blackstone.

"I want to be a good man like my real father," he said. "It's easy to punch and bribe and bully. It's a lot harder to win the hearts and minds of people by being good. That's the kind of person my real dad was. No matter what I do in life or how long I live . . . I intend to be the sort of person who would have made Theodore Blackstone proud."

Maggie's face shone in the lamplight, her eyes wide pools of admiration and understanding. "I get it. I feel the same way about my uncle Dino." She tilted in her chair to point across the street to Molinaro Ice Cream.

"Do you see that olive tree outside our ice cream parlor?"

He nodded.

"My uncle brought the cutting from Italy. Each Easter and Christmas, he cuts a twig from it and carries it to the church to dip it in holy water. Then we take it to the roof of the church, we face the east, and Dino holds the frond up high to send blessings to our family back in Italy." Her eyes sparkled and a hint of a flush illuminated her cheeks. "It reminds us of our blessings. We know it's silly, but I hope we never stop."

It wasn't silly. Liam sagged back in his chair to gaze at the olive tree across the street, astounded by the surge of sentimental longing her story triggered. Was it the late hour? The candlelight? Or maybe it was the odd sense of kinship he had for a homesick man who remembered and honored his family traditions with all his heart. Liam had felt adrift most of his life, but he didn't even know for what.

"Thank you for bringing me here tonight," he said. There weren't many memories in his life he wanted to lock away and treasure . . . but this was one of them.

⁕

It was almost midnight when Liam got home, knowing he had a long-overdue task to complete.

It was time to get rid of Darla's pill case.

He couldn't move ahead with a genuine courtship of another woman with the weight of the old dragging him down. It had been almost a year since he'd split with Darla, and during that time he cut a swath through the female population of the city. None of them meant anything to him, but Maggie might be different.

He sat in the dim light of the cardroom on the *Black Rose*, staring at a blank piece of paper while trying to write Darla a note. He didn't want to spill his heart and guts out to her all over again. All he wanted was to return her pill case so their break could finally be over and done.

He still remembered the day she gave it to him. His dog had

been violently sick. Darla came with him as they rushed Frankie to the veterinarian. The vet had worked his magic and sent Liam home with some pills to mash into Frankie's food for the next couple of days. Darla loaned him her little Tiffany pill case to carry the medicine home, and he'd had it ever since.

It was time to get this over with, so he began writing.

Dear Darla,
Here is your pill case. I'm sorry I had it for so long,
but it must have got lost on my ship, and I just found it.

That was a lie, something his father would never do. He balled up the page and threw it away. Telling the truth was important, even if it was painful, and everything about the swift breakup of his relationship with Darla Kingston had been painful.

A clicking of nails on the floor interrupted his thoughts as Frankie lumbered forward to plop down at his feet, looking up at him with sad, soulful eyes.

"You miss her too, eh, boy?"

Frankie kept panting and drooling as all overweight bulldogs did. Liam hauled the dog onto his lap, rubbing his wrinkly fur. "We'll be okay, Frankie," he murmured, then looked at the pill case again.

As painful as his experience with Darla had been, he was grateful for having known her. She made his early months in New York bearable. She accepted him, crude humor and all. Darla was a freethinking artist who made sculptures in both clay and marble. She asked him to teach her to weld so she could sculpt in steel. He'd been so flattered that he made her a blowtorch with his own two hands. He started with a little brass canister for the propane, welded on the pipe and nozzle, then added a polished rosewood handle that made the industrial tool look quaint and feminine.

Darla had been dazzled when he presented the blowtorch to her. He taught her to control the flame and bend metal into any

51

shape she wanted. Their first project had been a winged dragon made from thin strips of steel. She did most of the welding while he used tongs to shape the hot metal. A collector from Boston paid a fortune for that dragon, and Darla hoped she could make a name for herself sculpting in metal just as she had done for stone and clay.

It wasn't to be. She sent his blowtorch back a few days after he broke up with her. Why hadn't he been able to return her pill case? Why did he keep torturing himself with it? He couldn't ever trust Darla again, not after what he overheard her say. Darla wanted him for his money and laughingly told her smart, sophisticated friends that she didn't care that "he was as dumb as a stump." Those were her exact words, and they still scorched.

He once thought that he'd never get over Darla, but that was before he met Maggie. Unlike the society women who pursued him with overly bright smiles and pretended to like him, it was easy to drop his guard when he was with Maggie. They felt alike.

Before he got any deeper with Maggie, he needed to finish this letter to Darla. If he was honest, he'd say something like, *This pill case has always reminded me of you. Pretty and elegant, and I don't want to give it up. You made a world of difference to me those first horrible months after I came to New York when I was lonely and unsure.*

There were other emotions he could bring up. They would be a lot closer to what he'd thought in those angry days after their breakup. *I hate the way you pretended to respect me when all along you were waiting to get your hands on my money. I needed a friend, but you wanted a bank account.*

Frankie yelped, and Liam relaxed his grip. "Sorry, Frankie," he said, then picked up the pen again. This was harder than he thought it would be. Trying to find the right words made him lonely all over again. Uncertain. He never felt inadequate or overwhelmed before he came to New York, but he needed to quit wallowing in these old emotions and get down to business. He took out another sheet of paper and wrote.

Dear Darla, here is your pill case.

He signed his name and folded the page. The lousy note didn't capture his complicated feelings, but Darla knew he wasn't good with words. And yet . . . she deserved more than that blunt note. Despite everything, he owed her so much.

Bracing himself, he unfolded the page to add something straight from his heart.

You were a good friend, and I truly hope you have a bright future. Thank you for everything.

It was enough. It was the truth, and it was enough.

Walking to his stateroom cabin without the pill case in his pocket felt strange but in a good way. And instead of moping over Darla, that night he dreamed about the way the streetlamps sparkled in Maggie Molinaro's eyes.

5

After learning Liam came from *that* Blackstone family, Maggie wore her finest blue suit and a blouse with a lace collar to meet with his cousin about filing a claim against Charles Morse. She brought along two pints of her best hand-churned ice cream as a gift. Maggie might not be able to dress like a rich person, but her ice cream was the finest in the city. Liam carried the two pints in an insulated basket during the carriage ride to the Upper West Side. It was less than a mile from Gadsen Street but felt like another world.

Maggie stood agog before the Dakota apartment building where Liam's cousin lived. The ten-story building resembled a storybook castle with its high gables, turrets, and pale stone exterior. Inside, the ornate elevator had a uniformed footman to close the gate and pull the levers.

After arriving on the ninth floor, a servant opened the door of Natalia's apartment and led them into a spacious room with carved moldings and a coffered ceiling. Moorish tiles surrounded the fireplace, and tapestry panels framed the windows, but the best feature was the view. She stood in mute admiration before the windows overlooking Central Park and to the city beyond.

"I think I can see all the way to the East River," she said, peering into the distance.

"At night you can," a woman said from the other side of the room. Natalia Blackstone shared Liam's dark coloring, only she was willowy and feminine. It was embarrassing to be caught gaping out her window.

"Oh, hi. I brought some ice cream," she said, feeling a little foolish to offer such a humble gift in this grand home, but Natalia smiled warmly.

"Mischa loves ice cream," she said, glancing toward a little boy who hovered in the doorway, his dark eyes watching cautiously.

"He's shy," Natalia explained. "We adopted him a few months ago, and I'm afraid he doesn't speak much English yet. Mischa . . . *morozhenoye!*"

The boy straightened and babbled a string of words in a foreign language. Natalia laughingly replied in the same tongue.

During the carriage ride, Liam told her of Natalia's Russian heritage and how she recently married a Russian count who'd been hounded out of the country for political reasons. It was impossible to know what Natalia had said to the child, yet his eyes widened in astonishment as he gaped at Maggie.

Natalia supplied the translation. "I told him you live in an ice cream parlor, and Mischa is green with envy." Natalia pulled a velvet rope, and a maid soon appeared. Natalia asked for a dish of ice cream to be served to the child, who continued staring at Maggie in admiration as the maid led him from the room.

"Congratulations on your ice cream business." Natalia gestured for them to sit at the parlor table nestled in front of the spectacular view. "You must be so proud."

"Thank you, ma'am. We are."

"We?" Natalia asked.

"I've been partners with my aunt and uncle from the beginning. It's not a big fancy business like the Blackstone Bank, but we're proud of it nonetheless."

"As you should be," Liam said. "And no one should cheat you, even if it's only ninety-five dollars."

Maggie clasped her hands. "I confess I don't understand your plan," she said, but Natalia made it sound easy.

"Banks are regulated by the state of New York," she began. "Bank officers must be men of sterling character and play by the rules. Deliberately passing a bad check, no matter how small the amount, shows Mr. Morse in a poor light. The state should be put on notice."

Natalia provided additional details of the regulations that governed state-sanctioned banks. It was a revelation. The only side of banking Maggie knew was from the customer side, and she had no idea of the complicated rules behind the scenes to safeguard the finances of the nation.

Somewhere deep in the apartment a child began to howl. Natalia excused herself to deal with the crisis. Maggie seized her hostess's absence to stand before the floor-to-ceiling windows and gaze once again over the park.

"I've never seen a view so grand," she said. Words were inadequate to express the feeling of peace that came from this expansive view of greenery. This was what a bird would see while soaring over the city. "I can't imagine ever being sad if I lived in a place like this."

Liam moved to join her at the window. "Is that what you'd want if you had all the money in the world? A pretty view?"

There were so many things she'd want if she were rich. A roof that didn't need constant patching. A hot-water heater. If money were no object, she'd give out generous bonuses to her workers at Christmas and maybe even buy a pretty little pocket watch for herself. But at the top of her list would be this view.

"My bedroom window faces the brick wall of Mr. Lindquist's pharmacy across the alley," she said. "I'd trade views in a heartbeat."

Liam stood so close that the back of his hand brushed hers, sending a tingle up her arm. Did he realize they were touching? She ought to pull away, but didn't, and neither did he. The scent of his soap smelled clean and nice, and she tilted her head to see a faint stubble along his jaw. Such a fine masculine jaw, and the barest hint of a smile curved his lips. She missed being with a man. A daring, strong man who made her feel feminine and protected. Was that wrong? While she was perfectly capable of taking care of herself, it would be wonderful to be cherished by a man.

A flurry of footsteps sounded, and Liam jerked away.

"Forgive me," Natalia said as she returned. Maggie took a step away from Liam and managed a polite smile as Natalia made her apologies. "My son is at the age where a bruised knee can still be magically healed by a kiss. All is well now."

The brief flare of attraction Maggie felt for Liam was set aside as Natalia helped her fill out the paperwork to file a complaint regarding Morse's ethical violation. It seemed so easy, and afterward Natalia invited them to stay for lunch. How could she resist? Somehow the simple chicken salad sandwich tasted even better while enjoying the view of the park.

"How is preparation for the straw poll going?" Natalia asked, and Liam frowned.

"What is a straw poll?" Maggie asked.

"I'm sorry, I shouldn't have brought it up," Natalia quickly said to Liam.

Whatever a *straw poll* was must be upsetting because Liam's entire body looked tense. He glanced away and mumbled that the straw poll was tomorrow and assured his cousin everything would be fine. Yet it didn't sound genuine, and he seemed ill at ease for the rest of the meal.

Liam only reverted to his easygoing demeanor after they left the apartment. The dark cloud lifted and he was once again charming and genial, and she silently rejoiced when he offered to accompany her to file the paperwork with the regulatory agency on State Street.

He was the perfect gentleman during the streetcar ride across town. He paid her fare and swept aside a discarded newspaper from a vacant bench for her to sit. After they arrived at the government building, he opened doors and navigated corridors until they arrived at the correct office to submit the forms. She could have opened those doors and found the right office on her own, but it was nice to have someone to lean on.

They stepped back into the sunshine and headed to the streetcar stop. He would be taking the car to Pier 19 while she would board the Cross-Town line back to Gadsen Street. Now that their task was done, was this going to be the end for them? Their paths would never have crossed but for their chance encounter at Charles Morse's house. Now their mission was drawing to a close, and for the first time since meeting him an awkward pause stretched between them. She rushed to fill it.

"That was easier than I expected," she said.

"We did good work today," Liam said. "This meant a lot more than ninety-five dollars over ice cream."

She looked at him curiously. "What do you mean?"

Instead of answering, Liam scanned State Street, lined with government buildings and interspersed with boardinghouses and storefronts. Pushcart vendors navigated among delivery wagons and hustling businessmen. Liam gestured to a man standing outside a photography studio, who held up a hand-painted sign featuring a big red arrow pointing toward his shop. The man was putting on quite a show as he beckoned customers toward his shop.

"You see that guy? He probably took out a huge loan for his studio. Look how hard he's working to drum up a little business. I want that guy to succeed. Look around us," he continued. "The bookseller, the insurance agency, the coffee shop, and the dentist office. How many of them do you think took out loans to get their businesses started?"

"All of them," she answered with certainty.

"Thank heavens they took that risk because we need them," Liam said. "We need restaurants and bookstores and dentists. They make this city great. And, Maggie, by standing up for yourself today, you stood up *for them* too."

She caught her breath, unexpectedly moved. "That might be the nicest thing anyone has ever said to me."

"You deserved it," he said, smiling down into her eyes. She

ELIZABETH CAMDEN

didn't want this to be the end. She didn't want to go their separate ways. She scrambled for a way to prolong the moment, but anything she could think to say would sound hopelessly forward and not ladylike at all. Liam stepped up to the plate and spared her the embarrassment.

"Hey, if you aren't doing anything on Saturday, maybe you and I could go to Coney Island for a few hours."

She schooled her features to block the elation from showing because he must feel the hum of attraction too, but Saturday was a problem. "I work on Saturdays."

"Sunday?" Liam asked.

"Sorry, I work Sundays too, but I can do something in the evenings," she offered.

He grinned. "How about I take you out to the Porterhouse on Saturday night? I've heard they have the best steak in town. Do they?"

"I have no idea. I've never eaten there."

He pulled back to see if she was joking. "But it's right across the street from where you live."

"The Porterhouse wastes money on linen tablecloths and custom menus ordered from a printer each week. I don't believe in subsidizing those costs. If I want a satisfying meal, I go to the Jewish deli."

His laugh came from deep within his chest. "Then how about I take you to the Jewish deli? Or to the food cart that sells hot dogs if that will tickle your thrifty itch. If you'd like something a little nicer, I'll take you to the Waldorf or Delmonico's or the Porterhouse. Miss Molinaro, in case I haven't made myself clear, I'd like a few hours of your company. Just you and me. Name the time and place."

"Okay, the Porterhouse," she said. "Friday evening at six o'clock."

He touched the brim of his hat. "It's a deal."

Though Maggie didn't want this moment to end, the Cross-Town streetcar was heading their way. At least this wouldn't be the end. In four short days they would see each other again, and he was taking her to the *Porterhouse*! The fanciest restaurant in the city. She climbed aboard the streetcar and beamed at him as it pulled away.

Could all this really be happening? Over the past few days Liam Blackstone had become a friend, a partner who helped with her lawsuit troubles, and maybe even a new sweetheart. A powerful sweetheart who thought nothing of splurging at the Porterhouse or tackling a robber baron like Charles Morse.

Maybe it was too early to start building castles in the air, but everything suddenly felt new, exciting, and right.

6

*L*iam dressed with painstaking care the morning of the humiliating straw poll to determine if he would be subjected to an official vote of no confidence.

He shaved, slicked his unruly hair back with a sheen of macassar oil, and selected his best three-piece suit. The formal suit was fusty and uncomfortable, especially the high-stand collar. Back when he was a welder, he never realized those collars were detachable bands that needed to be fastened to a dress shirt by three collar studs, one at the back of his neck and two in the front.

He angled the mirror to catch the morning sunlight from his cabin porthole as he aligned the stud holes on his neckband, but a twinge deep in his belly was a painful reminder that he hadn't downed a glass of his daily medicine.

He finished anchoring the stiff collar on his shirt, wrapped his tie, then shrugged into a dress jacket before heading to the ship's galley kitchen. Every footfall triggered a fresh stab of pain in his gut, yet his mood shifted when he arrived in the kitchen where the crew heckled him over his fancy duds.

"Looking sharp, boss," the ship's cook said. Everyone else was dressed like a normal workingman. The cook wore a white smock and apron, the boiler room guys wore baggy coveralls, and the deck crew had on their blue uniforms. He was the only one trussed up like a stuffed turkey.

"And feeling awful," he said, taking a seat at the table. The white-enamel oven, stove, and icebox lined one side of the kitchen, while the crew sat at a long table on the opposite wall to take their meals. The tile-lined galley was a little loud when everyone was here, but breakfast with the crew was always fun. They were getting omelets seasoned with bacon, onions, and chili peppers, though it was all off-limits for Liam. He still made a joke about it.

"I'll bet you're all jealous there isn't enough fermented cabbage juice to share," he teased. Cabbage juice helped reduce the inflammation in his gut, and there was some good-natured hooting as the cook handed him a glass of the dark green liquid. Fermented cabbage juice was bad, but the other glass of his daily medicine was worse. The milky liquid had medicinal chalk ground up in it, but it helped neutralize the acid in his gut so he'd get it down.

He tackled the cabbage juice first, wincing at the bitter tang as he drained the glass. Now the milk. This was *the worst*. He held his breath while chugalugging the thick, chalky liquid in a continuous series of swallows, forcing it to stay down despite the powerful urge to throw it up.

He banged the glass down and raised both arms overhead like a champion. The crew roared with approval as he stood to accept the applause. The cheers were deafening in the narrow kitchen, and he still felt as if he might vomit, but the comradery of the others made it bearable.

The lighthearted mood faded as he set off to face the humiliation of witnessing his fellow board members decide if he was too incompetent to sit in their vaunted presence. He took the streetcar to the Financial District, his mood darkening a little more with each mile.

At least he had a secret weapon. Maggie's ethics complaint against Charles Morse was only a single page, but it would unleash an avalanche of embarrassment for any banker.

Patrick awaited him outside the U.S. Steel building, his face grim. "Ready?" he asked.

Liam gave a stiff nod, and Patrick launched into last-minute instructions as they entered the cool of the building. "Remember, all it takes is a simple majority for Morse to win the straw poll and move the resolution forward. We're going to lose today, but the way you present yourself is huge. Don't lose your temper. Don't fling insults or let Morse draw you into a duel of words. Got it?"

"I got it," he said, but defending himself with words had always been a challenge. Bare-knuckle boxing felt more natural to him, but he'd play by the rules if it meant saving his seat on the board. They strode to the elevator, where an attendant dragged the cage across the opening, clanging it into place. The door of a jail cell probably sounded exactly like that.

By the time he got to the meeting room on the seventeenth floor, his insides were knotted and his fists clenched. Regardless, he walked calmly to a chair, nodded to his fellow board members, and sat.

This was no ordinary conference room. The grandiose space reflected U.S. Steel's stature as one of the most powerful corporations in the world. The conference table had been made from rare black walnut and had room for thirty people to sit in the chairs upholstered with Sicilian leather. Raised gallery seating around three sides of the room accommodated shareholders, lawyers, clerks, and stenographers. Floor-to-ceiling windows on the fourth wall overlooked the Financial District of Manhattan.

The eleven other board members were already seated, with Fletcher at the head of the table. Once Liam and Patrick were seated, Fletcher banged a gavel to call the meeting to order.

"The first motion for business is a request for a vote of no confidence for Mr. Liam Blackstone. A report has been submitted to me by a board member outlining his concerns, and I will summarize it for the benefit of all—"

"Point of order," Patrick interrupted. "My client would like to know the name of the person who proposed the motion."

Fletcher shifted uneasily. "It was an anonymous request."

"My client has a right to know who has accused him," Patrick said in his lawyerly manner. Liam kept his eyes fastened on Morse, who raised a pugnacious chin but said nothing.

"What's the matter, Charles?" Liam asked. "Is there a reason you don't want your name associated with this?"

"Not at all," Morse said, then turned to Fletcher. "You may acknowledge my role in taking the initiative to improve the caliber of the board."

"Very well," said Fletcher. "It was indeed Charles Morse who requested the vote after the unfortunate incident on the *Black Rose*."

"Unfortunate incident?" Patrick said. "Is that what we're calling it when a grown man slaps a seventeen-year-old deckhand?"

Fletcher continued in the same unruffled tone, "However we refer to the incident, the issue is with Mr. Blackstone's lack of a formal education and executive experience."

"I think it's only fair to consider the source of this accusation," Patrick said. "My client brings a wealth of honest experience in labor relations, while Mr. Morse's reputation for financial integrity is in question."

"That's a lie!" Morse interjected.

"Is it?" Patrick turned to Liam. "Would you care to share your insight into what you witnessed between Mr. Morse and the woman from Molinaro Ice Cream?"

With pleasure. Liam handed a copy of Maggie's complaint to a clerk and asked for it to be carried to Fletcher. "Molinaro Ice Cream filed a complaint with the New York State Banking Department against Morse because he knowingly wrote them a bad check for his wedding reception. I was standing ten feet away and witnessed the entire incident."

Fletcher scowled as he read the complaint. "Charles?"

An angry flush tinged Morse's face as he glared at the document Fletcher held. "A complaint is not an admission of guilt, nor has it been adjudicated."

One of the other board members chuckled. "Careful, Charles. You're sounding like a lawyer."

"You had Molinaro Ice Cream at your wedding reception?" another board member asked. "Now I'm sorry I was in France when it happened. How is Mrs. Morse?"

"She's fine," Charles said tersely, but Liam couldn't resist a jab.

"I'll bet she's embarrassed that you stiffed the lady who supplied the ice cream to your wedding reception."

"Shut up, Blackstone," Charles growled. "I didn't stiff anyone."

"That will be for the ethics board to decide," Patrick said. "I suspect they will be shocked to learn that a man with a controlling interest in several New York banks would knowingly write a bad check. If a man will cheat a woman over an ice cream bill, can he be trusted at the helm of a banking empire that controls millions?"

Morse shot to his feet. "Why are we even discussing this? We're here to consider Blackstone's lack of qualifications to be sitting at this table."

"This is the first I've heard of an ethics violation," Rudolph Keppler said, surely the oldest, stuffiest, and most conservative of all the board members. Mr. Keppler was the president of the New York Stock Exchange and fanatically concerned about legal formalities. "What exactly is the charge this woman is making?"

Fletcher read the brief announcement aloud. "'Miss Margaret Molinaro has filed a complaint with the New York State Banking Department, charging Charles W. Morse with knowingly passing a bad check in the amount of ninety-five dollars. She requests relief and an acknowledgment of guilt.'"

Mr. Keppler's bushy gray eyebrows drew together in concern. "Is this true?"

"It's a bald-faced lie," Morse snapped. "That woman is trying to extort me. She is a liar, a swindler, and I will never pay her a dime."

"But why such a paltry amount?" Mr. Keppler asked. "Wouldn't a genuine swindler want more than ninety-five dollars?"

Fletcher nodded. "I once had a strange woman come out of the blue and accuse me of being her child's father. She wanted fifty thousand, a house in Rhode Island, and an annual stipend."

"What happened?" Patrick asked.

"I was able to prove I was in London at the time her child was conceived," Fletcher said dismissively. "We all know that men of power can become targets for extortion, but not over ninety-five dollars. That seems rather odd."

All eyes swiveled to Charles Morse. "Yes. She came after me for the ninety-five, but I refuse to be swindled out of money I don't owe."

"And I refuse to see this board become ensnared in anything that whiffs of an ethical violation," Fletcher said, sliding Maggie's complaint down the table toward Morse. "Pay the woman. Make this go away. There will be no public hearing or state investigation. Is that understood?"

Morse's face turned a deep ruddy shade, eyes snapping fire, but Fletcher proceeded to the business at hand. "My clerk will distribute ballots for the matter of Mr. Blackstone's continued membership on this board. If there's a simple majority vote in the affirmative, we shall proceed to an official vote at our September meeting." Fletcher sent him a conciliatory smile. "Liam, you will have plenty of time to mount a formal defense should the poll go against you."

His heart thudded as the clerk distributed the ballots to the other eleven men on the board of directors. This was the most humiliating moment of his life. For once he was grateful for the awful starched collar that forced his chin to remain high while he listened to pens scratching his fate onto the cardboard ballots.

The vote was 9–2 to proceed with a vote of no confidence. He might have succeeded in taking a little shine off Morse's stature on the board, but Morse had won the day.

7

Maggie was stunned when a check for $95.00 was suddenly deposited into her bank account. Liam had been right. The formal complaint was infinitely more efficient than letting the process slowly work through the court system, and she couldn't wait to share her good news with him. She'd been walking on air ever since he'd asked her to the Porterhouse, and nothing could dampen her mood.

Even bickering with the pushcart vendors didn't bother her as much as usual. Gary was the ringleader of the disgruntled employees who regularly complained about their schedules, their uniforms, and her meticulous cleaning standards. She was helping wipe down the carts and stock them with ice while listening to the litany of complaints.

Today's gripe was about the ice. "We're losing sales every time we have to stop in the middle of the day to restock the ice," Gary grumbled. "You're scrimping on ice, and it's costing us money."

She stopped polishing. "I'm not scrimping on ice. What are you talking about?"

"You aren't giving us a full twenty pounds anymore," Gary insisted. "It's melting before the end of the shift."

This was the first she'd heard of underweight ice. She glanced at Spider Mackenzie, their maintenance man since the beginning. Spider was as skinny as a beanpole, but still strong as he slid a block of ice into a pushcart's cold box.

"Yeah, the ice blocks are coming in smaller," he confirmed. "The new iceman claims they're melting because of the heat."

"Did he give us a break on the bill?"

Spider shook his head. "He said they're raising the rates. Twenty-five percent next month."

"No!" She'd only been using the Manhattan Ice Company for three weeks. They had a lot of nerve to raise her rates at the same time they delivered underweight ice.

"The guy said it's going to be a hot summer and to expect more price hikes," Spider continued. "He said all the ice companies are doing it."

That worried her. After the pushcarts were loaded and off for the morning, Maggie headed out to see if other restaurants on the street were faced with raising prices for their ice, and it was true. Even Mr. Lindquist, the owner of the pharmacy next door, who only needed small deliveries of ice to keep his serums cool, was being squeezed by the price hike.

With his dapper suit and bow tie, Mr. Lindquist always struck her as a grandfatherly sort. Maybe it was the way he sometimes slipped an extra peppermint stick into people's orders that made her like him. Today he was grinding headache powders behind the front counter as she asked him about his ice deliveries.

"It's been an unusually warm summer," Mr. Lindquist said. "I suppose it's only fair they raise prices when the supply gets low."

"Doesn't a twenty-five percent increase seem like a lot to you?"

"I guess it's the cost of doing business." Mr. Lindquist shrugged. "All the ice companies are saying the same thing, so it must be true."

Except it set off Maggie's warning bells. People on the street used different ice companies, and everyone's bill was rising in tandem. Maybe if she hadn't been forced to hire a new ice supplier only a few weeks ago, she might not be so suspicious. She'd always trusted Gabelli Ice and wouldn't have such misgivings if the price hike had come from them.

Mr. Gabelli's abrupt decision to close his business still seemed strange to her. She didn't trust her new supplier, but she trusted old Mr. Gabelli, who could maybe tell her the truth about whatever trouble was brewing in the ice industry.

The Gabelli family lived in a fine brownstone on the Upper East Side. While ice was a profitable business, the costs of starting an ice company were high. Harvesting ice happened up in Maine during the deep of winter. Horses drawing ice-cutting blades were driven across frozen lakes to cut checkerboard grooves into the ice. Teams of men followed with long-handled chisels to break the blocks free. Each block weighed two hundred pounds when it was delivered to an icehouse.

Mr. Gabelli once told her that his icehouse in Maine was longer than a football field and had four-foot-thick stone walls. Inside were a dozen well-insulated rooms, each with a window where ice was delivered directly from steam-powered conveyor belts. Although there was always some melt during the summer months, by opening only one room at a time he was able to keep ice available throughout the year. The Gabelli barge shipped ice to Manhattan every week, where his local crews delivered it to the customers.

The wide stone steps leading up to the Gabelli brownstone were testament to his four decades of hard work, yet she was stunned to see the worry lines on the old man's face as he welcomed her into his home. It had only been a year since she last saw him, but he seemed beaten down. Had he been ill? Perhaps that explained why he exited the business so abruptly.

"Come," he said, beckoning her into the parlor. A sofa and two chairs remained, but the carpets had been rolled up and everything else was in boxes. "I'm sorry I can't offer refreshment, but most of my kitchen is already packed."

"When are you moving?" she asked.

If anything, he seemed sadder. "I don't know. I can't afford to move until the house is sold, so it may be a while."

Perhaps the ice business had not been as profitable as she believed. Still, the timing of his move seemed strange. "Why did you close your company right before the hottest part of the summer when profits are highest?"

"It's not a business for me anymore," he said with a shrug, but he wouldn't meet her eyes. It was unsettling. When she asked if it was true that there was a shortage of ice this year, he was hesitant to confirm the rumor.

"I don't know about the supply. It doesn't surprise me, though, that the rates are going up," he said. "You should prepare for it to get worse."

"Worse?"

He nodded. She respected Mr. Gabelli, but he wasn't a fortune-teller who could predict how hot the summer would be.

"What aren't you telling me? I need to know what's going on."

Mr. Gabelli closed the door to the kitchen, then looked down the hallway before closing that door as well. He joined her on the sofa, leaning in to speak quietly.

"Forgive me, but this topic upsets my wife, so let me speak quickly. Some of the people in the ice business have formed a trust that will bind them together to share expenses. They don't like people who refuse to join the trust. I'm afraid I learned this the hard way."

Maggie listened in horror as he described an incident from earlier in the year. His foreman in Maine reported ongoing vandalism at the Gabelli icehouse. The building fronted a lake where the family had been harvesting ice for decades, but it was in a rural area and hard to guard. In February, Mr. Gabelli went to Maine to see if he could make peace with the troublemakers, but unless he agreed to join the trust, they weren't interested in peace.

"They sent an ice-cutting steamer to the portion of the lake

70

directly in front of my icehouse," he said. "They smashed my ice, so it was too small to harvest. I watched from the shore, and there was nothing I could do as they destroyed my season's entire stock. They scattered coal dust over it before they left."

He tried to stay in business by buying ice from others who had refused to join the trust. He was able to fill a barge, but the trust wasn't finished with him.

"Once I arrived in the city, I couldn't find a pier to dock the barge," he said. "In my forty years of doing business, it has never been a problem to dock, but the piers are controlled by the city. It's illegal to dock without permission, so I had nowhere to off-load the ice."

Maggie was flabbergasted. "I don't understand. There are a hundred and forty-four piers in New York Harbor."

"And not a single one was open to me." He drew a heavy sigh. "I had to sell my icehouse to someone who belongs to the trust, and he got it for a song. No one else would be foolish enough to enter this business so long as the trust is alive."

"Who controls the trust?"

Mr. Gabelli held his hands up. "I don't know, but he's got enough sway at the Department of Docks to drive men who won't pay graft out of business. I'm sorry, Maggie. This is going to get worse before it gets better."

Maggie didn't know anything about docking rules, but she knew someone who did. It was time to place a call to Pier 19 and draw on Liam Blackstone's insight for how to dock a ship in New York City.

8

Maggie stared in wonder at the ship where Liam lived. The *Black Rose* was possibly the prettiest ship she'd ever seen, with a sleek black hull and a scarlet stripe along her top. Brass fittings gleamed in the sunshine, cables stretched from towering masts, and a dark red smokestack dominated the rear of the ship. Liam called it "a yacht," but it looked more like a steamship to Maggie's untutored eyes.

How was she supposed to get on board? It wasn't as if there was a front door where she could knock or ring a doorbell. She walked the length of the ship until she finally spotted a crew member on deck.

"I'm looking for Liam Blackstone," she called up. "Is he here?"

"He's working at Pier 27," the crew member called down. "Testing out a new alloy on the pilings."

Maggie nodded as though she understood what he just said, and the crew member disappeared back into the bowels of the ship.

She walked the half mile to Pier 27, one of the municipal piers that included a long, multistoried warehouse stretching two acres into the Hudson River. Ships could dock alongside it to off-load cargo, while people used walkways on the roof to gain access to the warehouse.

Pier 27 was undergoing a renovation and looked like a steel skeleton. A dozen men scrambled over the exposed beams, some welding and others lifting new railings into place. Liam was straddling a partly disassembled wall two stories above. He wore tinted goggles and had his sleeves rolled up to expose tanned forearms as he wielded a blowtorch, directing its flame to a steel beam.

She stood on the pier a few yards away and shaded her eyes to look up at him. After a few minutes, he glanced down and spotted her. He cut fuel to the blowtorch, pushed the dark goggles up, and grinned down at her.

"What do you need, pretty lady?"

"Advice!" she shouted.

There was some good-natured heckling from the other men on the scaffolding, and she fidgeted a little. Venturing alone to the docks wasn't the smartest move she had ever made. Liam swung a leg over the railing and navigated a ladder with surprising agility. He jumped down the last few rungs and headed toward her.

"I'm sorry," she stammered. "I didn't realize you would be involved in something so daunting."

He shrugged away her concern. He looked different today, though she couldn't explain why. Happier? Sweat mingled with dirt and grime on his face, and his open collar revealed the strong column of his throat.

"I'm testing out a new alloy of steel our company has developed," he said. "There's no better way of seeing how it will behave than by giving it a whirl. This stuff is supposed to be stronger and more resistant to rust, but it takes longer to fuse."

"This is part of your job?"

"Nah," he said with a shake of his head. "We've got plenty of fancy scientists testing it in laboratories, but it's not the same as using it in the field. This alloy is going to be used by people climbing on skyscrapers and on ships' riggings. I don't want it going out before I can tell them what to expect. Hey, did Morse finally pay the ninety-five bucks he owes you?"

"He did," she said. "Thank you for your help with that." The breeze ruffled his hair, and she was struck once again at how different he looked today. More relaxed. "Is there somewhere we can go to talk?" she asked.

He nodded and led her to the Esplanade, which ran along the shoreline. New York City boasted the largest port in America, and it was always a hive of activity. Stevedores off-loaded cargo into lumbering wagons. Park benches and tables lined up along the Esplanade, and dozens of pushcarts offered everything from pork sausages to fried kippers.

"Well?" Liam asked once they were seated on a rickety wooden bench.

"I was hoping you could explain how docking fees in the harbor work."

"Well, the piers are owned by the city, of course," he said. "I pay a monthly fee for a berth."

"What about someone who only needs a few hours to unload cargo?"

"They pay by the day plus a tax if they're importing something from another country." He pointed to a pier straight ahead of them, where a crane was lowering barrels onto the deck of a steamer. "That's turpentine headed for the port of Rotterdam," he said. "Earlier today there was a fishing vessel off-loading tuna. On a typical day a berth turns over two or three times. Someone from the Department of Docks swings by to talk to the ship's bursar and collect the payments."

"That's it? As long as a person can pay the fee, they can use a pier?"

"Pretty much," he replied.

"I know someone who used to unload shipments of ice at this port for decades. Then last month they told him he'd have to dock somewhere else, that there was no room at the port."

"There's *always* room at the port," Liam said with a frown, and it confirmed Maggie's fears. Something shady was going on in the ice business, but she didn't know how to find out what it was. When she confided in Liam, he was matter-of-fact in his response.

"Follow me," he said, standing. "The folks who control docking privileges are at Pier A. I'll help you get to the bottom of this."

Maggie was both thrilled and frightened by his offer. The way he instantly stepped forward to help was a blessing, but it also confirmed her niggling anxiety. It looked like corruption had taken root in the ice business, and without a reliable source of ice, her company would collapse in a matter of days.

⁂

Liam held Maggie's elbow as they crossed the busy Esplanade toward the streetcar stop. He loved being able to help her out in a bind. Ever since he emerged as the missing Blackstone heir, women had been throwing themselves at him for no apparent reason other than his money, but he had *earned* the admiration shining in Maggie's gaze today. It made him feel worthy, like he was a man of accomplishment in his own right, when in truth he was merely good at making friends down at the docks. Hopefully it would be useful in shedding light on Maggie's questions.

They arrived at the streetcar stop, but Maggie wanted to proceed a little farther. "There's a free trolley on the next block if we wait twenty minutes."

"I haven't got twenty minutes." The streetcar would be here momentarily, and it cost a whopping five cents to ride. Even when he was a kid in the slums, he could always spring for a ride, especially on hot summer days. But someone must have beaten Maggie with the penny-pinching stick hard enough to make her permanently cheap, and he told her so.

"I prefer to call it frugal," she pointed out.

He paid her fare since he didn't want to shock her frugal sensibilities. It was crowded on the streetcar, and they grabbed the overhead straps as it set off for Pier A, where the Department of Docks reigned supreme and controlled all the goods flowing in or out of New York.

The city could be a tough place to do business. Tammany Hall still had an iron grip on commerce and wasn't above resorting to graft and bribery. If a business owner wasn't willing to cooperate, it wouldn't be surprising to suddenly lose access to a dock or a city contract.

The streetcar soon arrived at the southernmost point of Manhattan where Pier A stretched into the harbor. It was a showpiece at the entrance to the harbor and featured a white neoclassical building with arched windows, a copper roof, and an elegant clock tower. To some it might look like a welcoming entrance to the port. To others, it was where the Department of Docks and the Harbor Police ruled in tandem to oversee access to the city.

It was cool inside the building with ceiling fans slowly rotating the air as their footsteps echoed down the long corridors. The Blackstone name tended to open doors, so they didn't have to wait long before being shown into the office of Johnny Bartlett, the superintendent in charge of docking privileges. It was a modest office with plain walls and a few pieces of wood furniture, but the view overlooking the harbor was a showstopper with the Statue of Liberty in the distance. The windows were open, letting the salty breeze cool the room.

"Bartlett," Liam greeted, reaching across the desk to shake the superintendent's hand. Johnny Bartlett was a stout man with a head of curly brown hair and laughing eyes. He was always good for drinks at the end of a day.

"Please don't tell me you want to vacate Pier 19," Superintendent Bartlett said. "That crew of yours is popular with the restaurants on the Esplanade."

"No worries," Liam said. "I'm here about finding docking space for an associate."

"What kind of ship?"

Liam glanced at Maggie, and she supplied the answer. "A ninety-foot barge. The owner wants to make regular deliveries from Maine, and off-loading won't take more than two hours."

The superintendent smiled. "Easy as pie. We can cut you a better deal if the shipments can be scheduled in advance. What's the name of the company?"

"Gabelli Ice," Maggie replied, and Liam winced. It would have been better to lock Bartlett into a deal before revealing the name of the company, but Maggie was being forthright.

Bartlett leaned back in his chair, the hinges squeaking as he drummed his fingers on the desk. "Sorry. Gabelli is persona non grata."

"Why?" he asked, and Bartlett shrugged.

"The folks at Tammany Hall are keen on helping a new organization designed to support the ice industry, and anyone who doesn't sign up for it isn't going to be allowed to dock. Rules are rules. It's for the good of the city, I'm sure."

Maggie butted in again. "I've been doing business with Mr. Gabelli for years, and he's an honest businessman. He said he wouldn't pay graft—"

Liam sent her a warning glare, and she stopped talking. "What's the name of this new ice organization?" he asked.

"The American Ice Company," Bartlett replied. "It's a completely reputable organization, and they've helped grease the wheels for other ice companies that want to join and get prime access to New York business."

"Who controls American Ice?" Liam asked.

"Charles Morse."

Liam tried to block the surprise from showing on his face. Was there anything that man didn't have his hand in? Banking on Wall Street, copper in Montana, steel all over the nation, and now ice in Maine.

"Morse knows a lot about the ice business," the superintendent continued. "His father owns a bunch of icehouses up in Maine. Ice barges too. He's in a prime position to know how to improve the industry for the good of everyone. He's already helping drive bad actors out of the business." The superintendent's smile was relaxed and genuine.

He's lying, Liam silently thought. Johnny Bartlett was too congenial, too calm. The man had the ability to control the assignment of berths, which made him a critical part of the scheme. He was probably getting a payoff.

Liam stood and matched the cordial smile. "Thanks for explaining things. Hey, you should join me on the *Black Rose* one of these days when we have a sunset harbor party."

"I'd like nothing better," the superintendent said, standing to shake Liam's hand.

Maggie was fuming. With cheeks flushed and eyes flashing, it looked as though she couldn't decide whether to attack Bartlett or Liam. He slanted her a quick warning glance, and she seemed to understand, following him out of the office and down the hall.

"Don't say anything until we're alone," he whispered without breaking stride. She nodded and kept pace with him, but the moment they were out in the sunshine, she stopped and looked directly in his eyes.

"He's getting a payoff, isn't he?" she said.

"Bingo, but there's no point in confronting him. Besides, Morse is sitting on the throne of this particular scheme, and going after his underlings won't do much good."

"How did Morse get so much control in this city?" she asked. "This cannot be legal, and we ought to complain to someone."

"We?" Liam already had enough trouble with Charles Morse without taking on her battles again.

"You're a fair-minded person," Maggie said. "You didn't like what you just heard any more than I did, but I don't know how to fight this."

He shrugged. "People have been waging war against Tammany Hall for generations. You can't win against them. As soon as you cut off one head, they grow three more."

"What a comforting image," she said with a note of cynicism. "What happened to Mr. Gabelli was a crime. Isn't there anything you can do to help?"

Liam could probably use his influence to ease the situation, but he needed to choose his battles carefully. On September 30, the board would decide if he was worthy enough to retain his seat. That meant he had to keep his nose clean for the next three months.

He braced his hands on the railing, gazing at the tugboats scattered across the bay to lead oceangoing vessels in and out of port. There was a rhythm to life at the harbor, and he loved being a part of it, yet it was a dangerous place. No single person had control of everything, but powerful alliances operated behind the scenes. People who dared to stand up to those forces risked their businesses and sometimes even their lives.

He didn't want to worry about Tammany Hall or Charles Morse. In fact, all he could think about right now was how pretty Maggie looked in her pinstriped blouse and jaunty boater hat. But he was hanging on to his seat by a thread, and if he attacked Morse again, it would show him in a bad light. There were 160,000 men depending on him to represent their interests on the board. He had to put their well-being ahead of the charming lady looking up at him with such fresh-faced hope.

"I'm not going to be able to help with your ice situation, Maggie," he said. "I'm fighting too many battles to add another one to the heap, but can I still take you to the Porterhouse on Friday?"

She touched his wrist. "I'm looking forward to it," she said, and the zing that traveled from his wrist sent a shiver through his whole body.

He gave her a good-natured nudge. "Me too."

9

It was late in the afternoon when Maggie arrived home from Pier A. The news hadn't been what she wanted to hear, but her escalating relationship with Liam Blackstone was both thrilling and reassuring. He seemed so *competent*. Whether he was welding steel or navigating the political environment at the Department of Docks, he was strong and capable, and she liked that.

The bell dinged as she entered the ice cream parlor, where three people loitered before the service counter waiting for ice cream, but there was no sign of Dino.

"My uncle isn't here?" she asked in surprise. It wasn't like Dino to leave the counter untended.

A sour-faced matron frowned. "He went into the back room a few minutes ago to see to someone. He said he would be right back, but then an argument broke out. It's been over five minutes. Can I get a scoop of strawberry ice cream, please?"

Dino's angry voice could be heard even from here, and it wasn't like her kindly uncle to argue with anyone. Unbidden, the image of a steamship smashing and ruining Mr. Gabelli's ice rose in her mind.

"Someone will be right out," she said to the surly woman before opening the back door into the factory. Mercifully, it wasn't a frightening thug arguing with Dino, but Mr. Alfonso from the deli across the street. They spoke in Italian, both men nose to nose as they hollered at each other.

"What's going on?" she asked, kicking herself for never learning the language. Mr. Alfonso stifled his tirade but still had the flushed, angry look of a bulldog.

"Alfonso wants to use our refrigerator to store his salami and hams," Dino said. "I told him we can't do it."

"Why not?" Mr. Alfonso roared. "You've got plenty of space. You could do cartwheels in that walk-in refrigerator, but you can't spare a little room for a few smoked hams?"

It was unthinkable. Mr. Alfonso's heavily seasoned meats made his deli smell wonderful, but dairy picked up aromas easily. Exposure to spicy meat would ruin their cream.

"Why do you need our refrigerator?" she asked, and the answer was what she suspected. Mr. Alfonso didn't have enough ice to keep his own refrigerator cold. After the sharp increase in prices, Mr. Alfonso insisted on paying only what he had budgeted for, which meant he got much less ice than normal. He'd gambled and hoped the weather would be cool enough to make the ice last until the next shipment.

"How was I supposed to know the weather would be so hot?" Mr. Alfonso demanded.

"June is *always* hot," Dino retorted.

Mr. Alfonso turned to her, still scowling. "Can you at least loan me a few blocks of ice? Perhaps it will be enough to save the hams."

There was no such thing as "loaning" a block of ice. Ice melted, and Mr. Alfonso would never return the favor. Maggie bought an additional two hundred pounds on Monday because the weather had been so hot, and she never gambled when it came to business.

"I can cut a thirty-pound block for you," she said.

"Thirty pounds! That won't last until tomorrow morning in this heat."

It was all she could offer. Throughout her life she'd planned and saved, and never risked more than she could afford to lose.

She couldn't let Mr. Alfonso browbeat her into ruining their dairy supply.

"Thirty pounds is what I can give you."

Mr. Alfonso's face flushed a bright red, his eyes snapping in anger, but then he tried to sound conciliatory. "Thank you. Perhaps I can get enough from other people on the street, because my restaurant can't survive if I lose a week's worth of meat."

She turned away from his heated glare. "We have customers waiting out front," she said to Dino. "While you see to them, I'll take care of Mr. Alfonso." She headed to the freezer with an ice pick and a hammer to chisel the ice. It wouldn't be enough to save Mr. Alfonso's meat unless someone else came to his rescue, but she couldn't let his risky behavior damage her own business.

She suspected his downfall would not be long in coming.

⁂

The first casualty of Mr. Alfonso's poor planning arrived at Maggie's apartment that very night. It was ten o'clock when Frieda Neuman burst into the apartment to announce that she was being let go.

"He waited until my shift ended before he said I shouldn't come back tomorrow," Frieda said. With her smattering of freckles, she looked younger than her thirty years, but Frieda supported her widowed mother and had no other form of income.

"Did he pay you?" Aunt Julie asked as she poured milk into a glass at the sideboard.

Frieda shook her head. "He said to come back next week and he would pay what he owes. I hope he's telling the truth because things have been bad for him lately, and I'm not sure he's got it."

Julie tutted in sympathy as she brought the milk and cookies to set on the coffee table. Like the rest of the furniture in the apartment, the coffee table had come from a secondhand shop. It was a little scuffed, but Dino had buffed the scratches, and a fresh coat of varnish made it look brand-new. Same with the upholstered couch that practically swallowed Frieda in its tufted cushions. The damask fabric had held up well, and Julie had made lace coverings to hide the worn patches on the armrests. The care and attention lavished on the parlor and dining room made the apartment look as though rich people lived here. In truth, all three of them worked hard and saved harder, and they didn't squander money on luxuries.

Maggie sat beside Frieda. The two of them were different in all things except that they both knew what it was like to be a single woman working in a city that didn't have much room for people like them.

If Frieda had been smart, she would have spotted the warning signs at Alfonso's Deli and jumped ship before it started sinking. Mr. Alfonso paid his bills late and had started using cheaper cuts of meat. Yet her loyalty to the Alfonsos kept Frieda at the deli despite the warning signs, and it was a costly mistake.

"I don't know how I'm going to make it," Frieda said. "The rent is due in two weeks, and if Mr. Alfonso doesn't pay me, I won't have enough. And then what?"

Julie's soft gaze implored Maggie. They all knew the fear of poverty, but this shouldn't become their problem. Frieda wore a pretty new dress, and last month she bought herself a set of new stoneware dishes from a department store. She bought them brand-new, not secondhand like Maggie always did.

"Can we find something for Frieda to do?" Julie asked, her eyes pleading. Maggie handled the staffing and made the final decisions where the budget was concerned because she had a knack for getting the most out of every dime. She had been wanting to buy a mechanical egg breaker for months, but couldn't bring herself to fire Jake, the teenage boy who worked two hours a day cracking eggs. She had coordinated the purchase of the equipment to arrive the week Jake quit to follow his family to the West Coast. The expensive machine had just arrived and would pay for itself in five months . . . but not if she hired Frieda.

It probably wouldn't hurt to store the mechanical egg breaker in a closet for a few weeks, even though it was a shame not to put it to work.

"We could hire you to break eggs for a few hours in the afternoons," she said reluctantly, and Frieda's eyes teared up even more.

"Oh, thank you, Maggie!"

"It's only until you can find something permanent," Maggie rushed to say.

That night, she and Dino went downstairs to lug the hefty egg breaker into a storage closet so Frieda wouldn't see it the following day. Sometimes she had to set thriftiness aside to do the decent thing, but it wasn't ever easy.

∽

Anticipation for her coming dinner with Liam Blackstone tingled as Maggie wheeled another cart of eggs to the worktable.

"He's taking me to the Porterhouse," she confided to Frieda.

"My, my," Frieda said, reaching for an egg and cracking it into the five-gallon bowl.

Maggie couldn't stop smiling thinking about this evening's date at the Porterhouse. She liked everything about Liam. It was probably foolish to start hoping for something serious, but it had been so long since she'd felt such attraction for a man.

"Are you over Philip, then?" Frieda asked as she cracked another egg.

"Of course I am," Maggie replied. After all, she had been the one to walk away from the relationship, and Philip was long married by now, so of course she was over him.

But could a woman every truly forget her first love? She and Philip had been a mismatch from the start, but that didn't stop them from falling in love after they met while ice skating in Central Park. His parents had been appalled when their golden boy courted a girl who sold food out of a pushcart. They wanted so much more from their princeling, who was expected to join the family law firm like his father and grandfather before him.

Philip loved bucking his parents' expectations, and for three years while attending law school he spent every free moment with Maggie. They'd enjoyed picnics in the park, rowed together on the river, and frequented Philip's favorite haunt, the vaudeville theaters. They were young and innocent and in love.

Then Philip ruined everything when he dropped out of school two months shy of graduation and declared his intention to become "a lyricist," a job Maggie didn't even know existed.

"It means I'll write the lyrics to songs for vaudeville," he'd said, his eyes bright. "Don't you get it? I can break away from three generations of practicing boring probate law and do something creative with my life."

Maggie had been appalled. Philip didn't sing and couldn't play any instruments. His dream to write lyrics seemed farfetched and silly.

"Does it pay much?" she had asked him, but Philip was dismissive.

"Not at first. But who cares? I can live with some of the musicians who always need help paying rent. I can wait tables or work like you. I don't need my parents' money."

Philip might think genteel poverty was romantic, but Maggie knew better. So did his parents. They threatened to disown him if he didn't stop courting Maggie and finish college. Maggie hated being involved in the fallout between Philip and his parents and offered to go away, which only made Philip more determined. He moved out of his parents' home and into a shabby apartment next door to a seedy vaudeville theater.

He spent his time learning to read music, play a few instruments, and started writing songs. Yet he wasn't able to secure any sort of paying job, and just two months after moving in with his musician friends, he asked her for a loan to pay his rent.

Maggie was twenty-three years old and wanted to get married, but she also wanted a husband she could depend on. She loaned him the money, but of course when the next month's rent came due, he came to her again. They parted ways shortly after that.

"Philip is in my past," she whispered, even though she still worried if he had enough to pay rent and support his wife and child.

"What?" Frieda asked. The overhead motor and rasp of the pullies meant people had to raise their voices to be heard.

"I am completely over my youthful infatuation with Philip Altman," she announced a little louder. "Liam is different. He takes charge. When I had a question about docking rights at the pier where he lives, he went straight to the top. He's a real man. Someone who can be depended on."

"What do you mean, 'the pier where he lives'?" Frieda asked. "Doesn't he live in a normal house?"

A blush heated her cheeks at the memory of the fancy steamship Liam called his home. "He lives on a yacht," she answered, smothering a laugh at the sheer audacity of the idea.

"A yacht? Like the Vanderbilts have?"

"Like the Vanderbilts!" she said with a grin. She'd seen a photograph of a Vanderbilt yacht in a magazine, and Liam's ship seemed just as big. She hadn't been able to see what it looked like inside, but she suspected it was a floating palace.

Liam was rich, but he wasn't snooty like Philip's parents had been. He rolled up his sleeves, and it looked like he'd been having fun working alongside the other welders at Pier 27.

"He said he was taking me to the Porterhouse like it was no big deal," she said to Frieda. "When Philip courted me, we came to the ice cream shop because it was free. We never went to a place as nice as the Porterhouse."

"Money isn't everything," Frieda said as she broke another egg.

Maggie nodded. "Correct. Money isn't everything; it's the *only* thing if you don't have a good job. Philip walked away from a fine career in the law to pursue music instead. Music! It doesn't pay a pittance, and I'd be working my fingers to the bone for the rest of my life to support him."

She tossed an eggshell into the trash can and reached for another.

"Good afternoon, Maggie."

She gasped and whirled around. Liam Blackstone stood a few yards away beside the walk-in refrigerator. How much had he heard? The hard look on his face didn't bode well. She reached for a rag to clean her hands.

"Liam," she said. "You're early. How nice to see you."

"So, whatever happened to poor Philip?" he asked, and she drew back a little. Why did he seem so hostile? Her sad history with Philip was in the past and not something she wanted to discuss with Liam.

"He was nobody."

"I suppose most men who aren't rich are nobody in your eyes."

She lifted her chin. "That's a lousy thing to say."

"I think its lousy that you walked away from someone because he didn't earn enough money to keep you happy."

Her hand itched to throw the rag at him. Liam's money didn't give him the right to pass judgment on her.

"You don't know what it's like to be dirt poor," she pointed out. "You were a *welder*. Welders make good money. I'm not going to apologize for refusing to get sucked back down into poverty. I know what it means to be flat broke, and I am *never* going back."

If anything, Liam's expression grew even colder. "Congratulations on that," he said. "Knock yourself out working seven days a week in hopes of striking it rich. The weird thing about money is that it doesn't make you happy."

"That's easy for a rich person to say."

There was a lot more she wanted to add, but Liam had already turned his back on her. Foolish dreams began crumbling as she watched him walk out the factory door. Probably out of her life too.

Frieda stood beside her, holding a cracked eggshell suspended over the bowl as she stared at her in pained embarrassment.

"It's okay," Maggie said, even though it wasn't. She battled the temptation to run after Liam and defend herself, but she managed a smile for Frieda. "Let's get the rest of these eggs opened. Then I'll show you how we whip them up before mixing them into the cream." It didn't matter that the man she'd been dreaming about all week had walked out of her life. He wasn't the right man for her. She needed a man who would be supportive and could understand the pressures of having forty employees depend on her for a paycheck.

Even the two men packaging chocolate ice cream at the neighboring station had paused their work. Had they noticed how crushed she was?

"Everything is fine," she called out to them. "Time is money. No need to stop what we're doing."

The men went back to work while she continued showing Frieda the process for beating the eggs. Inside, however, it felt as if all her foolish dreams and hopes had just flown out the door with Liam Blackstone.

10

$\mathcal{L}$iam was grateful for his lucky escape as he strode toward the Porterhouse. He'd been so excited to see Maggie that he arrived early, which was a good thing because he caught a glimpse of her true colors about money and getting rich. It was better to learn that now rather than after he fell in love too deeply . . . like what happened with Darla.

He didn't have much of an appetite, but Patrick and Gwen were waiting for him at the Porterhouse. He'd had to plead with them to come. They had a seven-month-old baby Gwen was reluctant to leave, yet he'd leaned on them hard, bragging about how smart and pretty Maggie was, and how he needed them to help make conversation if he got tongue-tied. He probably ought to rein in his habit of running off at the mouth when he liked a girl, but Maggie had seemed so right. Perfect, really. So perfect that he neglected to consider how her obsession with getting rich would make it impossible for him to ever trust her again.

It was dim inside the restaurant. Mahogany paneling lined the walls, and rich maroon leather covered tufted seats. Crystal goblets and fancy silverware shimmered in the candlelight. Gwen and Patrick were already seated at a table near the back, and Liam headed their way.

"Where is Miss Molinaro?" Patrick asked as he rose.

"Sorry, she couldn't make it." He sat opposite Gwen, who always looked like she just stepped out of a fashion magazine. He and Gwen were brother and sister but couldn't be more different. She had been born after he was kidnapped, so he only met her for the first time two years ago. Gwen was lithe, blond, and serene, while he was dark, hulking, and annoyed most of the time.

He hadn't always been this way. He'd been happy in his old life working in the shipyards, throwing down his tools at the end of the day to take his dog to the park or spend the night carousing with the guys from work. No tense boardroom meetings, no feeling like an idiot for his eighth-grade education, and no armies of women trying to get their hands on his money.

He wasn't a greedy or stingy man. If anything, his generosity nearly caused Gwen a heart attack when he first came into his inheritance and started splashing it around on charitable contributions or impulsively buying dinner for everyone in a restaurant. He liked being generous, but it also made him a target, and he wouldn't forget it again.

"Shall we do this again when your young lady can join us?" Gwen asked. "I was looking forward to meeting her."

He flushed. "I won't be seeing Maggie again. It turns out she's like the other fortune hunters lining up for me."

Gwen's face softened in sympathy. "Liam, if you limit yourself to courting only women whose bank accounts rival your own, you will be fishing in a very small pond."

He understood that, but Maggie had already dumped one man she loved because he didn't earn enough money. Last year he'd had his heart thoroughly stomped on by Darla's pointy little heels, and he couldn't risk it again with another woman overly enamored with money.

It would be nice if he could turn off his feelings as easily as turning off a spigot, but he still cared about Maggie. He respected her and worried she might get into trouble with Morse again if she went poking her nose into docking rights. The

$95.00 she won had embarrassed Morse, but she might unwittingly stir up a hornet's nest if she meddled with his new ice trust. It worried him.

"I've got a legal question for you," he said to Patrick. "Can someone pay a government official to block a rival from getting access to public services?"

Patrick looked taken aback by the question. "They can try, but it's called graft and it's illegal. Are you running into it?"

Liam explained about the likelihood that Johnny Bartlett at the Department of Docks was on Morse's payroll to prevent rivals from docking at the public piers. Patrick confirmed that if proven, it could open both men up to charges of corruption and potential jail time.

Getting Morse convicted of graft and clapped in chains would remove Liam's biggest enemy on the board of U.S. Steel. Morse had escaped punishment for the bad check he wrote to Maggie, yet bribing the people who controlled access to New York Harbor was a far more serious charge.

Patrick had a surprisingly simple solution for how to do it.

"Demand an audit of the Department of Docks," he said. "See what percentage of the piers are vacant on any given day, and an accounting of people they'd turned away. I expect they'll find a way to cover their misdeeds, so you would need a complaining witness whose testimony will make the allegation stick. Do you know anyone?"

Liam smiled. "Gabelli Ice."

If he moved quickly, he might be able to strike another blow against Morse well ahead of the September vote.

⁓

Liam and Patrick paid a call on the owner of Gabelli Ice the following morning, but the old man was not interested in helping.

"I want to move upstate and enjoy my retirement," he said from an upholstered chair in his front parlor, where trunks were stacked high and ready to be moved. Thumping noises sounded in a back room where others continued packing up boxes and moving furniture. "Things are finally going well for me," the old man continued. "I sold my house and can move out of the city. That business with the Department of Docks is over and done."

"How many times did they refuse to let you dock?" Liam asked. "Can you give us the dates that it happened? That would be enough for us to start the process."

Mr. Gabelli seemed to shrink in his chair. "All my business files have already been sent upstate. I can't get it for you. I'm telling you it's done. It's over."

Liam recognized fear when he saw it. Mr. Gabelli couldn't meet their eyes, and his large callused hands were clenched. They were a workingman's hands. Mr. Gabelli had probably started out hauling ice, but he managed to build his own company and buy a fine house. Who could blame him for protecting the last of his investments?

"We can request that the auditors keep your name out of the complaint," Patrick offered. "And we can wait until the sale of your house has been finalized and you are out of the city."

It made no impact on Mr. Gabelli's decision. "They would know it was me," he said. "I have too much to lose, and I'm not talking about my property or my bank account. They've threatened my grandchildren. Do you understand? My whole life I worked to provide for and protect my family, but I can't keep them safe if the ice trust decides to make an example of me." His shoulders sagged and he tried to smile, but his eyes remained sad. "I don't mind settling for what I have left. I'm sorry, but my decision is final."

Liam didn't have the heart to keep pressing, but Mr. Gabelli insisted on serving them something to drink before sending them on their way. The kitchen was in a similar state of disarray with half-filled boxes as two workers continued filling them. Patrick visited with Mr. Gabelli, but all Liam could concentrate on was getting a soothing drink. His ulcer always hurt worse on an empty stomach, and water helped.

One of the workers kept looking at him oddly, trying to catch his attention whenever Mr. Gabelli was distracted.

Liam sent a surreptitious nod to the young man, then turned to Patrick. "We should be on our way."

Patrick agreed, and within a few minutes they were walking down the flight of steps in front of the Gabelli brownstone. "Let's wait a bit," Liam said, and sure enough the dark-haired man who'd been packing boxes approached them from the side alley.

"My name is Antonio Gabelli," he said. "I delivered ice for my grandfather for the past seven years. I know everything, and I'm willing to testify."

⸜⸝

Liam never understood the meaning of the expression "cold sweat" until he witnessed Antonio Gabelli testify before a board of auditors. Liam and Patrick accompanied him to the meeting held in a bleak, windowless room at city hall, where Antonio looked alone and defenseless sitting in a bare metal chair in the middle of the room, facing a panel of stone-faced auditors who didn't move a muscle during his testimony.

Charles Morse was the most powerful businessman in the city. Most of his influence was created through a network of allies planted among the city's bureaucrats, the firemen, the cops, the mayor's office, and those running the docks. Anyone turning to the city government for help was likely to encounter a Morse viper lying in wait. One of them might even be on the board of auditors hearing Antonio's testimony.

"Do you think it will do any good?" Antonio asked as they got ready to leave the office.

"Hard to say," Patrick responded grimly, but they all knew the truth. Unlike when Maggie complained about her $95.00 and the board at U.S. Steel swooped in to berate Morse, the city council might not risk taking him on.

"We planted a seed today," Liam said. "Maybe it will take

root, or maybe we'll have to wait for others to come forward and join the drumbeat, but you did the right thing, Antonio."

Liam only hoped there wouldn't be repercussions for Antonio, because Charles Morse was not a man who liked to be crossed.

11

As the summer went on, the ice situation in the city grew worse. Prices continued to creep upward, blocks were delivered smaller, and in the first week of July, Manhattan Ice failed to make a delivery for any of their customers on Gadsen Street. Even more ominous, Lieberman's Deli didn't get an ice delivery either, and they used a different supplier. Mrs. Lieberman's careworn face looked more lined than usual as she confided her problem to Maggie.

"We've used Knickerbocker Ice for the last ten years," she said. "They are expensive, but a top-notch company who has never let us down. It's not like them to miss a delivery."

Mrs. Lieberman had started the deli thirty-five years ago with her husband, Avraham. The young German immigrants invested everything they had in the restaurant, but Avraham died of a heart attack twenty years ago, leaving her with two sons only nine and eleven years old. Three days after her husband died, Mrs. Lieberman reopened the deli on her own, keeping the family business afloat through the awesome strength of her grit and the need to survive. David and Jonathan were now strapping young men whose tireless work at the deli had at last bought their mother a modicum of comfort, but the sudden lack of ice was a challenge they'd never confronted.

Mrs. Lieberman leaned across the deli counter to speak in a

low voice. "I don't think it's a coincidence that our ice company is failing us at the same time Manhattan Ice failed you."

Maggie feared the same, but before she could reply, the bell above the front door dinged and Aunt Julie hurried inside.

"Maggie, come quickly!" she said, her voice almost trembling with excitement. "There is a fancy businessman who wants a new contract for ice cream."

"Really?" Most of the contracts she negotiated with restaurants and hotels happened because she sought *them* out, not the other way around. "What sort of businessman?"

"I don't know," Aunt Julie replied. "But he must be important because he just signed a contract to supply all the prisons in the state of New York. Can you believe it?"

Mrs. Lieberman gave Maggie a friendly nudge across the counter. "Congratulations! Molinaro's is so famous that businessmen are knocking on your door for contracts."

But prisons? She'd never considered selling ice cream to prisons, but if true, it would be a huge windfall. This was an astounding opportunity and she bid a quick farewell to Mrs. Lieberman to follow Julie out the door.

"This will be our biggest contract yet," Aunt Julie gushed as they hurried down the street. Maggie agreed but wouldn't start celebrating yet. A windfall like this seemed too strange to trust.

Maggie crossed into the cool interior of the ice cream parlor, straightening her collar as she eyed the back of the man speaking to Dino, and her breath caught. Was it Liam Blackstone? He was tall and dark-haired like Liam, and he wore a fine suit. Maybe Liam came back to apologize for the appalling way he'd treated her last month. Should she take him back?

The man turned, and her hopes sank. The stranger had a heavy mustache and a long face that was handsome if a little imposing. For a middle-aged man, he certainly looked strong and fit.

Dino came around the counter to introduce her. "Maggie, this is Mr. Goldrick. He works for . . . who did you say, the Bureau of Prisons?"

The man smiled politely. "I did indeed sign a contract with the Federal Bureau of Prisons. I'd like to discuss additional contracts with Miss Molinaro."

Mr. Goldrick wore a three-piece suit despite the heat. Rarely did she conduct business with men who looked like him. She usually negotiated contracts with restaurant chefs, not the management. She put her misgivings aside and assumed her most professional smile as she gestured Mr. Goldrick toward the staircase.

"Our business office is upstairs. Will you follow me?"

The second floor wasn't nearly as impressive as the ice cream parlor. Crammed with supplies and spare equipment, it was intended for work, not impressing fancy businessmen. She lifted a crate of papers from the chair in the office and swiped a quick hand over the desk to clear the remnants of the bagel she'd had for breakfast. She hurried to her own chair and assumed a professional demeanor to face him across the rickety desk.

"You work for the prison system?" she asked.

"No, your uncle misunderstood," Mr. Goldrick said with an apologetic smile. "I merely secured a contract from them to supply their ice for the coming year. I'd like to offer you a similar deal."

Now she was more confused than ever. "Who do you work for?" she asked.

"The American Ice Trust."

The name landed like a fist in her gut. This was the group that had driven Mr. Gabelli out of business and used bribes to deny people docking rights. Mr. Goldrick wasn't here to buy ice cream. He was here to strong-arm her into complying with his demands. She strove to keep her voice polite but firm.

"I'm not interested in signing any new contracts at this time," she said.

"Are you sure? We are very well positioned to deliver reliable streams of ice. It was why the Bureau of Prisons agreed to our terms. Many agencies throughout the government have signed on—the Police Department, the Fire Department, and the Department of Docks."

Anxiety began to twist in her stomach. It certainly sounded as if American Ice was cozy with all the important city departments. Mr. Goldrick removed a few pages from his briefcase and set them on the desk before her.

"Here are the terms we are prepared to offer. They are not out of line with industry norms, and given the size and power of our operations, we can deliver a dependable supply of ice even during the hottest summer months."

She glanced at the prices on the page. High, but not extraordinarily higher than she was currently paying. The contract stated her current supplier would continue to be the subsidiary who delivered her ice, but they would answer to the American Ice Trust. Technically, she was already doing business with the trust, yet this contract would legally bind her to it. If she cut ties with Manhattan Ice, she would be obligated to buy ice from another company affiliated with the trust.

The thought of putting her name to this document was revolting, but what if Mr. Goldrick ordered Manhattan Ice to stop their deliveries? It might be weeks before she could find another supplier.

She shifted uneasily in the chair. "I'd like a few days to think about it," she hedged.

"I would like your signature now," he said. "The terms of the contract will not be so favorable tomorrow." Despite his cool demeanor, a hint of menace underscored his words.

She wanted to tell him to take this contract and stick it where the sun didn't shine. When she was alone late at night, she liked to imagine being fearless. A woman who would stand up before a crowd and shout through a megaphone that she would never capitulate. But those were only dreams. She didn't want to lead a crusade; she merely wanted to keep running her business like normal.

"I can't sign right now," she finally said, wishing she were braver. "I need to confer with my uncle first."

"Ah yes, Dino Molinaro," Mr. Goldrick said in an excessively polite voice. "He's Italian, correct?"

"Yes."

He tutted. "We are starting to have such problems with the Italians. Quite the criminal element in that group, isn't there?"

She stiffened. "My uncle came to this country with nothing. He worked hard for everything he has."

"Did he?" Mr. Goldrick pressed. "How comfortable would your uncle be with having his books audited for the past ten years? Not that I am accusing him of anything. Heavens! But so many of his countrymen have proven to be undesirable elements in society. So many Italians have had to be deported. But I'm sure your uncle has nothing to worry about, does he?"

She folded her arms across her chest. Dino was now an American citizen, and she doubted that could be taken away. Could it? She didn't know, and she clenched her hands to stop them from shaking.

A noise from the storage area caught her attention, but it was only Spider opening another box of packing tubs. She turned her attention back to Mr. Goldrick. She didn't want anything to do with the ice trust, but she couldn't afford to offend them either.

"I'm sorry we aren't able to do business," she said, sliding the contract across the desk toward him. "I'm sure that with all your government contracts, losing a small company like ours won't trouble you."

"Please read the clause at the bottom of page three," Mr. Goldrick calmly instructed. She reached for the contract and flipped to the third page. It was in small type, but it forbade anyone who received ice from the American Ice Trust to resell or even give away their ice. She glanced up at him in confusion.

"It means you can't buy ice on the secondary market," he explained. "If you want to have ice, you'll need to buy directly from us. Our prices are fair, and the trust is for the good of the entire city."

Again she pushed the contract away from her, swallowing

back a sense of panic as yet another escape door was slammed shut. "I'm still not prepared to sign," she said.

His eyes narrowed but not in annoyance. It almost seemed as if he were enjoying himself. "The American Ice Trust wants to help all the businesses in this city. If those businesses don't appreciate our good intentions, they will soon learn what happens to people who put their own interests ahead of the trust. It is going to be a very hot summer, Miss Molinaro. Take another look at the contract we are offering you. My terms are not unreasonable."

Spider was still out in the storage area, but now he was pushing a broom around. His presence gave her comfort.

"I can't sign this today," she repeated.

His face brightened. "But you'll think about it?"

"I'll think about it."

He smiled, but it felt more like a threat. "Good. I wish you and your uncle the best of luck. It would be a shame if something happened to throw a wrench into such a hardworking immigrant's life here in America."

He stood, adjusted the fall of his jacket, and left her office. Spider paused to lean on his broom as he watched Mr. Goldrick cross toward the stairwell door. The echo of his footsteps retreated down the stairs.

Spider hurried to close the door. "I heard about that guy," he said, turning to her.

"Oh?"

"He's Charles Morse's enforcer. Last year, Morse wanted the city elections to turn out a certain way, and Goldrick made the rounds at all the factories, telling people how to vote. Some of those factories had suspicious fires when enough people didn't show up at the polls."

Her chest felt tight, and it was hard to breathe. "You overheard what he said to me?"

"I heard every word. I expect he'll go after other people on the street too."

The thought of her neighbors being strong-armed was revolting. "Go and warn them about what you know," she instructed. Spider threw the broom down and ran down toward the fire escape so Goldrick wouldn't see him leaving.

She headed down the stairs. Dino hopped up off the stool behind the counter as she came bounding into the room.

"Did you see where he went?" she asked Dino.

"Next door, to the pharmacy," Dino replied. "Did we get a new contract?"

The hopeful look in Dino's eyes made her want to weep. She quickly filled him in on the threats from the ice trust, then ran to check the supply levels in their refrigerated rooms. Their ice would last only two more days.

Outside, Mr. Goldrick strolled out of the pharmacy, and she prayed the goon hadn't threatened kindly old Mr. Lindquist. She stepped outside to check.

Mr. Goldrick gave her a smirk as she brushed past him and into the pharmacy. Normally the scent of lemon soap and peppermint sticks was soothing, but today it did little to ease her anxiety. Mr. Lindquist was sliding a paper into a cabinet drawer as she approached.

"Did you sign a contract with Goldrick?"

He smiled. "Yes. A twenty-pound block of ice delivered three times a week." He must have noticed the sick look on her face, for his smile dimmed as he closed the drawer.

"Ice isn't a big expense for me, but I must keep my serums cold. I couldn't afford to say no, and he seemed . . . very adamant."

She nodded. It was likely Mr. Goldrick's campaign of intimidation was about to go into full swing.

<hr />

Maggie needed to strategize with Dino after the parlor closed for the night. Normally they discussed business with Aunt Julie at their dining table, but Dino claimed to have a sudden craving for sauerkraut and suggested a trip to the Jewish deli.

That meant he didn't want Julie to overhear. Her aunt's soft heart didn't handle stress well, and Dino had always protected her from bad news.

Mrs. Lieberman's sons took the late-night shifts, and David was behind the counter when they arrived. "Two corned beefs with sauerkraut," Dino said.

David scowled. "Sorry, no corned beef."

"No?" That was odd. Dino glanced up at the menu board behind the counter. Almost all the meat selections had a line drawn through them. There wasn't much left to choose from.

"I'll make it easy on you," David said. "We've got chicken noodle soup, bagels, lox, and plenty of my ma's potato knishes."

There were only a handful of customers at the counter, but Maggie didn't want them to overhear so she leaned in close. "Are you out of ice?" she whispered.

David's mouth pressed into a hard line as he gave a terse nod. His eyes were snapping mad, the veins in his neck pronounced. Without ice, the Liebermans had probably lost hundreds of dollars from spoiled meat.

"Two bowls of chicken soup," she said in sympathy. Hot soup wasn't what anyone wanted on a warm night, but she'd wait until it cooled. She and Dino retreated to a table near the plate-glass window at the front of the deli.

"All right, tell me how long we can last before we have to start throwing out inventory like the Liebermans have done," Dino said once they were seated.

The ice cream factory was the biggest consumer of ice on the street. On their last delivery they'd gotten three thousand pounds that had been divided up between the refrigerated room, the freezer, and the ice cream machines.

"Two more days," she answered. "After that, our ice cream will start melting."

David must have overheard because after he delivered the soup, he hunkered down beside their table with troubled eyes. "I hear the embargo is all over the city," he said in a low voice. "They want to teach everyone a lesson. Even folks who contracted with the ice trust are getting shortchanged. The trust is claiming that the heat wave is reducing supply, but I don't buy it. I think it's all an act to let everyone know we're at their mercy."

A trickle of sweat rolled down Maggie's neck as she scrambled for another explanation. "Maybe it's only a rumor," she said with fading hope.

But the very next morning, the newspapers confirmed a city-wide ice shortage was causing restaurants to close and grocers to stop selling milk, meat, and fish.

The entire food industry in New York City was now at the mercy of Charles Morse's ice trust.

12

The temperatures in her cold rooms began failing two days later. Noisy trickles of melting ice spattered onto the concrete floor as Maggie stepped inside the refrigerated room on Wednesday morning. Ice in the slotted bins was melting and dribbled toward the drain in the floor. The thermometer read forty-eight degrees, and dairy needed to be stored below forty.

The situation in the freezer was worse, where the ice cream was beginning to soften. It was still sellable, but not for much longer. She usually delivered four hundred gallons of ice cream each Thursday morning to the hotels, but if she could persuade some of them to take delivery early, her inventory wouldn't be a complete loss. In addition to the ice cream, she had hundreds of dollars of milk and cream that would go bad soon. Losing it all would be a blow to their monthly revenue unlike anything they'd ever suffered. Dino and Julie weren't up yet, so she left a note telling them she'd gone to see if any hotels would take early delivery of their ice cream.

Signs of trouble hit her the moment she stepped outside the ice cream parlor. The Liebermans had to close their deli two days ago, but now a sign tacked to the front door of the Porterhouse said they would be closed for the rest of the week. All the other restaurants on the street were shuttered too.

The Starwood Hotel was her first stop. Cool air surrounded her as she crossed the mahogany-paneled lobby and looked inside their restaurant. Silverware clinked with dozens of people at breakfast, their plates full of food, so obviously the hotel still had ice. She pushed through the swinging doors into the kitchen, where the head cook was shredding cheese.

"Mr. Ferguson, we owe you thirty gallons of ice cream every Thursday, but will you consider taking delivery early?" she asked, trying to mask the panic in her voice.

"Why would we do that?"

"We've got extra. I'll offer a ten percent discount if you take it today."

Understanding dawned on the cook's face. "Are you getting squeezed by the ice trust?"

"A little," she admitted. "Are you?"

He shook his head. "We signed a contract with them so they're delivering about half our normal amount. Not great, but enough for us to keep operating."

"Good!" she said brightly. "Can I deliver the thirty gallons today instead of tomorrow?"

"I'll have to check for space in the freezer." He headed to the walk-in freezer room, and Maggie crossed herself and prayed. At least he hadn't given her an outright no.

He returned quickly. "Sorry, Maggie, space is tight. We can take ten gallons, though, so long as you're still offering the discount."

She swallowed back the disappointment. Ten gallons was better than nothing. "Excellent. We'll have it over to you before lunch."

News at the other hotels was worse. Most hadn't gotten ice in days and were forced to close their restaurants. The few restaurants who still had ice feared they would be in trouble soon and weren't buying frozen food.

Heat pressed down on her as she began the long walk home. How could this be happening? What was Morse trying to prove by depriving the city of ice? She was hot, thirsty, and out of breath by the time she returned to the factory. There, the push-cart vendors had arrived and had surrounded Aunt Julie.

"What do you mean there isn't any ice?" Gary Johnson roared. "I have a wife and two kids to feed, and how am I supposed to do that if you say I can't work today?"

"I'm s-sorry," Aunt Julie stammered. "The ice cream is getting soft and—"

Maggie cut her off. "I explained this to you yesterday. Unless we get a delivery of ice, we can't send out the pushcarts. You can wait and see if a delivery arrives, but don't you dare yell at my aunt."

"Are you still going to pay us?" another vendor asked.

"You get paid on commission," she pointed out. "I can't afford to pay you today. Julie, could you please prepare a single cart. We've got a delivery to the Starwood Hotel and then everything is closing down."

"Why can't you pay us?" Gary demanded. "You own a four-story building. You're rich and can afford something."

She was in debt up to her eyeballs and paying the mortgage was going to be a challenge if her factory shut down, but Gary didn't care about her problems. "Once this is all over, I'll try to find some way to compensate you, but don't count on anything this week."

Julie emerged from the freezer with a thin sheet of ice. Normally they stocked the delivery cart with ten-pound blocks, yet all their ice blocks had melted to a fraction of their size. Julie carefully walked the thin sheet of ice toward the delivery cart, but before she arrived the ice split down the middle and smashed on the floor.

Julie burst into tears. Covering her face with an apron, she fled from the factory floor.

"You made my aunt cry," Maggie accused Gary.

"She's the one who broke the ice," he retorted. "We could have used that ice!"

Other vendors were just as surly, and her temper boiled over.

"I changed my mind. All of you get out of here. If any ice arrives, I'll send word of it. Until then, go home."

Some of the vendors seemed to understand as they drifted away, while others were as rude as Gary. She met their glares with her chin held high, relieved to see them go, but asking the factory staff to leave was much harder. Their eight employees felt like part of the family. They never complained as they manned the machinery and boxed the ice cream, faithfully serving the company for years.

"I'm sorry, Alfred," Maggie said to the oldest of the machine operators. "I'll let you know as soon as we're up and running again."

Her heart nearly split watching the old man's sad smile of understanding. He took off his net cap, carefully hung it on a peg, and walked away. The others followed, their footsteps shuffling on the concrete floor as they left the factory.

Spider filled the delivery cart with enough slivers of ice to safely deliver ten gallons to the Starwood, leaving Maggie alone in the unusually quiet factory. The hum of the overhead motors went silent—no rotating belts or sloshing ice in rotating vats. The only sound in the factory was a faint buzz from the compressor working to keep the refrigerated rooms cool, but it would fail soon. Electric cooling depended on a boost from ice-chilled air to operate properly, and there simply wasn't enough ice.

Like everyone else on the street, Maggie hung the *Closed* sign on the front door of the parlor. She and Dino stacked chairs atop the tables to sweep and mop the floor. There wasn't anything else for them to do. Aunt Julie soon returned, determined to help. Her mood had improved, and she feigned cheerfulness as she made a list of all the chores they could accomplish now that they had the time.

Dino began waxing the parlor floor while Julie pruned the blooms in the flower boxes outside. Maggie oiled the fan belts, all the while casting a baleful eye at the cold rooms, where eight hundred dollars of inventory was on the verge of spoiling. Why was she delaying the inevitable? There wasn't going to be a miraculous delivery of ice. Still, she wouldn't start throwing it out until all hope was gone.

At two o'clock she checked the temperature of the cream in the refrigerated canisters. It was now at room temperature and starting to smell.

"We need to dump it," Dino said, his voice heavy.

Everything inside her rebelled, but Dino was right. She balanced a thirty-gallon canister on a hand truck and wheeled it to the alley behind the building. She hated it back here. It had the same stink of wet, dirty brick as the back alleys where she and her father sometimes had to sleep before Dino took them in. Back then she'd been cold, scared, and hungry.

Today she was hot, scared, and dumping hundreds of dollars of cream into a sewer. The metal rim cut into her palms as she hefted it off the cart and tipped the canister toward the sewer drain. The clang of it hitting the bricks echoed down the alley as the thick cream sloshed toward the metal grate.

Two men from O'Donnell's Pub lugged a keg of beer between them, wobbling in an unnatural gait as they trudged toward the same drain.

"You too?" Michael O'Donnell asked, wiping his face in the sweltering heat.

"Us too," she sighed. She stepped aside as the beer washed toward the drain, the amber liquid sweeping away the remnants of pale, thick cream in a swirl of waste as it funneled into the city drain. It stank back here. With so many restaurants making use of this alley to collect their rubbish, it was never pleasant, but the hot stagnant air made it rank. The rats would feast tonight.

Up and down Gadsen Street, the waste continued as spoiled meat, fish, and cheese overflowed the garbage cans. Mr. Prescott, the owner of the Porterhouse who was usually such an elegant man, had his shirtsleeves rolled up and angrily suggested they document every gallon of milk or ounce of produce they lost.

"I intend to sue," he said. "I had a contract, and Manhattan Ice failed to deliver on it. I've lost six hundred dollars of prime beef, and someone must be made to pay. We should all document our losses."

It was a worthwhile suggestion, but Mr. Goldrick's oily smirk haunted Maggie. Mr. Goldrick enjoyed playing dirty and would be prepared for any feeble attempts the small businesses of Gadsen Street could mount against his ice trust.

The scandalous shortage of ice made the front page of all the morning newspapers. It was ninety-eight degrees yesterday, and hundreds of restaurants had been forced to shutter, and the crisis was spreading. The fish markets, the meat-packers, and the dairies all ceased operations for want of ice. Canneries were turning workers away. Several breweries stopped production because without ice they couldn't keep the temperature of the lager cold enough for fermentation to occur.

One of the newspapers quoted the owner of Whelan & Sons, the famous brewery from Philadelphia that recently opened a second factory in Brooklyn, who said, "Without ice to keep the lager cold during fermentation, we'll have a cloudy, sour-tasting mess. I've got two hundred employees out of work because of the American Ice Trust."

Julie shook her head. "What bad timing to open a brewery this month, but who could have seen this coming?"

"Maybe they're having ice troubles in Philadelphia too," Dino said, but Maggie wondered. Did the American Ice Trust have a stranglehold on the entire East Coast? If this was a natural ice shortage due to the heat, other cities would be suffering as well. The newspaper listed the name of the manager for the new brewery that just opened in Brooklyn, and she had questions.

"I'm going next door to use the telephone," she impulsively said. Mr. Lindquist had a public telephone in his pharmacy that could be used for a nickel, and she suddenly had a very important telephone call to make.

It took only a few connections for the telephone operator to plug her call through to Mr. Whelan in Brooklyn, and she got straight to the point of her call.

"The American Ice Trust claims the shortage is because of the heat wave," Maggie explained. "It's even hotter in Philadelphia. Is there a shortage at your father's brewery in Philly?"

"No," Mr. Whelan replied. "The price has gone up ten percent, but that's normal for this time of year, and there is *plenty* of ice in Philadelphia. My thoughts are exactly yours, Miss Molinaro—something about this new ice trust stinks to high heaven. I've had to furlough two hundred employees because of someone's greed."

It was as she suspected. After completing the telephone call, she remained sitting motionless on the stool, counting her heartbeats in the dim quiet of the pharmacy. Her ice cream factory was a small operation compared to the breweries, but her panic was just as large. Outside the pharmacy's plate-glass window, Gadsen Street looked lonely and vacant because of this manufactured crisis.

The blame rested entirely on Charles Morse and his ice trust, but what could she do? She couldn't exactly take a train to Philadelphia and come back with two thousand pounds of ice. Or better still, to Maine where there were icehouses bulging with ice that couldn't be sold because they had no docking privileges in Manhattan.

A ship could do it.

The thought hit like a jolt of electricity. A ship could bring ice down from Maine and save every restaurant on Gadsen Street, and she knew someone with a ship. Liam disliked her, but he disliked Charles Morse a lot more, and maybe that would be enough to convince him to lend her his ship.

13

Ever since he was a ten-year-old kid growing up on the wrong side of Pittsburgh, Liam had an embarrassing hobby he hid from most of the world. Stamp collecting was a great comfort during his painful years growing up. He hadn't been good at school or book learning, but stamp collecting was different. Something about seeing a stamp that came from a foreign land captured his imagination. It was tangible proof there was more to the world than could be seen in the sooty streets outside his window. When he saw a stamp from a place like Scotland or Germany, he would hold it in his hands like a sacred relic, dreaming about those distant lands.

His father led the steelworker union in Pittsburgh, so letters from international labor unions sometimes came to their house, and Liam always waited until after dark to retrieve the discarded envelopes from the trash. If Crocket Malone ever learned about Liam's fascination with the stamps, he would have taken delight in tossing his fledgling stamp collection into the fire and laughing at Liam's dismay.

So Liam collected the stamps secretly and pasted them into a cheap pamphlet of blank pages he kept hidden under his bed. When he was a kid, that pamphlet held the most important sixteen pages in the world for him. Wanting to learn more about all the foreign countries, he checked out an atlas from the public library and studied the maps for hours on end.

It had been a mistake. Crocket found it and wanted to know why Liam was wasting time with a useless atlas when he wasn't reading books that had been assigned for school. He demanded an answer, but Liam would rather die than let Crocket know about his stamp collection, so he stayed silent and let Crocket pound him into a bloody mess that night. He smacked Liam in the face with the atlas, which accounted for the scar splitting his eyebrow.

That was the last time Liam checked out a book from the public library. After that, he used the globe in his classroom, even though it didn't have nearly as much information as the atlas. Then Crocket yanked him out of school in the eighth grade, so that marked the end of his ability to learn more about the world outside of his grubby neighborhood. It wasn't that Liam had any real hope of seeing those faraway lands; the stamps simply represented hope that he might someday aspire to more than his dark world of smokestacks and dead ends.

He never stopped collecting stamps. Now he had an expensive leather stamp album and attended fancy auctions in search of rare stamps. He once bought a collection from the estate of a German duke with over three thousand unique stamps. He had another from Japan with hundreds of stamps from the Far East.

But his most precious stamps were the ones in the sixteen-page folio he'd collected in Pittsburgh. The fragile pamphlet had yellowed with age, but he carefully repaired the pages whenever the old glue failed and kept the pamphlet in a place of honor boxed up alongside the fancy leather albums.

The stamp showing the cathedral in Heidelberg was about to fall off. Liam wielded a pair of tweezers as delicately as if he were performing surgery. If he pried too hard, the rigid stamp might tear, and these stamps were irreplaceable.

A knock at his cabin's door intruded. He looked up to see

Mr. Ashton, the first mate of the ship, who announced a visitor to see him.

"It's the lady you took to the Department of Docks."

Why was Maggie here? It was almost nine o'clock at night and he had no interest in seeing her. "Find out what she wants and send her away. I'm too busy to see her."

Mr. Ashton nodded. "Yes, sir."

Liam went back to his surgery on the German stamp. This was one of his better old stamps because its etching of the Heidelberg Cathedral was both rare and pretty. He nudged it a little harder but couldn't concentrate.

He had to find out what Maggie wanted.

He dropped the tweezers and vaulted up the companionway, taking the steps two at a time until he reached the top deck. Mr. Ashton was delivering the bad news to Maggie, who stood on the pier, craning her neck to look up at the ship.

"Ashton!" he called. "Hang on. Tell her I'm coming down."

She looked a bedraggled mess. Her clothes were sweaty and stained, and a few strands of hair stuck to the sweat on her face. It ought to make her less attractive, but to his eyes, she looked strong. And kind of appealing.

Mr. Ashton accompanied him down to secure the gangway, and Liam's feet thudded on the pier as he headed toward her.

"What happened to you?" he asked, bothered by how much her distress got to him.

"Do you remember how Charles Morse is blocking off the harbor to anyone who isn't signed up with his ice trust?"

"I remember," he admitted.

Mr. Ashton turned to head back, but Liam stopped him. "Stick around. I'll be heading back inside in just a minute." Ashton's presence meant Liam wouldn't do anything stupid like start flirting with Maggie again. He turned back to Maggie. "What's Morse done now?"

"He's punishing people who didn't sign a contract with his new trust, but he's covering his tracks by denying everyone ice and claiming it's because of the heat wave. He's lying. He's doing this to show us how dependent we are on his trust. Factories are shutting down. Restaurants and grocery stores are throwing out spoiled food, all because of him."

It sounded like something Morse would do, but Liam couldn't afford to get involved. He had his own battles just to keep his seat at U.S. Steel.

"Maybe the shortage really is because of the heat wave."

Maggie shook her head. "One of Morse's oily men confronted me in my own office and warned this was about to happen. He said that the people of this city were about to learn how easily the ice could stop appearing if we didn't cooperate with the ice trust, and now it's happening."

"The ice trust is a nasty piece of work," he said in genuine sympathy. "Hey, keep your chin up. He'll find someone else to harass sooner or later—"

"You have a ship," Maggie cut in, "and a dedicated berth here on Pier 19. You could take the *Black Rose* to Maine and pick up a load of ice and be an absolute hero to every grocer and restaurant owner in the city."

He muffled a snort of laughter. "This is a yacht, not a barge."

"I know it seems a little odd to use a yacht for this sort of trip, but it would still work, wouldn't it?"

Liam crossed his arms across his chest. There had to be a good reason it wouldn't work. Plenty of reasons, but after a few awkward moments he was forced to turn to the first mate for help. "Ashton, you explain it to her."

Mr. Ashton had ten years with the merchant marine before signing on with the *Black Rose*, so he should be able to come up with a good excuse.

"Barges and cargo ships have wider openings for loading supplies," Mr. Ashton said. "The supply door for the *Black Rose* is smaller. And we don't have as many storage rooms." But Ashton's patient, rational explanation made no dent on her.

"So you're saying that it's not practical, but it can be done," Maggie stated.

"Yes," Ashton confirmed.

Liam silently groaned as Maggie turned to him in flushed excitement. "You see? Mr. Gabelli knows some ice harvesters who will provide the ice for free. It wouldn't cost you a dime to go get it."

"It would cost hundreds of dollars in fuel," Liam pointed out.

"Oh." She seemed so deflated when she said the word, making him feel like he'd yanked a cookie away from a hungry kid. He admired her gumption for coming up with a clever way to fight back, but he couldn't help her.

"Look, I'm sorry about your troubles, but if things are as bad as you say, it will work itself out pretty soon. Right?"

Her shoulders sagged. "I'm sure you're right."

She left, but he worried about her long after he returned to gluing stamps into his faded old pamphlet.

⚬⚬

It was stinking hot the following morning as Liam rolled from bed and put on a suit to meet with Patrick. They needed to start putting together a defense to keep his position at U.S. Steel, but even thinking about the looming vote of no confidence made him sick with anxiety because maybe Charles Morse was right. Liam didn't know what he was doing and was literally making himself sick over this job.

Which was why Liam wanted to figure out a way to get Patrick to serve in his place. He and Patrick were kindred spirits. They both came from hardscrabble backgrounds, though Patrick had received a free college education compliments of the Catholic Church. His law office was dedicated to helping the poor, and he could be trusted to fight for the workers in the mills. After Patrick married Liam's wealthy sister, he could have moved his office to the Financial District and started taking on a better class of clients, but instead he remained steadfast to his calling.

The air was stifling hot after climbing the two flights of stairs to reach Patrick's third-floor office, and Liam was grateful for the tall glass of ice-cold water Patrick poured for him when he sat opposite his desk.

"Thanks," Liam said before downing the water. The windows were open, a fan slowly rotating overhead, but it was still sticky and warm. It was hard to draw a full breath of air when it was this humid. He set the empty glass on an end table, wishing he didn't have to have this conversation.

"I don't think I can win," Liam said. "The preliminary vote was nine to two, and I don't know how I can convince enough people to switch sides between now and the end of September. I think we should plan for a way to get you appointed in my place."

Patrick looked away. "That's what I was afraid of."

"And my gut is getting worse," Liam continued. "Even thinking about this feels like I just swallowed a spoonful of acid. I wake up at night balled up in pain. It's bad, Patrick."

He picked up his glass and reached for the pitcher, but the ice had melted. "Is there any more ice?"

There wasn't. "The iceman came by this morning, but I didn't have the heart to take any," Patrick said. "I bought out the entire cart and asked him to deliver it to the hospital."

"Why would you do that?"

"There's some kind of ice shortage," Patrick said. "It was all over the newspaper this morning. Folks have been dropping from heatstroke and filling up the hospital. A couple of kids died at the orphanage on Hester Street."

Liam straightened, not sure he had heard correctly. "What do you mean, 'a couple of kids died'? From the heat?"

Patrick nodded. "A glass of cold water and a cool compress might not sound like a lot, but it can be the difference between life and death if you lack it. It was ninety-eight degrees yesterday, and it's supposed to get just as hot today."

"And these kids died?" Liam still could barely believe it.

"Yes, they died," Patrick confirmed, passing him the newspaper, where the front page reported the suffering throughout the city from the heat wave. Three children, all under the age of five, had died at the orphanage. The coroner couldn't provide a definitive cause of death, but the children had been healthy earlier in the week, and heatstroke was suspected. A dozen more children showed similar symptoms and had been moved to the nearest charity hospital for better care.

Liam scanned the rest of the front page in growing alarm. Factories were shuttered until the heat wave broke, turning thousands of people out of work. Fishermen couldn't unload their boats because the fish markets wouldn't pay for seafood destined to go bad within a few hours. The morgues were refusing to take bodies, claiming it was unsafe to store them without ice.

"Morgues?" he said in disbelief.

"I gather people are being urged to bury their dead immediately," Patrick said. "You can't blame the morgues for refusing to take bodies if they don't have ice."

No, he blamed Charles Morse.

Liam cursed under his breath and looked away. He should have believed Maggie. This time yesterday, maybe even while he was turning down Maggie's plea for help, those little kids had been dying of heatstroke. It was galling enough to let Morse bully the restaurants on Gadsen Street, but the orphanages? The hospitals and morgues? No. He couldn't just sit by and let Morse get away with it. He abruptly stood.

"I'm canceling our meeting," he said. "I've got a bigger battle to fight today."

Patrick lunged in front of Liam. "If you're thinking of confronting Charles Morse, think again," he warned.

"That's exactly what I'm thinking, and I don't need to think again," Liam said. "Morse could lift the embargo *today*. For once he could choose to do the right thing instead of bleeding every penny out of the people of this city."

Patrick was not swayed. "You'll dig yourself into a deeper hole by going after him. Don't stir up more bad blood with Morse."

The prospect of going after Morse stoked hot, savage anticipation. "I'm looking forward to stirring up more bad blood," he said over his shoulder as he strode out the door.

Ignoring Patrick's advice was always risky, but it was time to confront the spider sitting at the center of this web.

~ ∞ ~

Liam went straight to Morse's fancy banking headquarters in the heart of the Financial District, where his secretary sat at a desk blocking access to Morse's private office. The secretary's name was John Bowdler, a man so muscular he could barely fit into his three-piece suit. Liam doubted Bowdler had been hired for his secretarial skills. Men like Morse needed bodyguards, and Bowdler went almost everywhere with Morse.

Liam approached the secretary's desk. "I'm Liam Blackstone, and I sit on the board of U.S. Steel with Morse. I need to see him right away."

Mr. Bowdler's response was polite but firm. "Mr. Morse is occupied. I can make an appointment for you early next week."

"Too late," Liam said. "I need to see him now. It's an emergency."

"Tell me what's going on and I'll see what I can do," the secretary said.

"For once in his life, Morse needs to act like a decent human being instead of a bottom-feeding parasite." Patrick would probably warn Liam to pipe down, but sometimes a show of force was the best way to handle a bully.

The muscle-bound secretary stood, his formidable height even taller than Liam. "Mr. Morse is occupied all morning. I suggest you leave."

In three strides Liam skirted around the man and flung open the door to Morse's office. A woman gasped and leapt off Morse's lap, hastily arranging her blouse.

"What is the meaning of this!" Morse shouted, rising to his feet.

"Sorry, sir," the secretary said in a groveling tone. "He barged in without warning."

Liam took in the situation quickly. The woman looked around his age, respectably dressed with piles of chestnut hair starting to slip free of its bun. As a newlywed, Morse might be forgiven for indulging in some morning affection with his wife, but Liam doubted the woman was his wife and decided to show no mercy.

"Mrs. Morse?" Liam asked with a cordial smile. "We haven't had the opportunity to meet each other yet, but congratulations on your recent marriage."

"Shut up, Blackstone!" Morse barked, then sent a conciliatory look at the woman who was pinning up her hair. "Wait for me in the foyer, Katherine. I'll dispose of Blackstone in two minutes. He has no prayer of reversing my decision about the vote to kick him off the board, so this won't take long."

"I'm not here about the vote," Liam said, holding the newspaper aloft. "I'm here because the city has you to thank for three dead kids at an orphanage."

"What in tarnation are you talking about?" Morse seemed genuinely puzzled, and Liam tossed the newspaper onto his desk, folded open to the article about children suffering from heatstroke after no ice could be found to bring their temperatures down. His brows lowered as he scanned the story, and even Katherine leaned in close to read over his shoulder.

Morse's wife was named Clemence, not Katherine, and this woman surely had something to do with the rumors of marital trouble. She held a hand to her throat as her eyes traveled in dismay across the various stories about the heat wave.

In contrast to his mistress, Morse was unsympathetic. "You can't blame this on me. Who can prove how those children died? It's hot! Everyone is suffering from the heat."

"But not everyone is bribing government officials to block rival ice barges from docking in the city. Lift the embargo and let all the ice companies go back into business whether they're part of your trust or not. It would be the decent thing to do."

A pause stretched in the room. Morse's face twisted in frustrated annoyance as he drummed his fingers on his desk.

"Charlie?" The smidge of compassion in the mistress's voice seemed to harden Morse's resolve.

"Don't let him fool you, Katherine," Morse said. "This isn't my fault. Blackstone is only trying to stir up trouble against me, and it won't work."

Liam strove to keep his temper under control. "This isn't about a grudge; it's about doing what's right for the people of this city."

"What would you know about that?" Morse scoffed, then looked at his mistress. "Liam here comes from Pittsburgh and never went to high school. He's a semiliterate welder who needs his brother-in-law to interpret his shareholder reports for him. He's an embarrassment to the entire board of directors when we dine at respectable restaurants because he uses a bread roll to soak up soup and then *licks his fingers* when finished."

Liam's jaw tightened. Morse was only trying to goad him, though every word hurt because it was all true. Morse must have sensed the tide was turning in his favor because he stood and began walking around his desk, a taunting smile on his face.

"Liam has been arrested for brawling, he carouses with the crew of his yacht because he doesn't have any real friends, and he speaks like a vulgarian."

Liam lifted his chin. "No kid ever died because I denied him a drink of cold water."

The woman was still reading the newspaper with a pale look on her pretty face. "Charlie, it says here that the morgues are closed. The morgues! What are people to do?"

"Yes, Charlie," Liam said, "what are people to do?"

Morse snatched the newspaper from his mistress and threw it in the wastebasket. "I can't wait until September when we vote you back to Pittsburgh where you belong. Now get out of my office before Mr. Bowdler throws you out."

Liam nodded to the bodyguard. "No need, I'm leaving."

Maybe he hadn't won Morse's capitulation, but Liam had an oceangoing vessel, held docking privileges at Pier 19, and knew where he could get ice for the people of New York City.

⌘

Liam's first obstacle was in getting the ship's captain to agree to the trip six miles up the Kennebec River to the Norberg Icehouse.

"The *Black Rose* is a yacht, not a cargo barge!" Captain Macauley said. They stood in the wheelhouse of the ship, where the windows on three sides of the captain's chair provided a panoramic view of the harbor.

"A yacht is just a fancy term for a ship," Liam argued. "It means people like to sail on it because it's got parlor games and comfy beds and decent food. Give me a month in dry dock with a blowtorch and I could transform this thing into a tanker, a freighter, or a battleship."

It wasn't idle talk. He'd spent fourteen years building ships from the ground up. He loved the *Black Rose*, but in her current state it was a playground for rich people. It was time to use the vessel to do something great, except Captain Macauley was determined to stop him.

"We don't have a month, and you want to sail today?" the captain said.

It would be the only way to get back in town with the ice within two days. The *Black Rose* had been designed for speed because his uncle liked racing against other hypercompetitive millionaires. At least now Liam could put that speed to use.

"This ship has a cargo hold larger than a ballroom," Liam argued. "We open it up and stack it to the gills with ice."

"That's what I'm trying to warn you about," Captain Macauley ground out in frustration. "You are exceeding the operational limits of this ship. The doors to the hold are meant for wheeled crates, not conveyor belts hefting tons of ice. Not to mention we just painted the hold, and this sort of thing could damage it."

"The hold can be repainted. As for loading the ice, I'll figure that out once we get to Maine. My mind's made up—prepare to sail at sunset."

Captain Macauley pressed his lips into a line. "I'll do it, but I want you to sign a document acknowledging my objections.

121

If this ship runs aground or capsizes, it could ruin my reputation. I want a signed statement acknowledging that I attempted to warn you of the dangers and releasing me from any legal consequences."

"Agreed," Liam instantly said.

Twenty minutes later, Liam's gut began to sour as he read the statement drafted by Captain Macauley. Potential hazards included running aground, capsizing from imbalanced cargo, damage to the bilge pumps if they got overwhelmed from melting ice, and a mortifying hairpin turn at a spot in the Kennebec River named Squirrel Point. Captain Macauley showed him the promontory on a map pinned to the wall of the wheelhouse.

"Squirrel Point is four miles up the Kennebec," he explained, pointing to the spur of land jutting into the river.

"Can the ship handle the turn?"

"It can, but it's dangerous."

So was letting little kids swelter in the heat without anything cold to drink. His resolve strengthened as he began initialing each warning on the document, but his ulcer began to pinch. The *Black Rose* wasn't merely a ship; it was his home. The only real home he'd ever known, and now he was risking it just to stick a thumb in Morse's eye.

And maybe also save a bunch of companies from going out of business. What was the point in having money and power if he didn't use it on behalf of common decency? For a split second it felt as if his father were standing nearby, watching him sign the document. Somehow he knew that Theodore Blackstone would approve of this action.

A smile hovered as he signed his name at the bottom of the document with a flourish.

14

For the first time in years, Maggie had nothing to do. The ice cream parlor was closed, the factory had ceased operations, and their cold rooms had been emptied and cleaned. That meant she had the time to start strategizing how to take down Charles Morse and break the ice trust wide open, and she quickly identified her first ally.

His name was Rupert Pine, the newspaper journalist who had written several articles detailing the ice shortage. Although his coverage about the health crisis at the orphanages had been given the most prominence, Mr. Pine's brief article buried in the back of the newspaper was even more revealing. It divulged that several members of the city council owned stock in the American Ice Trust. The journalist had obviously been paying close attention to the underhanded ways Morse had built his empire, and his insight might prove useful.

Maggie fanned herself with the folded section of the newspaper as she rode a streetcar down Centre Street. Businessmen had shed their coats and rolled up their sleeves, women had their collars open, and fussy children sprawled on the seats. Everyone was hot and miserable, but a weak breeze from the window cooled the sweat on her face as the streetcar funneled on the electric tracks sunk into the pavement.

The *New-York Tribune* occupied the tenth floor of a nineteen-story building that towered over the Financial District. The red-brick edifice spoke of power, strength, and wealth, but the elevator was out of order, so she had a long hike to get upstairs. Her boots echoed in the dank stairwell, and she was breathless when she finally arrived at the tenth floor. She paused at the top of the stairs to catch her breath, blotting her face with a handkerchief and pinching her blouse to wiggle the damp, sweaty fabric in a hopeless attempt to help it dry.

A young lady occupied the secretary's desk in the lobby, the top buttons of her blouse open as she waved a bamboo fan.

"Do you know where I can find Mr. Rupert Pine?" Maggie asked.

The lady smiled. "You look even hotter than me," she said, flicking her wrist to offer Maggie a few twitches of the hand fan.

"Bless you!" Maggie said with a laugh. Unfortunately, Mr. Pine was a night reporter and wasn't expected in until seven o'clock this evening. Maggie tried to pry the reporter's home address from the secretary, but the woman hedged.

"Please," Maggie pressed. "I have some valuable insight into a story he is covering. He seems to be taking the lead in writing about the ice trust, and I know a lot about it."

A bead of perspiration rolled down the secretary's forehead. "All right," she whispered and cracked open a leather book. She wrote the address on a slip of paper.

Maggie blinked twice at the address. It was the same boarding-house where she once lived with Dino and Julie during their lean years when they owned a single pushcart. Was this a good omen or a bad one?

She rode a streetcar to her old neighborhood, noting how quickly the quality of the streets declined. It had been eight years since she left this dilapidated street, but the changes were everywhere. Back then it was mostly Irish immigrants with a smattering of Italians. Now Italian flags hung outside several storefronts, and the language was alive on the street. The boardinghouse was the same, however—the red brick, the narrow windows, and the musty smell inside. Entering the building stirred long-lost memories she wished to forget.

She passed the third floor where she used to live and continued up to the fourth. A dim lightbulb in the hallway illuminated peeling paint and stained tiles. She found Mr. Pine's door and knocked, but there was no answer. She knocked louder, hurting her knuckles. Still no answer.

"Mr. Pine?" she called, wiggling the doorknob. She didn't want to come back. The dank smell of this ramshackle building brought back too many bad memories. "Mr. Pine, if you're in there, please open up."

"Go away!" came a gruff voice from behind the door.

"Mr. Pine, I need a few minutes of your time." A thud and some grumbling followed, and then the door flew open to reveal a bleary-eyed man with a shock of honey-blond hair, wearing nothing but his knickers and an unbuttoned shirt.

"Lady, I work nights, and you just woke me up. Go away!"

She stuck her foot in the doorway before he could slam it shut. "I have insight on how Charles Morse is running his ice trust scheme."

Interest flickered in Mr. Pine's tired eyes. After a moment he opened the door wider. "Come in," he said, his voice calmer but still annoyed.

Mr. Pine was about her age. He had long, lanky limbs and curious blue eyes as he gestured her toward a table beside his rumpled bed. He hopped on one foot while dragging on a pair of pants, flipping his suspenders over his shoulders before joining her at the table. There was only a single chair, so he sat on the mattress, elbows braced against his knees as he looked at her. By now all traces of annoyance were gone.

"What have you got?" he asked.

"I know how Morse is strong-arming ice companies to join his trust."

He reached for a notepad and a stubby pencil. "Tell me," he said, and she began speaking. It seemed like he already knew about the pressure ice companies were under to join the trust.

He even knew how customers had been forbidden from selling so much as a pound of ice to other companies. But the situation at the pier was new to him.

"The Department of Docks is answering to Morse alone," she said. "No one is allowed to dock in the city unless they are part of the ice trust."

"Can you prove it?"

"I know the man who submitted a sworn affidavit to the city council. I have a copy of it at my office at the factory." Antonio had dropped off a copy of his testimony as soon as it had been printed and published in the city's official records. So far, the city had done nothing with it, but Mr. Pine seemed more determined.

Mr. Pine stood, a broad smile on his face. "Let's go to Gadsen Street. I want to see that document."

It was early afternoon by the time they arrived at Gadsen Street, but with all the restaurants shuttered, it seemed depressingly vacant. She'd never seen it so deserted.

"Our shop is ahead on the left," she told Mr. Pine as they walked past O'Donnell's Pub.

Surprisingly, the interior of the ice cream parlor looked crowded. Why would every table be occupied when they had no ice cream? She quickened her steps and hurried inside, spotting the Lieberman brothers, folks from the Irish pub, even Mr. Alfonso. Dino stood at the front of the group.

"Maggie, look who's here," Dino said, pointing to a broad-shouldered man near the counter. The man turned to her, and she caught her breath at the sight of Liam Blackstone, his face flushed with excitement.

"He's going all the way to Maine to get ice for everybody!" Aunt Julie said.

Had she misheard? It was too astonishing to believe, but people clapped and cheered so it must be true. And Liam looked fabulous. With his shirtsleeves rolled up, he braced his hands on his hips, looking like a pirate ready to go forth and conquer.

"I'm taking my ship to Maine like you asked," he said with a grin, and she couldn't help herself. She reached out to frame his face between her palms and kissed him on both cheeks, then directly on the mouth. The crowd roared, and he returned her kiss for a fleeting second before pulling back to laugh along with those cheering.

"What do you mean, you're going to Maine for ice?" Mr. Pine asked. When Liam explained how he intended to set sail on the *Black Rose* this very evening, the journalist asked to come along. "I want a front row seat to watch someone deliver a knockout punch to Charlie Morse!"

"I don't care about any knockout punch," David Lieberman said. "I want to see my ma's face when we wheel a big cartload of ice into the deli."

Had there ever been a moment like this? Dino hugged her, the Lieberman brothers clapped Liam on the back, and someone popped a cork. Maggie didn't know why Liam had changed his mind, but for tonight she intended to celebrate.

⁓

Liam savored the way everyone here treated him like a conquering hero, but he couldn't stop thinking about Maggie's impulsive kiss. Had she meant anything by it? Maybe she was one of those physically affectionate people. In the past hour, he'd seen her uncle Dino hug and kiss almost everyone here. Was her kiss nothing more than that? Because he kind of liked it in a different way, and that bothered him.

Someone brought in a few bottles of wine from the Porterhouse and an impromptu celebration began. He tugged on Maggie's elbow. He was about to have the world's most awkward conversation, but it was important and he didn't want an audience.

"Can I talk to you?" he asked. "Outside."

"For you? Anything!" she said with a blinding smile. Frieda winked at Maggie as they wove through the others and out the front door. Some of the party had already spilled outside, but the space beneath the olive tree was clear, and she looked as pretty as a peach standing before its pale-green leaves.

"I want you to know . . ." He cleared his throat and started again. "What I mean is, I'm glad I can go get that ice for you, but I want you to know that it doesn't mean anything, okay?"

Her eyes widened. "No? It means everything to the people on this street."

"Okay, yeah, I get that. But it doesn't mean anything between you and me. I still don't want . . . I mean, your kiss . . ." There wasn't an easy way to say this, so he needed to simply spit it out. "I still don't want anything special between you and me."

He shouldn't have worried about offending her because it looked like she was trying not to laugh. "Because you think I'm a gold digger?"

"Yeah, that's the gist of it." Maggie was way too fascinated with money for him to ever trust her interest in him was real. "This trip to Maine is a onetime deal. You and I are just friends, okay? We obviously have no future together other than this crusade to bust up the ice trust, right?"

"Obviously," she said, still looking as happy as he'd ever seen, and he breathed a sigh of relief. Her impulsive kiss hadn't meant anything, so that meant they could go back to just being friends and partners. He liked her before the money thing got in the way. He crossed to the table beneath the olive tree and gestured for her to join him.

"I'm glad we'll have that journalist along for the ride because Morse hates bad publicity," he said. "We can use Mr. Pine to stoke up outrage in the press."

She nodded, then asked a question he hadn't seen coming. "Can I come with you to Maine?"

"Why?" he asked, his misgivings awakening again.

She held up both hands. "Don't worry. I'm not hankering after your vast fortune, but I want to see where the ice comes from. I've never traveled more than ten miles from this exact spot. All my life I've heard stories about Italy, and Mrs. Lieberman can ramble on forever about Germany. I import peaches from Georgia and blueberries from Michigan, but I've never been to any of those places. I've always wanted to see beyond my own horizon, you know?"

He understood. He had an old stamp book to prove it. Taking her with him went against every sensible instinct, but how could he deny her? Inconvenient romantic attraction aside, he respected how hard she worked, and she deserved a chance to see something of the world.

"Yeah, you can come . . . provided you keep your hands to yourself. I can't risk my purity by having you throw yourself at me again." He couldn't quite block the humor from his voice, and she beamed the most charming smile back at him.

"After all, we obviously have no future together," she teased, throwing his own words back at him.

"None at all," he said and couldn't resist a quick wink at her. "If you get your uncle's permission, we sail at five o'clock."

And against Liam's better judgment, he looked forward to sailing with her.

15

Getting Dino's permission wasn't a problem. Maggie was twenty-nine years old, and Dino trusted her. When she assured him there would be separate cabins on the yacht, he gladly gave his approval.

Two hours later, she and Rupert Pine arrived at Pier 19 and trudged up the gangplank to board the *Black Rose*. Rupert craned his neck to scan the teak deck and collection of elegant tables, chairs, and lounges clustered near the front of the ship, but Maggie's gaze was immediately drawn to Liam.

Something seemed wrong. The laughing man from earlier was gone, and now Liam looked grim and tense as he conferred with the crew. He barely acknowledged her before directing a young deckhand named Caleb to show her to a cabin.

"This place is as long as a city block," Rupert said in admiration, but the deckhand disagreed.

"The *Black Rose* is two hundred thirty feet and eight inches long," Caleb said. "A city block is three hundred feet long, so the ship is shorter."

"Okay then," Rupert said agreeably. "It's still the biggest ship I've ever been on."

It was the *only* ship Maggie had been on. The teak deck was varnished to a high shine, and everything looked spotless.

Flags snapped in the breeze, and the briny scent of the sea was invigorating.

"Please wipe your feet before we head belowdecks," Caleb said, gesturing to a sisal mat just inside the doorway. "Liam likes things to be spick-and-span, so everyone has to clean their shoes coming off the deck."

"Can I see him before we go below?" she asked Caleb. "I brought a gallon of ice cream just for him." This afternoon she ran over to the Starwood Hotel to buy back some of the ice cream she'd sold them. Liam said ice cream helped with his ulcer, and she wanted him to know she was grateful for what he was doing.

Caleb shook his head. "Liam is in a bad mood. Sometimes he gets that way when he's upset about business."

She'd been looking forward to personally giving the ice cream to Liam, but Caleb already took the bucket and handed it to another crew member to carry below. Getting it into an icebox was probably more important than her grand gesture, but she wanted to thank him. This trip to Maine was the most gallant act of generosity anyone had ever done for her. She obediently wiped her feet on the sisal rug and headed down the steps.

The ceiling was low down here, yet everything else was pure luxury. Fine carpet led down a narrow corridor with elegant brass lanterns anchored to the walls every few yards. Caleb narrated what they were seeing as they walked.

"This deck is for entertaining," he said, pointing out a dining room, a cardroom, even a bowling alley. The next level down had the bedrooms, or "cabins" as Caleb called them.

Then Caleb opened the door to her cabin, and she caught her breath in wonder. It was the most delicate, feminine room she'd ever seen. Polished rosewood lined the walls, and a shimmery coverlet of champagne-colored silk lay across a bed mounded with pillows. The slim dressing table featured an oval mirror and a vanity tray to keep crystal bottles of perfume and other toiletries safely secured to the table. Everything looked far too pretty to touch.

"Oh my," she whispered as she stepped inside.

"Just pull on that rope if there's anything you need," Caleb said with a nod to a braided silk cord with tassels on the end. Then he left to show Rupert to his cabin, leaving Maggie alone among the splendor.

She lowered herself onto a tufted chair before the dressing table, whose drawers featured ivory knobs carved to look like seashells. The drawer slid open with barely a whisper. What should she put inside it? Rich ladies probably had all kinds of powders and mysterious jars of cosmetics, but all Maggie brought with her was a comb and a toothbrush.

Nevertheless, she loved setting them inside the empty drawer and pushing it closed. She opened and closed it twice more to savor the sleek glide. She helped herself to a spritz of perfume from the vanity, the bottle heavy in her palm. She'd never tried real perfume before, and the lemony scent was divine.

Then it was time to try the mattress. It was springy and soft and like nothing she'd ever sat on. The pillows were just as nice, and there were so many of them—two big ones for sleeping, lots of little square pillows, a round one, and a rectangular one. Why did rich people need so many pillows?

From somewhere deep inside the ship came an abrupt thud, then a clank. She set the pillow aside as a rattling of chains and two long blasts prompted her to stand.

Was she supposed to do something? She reached for the silk rope, feeling horrible about summoning a crew member like a hoity-toity person, but she didn't know what to do. Was she supposed to stay put in her cabin or go up on deck? All of a sudden the whole ship seemed to jerk.

"Do you need something?" Caleb asked when she opened the door to his knock.

"I don't know what's happening. Is there something I should be doing?"

"The ship is leaving berth. You can come up on deck if you want to watch."

She did. Every minute of this voyage was an adventure she

wanted engraved in her memory forever. She followed Caleb up two flights of the steep, narrow staircase until bright sunlight on deck made her squint.

Liam was straight ahead, his arms braced on the railing as he stared out at the river. Even from behind, it was obvious every muscle in his body was as taut as a bowstring.

"Is everything all right?" she asked as she joined him. She followed his gaze to a tugboat drawing alongside them.

"Yeah," he said after a pause, his attention on the tugboat that would guide them out of the harbor. "Captain Macauley has done this a thousand times before."

"Why do you seem so anxious, then?"

Liam drew in a deep breath, then blew it out in a heavy gust. "We've never loaded this ship with ice before. I got worked up in the heat of the moment this morning, but everything is a lot more real now."

She fidgeted, trying not to dwell on how much she, Dino, and every other restaurant on Gadsen Street needed ice, and she clenched the railing. "It's not too late to back out," she said, holding her breath and praying he wouldn't.

"Everything in me is warning against it, and Captain Macauley hasn't stopped yammering about how bad an idea it is."

"Then why are you going?"

The breeze carried her question away, but he heard it. He watched a flock of pelicans skimming across the waves, his expression tormented. "I want to best Charles Morse," he admitted, "and prove to the world I'm the better man, but it's a risk." Then his eyes softened as he gave her an amused look. "Hey, what's this I hear about you bringing us ice cream? I thought yours all melted."

"It did, but I sold some to a hotel that still has ice and I bought it back from them. There's enough for the whole crew."

"Careful," he teased. "You're in danger of ruining your reputation as a penny pincher."

"Don't worry. The whole world already knows I'm a penny pincher, and that will never change."

The wind blew a lock of his dark hair, and the corners of his eyes crinkled as he smiled down at her. "I kind of like that about you," he said. The open admiration in his expression stirred a dangerous tug of attraction, making her wonder if there might be a future for them after all . . . but then a voice broke into her wayward thoughts.

"Great ship you have here."

Maggie pulled away from Liam as Rupert Pine joined them at the railing.

"Thanks," Liam said a little formally. "Did you find everything you need in your cabin?"

"Absolutely," Rupert said. "It must be nice to live on a floating palace like this."

Liam nodded. "It is, but its going to be hot and humid belowdeck tonight. When the weather is this hot, I usually sleep up top. You might be more comfortable up here. You can't get much of a breeze from the portholes." He glanced at her. "You're welcome as well. We set up the reclining chairs at the bow where no one will bother you."

It might be cooler on deck, but for once in her life Maggie wanted to know what it felt like to sleep on a top-notch mattress with silky sheets and fancy plush pillows.

"I'll be fine below," she said, trying not to notice the way Liam's open shirt collar exposed the strong column of his neck.

Yes, it definitely would be safer down below. He'd made it perfectly clear that this was a humanitarian mission for him with no possibility of a romantic future between them.

Liam disappeared into the wheelhouse to confer with the captain while she and Rupert stayed on deck to watch the tugboat guide the ship out of the harbor. As soon as the sun began setting and they were out to sea, Maggie headed below to begin enjoying her lavish cabin.

A little brass lantern illuminated her cabin, the amber light making the room seem even grander. She trailed her fingers along the counterpane and drifted to the dressing table to unpin her hair. Maybe it was the lighting or the fancy setting, but she looked prettier than usual in the oval mirror. This must be how rich people felt every evening. She combed her hair and tied it into a braid for sleeping, then proceeded to open and close every drawer in the dainty dressing table just for fun.

The drawer on the left wasn't empty. Someone had left their things there, and Maggie suddenly felt like an intruder. The jar of face powder looked like pure silver, entwined with ivy leaves and little blossoms. There was a silver cigarette case too.

She should leave it alone. This cabin wasn't hers; she was only a visitor. But she couldn't help herself . . . She lifted the cigarette case and flipped the lid open. It was empty. The inside of the lid, though, had words inscribed on it. She tilted the case before the lantern to get a better look.

> Happy birthday, Darla.
> With all my love, Liam.
> July 8, 1901

A heavy lump landed in her stomach. This gift was only a year old. Was he still in love with this unknown woman named Darla? A closer scrutiny of the lid revealed the silver cover wasn't a mere floral decoration. The vines were in fact two entwined initials—D and L.

Liam must have spent a fortune on the cigarette case. She quickly put it back in the drawer and closed it. Yet her curiosity won out until soon she was opening other drawers in the bureau. The top drawer held expensive lace handkerchiefs, all monogrammed with Darla's initial. There was another bottle of the lemony perfume, this one unopened.

Suddenly the lemon scent on her skin was cloying. Had Liam noticed that she'd worn Darla's perfume earlier? She went and dunked a cloth into the washbasin, then wiped the scent from her skin, though it lingered even after she dimmed the lantern and slipped into bed.

The deep comfort of the mattress and silky sheets felt divine, but all she could think about was Darla. Who was she?

Liam told her there was no future for them as a couple. *He told her!* But she ignored it because it had been fun to imagine a strong, adventurous man being attracted to her.

She rolled onto her back to stare at the ceiling and listen to the slosh of waves outside the open porthole. The lift and fall of the ship made lying in this strange bed unsettling. She didn't belong here. It had been foolish to let herself become attracted to Liam when he warned her they had no future. For pity's sake, there was a woman named Darla he adored!

It was so hot down here. The air was stagnant, reeked of lemon, and seemed to get warmer the longer she lay on the overly soft mattress.

An hour went by. Then another. It was impossible to get comfortable in Darla's bed, and by midnight she concluded it would probably be easier to sleep on a lounge chair on deck after all. She dressed quickly, then headed up the companionway and onto the deck.

A cool breeze immediately soothed her. Half a dozen men sprawled on lounge chairs near the front of the ship, and she crept toward them in search of an empty lounge chair. There wasn't enough moonlight to identify the sleeping men, but it was easy to see there weren't any vacant chairs. Would she be able to find one at the rear of the ship? A few snores mingled with the roar of waves, and she crept carefully to ensure her footsteps were silent.

"What are you doing up here?" a raspy whisper asked.

She nearly jumped out of her skin, but it was only Liam, sitting upright in a lounge chair hidden beneath the eaves of the wheelhouse.

"Looking for a lounge chair. It's too hot below." She'd die before admitting it was impossible to sleep in Darla's bed.

His teeth flashed white in the dim moonlight. For some inane reason, that quick, confident flash of a smile unknotted the tension in her neck.

"Follow me," he whispered. "There are empty lounge chairs near the stern." Her eyes soon adjusted to the dark, and by the time she arrived at the rear of the ship, Liam had spread a blanket across a reclining lounge chair for her.

"Make yourself at home," he said. The breeze was so cool that she welcomed the blanket as she stretched out on the chair.

"Who's steering the ship?" she whispered. With so many people sleeping up here, it felt only right to keep her voice low. Liam moved to a lounge chair a few feet away and dragged a blanket over himself to settle in.

"Captain Macauley had bridge duty until midnight, but the first mate is on duty now and will be there until sunrise," Liam replied.

She stared up at the crescent moon that cast its faint glow over the water. It was still hard to believe that her impulsive, starry-eyed suggestion to fetch ice from Maine had been set in motion. No matter how long she lived, it was doubtful any man could ever top the gallantry of Liam's offer on her behalf.

"Who is Darla?" she asked, shocked by her own audacity.

Liam stiffened a little, then cocked a brow at her. "Who's Philip?"

She should have expected it. She and Liam had gotten along since the instant they met, and it wasn't until he overheard that bit about why she left Philip that his attitude cooled toward her.

"Why should you care?" she teased. "After all, we obviously have no future."

"True." He grinned. "So, who's Philip?"

She settled deeper into the lounge chair, her eyes fixed on the moonlit clouds. "Philip was a great dreamer. He comes from a rich family, and his parents were appalled that he fell for a pushcart vendor. The irony is that my business turned into something, while he's still struggling to write songs."

"You left him over money," Liam said. There was no judgment in his voice, just a flat statement, as though he hoped she would deny it. She rolled onto her side to look at him in the neighboring lounge chair.

"I left him because I know what it's like to be poor and I'm never going back." She said the words lightly, as if threat of poverty was nothing more than a long-vanished figment of her childhood fears, and yet she had lost more than a thousand dollars in inventory this week alone. In truth, her fear of poverty had come roaring back with a vengeance.

"Okay, I get it," Liam said. "I'm sorry I jumped to conclusions, but I've had women throwing themselves at me because of money ever since I came back to New York."

"I don't want your money; I just want your ship." That got a laugh from him. It was rich and warm, a wholesome laugh from deep inside that made him even more attractive to her. Which was probably wrong, especially because she still smelled the lemon on her skin, and it still annoyed her.

"And Darla?" she asked. "The stateroom I'm in is filled with her things."

Liam sobered. "Darla was one of those women who threw herself at me because of my money." He stared at the deck, his face bleak as the faint roar of waves came from below. "It didn't stop me from loving her, though."

For the first time since she'd met him, Liam seemed vulnerable. There was an open, aching quality to his voice that made her want to comfort him. Always before, Liam came across as strong, courageous, funny, or challenging. This raw ache of his was a surprise, but she understood it.

There was no need for her to say anything. She rolled onto her back again, wondering why learning about this new facet of Liam's personality made him even more attractive in her eyes.

It was a long time before she could fall asleep.

16

By ten o'clock the following morning, Maggie stood at the railing of the ship to peer at the rocky coast of Maine, savoring the cool breeze wafting over her skin. No wonder rich people came to places like Maine during the heat of the summer. As someone who'd never set foot outside New York City, Maine seemed like a primeval wilderness. Granite boulders lined the shore, and spires of pine trees shot up toward the sky. Every now and then the wind carried a hint of pine scent mingled with the brine from the sea.

By noon the *Black Rose* had arrived at the mouth of the Kennebec River.

"Can you believe it?" she said to Rupert Pine, who drew up alongside her as they waited for a tugboat to guide them six miles upriver to the icehouse that was waiting to fill the decks and cargo hold with the precious commodity.

"I didn't know there were this many trees on the earth," he replied, gazing at the coastline.

Rupert was good company, unlike Liam, who had reverted to being a nervous wreck this morning. He'd risen before dawn to start barking out orders to his men, his anxiety over the coming day apparent to everyone.

Had she been selfish in asking Liam to come? This ship was

his *home*, and he was putting it at risk for her and the others. She glanced to the far side of the deck, where Liam stood beside Captain Macauley.

"Here she comes," Liam called to a deckhand, pointing to the tugboat bobbing in the water and heading their way.

"Raise anchor!" Captain Macauley shouted, and a couple of crew members scrambled to obey the order. Others lowered a ladder for the tugboat pilot to climb aboard. The pilot was a seasoned expert whose knowledge of local conditions qualified him to guide the *Black Rose* safely up the river.

"This is a lot bigger than most ships sailing up the Kennebec," the pilot said as he considered the *Black Rose*, his gaze moving from bow to stern.

"Can it be done?" Liam asked tightly.

"I'll get her there." The confidence in the weather-beaten grooves of the pilot's face was reassuring, but it did nothing to ease Liam's anxiety, who crossed himself and muttered some sort of imploring prayer.

Maggie listened as the river pilot conferred with Captain Macauley about the best way to navigate the Kennebec. The wide and deep river ran almost directly north with only a few dangerous twists in the route. It had been used for over a hundred years to support the timber mills, ironworks, and shipbuilding companies located in towns up and down the river, but ice had always been the Kennebec's main commodity.

Liam retreated with the tugboat's pilot and Captain Macauley into the wheelhouse as the journey began. She and Rupert were the only ones without a job, so she joined him at the railing to watch the ship edge toward the mouth of the river.

"What caused you to have so much interest in the ice industry?" she asked him.

"I don't like Charles Morse," he said lightly, watching a pair of seagulls wheeling on the breeze. It seemed as if he wanted to add more, and she waited, watching Rupert's expression turn dark. "Charles Morse ruined my father."

She sucked in a quick breath. "How?"

"My father tried to run for city council. Morse wanted someone else to win, and he doesn't mind playing dirty."

Mr. Goldrick's ironhard face rose in her mind as Rupert continued speaking. His father had owned a fish cannery in Brooklyn for decades, but when he wouldn't pay bribes to the borough's police force to "keep his building safe," the elder Mr. Pine decided to run for city council to clean up the New York City Police Department as a whole.

"There was a fire at our cannery the week before the election," Rupert said. "Everyone knew who was behind it. Then people in the neighborhood started getting late-night knocks on their doors, reminding them what happens to people who vote the wrong way. Was it any wonder that my dad lost the election? He had fire insurance, but not enough to replace what he lost. To make matters worse, he had to pay the city to clear the land after the cannery burned down. That put him into debt. All for challenging Charles Morse."

Maggie gripped the railing, her nerves ratcheting tighter as the ship entered the mouth of the river. This trip to Maine was about more than ice, and she could only pray it would be a success.

❦

From his position in the wheelhouse, Liam eyed the rocky promontory of Squirrel Point straight ahead, bracing himself to endure the next ten minutes.

"Order the engines into lower gear," the pilot said. Captain Macauley obeyed, and the *Black Rose* slowed to a crawl. Liam's heart pounded so hard that it became a roar in his ears, and a whimper escaped his throat.

"Have you got insurance on this ship?" the pilot asked.

"I do," Liam replied.

"Good, because I've never led a ship this big around Squirrel Point."

Liam let out a string of curses. "Why did we sail up this far if you've never done it before?"

"I said it can be done, but I never said I did it," the pilot said. "Don't work yourself into a lather. A ship is only wood and steel, nothing that can't be replaced."

"No, this ship is the only thing I have left from my father," Liam bit out. "You're going to treat it like it's made of glass and carrying the Holy Grail."

Captain Macauley's voice cut through Liam's tantrum. "Let the man do his job. We're almost there."

Liam bowed his head and closed his eyes. He couldn't look. He only had one single, fleeting memory of his father, which happened right here on the *Black Rose*. They had been at the bow, and Liam was no more than a toddler, throwing scraps of bread to the seagulls hovering overhead. He'd been too little to toss the bread very high, but his father had been endlessly patient, showing him the proper stance and wide arc to toss the bread higher. That was all, just a fleeting memory and the feeling of complete love and happiness. To this day, Liam sometimes stood at the bow to summon the memory of that golden afternoon.

"Softly now," the pilot murmured to himself.

Liam crossed himself, silently reciting a Hail Mary. What if the ship ran aground and had to be scuttled? It would be the ultimate failure, proof he wasn't worthy of the legacy left to him by his father. Liam had already become a laughingstock on the board at U.S. Steel, but if he ruined this ship . . . well, it didn't bear thinking about. He closed his eyes and prayed harder.

"Aaaaand there we go," the pilot said.

Liam looked up to find Squirrel Point behind them. "We're safe?"

"Safe," the pilot replied.

Liam nodded, letting out a pent-up breath. *Thank you, God!*

Twenty minutes later, the ship approached the Norberg Icehouse, built only fifty yards from the riverbank. The brick building was four stories high and painted white to deflect the heat. Instead of windows, a series of hinged doors ran across the front of the building, and a conveyor belt mounted on a rolling gurney lowered blocks of ice from the upper stories to the ground below.

Captain Macauley cut the ship's engine. Water sloshed against the hull as the *Black Rose* drifted in the current, the tugboat gently nudging it toward the Norberg pier. Deckhands lowered rubber bumpers to protect the hull as they drifted closer to the pier. Half a dozen men came running from the icehouse, waving their caps and calling out greetings. They came to the end of the pier to catch the mooring ropes tossed down by crew members.

Liam blotted sweat on his forehead as the men from Norberg Ice caught the ropes and began pulling the ship closer to the pier. The *Black Rose* made contact with the pier's bumper with barely a sound.

"Perfect!" Captain Macauley boomed, and relief at the successful mooring almost drove Liam to his knees. The crew swung into gear quickly, lowering the gangway and welcoming men from Norberg Ice aboard to have a look at the mighty yacht.

Mr. Norberg was a wiry old Swede who clambered over the ship inspecting the holds, the decks, and the cargo doors. Liam escorted the man belowdeck to show him the cargo holds that had been cleared for ice.

"There's not a lot of room down here," Mr. Norberg said. "We'll need to cut smaller blocks to get them through that door."

"Can it be done in time?" Liam asked. He wanted to set sail tonight so they could be back in New York by tomorrow.

"I'll start a couple of boys on the cutting right away," Mr. Norberg said. "In the meantime, start filling the top deck, and we'll tackle the cargo holds last."

The Norberg crew flew into action loading the ship. Chains rattled as block after block of ice traveled down by conveyor belt from the icehouse. The belt system snaked all the way down the pier directly to the *Black Rose*.

They filled the rear deck first. The furniture had been carried down for temporary storage in the bowling alley, leaving the deck clear for the knee-high blocks of ice.

"The ice is going to ruin the finish on your deck," one of the Norberg men warned, and Liam had to tamp down his persnickety impulse to protect his fine teak decking. The deck could be refinished, but restaurants that had been years in the making were on the verge of going under without ice. The orphanages and hospitals would get the first delivery of ice, but there should be plenty left over for every restaurant on Gadsen Street.

As soon as a single layer of ice filled the stern, workers sprinkled an inch of sawdust over the ice to prevent it from fusing with the next layer. Then more ice was brought aboard, eventually piling higher until the ice was stacked eight feet high. Next they began filling the bow with ice.

Stacking hundred-pound blocks of ice was tiring work, prompting Liam to join in. Rolling up his sleeves and making himself useful always felt good. Soon the air smelled of sawdust and sweat, but he loved it. Even Maggie helped. With the strongest men hefting blocks on their own, Maggie paired up with Caleb, each of them using a pair of ice tongs to share the burden of carrying a hundred-pound block of ice between them.

Liam's back hurt, the ice tongs had rubbed blisters into his palms, and the muscles in his biceps felt like limp noodles. But then he'd catch a glimpse of Maggie, looking at him as if he were a hero out of a storybook, and a bolt of pure energy renewed his spirit.

At one point the conveyor belt leading to the pier jammed, but Maggie helped Mr. Norberg remove the belt and oil the gears to get it operational again. It was the same sort of task he'd seen her do the first day he visited her factory. After finishing the repair, she stood to clean her hands with a rag. She was dirty and exhausted, but to his eyes . . . she was perfect.

The deck was completely filled by three o'clock. Captain Macauley blew a whistle for a break, after which they would start filling the cargo holds with smaller blocks. Mrs. Norberg set out platters of sandwiches and jugs of lemonade in the grassy area beside the icehouse, where everyone congregated for a well-deserved rest. Liam sat on a blanket next to Maggie in the shade of a large oak tree. He leaned in to tease her, but quietly so that no one would overhear him.

"I want you to know that even though you're a complete skinflint and we obviously have no future together, what you did with the conveyor belt was a thing of beauty."

"Yes, it was," she said proudly.

He stretched out on the blanket, thoroughly exhausted but content. It had been a good day so far. He'd never been a very admirable man, but since coming back to New York, he was hoping to change that. No more back-alley brawling or letting his temper get the better of him. Now he went to church, walked a straight-and-narrow path, and tried to make his father proud, both Theodore Blackstone and his heavenly Father.

He would never know who those three orphans might have grown up to become had they not died from heatstroke. Liam wasn't a theologian like Patrick or brilliant like Theodore Blackstone, but at least he knew that rushing ice to the city was a good and selfless thing to do.

He could lie here in this sunlit meadow all day, but a shadow suddenly blocked the sun, and he opened his eyes to see Captain Macauley standing over him. "We need to talk," he said. "Let's head over to the ship."

Liam sat upright, wincing as the muscles in his back protested. He lowered a hand to help Maggie up as well.

"Should I come too?" she asked, but Captain Macauley asked her to join the others at the picnic table.

Liam followed the captain while listening to the grim news. "Mr. Norberg says we've got a problem with the cargo holds," he began. "Come aboard and he'll show you." All Liam's senses went on alert as he followed the captain to the cargo area ready to be filled next.

Mr. Norberg was waiting for them. "These rooms aren't going to work after all," he said. "It's too warm in here. Once the ship starts sailing, heat from the boiler rooms is going to melt this ice faster than what's up on deck. As the meltwater drains, it can lead to an unbalanced load."

"Why not load a little more ice on the port side of the deck to balance it out?" Liam asked, but Captain Macauley rejected the suggestion.

"We can't predict how fast the ice will melt in the holds. The only safe way to operate the ship is to stop loading now."

That meant they'd be returning home with only half the ice he anticipated carrying. The hospitals, morgues, and orphanages would get the first deliveries, and there wouldn't be enough left for Maggie's factory or any of the restaurants on Gadsen Street.

As he emerged up on deck, he gazed at Maggie, standing alongside a cluster of men from Norberg Ice at the lemonade table. She looked so happy, the stress gone from her face as she relaxed with the crew. For a while today she had been looking at him like a hero. Maybe he'd be a hero to the orphanages and the hospitals, but disappointing Maggie was going to hurt.

He turned to Captain Macauley. "Let's weigh anchor and set sail as soon as possible."

Macauley nodded, then blew a series of whistle blasts to summon the crew back to the ship, and Liam headed toward Maggie. There was no point in delaying what had to be said; he just regretted that her current happiness was about to fade. Members of the crew were already leaving the picnic tables while Maggie lingered with the icehouse team. This was going to be a difficult conversation, best handled privately.

"Hey, Maggie. Can you follow me over to those trees?" The cluster of oak trees shaded the hitching post where they could be alone.

Her smile was radiant. "For you? Anything!"

By the time they got there, she must have realized something was wrong because Mr. Norberg was already rolling the conveyor belt away from the ship.

"What's going on?" she asked.

"Captain Macauley says we won't be able to fill the cargo holds because of melt and balance issues."

"What a shame. Is that why we're leaving early?"

He nodded, dreading what was about to come. "We'll wire a message to Mr. Gabelli to meet the ship tomorrow at noon to start distributing the ice. He can notify the hospitals and the orphanages to expect delivery before the end of the day."

Maggie continued looking up at him, waiting for him to say more, but he couldn't. It took a few seconds for understanding to dawn. She kept her chin up, eyes locked with his, and asked, "Will there be anything left for Gadsen Street?"

"I'm sorry, Maggie. We won't even have as much as the hospitals need."

She took the news like a champ. She didn't complain or try to twist his arm, just looked away and nodded. Her sigh had the weight of crushed hopes and dreams wrapped up in it, but she still managed a hint of a smile. "I understand," she said. "And I still think you're a knight in shining armor for doing this."

Her brave words made him feel even worse. "If things are still bad after we get back to New York, we can make another run," he assured her.

She tilted her head to meet his gaze. "I thought this was a onetime deal."

"I did too." He gave her a smile. "Sometimes I change my mind."

"I'll be okay. I just dread telling Dino. He was so hopeful."

How close to the bone did they live? He had no business digging into her personal finances, but they'd grown close in the past few days and he needed to know. "If you don't mind my asking, what sort of outstanding debts do you have?"

She didn't hesitate to answer. "The mortgage on the building is six hundred a month, and I owe another two hundred and fifty a month on a bank loan for the equipment."

"Will you be able to pay?" If not, he could loan her whatever she needed.

"I can pay," she said. "All my life I've lived in terror of debt, so I have a solid rainy-day fund." She wasn't meeting his eyes anymore, just picking at the bark of one of the trees as though it were the most fascinating thing in the world.

"How long will your rainy-day fund last?"

She closed her eyes. "Could we please talk about something else?"

He wasn't responsible for shoving her business toward the edge of a cliff, but he still felt lousy on her behalf and wished he hadn't teased her about being a skinflint. "I want you to promise me something. If you need help with money or with Morse . . . or whatever, I want you to know you can come to me."

"Even though we obviously have no future together?"

He chuckled. "Yeah. Just say the word and I'll help you out, okay?"

She stepped back from the tree and dusted off her hands. "Okay," she said, but she didn't meet his eyes and he didn't quite believe her. What an irony it would be if after dismissing her as a fortune hunter, Maggie turned out to be too proud to accept his help.

Maggie battled a range of emotions during the voyage home. Even though they didn't get ice for Gadsen Street, they still accomplished a miracle. Tons of ice would go to the neediest people in the city, and she got the chance to see the glory of Maine. Now the adventure of a lifetime was over. As the *Black Rose* sailed toward its berth at Pier 19, she dreaded telling Dino they had no ice to restart their factory.

Rupert Pine stood beside her at the railing. He had been documenting everything about their momentous voyage, and soon news of the trip would be splashed all over the city, sticking a thumb in Charles Morse's eye and possibly shaming him into doing the right thing.

"Look!" Rupert said with a nod toward the pier. "The ice trucks are already waiting for us."

Gabelli Ice had come through for them. A fleet of six trucks lined up at the base of the pier, ready to receive the ice. Antonio Gabelli stood at the front of the line, waving at her as crew members began mooring the ship. Even old Mr. Gabelli was there, admiring the towers of ice stacked along the deck.

They weren't the only ice trucks. Two ambulances from St. Cecelia Hospital were also on the pier, their rear hatches open and ready to take as much ice as could be shoved inside.

Then her heart sank. At the end of the pier was every pushcart Molinaro Ice Cream owned. Aunt Julie and Uncle Dino waved at her, their smiles wide.

She waved back. What else could she do? They would learn soon enough there would be no ice for them or anyone else on Gadsen Street.

Docking procedures took forever. Crew members at the bow and stern prepared the mooring lines as the ship pulled slowly alongside the empty berth at Pier 19. Tugboats hovered nearby to ensure a smooth berthing. Was it always this slow? Power to the engines had been cut, and only friendly nudges from a tugboat inched the ship closer to her berth.

Maybe it was her anxiety over Dino and Julie waiting for her, but the July sun was broiling hot. It was probably the same for Dino and Julie—this sort of heat could cause heatstroke in older people, and it seemed cruel to make them wait at the end of the pier when there wouldn't be any ice for them.

Crew members finally lowered the gangway. Liam came alongside her as she prepared to go ashore, his face drawn in concern.

"Do you want me to go with you to explain?" he asked.

She shook her head. "They'll be decent about it." Dino and Julie were always decent. The pushcart vendors were another story, but she'd deal with them later.

She stood on tiptoes and kissed his cheek. "Thanks, Liam." His eyes crinkled in pained sympathy, and she turned away before it could put a dent in her armor.

"There's our girl," Uncle Dino boomed, waving a clipping from their olive tree to welcome her home. The Lieberman brothers were there too, and even the pushcart vendors cheered her arrival.

"You might want to wait on that," she told them. "We got some ice, but there won't be enough for Gadsen Street."

Surprise, then despair settled on Dino's face as she explained how the hospitals and orphanages would get most of the ice. Anything left over would go to the morgues. As she predicted, Dino tamped down his disappointment and was thoroughly decent about it.

"Okay, sorry, boys," he told the pushcart vendors. "Let's head back to the garage and lock up the carts. Maybe in a few days we'll finally have some ice."

Dino strove for a tone of hearty good cheer, and some of the vendors sent him nods of understanding, but most looked annoyed. Maggie tried to ignore them as she accompanied Dino and Julie back to Gadsen Street.

How long would God make them wait for an answer to their prayers? Was He even listening? A fully loaded Gabelli ice truck rumbled past them on its way to an orphanage, and a tiny bit of satisfaction lifted her gloom. Those orphans needed the ice more than she did. Maybe her trip had been God's plan to alleviate the suffering among the neediest in the city and to teach her a better appreciation for her blessings.

But as her factory continued to sit idle, the prospect of drowning beneath an avalanche of debt was becoming more ominous.

17

Although the press was falling over themselves in praise of Liam's daring jaunt to fetch ice for the poor and needy, the trip was not without consequences. Journalists were quick to point out that the villain in this drama was Charles Morse, a man who sat on the board of U.S. Steel. While Liam was happy to see Morse suffer for his role in the ice fiasco, most of his family disapproved.

Oscar Blackstone in particular. Uncle Oscar had been his father's brother. While Theodore was universally acclaimed as the embodiment of humanitarian virtue, Oscar was the opposite. It had been said that the term *robber baron* had been coined to describe Oscar Blackstone, a ruthless man of ambition whose legacy of corporate machinations stood in stark contrast to his younger brother's compassion. The good brother and the bad brother. The good brother died from a heart attack after a lifetime of stress and grief, caused in part by Liam's kidnapping. The bad brother was alive and well and still fomenting schemes on Wall Street.

Oscar was incensed by the public airing of a feud on the board of directors of U.S. Steel and summoned Liam to his office on the top floor of the Blackstone Bank the day after he arrived home from Maine.

Oscar didn't rise when Liam was shown into his office. With a black patch covering one eye and a hand braced atop the silver handle of the cane he relied on to walk, Oscar looked like a villain straight out of a vaudeville play.

They'd never liked each other. From the day Liam returned to the family, he and Oscar had locked horns over business values, about Oscar's snotty wife, and about ownership of the *Black Rose*. So far, Liam had won every battle, mostly because Patrick was by his side, sending up one legal salvo after another. Today Liam simply needed assurance that Oscar wouldn't revoke his support for Liam's membership on the board after the stunt in Maine.

Liam took a seat opposite Oscar's desk. For a one-eyed man, Oscar sure liked to keep his office dim. The maroon velvet drapes were drawn closed, leaving only a few electric lamps beneath amber glass shades to illuminate the cavernous space. A ticker-tape machine on the corner table gave a monotonous rattling sound as it tracked stock prices, there because Oscar liked to pounce the instant he sensed trouble in the market.

Oscar got straight to the point. "Why are you antagonizing Charles Morse?"

"He jacked up the price of ice too high for poor people to pay."

Oscar shrugged. "I don't care if you disapprove of his ice trust. Your stunt endangers the health of the U.S. Steel board and is going to boomerang back on you. When you strike at a king, you need to kill him, and you didn't."

Liam snorted. "Morse is no king."

"Don't underestimate him," Oscar warned. "When evaluating an enemy, always look to the intelligence and cunning of the men he surrounds himself with. Morse is strong. He hires the best men he can corrupt and control. They're powerful, mean, and dangerous. You're underestimating him, and in so doing are costing me money, and I won't tolerate it."

Liam shifted uncomfortably in his seat. Uncle Oscar wasn't a member of the board of U.S. Steel, but he could still wield

152

influence merely by picking up a telephone and speaking to a few key individuals.

A knock interrupted them, and Oscar's man of business stepped inside. "Mr. Morse is here to see you, sir."

Liam stiffened. Had speaking of the devil actually summoned him? Oscar instructed the secretary to ask Morse to wait a few minutes, then turned his attention back to Liam after the door closed.

"I want to broker a peace between the two of you," Oscar said. "A fractured board of directors is bad for business. Either the two of you learn to get along or I'm going to use my influence to pull you from the board. I don't need to wait for the vote of no confidence in September. I'll simply exercise my authority as the largest investor in the company to get a different Blackstone appointed in your place."

Liam sputtered, "You can't do that!"

"I can, and I will," Oscar said. "My father has been retired from active management of the bank, but he'd step onto the board if I asked him."

Liam's mind whirled. Frederick Blackstone was his grandfather and the one who had originally pulled strings to get Liam appointed to the board. If Frederick lost faith in him, it would be a body blow. He leaned forward, scrambling for a way to save his seat.

"Don't do this," he urged. "Tell me what I can do to keep your support. Please . . ."

Oscar retrieved a cigar from a humidor that probably cost more than most men earned in a year. His expression was thoughtful as he went about the motions of clipping the end, lighting the cigar, and drawing several puffs before he looked at Liam, his expression not unkind.

"You've already lost my support and are going to be ousted from the board, if not now, then in September," he casually said. "The question you should be asking yourself is how to best capitalize on a bad situation. I'm going to ask Morse in here so we can settle this here and now."

Liam tugged on his collar, wishing it weren't so stinking hot. He should have brought Patrick with him. Oscar was a master of Machiavellian tactics, and Liam didn't have a prayer of getting the upper hand.

"I'm not going to quit," Liam warned.

"You are if I withdraw my support," Oscar said. "Charles Morse's goal on the board is to make money for the shareholders. So is mine. That's not to say I won't pressure him to turn this situation in our favor. Sit back, shut up, and let me steer the ship."

Oscar pushed a button on his desk, signaling his secretary to bring Morse in. Liam felt like a brick had just landed in his stomach. How had the situation spiraled out of control so quickly? This was going too fast. He'd run to Patrick's office as soon as this meeting was over and try to salvage the catastrophe.

The door opened, and Charles Morse strode into the office. He flashed a quick smirk at Liam before nodding a greeting to Oscar. "Mr. Blackstone," he said cordially, then seated himself in the chair closest to Oscar. The game was now two ruthless robber barons ganged up against one uneducated welder. Liam braced himself for the onslaught, but to his surprise, Oscar's attitude to Morse was chilly.

"What's this I hear about your call for a vote of no confidence in my nephew?" Oscar demanded. "If you weren't happy with Liam's performance on the board, you should have brought your concerns to me, not the other board members."

Morse didn't flinch in the face of the arctic blast from Oscar. "I was in the room when you and your father jammed Liam onto the board," Morse said. "You were wrong then, and you're wrong now. You valued blood over profit. Liam may be a fine man in his personal life, but he is not qualified to be on the board. For the next ten years we are handcuffed to the labor contract he negotiated on behalf of the steelworkers."

Liam sat up straighter. "It's been the only decent thing the board has done all year. The dignity of the workers is more important than the wallets of rich shareholders."

Morse jabbed a finger in Liam's face, his voice lashing out. "And *that* is why you don't belong on the board."

Oscar raised a calming hand. "Settle down," he cautioned. "I've brought you both here to lower the temperature between the two of you. Liam, I don't want to see any more damaging stories in the newspaper. And, Morse . . . no more underhanded calls for votes of no confidence. I want to settle our differences as gentlemen."

"What are you suggesting?" Morse asked.

A long pause stretched in the room. The rattle of the ticker-tape machine in the corner recorded fluctuations in Oscar's personal fortune while a crafty look hovered on his face.

"I want to replace Liam on the board with my father," Oscar said. "Frederick Blackstone is eminently qualified to serve, and in return the board will pay my nephew a fortune to walk away quietly. If you balk, Liam will rally the unions to strike on his behalf. I predict that carefully planted rumors about a rift on the board are likely to start circulating in the press. Shareholders hate that. The stock price will crater, the board's influence will suffer, and soon you will be begging me to put out the fire of bad publicity. Then I will double my demand for Liam's cash settlement and still get to appoint my father in his place." Oscar smiled as he drew on the cigar.

Oscar's audacious demand was probably a bluff, but one never knew with Oscar. In the center of Oscar's calculating heart, he'd always wanted controlling interest on the board of U.S. Steel. He couldn't control Liam, but he could control Frederick, so Oscar might be willing to foment trouble to make it happen.

Morse's face darkened. "You're bluffing."

"Try me," Oscar said without a flicker of change in his iron-hard expression.

To Liam's surprise, Morse sat back in his chair, mulling over the offer. "How big of a settlement?" he finally asked Oscar.

"One thousand nonvoting shares in the company," Oscar replied. "It will be enough to inspire Liam to play nice with the unions and salvage his pride in the press."

Liam's mind whirled as Oscar and Morse continued thrashing out the terms of his departure. They couldn't do this, could they? He kicked himself again for walking into this meeting without his lawyer. Oscar and Morse conversed in easy tones, flinging around terms and details Liam didn't understand. Every time Oscar seemed to score a point, he gave a concession to Morse as well. The two most ruthless men on Wall Street played a game of high-stakes poker with seeming ease and enjoyment until Morse committed a fatal mistake.

He insulted Oscar's wife.

Poppy Blackstone was Oscar's only weakness. She was his second wife, whom he met when he was aging, infirm, and slowly headed toward the grave. The athletic young woman inspired Oscar to get out of his wheelchair, pick up a golf club, and join her on the golf course. As Oscar's health returned, his infatuation with Poppy deepened. He would tolerate no criticism of his wife, even though Poppy, the working-class daughter of the golf course manager, married Oscar for his money. Everyone knew it, including Oscar. He didn't care. He loved the flighty young woman who had adapted to her new lifestyle like a predatory duck taking to the water for the first time.

Morse's error occurred when he let down his guard while Oscar admitted that Liam never learned to master his impulses, which was ironic because throughout the entire conversation, Liam sat only six feet away, clenching the arms of his chair and brilliantly mastering the impulse to punch both men at the same time.

"I confess, even my wife has been frustrated with Liam," Oscar conceded.

"Ha!" Morse chortled. "That's the first sign of intelligence I've ever heard coming from Poppy Blackstone."

A pall settled over the room. Worse than the actual insult was the tone in which Morse said Poppy's name, as if it were gum stuck to the bottom of his shoe.

Morse immediately realized his gaffe and tried to backpedal.

"What I meant to say was . . ." Morse swallowed and glanced around the room, stammering as he tried to repair the damage. "I meant that your wife is uniquely clever in her own particular way."

"Get out," Oscar said with lethal calm. Morse sat up straighter and raised his chin. "Sir, I apologize for misspeaking, but we mustn't let a minor issue foil an important business decision."

Oscar pushed himself to his feet. "I will never consider an insult to my wife to be a minor issue," he said. "I am old and rich enough to tell anyone who disrespects my wife to take a flying leap off the tallest building in the city. The deal is off, and I want you out of my office."

Morse made a few more attempts to salvage the deal. Oscar responded to none of them. He merely pushed the button on his desk, which summoned a clerk to show Mr. Morse out of the building.

Liam quietly smiled. He and Poppy locked horns often and with gusto, but they did so openly, each begrudgingly respecting the other. Perhaps that was why Oscar had been willing to tolerate him. Oscar might never warm up to Liam, but they were family, and at least for today, Liam maintained his seat on the board.

Perhaps more importantly, Charles Morse had just made a powerful enemy.

<hr>

Maggie tried to keep her nerves at bay as she watched Mr. Lindquist methodically grind another batch of her aunt's headache medicine in the old mortar and pestle. Julie's painful stress headaches were alarming enough without listening to the pharmacist's nonstop stream of commentary about the lackluster business on Gadsen Street.

"You're the first customer I've had all day," he said. "My serums have all gone bad. How am I supposed to keep them cold without ice?"

"None of us have ice," Maggie pointed out, hoping she didn't sound as short-tempered as she felt. She waved a hand fan before her sweaty face, but it did little to alleviate the heat.

"But I signed a contract with the ice trust! Shouldn't they be supplying me with ice even if they withhold it from people who didn't sign?"

It had been a week since the *Black Rose* returned from Maine with ice. The newspapers showered Liam with words of praise like rose petals on a returning warrior. They celebrated his selfless gesture, and like magic the ice shortage in the city began to ease. Ice trucks resumed their routes, prices stabilized, and companies were able to reopen.

All except the businesses on Gadsen Street. For some reason, not a single customer on Gadsen Street was getting ice.

"It seems like every other neighborhood has plenty of ice except us," Mr. Lindquist continued. "The fish markets and the canneries are open again. Even the breweries are getting ice. Breweries! You should think that a pharmacy would get ice before they give it to a brewery."

Except the pharmacy in question was next door to Molinaro Ice Cream, and Maggie had a nagging fear that she might be the cause of the ice drought on Gadsen Street.

The bell over the front door chimed as a customer entered, and Mr. Lindquist looked up with a hopeful expression. "Can I help you, sir?"

The portly gentleman removed his bowler hat and met Maggie's gaze as he fanned himself with the hat. "I'm looking for Maggie Molinaro. Is that you?"

She pushed away from the counter to stand upright. "That's me."

"Good," the man said. "Your uncle said you were probably over here. I'm John Ambrose, a clerk for the attorney general of New York. I'd like to speak to you."

She blinked. "Have I done something wrong?"

"Forgive me," Mr. Ambrose said with a smile. "There is an ongoing investigation into problems associated with the new ice trust. Your name keeps popping up in the discussions, and we'd like to speak to you about it."

He handed her a business card. It was on fine linen cardstock with raised type. "My goodness, I didn't know clerks got such fancy business cards."

Again, his smile was friendly. "Being a clerk for the attorney general means I am a lawyer who does the preliminary legal research for him. It doesn't pay well, but I get nice business cards."

The quip broke the tension, and Mr. Ambrose outlined how the ice shortage during the heat wave prompted the state's attorney general to investigate potentially unfair business practices by the American Ice Trust. He explained there was a fine line between honest competition and illegal collusion to rig the system.

"We need to hear from people like you to determine if American Ice has stepped over that line," he said, his face unaccountably serious. "Would you be willing to come forward and offer sworn testimony about your experiences?"

Willing? She would pound down the door to find someone willing to listen, but Mr. Lindquist spoke first.

"Can you guarantee her safety?" The concern in the pharmacist's voice worried Maggie, but Mr. Ambrose shrugged it off.

"She'll be perfectly safe," he answered. "All she has to do is tell her story to the attorney general and answer a few questions. The report will be entered into our docket, and eventually the attorney general will decide if the case warrants further investigation."

Her gaze strayed out the window, where empty tables and failing restaurants lined Gadsen Street. Antonio Gabelli had offered his testimony about the docking situation, and she ought to be just as brave.

"I don't know, Maggie," the old pharmacist said. "It could take months before anything happens, and we need ice today. Talking to these people might make the ice trust mad at you."

They were already mad at her. Testifying might not save her

business, but it would be the right thing to do if it would stop the trust from trampling over other honest businesses.

"I'll do it," she said, her chin held high as she tried to ignore the worried gaze of Mr. Lindquist.

"Excellent!" the clerk enthused. "Our calendar is booked solid for the next two weeks, but I shall put you down for an appointment with the attorney general on the first of August."

Somehow having a date for the appointment made it seem a little more ominous, like a pending trial or execution. Would it do any good? Given the worry in old Mr. Lindquist's face, it might make things worse than ever. But letting the ice trust get away with what they'd done to her was not a possibility.

After nine years of running a successful business, the moment Maggie always feared had arrived. They didn't have enough money in their operating budget to pay their monthly expenses.

She and Dino discussed the matter as they repainted the flower boxes on their front walk. With no customers anywhere on Gadsen Street, it was the perfect opportunity to spiff up appearances. Her knees hurt as she knelt on the pavement to take out her frustrations while sanding the chipped paint from the wooden flower box.

"Do we pay the mortgage on the building or the loan on the factory equipment?" Dino asked. "Or I suppose we could pay a little for both."

"We need to save the building," Maggie said. It was their home. They lived on the top floor, and the building was worth far more than the equipment. No matter what, they needed to safeguard their investment in the building.

"How fast will they repossess the equipment if we don't pay on the loan?" Dino asked, and Maggie frowned as she continued sanding. The same bank held both the building mortgage and the equipment loan. Surely they'd want her to keep the factory equipment so that when the crisis was over, they could swing back into business and start paying their bills again.

"I think they'll give us a few months," she said. The bank manager, Mr. Longmire, had been so good to them since the day they walked into his office all those years ago. This would be the first time she'd let him down by missing a payment.

"Maybe we should dip into our savings," Dino said. "We have enough money. We could last for at least three more months if we crack open our nest egg."

Maggie straightened, looking down at the vacant street. All the restaurants on the street were closed. Although most of the city was now getting ice, some streets were mysteriously without. The ice embargo was now personal. Charles Morse knew of her trip to Maine with Liam and wanted to punish not only her but every restaurant on Gadsen Street. Years of hard work were evaporating before their eyes.

"I won't pay until I know what will happen with the ice trust. What if this goes on for months? For a year?"

"Then we move to a city where Charles Morse and his corrupt ice business has no power."

She hunkered back down to continue sanding the flower box. "I agree. And if we have to move, we'll need money to start over somewhere else. We can't drain our savings just yet."

Her knees hurt from kneeling so long, but at least she was putting her time to good use. As soon as she finished repainting the flower boxes, she'd do the same for the flower boxes on the rest of the street. Careful attention to appearances was one of the things that made Gadsen Street famous for its charm.

"Maggie!" someone shouted. It was Frieda Neuman, running down the street with her skirts hiked up in one hand, waving a piece of paper over her head with the other. Frieda's skirts were so high she exposed her scarlet leather shoes and black stockings. Maggie stood, rubbing the ache in the small of her back.

"Good heavens, what is it?"

Frieda's hair was tumbling down the side of her head, and she was breathless and beaming. "Look," she panted, thrusting the piece of sheet music into her hands. "A new song," she panted. "They're singing it in all the music halls. It's by Philip. Your Philip!"

Maggie stared at the brand-new piece of sheet music. The song was titled "The Ballad of Gadsen Street," written by Philip Altman. News of the shuttered restaurants on Gadsen Street had been reported in the newspapers, but how had Philip composed a song so quickly?

Frieda yanked the paper from her hands. "He mentions you in the lyrics," she said. "See? He calls you 'Sweet Miss Maggie of Gadsen Street.' And here he talks about piano music from O'Donnell's Pub and Mrs. Lieberman's bagels."

"And the song is popular?" Maggie asked in disbelief.

Frieda nodded. "Yes! The music store sold out of it, and I had to get this directly from the publisher."

She blinked back the prickle of tears to scan the lyrics. Philip mentioned lots of the restaurants by name. He spoke of the scent of baking bread and the glow of the streetlamps as the sun went down. The sounds of laughter mingling with mandolins and the clinking of glasses. He wrote of everything that made Gadsen Street so special.

Maggie couldn't read music, but the pub had a piano and Mrs. O'Donnell could probably play it for her.

It didn't take long to summon others on the street over to the pub, which was depressingly vacant as they entered. The chairs had been upended on the tables, the barstools empty, and the hanging glass racks full. One of the O'Donnell boys rolled the upright piano across the wooden floorboards to the front of the pub while their mother studied the sheet music. Even the persnickety Mr. Prescott from the steakhouse came to listen.

Soon Mrs. O'Donnell started playing the notes while one of her boys took a stab at the lyrics in a hearty tenor.

It was bittersweet. The tune was charming and spritely, the lyrics full of praise, but every few measures a hint of melancholy crept in. How could a song be happy and sad at the same time? But it was joyous and clever and wonderful, laden with wistful memories and a sad sort of joy.

Old Mrs. Lieberman was the first to press a balled-up handkerchief to her eyes, but others looked misty-eyed too. The song was a hymn to the spirit of Gadsen Street in all its culinary delights, all its backbiting competition and irrepressible dreams. How many long summer evenings had she and Philip sat in this very pub, listening to the music and dreaming of their future? He had captured it perfectly, but the final line of the lyrics hinted at trouble: "After the last light on Gadsen Street fades, its memory will shine forever."

They were in trouble, and even Philip knew it. The restaurants of Gadsen Street were now a cautionary tale for the city.

18

Maggie wore her spiffiest business suit to meet with the bank manager. Mr. Longmire probably wouldn't notice that the blue poplin jacket with its nipped-in waist and matching white tie was the same colors as the Molinaro Ice Cream brand. The navy stripes matched the awning on their store and every umbrella on their pushcarts. The colors of her suit reminded her what she was fighting for.

The bank manager might show sympathy for her plight. She'd lost a thousand dollars of inventory because of the ice trust. Hundreds of other businesses had been hit as well, so she probably wasn't the only one in trouble. Hopefully her years of prompt mortgage payments would buy her enough goodwill to extend a bit of grace until the ice situation got resolved.

Thick granite walls kept the bank cool inside and muffled noise from the street as she entered. It was quiet enough to hear the pounding of her heart as she headed toward Mr. Longmire's office.

He hadn't changed much in the years since extending her the loan, still sporting the same head of thick auburn hair, the same full mustache, and the same imposing desk. Her mouth went dry, and she clutched the briefcase as she stood before his desk, feeling awkward and overheated.

"Please have a seat," he offered. "Would you like something to drink?" A silver pitcher beaded with condensation sat on the corner of his desk.

"Yes, please."

Ice tinkled in the glass as he filled it from the pitcher.

"You have ice," she said.

"Yes. It is widely available."

Not to the people of Gadsen Street. She took a sip of the blessedly cold water, then rolled the glass in her hand, savoring its chill.

"Mr. Longmire," she began, "for some reason, no one on Gadsen Street has been able to get ice. I know you have been patient with some of my neighbors in the past. Alfonso's Deli has often been late on their obligations—"

"I would not suggest using Alfonso's Deli as a shining example of business acumen."

"Well, you know Molinaro Ice Cream has been successful. As soon as the ice situation is resolved, we'll swing back into production and start paying on our loans. Can you extend us a few months of leniency?"

Mr. Longmire shifted uneasily in his seat. It didn't look like he was enjoying this conversation any more than she was. "Surely you have been able to put funds away in the event of an emergency. How much can you pay?"

It was a question she didn't want to answer. They *could* pay but had excellent reasons for safeguarding their nest egg.

"We can pay the building's mortgage in full, but not the loan for the equipment."

"None of it?" Mr. Longmire asked.

"None of it."

"Then I'm sorry," he said. He took several long, measured breaths before leaning forward to speak in a low voice as if he feared being overheard. "Maggie, I want you to succeed. You and your uncle are the kind of people who make this country great. Please don't force my hand by not paying both loans in full."

165

Fear clouded the edges of her vision. Mr. Longmire was a kind man, which made his reluctantly delivered threat even more ominous. Someone else was pulling his strings, and she feared who it might be.

Charles Morse made his fortune in banking. He had a stake in half the banks in the city. She glanced around the well-appointed office, noting the expensive mahogany and upholstered chairs. Was this one of Morse's banks? It was called the First Mercantile Bank of New York, but she never thought to ask who controlled it.

Maggie looked Mr. Longmire in the eyes. "Who owns this bank?"

"It's part of the Morse Consolidated Financial Corporation," Mr. Longmire said quietly. "I urge you to pay your loans in full. You can't win. Do you hear what I'm telling you?"

"I hear you," she said before collecting her briefcase and heading out the door.

Her heart pumped so hard that she was perspiring even before stepping into the harsh glare of the July afternoon sun. It was *so* hot, so stinking, horribly hot as she headed to the shaded awning of the streetcar stop. It didn't offer much relief from the heat, but it was better than nothing. She yanked the hat from her head and used it to fan herself while waiting for the streetcar.

It would cost five cents to ride home, and now more than ever she needed to guard her pennies. The walk home would be brutally hot with no shade, but it was the thriftiest option. She jammed the hat back on her head and started walking, almost bumping into a tall gentleman.

"Pardon," she muttered and prepared to pass by, but he grabbed her elbow.

"Good afternoon, Miss Molinaro." The handsome middle-aged face with a full mustache summoned a raft of sour memories.

"Mr. Goldrick," she said, jerking her elbow away. His sudden appearance probably wasn't a coincidence, especially after he started speaking.

"How did your meeting with Mr. Longmire go?" he asked cordially.

"How did you know I met with Mr. Longmire?"

"My office is on the top floor above the bank. Not much goes on down there that I don't know about."

She glanced up. There were three floors of residential apartments above the bank. How convenient for Morse's goon to keep an eye on the minions working in his bank. He'd probably overheard every word of her meeting, and it felt like a noose tightened around her neck. Frustration boiled over.

"Why do you people want to drive me out of business?" she blurted out.

Mr. Goldrick laughed. "Heavens, that's not what we want." Then his humor evaporated, and he lowered his chin to skewer her with piercing eyes. "What we want is for the bad press about Mr. Morse to stop. I think you can do that."

"Me? I don't have any control over what the newspapers print." Journalists all over the city had made Charles Morse a punching bag because of his callous grip on the ice market, but he deserved every bit of their criticism.

"You know Rupert Pine," Mr. Goldrick said. "He was on that ship when it sailed to Maine, and I suspect you're in cahoots with him."

"I barely know Rupert Pine." She crossed her arms and hated the tremor of fear in her voice.

"Too bad," Goldrick replied. "He's the ringleader behind these stories, and you know how to contact him. I want him stopped. For every day of additional bad press Mr. Pine spills in his newspaper, you and every other merchant on Gadsen Street will suffer an additional week without ice."

She gasped. "You can't do that!"

"I can, and I will," Mr. Goldrick said in his smoothly elegant voice. "I will grant you a single day of mercy before your clock starts. Beginning the day after tomorrow, you and your fellow merchants on Gadsen Street will swelter without ice for a solid week until the bad press from Pine stops."

Anxiety prickled like insects crawling over her skin. The streetcar was approaching, and she hurried aboard to escape Mr. Goldrick's oppressive stare. She didn't have the strength to confront this sort of evil on her own, but perhaps if she rallied the others on Gadsen Street, they could defeat this monstrous plot together before they all went bankrupt.

～ ∽ ～

Liam took Caleb with him to restock the larder of the *Black Rose*. He was bored to death of the bland diet his doctor recommended and was on the hunt for something without much spice but that didn't taste like sawdust. He'd overdone it on the trip to Maine when he'd lifted and hauled ice. His ulcer had been worse since then, but he'd redouble his efforts in obeying his doctor's orders. He was heading to the health clinic upstate soon and would shop with renewed determination to follow the recommended diet.

He and Caleb stood before a high-end grocer's display window, scanning the baskets brimming with colorful fruit, jars of seasoning, and ropes of sausages dangling from hooks. All of it was too spicy or acidic for his gut to handle.

"What does *au naturel* mean?" Caleb asked, pointing to the label on a bottle of olive oil. Most of the bottles were infused with herbs or peppers, but the plain versions were labeled *au naturel*. It wasn't until he joined the Blackstone family that Liam started learning the endless variety of food wealthy people considered normal.

"It means it doesn't have any extra flavoring added to it," he said.

Caleb scowled. "Then why did Darla say that she was stupid for going au naturel for the Frenchman? I don't understand."

Liam startled in surprise. He knew all about Darla's act of youthful rebellion when she posed in the nude for a famous French sculptor. She'd confessed the incident to Liam, just like he'd confessed his string of arrests for brawling and vandalism when he was a kid. Neither of them was proud of their wild youth, but that was all in the past, and he didn't want Caleb babbling about Darla's indiscretions.

As a cabin boy, Caleb tended to pick up a lot of gossip and his brain was like a steel trap. Caleb remembered everything exactly as he heard it, even if he didn't understand nuance or figures of speech.

"When did you hear Darla say this?" he asked Caleb, who reported it was during one of Liam's weekend parties when he hosted Darla and a bunch of her artist friends on the *Black Rose*.

"Darla said that she posed au naturel 'to renounce her mother's stuffy ways, but it just proved that the folly of youth can be more dangerous than the prudery of the aged.' That was exactly what she said."

It sounded like Darla . . . smart and cynical but with a dash of wisdom. "Try to forget about what Darla said, okay? Let's get some ice cream before we head back to the ship. Molinaro's should be back in business now."

Ice cream was the one vice his ailing gut could tolerate, and it had been too long since he'd indulged. He and Caleb navigated the crowded avenue, scanning both sides of the street for the familiar blue-and-white umbrella of a Molinaro pushcart.

They walked half a mile but only saw two ice cream vendors, neither of them belonging to Maggie. So they headed to Pier 15, where supposedly she earned more than she did at Pier 19. Liam came upon a rival ice cream vendor parked at the pier.

"Doesn't this spot belong to the Molinaros?" he asked the wiry young man staffing the rival pushcart.

The man shrugged. "We thought so too, but we haven't seen a Molinaro pushcart in over a week—not since the heat wave began. What can I get for you?"

While the news was worrisome, Liam ordered enough chocolate ice cream for his entire crew. It wasn't like Maggie to keep her carts off the streets, and she should have been back in business by now.

That meant she was in trouble.

Once he and Caleb had returned to the ship and dropped off the ice cream, Liam set off for Gadsen Street to find out what was going on at Molinaro Ice Cream.

∞

Word spread quickly on Gadsen Street after Maggie reported what she learned after her bank meeting. With all the restaurants closed, everyone was free to gather and discuss the situation. She and Frieda sat on the front stoop of Lieberman's Deli while older people sat at the café tables. There was universal outrage over the threat to embargo their ice unless they could persuade Rupert Pine to quit writing his articles about Morse.

At first Uncle Dino wondered if they should ask Rupert to back off his reporting. Most of the other journalists in town had lost interest in the ice scandal, but Rupert continued banging his drum. Rupert's animosity against Morse might be rooted in resentment over what happened to his father, but what did it matter? It wasn't right for a single individual to control an essential commodity like ice, and Charles Morse had proved himself unworthy to wield that much power.

The Lieberman brothers agreed with Maggie. "Today he wants a journalist to stop writing articles about him. What will he want tomorrow?"

"Who cares?" Mr. Alfonso demanded. "We'll cross that bridge when it happens. For now, I want ice."

"I say we hire a lawyer," the owner of the Porterhouse said. Even though his restaurant was closed, Mr. Prescott still looked immaculately dressed in a three-piece suit and a fine gold watch chain. "A lawsuit is the only thing a man like Morse will respect, and a jury of our peers will give us justice."

"But it will take years," Mrs. Lieberman said. "What about your meeting with the attorney general? Can that help us?"

Maggie sighed. "My appointment with him isn't until next week. And I have a hunch it will be a slow process."

ELIZABETH CAMDEN

The heated discussion continued as Maggie leaned against the side of the deli. At least they were all in this together. Over the past few weeks, their street filled with rival businesses had become an unlikely band of brothers and sisters. A community—Christian and Jew, rich and poor, Italian, Irish, German, Ukrainian, and native-born Americans—all here as one in this East Village neighborhood. It was a refreshingly cool evening, and there was no work to be done. No food to prepare or dishes to clean, just a forced idleness that none of them wished for but must endure together.

A man walking down the street toward them was a dark silhouette against the setting sun. He looked big and muscular, but he moved gingerly, as though in pain. She stood. "Liam?"

He grinned and raised a hand in greeting. It had been more than a week since she'd seen him. She thought of him daily but had been too ashamed to reach out to him. Her inability to get her factory back in action was embarrassing, but that didn't stop the surge of admiration the sight of him triggered.

"I've been looking for some Molinaro ice cream, but I have a feeling I'm not going to find any." He glanced at the shuttered restaurants, then back at her.

"No ice," she said simply. "We're still out."

"All of you?"

"All of us," David Lieberman interjected. "Someone has it in for Gadsen Street." Jonathan went to fetch another café chair, and Liam sat as the others filled him in on the ice embargo that would continue unless Rupert Pine stopped publishing his incendiary articles.

Liam's outrage spoke well for his sense of justice. "Don't cave in," he said. "I'll get you more ice from Maine. I'm not well enough to make the trip, but I'll send my ship for it. The ship can sail tomorrow and deliver a load of ice exclusively for Gadsen Street."

"You would do that for us?" Maggie asked in wonder.

Liam nodded. "I hate bullies. I also think we should send Rupert Pine along for the ride. He's about to get a story that ought to be splashed across the front pages of every newspaper in the country. Let's stoke the press about what's happening here."

"Don't forget the song," David Lieberman said, passing a copy of "The Ballad of Gadsen Street" to Liam. Maggie watched his expression carefully as Liam scanned Philip's song, but why should she be worried? Philip wrote about the whole street, not just her.

"That song is playing in all the music halls," David said.

"Really?" Liam asked. "I have a cousin in the music business. If the song is any good, maybe she'll make a record of it."

Maggie's jaw dropped. Did Liam realize who had written the song? He knew she once had a sweetheart named Philip, but that was only until Mrs. Lieberman spilled the beans.

"Oh, Maggie! Wouldn't that be heavenly for poor Philip? Maybe the two of you could get married after all."

Maggie bit her lip as the muscles in Liam's face froze. "This is from *that* Philip?"

She nodded reluctantly. "Yes. That Philip." She glanced at Mrs. Lieberman. "And he's already married, so there's no need to think we'll start anything up again."

"He's married and still writing songs about you?" Liam asked.

"It's not about me; it's about the whole street. It's about the feeling people get when they come to Gadsen Street and why it's so special."

Liam's brows lowered as he scanned the lyrics again. Soon his expression softened and grew a little wistful. What on earth was he thinking? It seemed to take forever before he lowered the sheet and looked at her.

"Yeah," he said, "I feel the same way about this street, Sweet Miss Maggie."

"You'll still help us, then?" Her heart pounded so hard he could probably hear it, and he winked at her as he returned the sheet music.

"I'll still help you," he said, looking pale and exhausted. "I'm heading to a health clinic for a while, but my ship and crew are at your command."

Liam looked weak and clammy, but the excitement in his eyes nearly set the street ablaze. A celebratory cheer rose from the crowd. David Lieberman promised to name his firstborn son after Liam, and Dino grabbed Liam's face to kiss both cheeks.

A swell of emotions ran amok as she gazed at him. Falling in love with Liam Blackstone was hopeless—he'd warned her many a time that they obviously had no future together—but for now she basked in the sensation of admiring a thoroughly good man.

⸺ ⸙ ⸺

Liam frowned as he inspected the deck with Caleb as the crew prepared the *Black Rose* for another trip to Maine. Tons of melting ice and sawdust had ruined the varnish after his first trip, and there would be more this time. It made him shudder each time he saw the formerly pristine teak deck.

"I thought you said we were going to repair all this," Caleb said as he stared at the splotchy stains on the deck.

"Yeah, we're going to have to wait on that," Liam replied.

"But you said the minute the weather was clear, we were going to strip, sand, and lay down six perfect coats of the world's best marine spar," Caleb said. "Those were your exact words, and this is the first clear day. We need to strip, sand, and lay down six perfect coats."

Caleb was a good kid, but sometimes his memory could be annoying. "There's no point in fixing the deck until we're done hauling ice." Charles Morse had it in for Gadsen Street, and it was anyone's guess how long his embargo would last, so this might not be his last trip to Maine.

Using the *Black Rose* to haul ice was expensive and inefficient, but it made Liam feel good, like a swashbuckling pirate out to save the city. Last night he lingered with Maggie beneath her uncle's olive tree until midnight, laughing and swapping stories. She respected him. He could tell by the way she was eager to hear his stories about working in the steel mills. She didn't look down her nose at him for his tough upbringing. Instead, she admired him for it. They spoke the same language. They clicked and hummed along like a well-oiled machine. Maybe she was a little too enraptured by the prospect of getting rich, but weren't most people? It shouldn't be a fatal flaw.

"Is she coming with us again?" Caleb asked, and Liam followed the young man's gaze, surprised to see Maggie hurrying toward the ship. He had no idea why she was here, but he braced his arms on the railing for a better look.

"Hey, pretty lady," he shouted down. He was about to ask her aboard, but she was a mess! Black gunk tracked all over her white blouse, and she held her straw boater at arm's length from her body. The closer she got, the worse she looked.

He raced to the gangway that was already lowered and arrived on the pier in short order. The tradesmen and delivery guys all cut a wide berth around Maggie.

"What happened to you?" he asked, gaping at the black gunk all over her blouse. Oil?

"An accident at Pier 15, and I'm a mess. Can I come aboard and clean up?"

He took a large step to block the gangway. "You're not boarding my ship like that."

"I can't ride a streetcar home covered in oil."

"Well, you're not boarding my ship either!" The crew teased him for his persnickety tidiness, and he was trying to ease up a little, but this was beyond the pale. The glob of oil on her blouse had already starting smearing all over the rest of her. It had dribbled on her skirt, smeared on her hands, and a smudge stained her cheek. Dark fingerprints stained the brim of her straw hat.

"Liam, please," she implored.

"Caleb, bring down some rags!" he bellowed up to the deck, then looked at Maggie again, careful to keep his distance. Longshoremen stifled laughter as they passed, and even Captain Macauley let out a snort of amusement when he saw her.

"Tell me what happened," he said.

"I was at Pier 15 to renew a lease for space and a stevedore dropped a barrel of oil from the top of the warehouse. I got splattered with a big glob of it. I've been trying to be careful, but it's getting everywhere."

Caleb came down with the rags and handed them over. Maggie started blotting the biggest stains, but her efforts only smeared the oil around. And now she had dirty rags that needed disposing of. All she managed to accomplish was to make a bigger mess.

"Come aboard," he reluctantly agreed. "We've already watered the ship, so you can clean up in the crew's washroom. You're not using mine when you're a gooey mess. Don't touch *anything*."

She oozed gratitude as she followed him aboard. He kept several paces ahead of her, opening doors, pulling deck furniture aside, warning the crew away. Getting down the narrow staircase was the worst.

"Lift your skirt, step carefully, and *don't breathe*," he said. He was kidding about the breathing part, but she was indeed holding her breath as she tiptoed down the steps, her skirts held tightly to her body. He continued opening doors on their journey through the center corridor, down another flight of stairs, and to the crew's washroom on the lower deck. He popped his head inside to be sure it was empty before holding the door for her.

"All clear," he said. "I'll stand guard outside the door while you strip down and wash up. Caleb is about your size, and you can borrow some of his clothes."

She clutched her arms to her chest and looked with trepidation into the stark tile washroom. The urinals and the long metal pipe with exposed showerheads probably looked odd to her, but the room had plenty of soap, sinks, and hot water to get cleaned up.

"Please don't leave that spot," she whispered.

He winked at her. "I'll stand guard until you're finished. Vinegar and baking soda are on the way. They'll help cut through the oil, and the soap will do the rest. Dump those clothes in the garbage. You've got a clean set of deckhand's clothes coming right up."

She nodded, still the picture of mortification as she stepped into the washroom and he closed the door. The hiss of the water taps indicated she was getting started. Soon Caleb arrived with a spare set of clothes, a bottle of vinegar, and a box of baking soda. Liam waited until Caleb was gone before tapping on the washroom door.

"I've got the vinegar and baking soda and fresh clothes. Can you open up?"

"Keep your eyes closed," she said. He squelched a smile but obeyed. The door creaked, and she snatched the supplies from him before slamming the door closed again. "Thank you," she called. Then the water taps turned back on.

This was going to take a while. He folded his arms and leaned against the door. "So," he called out, "it must feel pretty good to be the star of that song, 'Sweet Miss Maggie of Gadsen Street.'"

For a while he didn't think she was going to reply, but then she got around to it. "I feel good and bad at the same time," she said. "If that makes any sense."

It made perfect sense. It was what he'd been feeling over Darla before he finally threw in the towel and sent her pill case back to her.

Darla and Maggie were complete opposites. Darla ran with an arty crowd, liked high living, and had a racy past, while Maggie was wholesome, hardworking, and the most frugal woman he'd ever met. He cared deeply for both but couldn't fully trust either of them. Maggie was too wrapped up in monetary concerns for him to believe her interest in him was entirely genuine. And she might still have feelings for Philip.

"Are you still hankering over him?" he asked through the closed door.

"Ha! He's married," she replied. "With a new baby too."

That didn't mean they weren't still carrying a torch for each other. "Why is he writing songs about you if he's married?"

The door cracked open, and her face appeared in the tiny opening. "I told you—the song isn't about me. It's about Gadsen Street. He used to come there all the time. He feels bad about what's happened to us, but I doubt he thinks about me at all anymore."

The door closed, but he still had more questions. "And you? Do you think about him?"

"We weren't right for each other. I buy his sheet music because I feel sorry for him."

He rotated so he could lean back against the door. His smile started slowly, then stretched until it was so wide that his face hurt. He liked not having a rival. A little whimpering came from behind the door, and he straightened in concern. "Are you okay in there?"

"No more hot water."

He grimaced because the boilers had been turned off during the coaling process. He should have remembered that she'd run out of hot water quickly, but a cold shower never hurt anyone.

"When I was a kid, I had to break a layer of ice off the wash bucket in the mornings because my dad was too cheap to buy coal. Of course, folks from Pennsylvania are a lot tougher than New York lightweights."

"I'm a tough cookie," she called. "You said so yourself. Have you got a sack I can borrow?"

"What for?"

"To take my clothes home," she replied. "I'm not throwing out perfectly good clothing just because of a few stains. I can wear them when I clean the factory. I need to be thrifty since I won't be able to depend on your bottomless wealth, Liam."

He stifled a laugh as he went to find a sack. By the time he returned with a canvas sack, she stood in the passageway wearing Caleb's blue slacks and light gray button-down shirt. The hems and cuffs were rolled up, and her wet hair had been braided over one shoulder. Everything was a little too big, but a belt kept the pants up and the self-deprecating humor in her expression made her look impossibly charming.

"Much better," he said, handing her the sack, into which she stuffed the oil-stained clothing. She'd tried to wash the oily fingerprints from the straw boater, but shadowy smudges remained. The hat was a goner, but she plopped it on her head anyway.

As they crossed the deck, she craned her neck to gape at the activity as the ship prepared to sail. Workers disconnected the hose supplying water to the ship. Stevedores wheeled in crates of food, and the boiler room crew carted away sludge oil. Maggie couldn't stop asking questions as she watched every step of the coaling, fueling, and bunkering.

"I didn't understand how much work went into sailing a ship during our first trip to Maine, but now I do. Thank you," she said.

A pause stretched between them, and he was surprised by how appealing she looked even in boys' clothing and a stained boater hat. The hat was beyond salvation, but Maggie would probably never admit it. He snatched it from her head and flung it into the harbor. The wind lifted it before it finally plopped into the choppy surf, bobbing on the surface.

"Hey!" she said.

"I'll buy you a new one. You won't be able to get oil out of the straw." He prayed she wouldn't argue with him, and she didn't.

A hint of amusement gleamed as she looked up at him. "It must be nice to be rich."

"It is, but even if I was still a welder, I wouldn't let my woman walk around in a shabby hat like that."

Her eyes gleamed with humor. "When did I become your woman?"

Heat crept up his neck when he realized what he just said, but he didn't regret it. "You know what, Maggie? I've been kicking myself for accusing you of being a fortune hunter that day at your factory. You and I were on course for something

178

great before I let my temper get in the way. I'm sorry for what I said that afternoon. Can I take it back?"

"You can take it back," she said and turned to face him, looking fresh and pretty despite Caleb's clothes. Opening up and talking frankly about his feelings felt kind of good. He touched the thin white scar that split her eyebrow, then traced his finger down her cheekbone and along the curve of her jaw. She held his gaze, and he lowered his voice so the crew couldn't hear them.

"And that part about how we obviously have no future together . . . will you let me take that part back too?"

"Only if we might have a future together after all."

Oh, they had a future. Now that he'd cleared away his stupid gaffe, he wanted a future with her morning, noon, and night. He wanted to sail with her to Maine and across the Atlantic and to the moon and stars and back. He tamped his excitement down and lowered his nose to touch hers.

"Good," he said, then leaned down to kiss her. She kissed him back, and he took a gamble by drawing her in closer, wrapping his arms around her, and deepening the kiss. If he were physically capable, he'd lift her up and twirl her about with pure joy, but that would have to wait for another day.

He pulled away and impulsively lifted her hand to press a kiss on her palm. Her callused hand with short fingernails and no jewelry. It was a beautiful hand, the kind that made ice cream, cleaned factory floors, swapped out fan belts. It was the kind of hand that could change diapers, fight battles, and make the world a better place.

His trip to the health clinic couldn't have come at a worse time, but hopefully when he returned, he could court her like a healthy man who wasn't always doubled over with a tummy ache.

They spent an hour nuzzling at the railing until it was time for departure. He walked her down the gangplank, then held her loosely in his arms to say goodbye. The hazy glow of the sunset made her look even more beautiful.

"When I get back from the health clinic, you and I are going shopping for a new hat. Okay?"

Her smile was radiant as she agreed, then stood up on tiptoes to kiss him goodbye a final time. A strange, buoyant sense of hope began to surge as he held her, and he savored the growing conviction that they had a future together after all.

19

*L*iam had been at the Woodlands Health Clinic for ten minutes when he started searching for ways to break the rules. How was he supposed to go an entire month with no telephone calls, no newspapers to track the steel business, and no contact with his ship? The *Black Rose* was on her way to pick up another load of ice, and he needed to keep an eye on her progress.

His bossy sister wouldn't hear of it.

"You need to trust that Captain Macauley will know how to handle things," Gwen said, unpacking his socks into the top drawer of his bedroom bureau. His room was on the top floor of a three-story building an hour north of the city, secluded in the woods and already starting to feel like a prison. The private room overlooked a grassy lawn sloping down to a lake with white swans gliding on its surface. Some people would probably appreciate the view, but Liam only wanted to get back to the city and see Maggie again.

Their first kiss yesterday had been sweet. While lingering on deck to watch the activity onshore, their kisses had been playful and fun. But the evening ended with that incendiary embrace on the pier, and he wanted to get back to it. It was hard to sit on this cane-backed chair like an invalid while Gwen continued unpacking for him. She hung up his shirts and set out his toiletries as though lifting a toothbrush were too strenuous for him to handle. He drew the line when Gwen reached for a stack of his skivvies.

"I'm not completely helpless," he growled, elbowing her aside to grab his undergarments and stuff them into the dresser drawer. He commenced rearranging things more to his liking while Gwen opened the second suitcase.

"What's this?" she asked, her tone frosty. She held aloft a stack of papers, and on the top was "The Ballad of Gadsen Street."

"I'm going to get Natalia to make a recording of the song," he said. "Gadsen Street still isn't getting ice because Charles Morse is carrying out a vendetta against Maggie, and that song can help blow the story—"

Gwen tucked the pages into her canvas satchel. "Absolutely not," she said. "This is exactly the sort of stress you need to avoid."

He grabbed the sheet music back and held it aloft. "This is ammunition in a war," he said. "Natalia can help spread it far and wide, and it's best done now while the iron is still hot. Most of the city is already forgetting about the ice crisis last month, but I'm going to keep it stoked."

He stashed the sheet music in a bottom drawer and tried not to notice Gwen's disappointed look. She meant well, but Gwen always made him feel like a failure. She never struggled with doing the right thing or being polite and was always quietly, annoyingly perfect. She wouldn't even let his bad mood interfere with her thoughtful gestures as she helped him unpack.

"Here," she said, pushing a fat book into his hands. "I know you've been trying to learn more about religion, and this was our father's Bible. He used to read a few pages each evening, and perhaps you would like to do the same."

His breath caught. "You don't want it?"

Gwen's eyes glimmered. "He would have wanted you to have it, Liam."

He traced his fingertips across the well-worn leather cover.

This was like inheriting a sacred relic. Inside the front cover was the family tree written in his father's own hand—birth, marriage, and death dates going back several generations. Theodore had recorded the death of his own wife, the mother whom Liam didn't remember at all. Liam's birth had been written in his father's hand as well, but no death date was recorded. Theodore had gone to his grave still hoping.

Liam started paging through the Bible, dismayed at the tissue-thin paper and tiny letters. He'd already tried to study the Scriptures a couple of times, but reading was a struggle for him and he gave up pretty quickly. But if this was his father's Bible, the one Theodore Blackstone had held in his hands to read and glean insight each evening? It didn't matter that the text was small. Liam would make a point of studying it every night just like his father had done.

Gwen's generous gift had taken him by surprise. He and Gwen rarely got along. They both tried, but he was a bull in a china shop, while she was the most cultured lady he'd ever met and practically walked on water.

From now on, he would try harder to get along with her. He would read his father's Bible and start putting its principles into action. No more losing his temper. He'd quit needling Gwen and resenting her prissy, overly ladylike ways. Gwen was exactly the sort of woman their father raised her to become: cultured, generous, and kind. He set the Bible on his bedside table.

"Thanks," he said. "This means a lot to me, Gwen."

His father would have wanted them to get along, and Liam would do so, even if it didn't come naturally to him. Nobody said being a good man was easy, and he needed to try harder.

⁂

The days blended into one another during Liam's enforced seclusion. His ulcer was no better. If anything, worrying about Maggie and the pending vote on September 30 made it ache even more, but it had only been a week, so maybe he needed to give it more time.

At least he had plenty of time to read his father's Bible, which hadn't been an easy read. After a terrific beginning, it was a heavy slog through Numbers and Deuteronomy, and Liam finally gave up and started flipping around, which worked okay too. He kept studying, trying to let the timeless wisdom seep into his soul and become second nature.

Surprisingly, not all the good guys in the Bible were too holy to emulate. He liked Samson and David and Moses because they all blew their stack sometimes but managed to redeem themselves in the end. It gave Liam hope. Most of his life he'd given in to temptation, whether it was women, wine, or his temper. He used to play dirty to score victories for the unions. These days he was trying to do everything by the book, but he couldn't quite squelch the desire to rub Charles Morse's nose in the dirt, which was probably something Jesus would frown on.

So, in addition to worrying about the September vote and Maggie and the trip to Maine for ice, he added stressing about his immortal soul to the list of ways he was failing.

Everything brightened the day he received his first letter from Maggie. He sat on his bed to savor every line.

The ice had arrived! Maggie gleefully wrote about how people on Gadsen Street poured out of their buildings as Antonio Gabelli led a line of four wagons to deliver ice to everyone on the street. Within a day, all the restaurants had reopened, though it took the ice cream parlor a little more time to buy milk and cream, fire up their machinery, and get busy making ice cream.

> We operated the factory around the clock. Even the pushcart vendors showed up to help during the overnight hours, but by sunset the next day we had three hundred gallons made, which was enough to stock every pushcart and reopen the ice cream parlor. Today we are making vanilla ice cream so I can deliver to the hotels and restaurants.
>
> Liam, you are our hero, and I am lucky and proud to

know you. Please follow the doctor's orders so you can come home. I think about you all the time . . .

He lay back on the mattress, Maggie's letter clutched to his chest, his heart pounding. Every instinct told him to spring off his bed, catch the nearest train back home, roll up his sleeves and help her make ice cream. He wanted to kiss her until they were both breathless. He wanted to sit beneath her uncle's olive tree and dream about the future with her, because at long last he suspected she might be the right woman for him.

He took a deep breath and concentrated on slowing his heartbeat.

He wanted a future with Maggie by his side, but he couldn't have it until this ulcer healed.

That meant he needed to keep eating the bland food, keep relaxing, and keep studying the Bible, praying for a way to tame his moods and live a decent, God-fearing life that would have made Theodore Blackstone proud.

20

Maggie was cleaning the overhead machine belts that crisscrossed the factory near the ceiling when the first hint of trouble arrived. She had just positioned the ladder in a new space to start on the motor box when Dino came inside, worry etching his careworn face.

"There are a couple of police officers here," he said. "They want to talk with you."

"Why?" Unexpected visits from police officers never boded well. She scrambled down the ladder.

"I don't know," Dino replied. "They wouldn't talk to me; they want to see you."

She hurried into the ice cream parlor, which wouldn't open for another hour and was empty except for the two policemen wearing their dark blue uniforms with badges prominently displayed. The older one had a shock of white hair, while the younger casually gnawed a stick of black licorice.

"Can I help you?" she asked, nervously wiping her hands on a clean rag. They looked hot in their wool uniforms, and she considered offering them some ice cream. Anything to soften those serious expressions of theirs.

"Let's step outside for a chat," the older one said in a grand-fatherly tone.

She met Dino's gaze, who sent her a brief nod. She set the cloth on a table and led the way. It was bright outside and seemed hotter than usual, but maybe it was just her nerves. The older policeman used his billy club to point at one of the flower boxes bordering the sidewalk.

"Do you have a permit for those things?"

"I don't think I need one." She and Julie had built them nine years ago when they opened the ice cream parlor, and no one ever complained about them.

The police officer shrugged it off and looked at her with a kindly smile. "So you're the famous Miss Maggie of Gadsen Street."

She gave a weak smile. "So they say."

She had a hunch that Philip's affectionate nickname for her was going to be around for a long time. The silence became awkward as the younger officer chewed another bite of licorice, staring at her rudely. Was she supposed to say something more? The broiling sun made her even hotter as the older officer reached into a pocket and retrieved a slip of paper. He unfolded it, scanning its contents and shaking his head with a sorrowful expression as though disappointed. He finally turned the paper to show it to her.

It was the sheet music for "The Ballad of Gadsen Street."

"I don't like this song," he said. "It makes heroes out of people who didn't do anything to deserve it." He glanced at his younger partner. "What about you, Cardello? Do you like this song?"

"I don't like that song," Officer Cardello replied.

They were standing too close to her. She shouldn't be afraid because there were plenty of people around. Spider had emerged from the factory and watched from the sidewalk next door. A couple of workers over at O'Donnell's Pub were replacing the front window across the street and could see them as well.

"I heard through the grapevine that you've got a meeting with the attorney general pretty soon," the older officer said.

How could he have heard that? She crossed her arms and

tried to stay calm. "I do," she admitted, swallowing back a hint of misgiving.

Officer Cardello finished the licorice, then reached for his billy club. He used the tip of it to lift the vine of ivy spilling over the rim of the flower box. "Are you sure you don't need a permit for this thing?" He whacked the wooden planter with the club, leaving a chip in the new paint. "Because I'm pretty sure you do. It's obstructing the sidewalk so it shouldn't be here."

The older officer waved a calming hand at the younger one. "Not now, Cardello. I suspect Miss Molinaro will want to be helpful. She doesn't have anything to say to the attorney general. This ice situation is just a fallout from the hot weather, and soon everyone will be getting ice on a regular schedule again, so there's no need to meet with the attorney general." He took a step closer to scowl down at her. "Right?"

She took a step back. Others had started to gather on the sidewalk. Dino and some men from the pushcart crew stood alongside Spider, and Mr. Alfonso came out from across the street. She shouldn't let these policemen intimidate her. This was scary, but the momentum against the ice trust would stall if she backed down.

"What I do with my time is my own business," she hedged.

"Lady, this ugly planter is a safety hazard," the younger officer said. "It interrupts the free flow of people on the sidewalk." He braced his boot against the planter and shoved it over. The flowers tumbled out, and dirt spilled onto the street. He lifted the billy club high and began pounding on the planter, wood chips flying.

"Hey, you can't do that!" Spider said.

"That's private property," Dino said, charging forward, but Maggie blocked him. If Dino laid a finger on the officer, he would be arrested. Terrible things could happen.

The older officer kicked over another flower box and then stomped on it, splitting the wood with a loud crack. With his foot he shoved it into the street, crushing the petunias and marigolds. She turned away but heard everything. The snapping of boards, the cracking of batons, the laughing coming from the younger officer.

Her neighbors started shouting in protest. "Don't do anything," she warned them. "You can't touch a police officer." It would go much worse for them if they did.

"What about that ugly thing?" Officer Cardello said, pointing at the olive tree. The shrub Dino brought from Italy had grown tall, its limbs arcing out over the sidewalk to provide shade.

"Yeah, that's got to come down too," the older officer said.

Maggie couldn't bear to look at Dino's face as the two men wrapped their dirty hands around the silvery bark of the olive tree. It took them several tries, rocking the tree in its heavy planter, the limbs swaying wildly, scattering leaves and olives onto the ground. Maggie pulled Dino back because the tree was about to topple, which could be dangerous. Dino crossed himself and muttered a prayer in Italian. Maggie's fists clenched so tightly her nails bit into her palm, but there was nothing she could do.

The tree reached a tipping point, hanging suspended for a second before crashing down, olives bouncing across the cobblestones as its graceful limbs smacked against the pavement.

A chorus of boos erupted along the street. Officer Cardello tugged his uniform back into place, dusting some grit from his shiny copper badge. The older officer panted from the exertion, his face flushed and sweaty. He glanced over at the large plate-glass window at the front of the ice cream parlor. One smack of his club would smash it to pieces, and she held her breath.

"You folks have a real fine place here," he said, casually standing before the window. "I'm glad we could take care of that permitting problem you just had. Are you sure you still want to talk to the attorney general?"

Revulsion rose in her throat. She hugged herself, inexplicably cold as she glared at the officer. He strolled closer. Beads of sweat covered his face, and he stank of perspiration. "You decided there's no need, right?"

Rumors claimed that Charles Morse had the Police Department, the Fire Department, and the Department of Docks in his back pocket. There wasn't anyone she could complain to; she just needed to keep safe until she could talk to the attorney general and hopefully turn the tide in her favor.

"I know who you answer to," she said.

"Then you ought to be smart enough to know what to do." He stepped away and snapped his fingers. "Come on, Cardello. We're done here."

The two police officers seemed fearless as they strolled down Gadsen Street, ignoring the glares of the silent bystanders. She held her breath with each restaurant they passed. All of them had planters brimming with flowers, and they could make more trouble if they chose to.

Officer Cardello leaned down to pluck a marigold from the planter outside the Porterhouse. He paused to turn around and smirk at Maggie, his message clear. He could topple every planter on the street and there would be nothing they could do. Windows could be broken. Power and water lines cut. Garbage could go uncollected.

But Maggie still intended to speak with the attorney general next week.

It took four men from the pushcart crew to get the mangled olive tree propped back up. Dino had been too upset to participate and went upstairs while others pitched in to help. David Lieberman worked with Maggie to trim the broken branches, leaving the tree looking shorn and pitiful, but it might survive.

That was more than could be said for the marigolds and petunias. The officers had stomped on them until the wooden planters were beyond repair. Within the hour the ruined planters had been carted away and the dirt swept up. Mr. Lindquist was too old to help with the physical labor, but he brought everyone bottles of ginger ale from his pharmacy after the work was done. It was refreshing as they sat outside to commiserate.

190

Who would have guessed the people on this street would have all become such friends? Maybe it was only natural that having a common enemy was a uniting force, but it seemed like more than that. The pushcart employees who rarely spoke to her except to complain seemed friendlier now, and she saw a side of Mr. Alfonso she hadn't known even existed. Over the past few weeks, she had gotten to know her neighbors as friends instead of competitors.

All except for Mr. Prescott from the Porterhouse. He still wore his businesslike persona like a suit of armor. "We need a lawyer," he ranted for the tenth time. "We cannot operate our businesses in a lawless environment where the police can run roughshod over us."

"It's too dangerous," Mr. Alfonso said. "If we file a complaint against the police, those two cops will hear about it and be back."

"That's why we get a lawyer," Mr. Prescott stressed.

The short-lived spirit of comradery vanished as people began to bicker. Consulting a lawyer would raise the stakes even higher, but sitting around doing nothing was intolerable, and Liam's brother-in-law was a lawyer. Patrick O'Neill already knew everything about Liam's difficulty with Charles Morse, and he'd be a good person to ask for help.

"Can I use your telephone?" she asked Mr. Lindquist.

Twenty minutes later, she had an appointment with Patrick O'Neill.

⁓

The O'Neill law office was located on a street that looked like it couldn't decide if it was part of a respectable neighborhood or would be more comfortable slinking into urban decrepitude. Second-rate boardinghouses were next door to quaint shops selling millinery goods and stationery. Some storefronts boasted fresh paint and nice awnings, while others had streaks of rust from lopsided gutters.

The law office seemed pleasant. A secretary sat in the front lobby, and the door leading to Mr. O'Neill's private office had a clear glass panel set into the oak door. Inside, the broad-shouldered Irishman was casually dressed in a plain white shirt with suspenders. He gestured her to a chair across from his desk as he welcomed her inside.

"You're a friend of Liam's, correct?" Mr. O'Neill's tone wasn't the friendliest she'd ever heard. He had the trace of an Irish accent and a rugged, intelligent look as he scrutinized her.

"Yes. He said you're a good lawyer and he'd trust you with his life." The praise did nothing to thaw the lawyer's cool reception, even though he remained entirely polite.

"How can I be of help?" he asked.

His brows lowered in concern when she reported the unexpected visit from the police this morning. She told him about the destruction of her property and their strongly worded suggestion to cancel her meeting with the attorney general. Mr. O'Neill let her speak without interruption, then waited several seconds after she completed her story.

"Did you have a permit for the planters?" he asked.

She shook her head. "I didn't realize I needed one."

"You do," he said. "You should have been given the opportunity to remedy the situation before the police destroyed your property, so it was clearly an attempt to intimidate you. Nevertheless, your lack of a permit will protect them if you file a formal complaint."

She shifted uneasily. "What am I supposed to do about meeting with the attorney general? That's my main concern."

The lawyer leaned back in his chair and studied her with a brooding expression. It made her uncomfortable and a little bit angry too. Wasn't he supposed to be on her side?

"The attorney general is already working behind the scenes to bring the ice trust in line with common business practices," he replied. "He won't need your testimony to make a case. You are under no obligation to testify if you fear for your safety."

It would be safer to do nothing, but Antonio Gabelli had stuck his neck out to do the right thing. Liam Blackstone rolled up his sleeves to do the right thing over and over in confronting Morse. She needed to be just as brave and so leaned forward to speak her mind.

"Charles Morse is a scoundrel who has driven the honest ice brokers out of business. Liam said he's done the same in other lines of work. Liam says—"

"I don't like seeing Liam dragged into this fight," Patrick said, interrupting her. "His enmity with Morse is already bad enough without opening up another front in the war over ice. At this very moment he's in a clinic because he's been taking on battles beyond his control and it's ruining his health. This isn't his fight. He shouldn't be butting into the ice industry or doing anything other than being an advocate for the employees of U.S. Steel."

She blanched but refused to back down. "Liam had trouble with Morse before he ever met me."

"Of course he did," Patrick said. "That's because Liam's instinct is to swoop in wherever he sees injustice, pick up a sword, and attack without any regard for the consequences. What's happening between him and Morse is ugly. It's making him look impulsive and unsuitable for his position on the board of U.S. Steel. He needs to focus on regaining his health instead of getting dragged into another fight."

Maggie stood. "Who is going to tell him to quit fighting? To drop his sword and let the Charles Morses of the world trample anyone who dares to disagree? Is it you?"

"I've told him that ever since I met him," Patrick said. "Liam needs to control his temper and focus on a single mission." He sighed, leaning over to brace his hands on the desk, his annoyance draining away. When he looked up, his expression and his tone had softened. "As for the police, I will pass along your complaint to the police commissioner, a man I trust who isn't corrupted by Morse. That should stop the police harassment, but you still need to brace yourself. Unless you announce that you've canceled your meeting with the attorney general, a corrupt police officer can still carry out Morse's dirty work while he's not wearing a uniform, and I can't insulate you from that."

It wasn't what she wanted to hear, but Maggie would keep her appointment with the attorney general no matter how much the police tried to bully her.

21

A clatter woke Maggie, and she jerked upright in bed. She held her breath, trying to identify the sound, but her bedroom was dark and everything was quiet now. Only the soft chirping of crickets came from her open window. But *something* had woken her up, and it came from downstairs.

The factory had been running for fifteen hours a day ever since Liam's delivery of ice, and that was a lot of stress on the electrical equipment. It would be impossible to sleep until she checked the wiring downstairs to be sure there wasn't a problem. She slipped out of bed and dragged on a robe.

The stairwell's concrete felt cool on her bare feet as she made her way downstairs. Light from the streetlamps outside cast a faint glow across the interior of the ice cream parlor. Everything looked fine here, so she moved to check the electrical equipment in the back of the factory.

Crack.

She stilled. The noise came from inside the factory, and she hurried toward the doors, flinging them open, revealing the hulking figure of a man near the worktable. Her gasp echoed in the darkness, and he froze.

She dashed back toward the safety of the parlor, trying to

195

lock the door behind her, but the man kicked it open. An arm clamped around her throat, dragging her back into the factory.

Her breath cut off. She couldn't scream. The arm squeezed harder, choking her, lifting her toes from the floor. She thrust her elbow into his torso.

"Knock it off, lady."

She thrashed about, struggling to break free, but he hauled her across the factory floor as if she weighed nothing. She clawed harder at the arm choking her and managed a tiny gasp of air.

"Take it easy," he ordered. "Just calm down."

He had licorice on his breath. He shoved her facedown over a worktable, scattering tools everywhere. She reached out, fumbling for anything she could use as a weapon.

Her fist closed around the handle of an ice pick. She flailed, then managed a jab at his leg. He howled. She jabbed again and twisted from beneath his weight, dragging in a huge gulp of air before lunging away. But he tackled her again, slamming her onto the concrete, the ice pick skittering out of reach.

The arm was around her neck again, stopping her from screaming. He pulled her deeper into the factory. The freezer door opened with a creak. Then she was airborne for a second before crashing into the steel canisters at the back of the freezer. They toppled over in a hail of clanging. She tried to get up and escape, but the door slammed shut.

She was trapped in the freezer. She pounded on the door and screamed, "Let me out!"

"Sorry, lady," he said. She jerked at the door handle, but he must have jammed it shut. Again she pounded on the door with the side of her fist but heard nothing more from the stranger who'd just locked her in.

It was pitch-black. It was freezing.

Was he gone? She tried to listen, but her ragged breathing made it hard to hear anything. Her throat hurt. The cold went straight into her lungs. She kept gulping air, still dizzy, her heart racing in panic. She couldn't see, and the soles of her feet were freezing on the concrete floor.

196

"Oh no," she whispered, her teeth starting to chatter. "Oh no, oh no, oh no . . ."

What time was it? Morning was hours away and she'd be dead by then if she couldn't figure out what to do. A tiny bit of gray light shone through the fan box at the top of the freezer, but it wasn't enough to see much of anything.

Could she wake up Dino or Julie? The apartment was on the top floor, but maybe they'd hear her if she made enough noise. She fumbled for an empty dairy canister and banged it against the concrete floor. The clang of steel hurt her ears in the cold air as she banged it harder and faster, screaming with everything she had.

But the freezer room was well insulated, the apartment three stories above. They'd never hear her. Fear and frustration boiled over, and she threw the canister against the shelves, not caring what damage it did as she sank into a crouch on the floor, pulling her nightgown and robe over her face and nose to capture her breath. She had to keep warm. Keep warm and quit panicking. Yet the whirring of the fan was a constant reminder of the cold air being pumped into the room with every second. Was that awful whir going to be the last thing she heard on this earth?

She had watched the electricians install the fan. She'd been here when they wired the freezer system. She knew how the equipment worked, and if she kept her head, maybe she could dismantle it.

The compressor was located on the other side of the wall and there was no way to reach it. The pipe for the ammonia condenser ran along the top of the room and was powered by an electrical pump mounted on the wall outside. If she could yank the evaporator pipe leading to the pump, it would shut down the entire system.

She groped blindly toward the back of the room until she felt the icy evaporator coils. She ignored the cold burning her fingers as she traced the line to the floor, poking until she found the heavy evaporator pipe. With her hands wrapped in fabric from the robe, she grasped the icy metal and tugged hard.

Nothing happened.

She pulled harder. Then harder still, screaming with the effort. The metal squeaked but remained firmly attached to the pump on the other side of the wall.

If she didn't pull harder, Uncle Dino was going to find her dead body in the morning, and that was *not* going to happen.

Dear God, please give me enough strength to pull this pipe free.

But maybe pulling wasn't the right thing. She let go of the pipe and stood, rising cautiously in the darkness. Her body weight might knock it free. She positioned her heel atop the pipe, then shifted to place all her weight on that heel.

Nothing.

She did a little jump. The pipe clanged against the floor and broke free of the wall.

She stood motionless, listening to the whirring hiss of the evaporator fan as it slowed, then stopped. Everything was silent except for the shaky noise of her own breathing. It had worked!

Was she laughing or crying? It was going to be a wickedly cold few hours until someone opened the factory, but she wouldn't die. It would be painful, but she wouldn't die.

She groped around for the wooden pallet. It would be better than sitting on the concrete floor. Her toe stubbed against it, and she pushed it into the corner, then huddled on it, drawing her knees in close. Maybe in time she could warm up this tiny corner, but her bare feet were freezing and she began shivering uncontrollably. Without the noise from the fan and compressor, all she could hear was her chattering teeth and shaky breath.

"'The Lord is my shepherd, I shall not want,'" she said, her voice quavering in the darkness. Praying felt right and distracted her from the mind-numbing cold. She'd always loved this psalm, even though the words didn't ring true, especially the part about the valley of the shadow of death and fearing no evil because she *did* fear evil, and she *did* fear death.

She prayed the psalm over and over, then said a rosary. Then she recited the names of the presidents in order. Then back to the psalm.

How much time had passed? An hour? Two? It became hard to keep praying because she couldn't remember the words anymore. Wasn't that strange? She must have prayed Psalm 23 a thousand times in her life, but now the words were coming out jumbled and confused. And she was too sleepy to remember them.

But after a while it wasn't so painfully cold anymore. And the shivering stopped. She leaned her head back against the wall. This was almost . . . pleasant. Though it was still cold, everything felt numb. A nap would feel good.

Actually, she'd been napping on and off for a while. Maybe sleeping wasn't such a good idea. Was it dangerous to sleep when it was this cold? If she stood, maybe she could stay awake, but it would take a lot of effort to get her feet underneath her and stand up.

In the dim edges of her mind, it sounded like someone was shouting from far away. Yelling. It sounded like Uncle Dino, worried about blood on the floor.

Blood?

There were two voices now. Worried voices. They could help. She tried to shake the fog of confusion away and fumbled in the darkness to grab the empty canister, though her numb fingers didn't work. She kicked it, and the clang hurt her ears. She kicked it again to keep making noise.

The door opened. Light poured in, blinding her.

"Maggie?" Dino's frame blotted out the light. He shouted something in Italian and reached inside. "Spider, help!" Dino scooped her up and carried her outside into the bright light of the factory. It was warm out here, and the shivers started again.

Dino deposited her onto a table and began rubbing her right hand between his large warm ones. Spider took her other hand and did the same. It hurt.

"What happened?" Spider asked.

"I don't know," she said, but that was wrong. She did know. That horrible man with licorice on his breath had done this.

The next hour was a blur of pain and mortification as her body warmed and she started thinking clearly again. Memories of exactly what happened came back, and she recounted it for Spider and Dino. Soon the Lieberman brothers were there, looking as tautly angry as the others.

The man who attacked her was almost certainly Officer Cardello, and he cut all but two of their mixing belts before she surprised him. The belts were ruined and would cost hundreds of dollars to replace.

Reporting the problem to the police seemed pointless, but Dino insisted, and within an hour a police detective came to take her testimony. Detective Brady was a slim, serious man devoid of emotion as she described what had happened. His face was impassive as he jotted notes on a pad, and it was worrisome to Maggie. Was Officer Cardello friends with the detective? Accusing a man based on smelling like licorice was a stretch, but if Officer Cardello had a fresh wound from an ice pick on his thigh, it would be hard for him to deny her accusation.

"Are you going to arrest him?" Dino asked.

Detective Brady snapped his pad shut. "First I need to find him. Then I'll see if he has a wound such as Miss Molinaro described."

She remained motionless until the detective left the building. Maybe Detective Brady was an honest man and would carry out his investigation with integrity, or maybe he was friends with Cardello and nothing would happen. Either way, she knew one thing for sure.

She intended to testify before the attorney general no matter who threatened her.

22

Mandatory relaxation at the Woodlands Health Clinic was proving unexpectedly stressful. How was doing *nothing* supposed to help Liam's ulcer? In the mornings he was instructed to sleep as long as possible, and in the afternoons he reclined on a lounge chair overlooking the lake. Nurses spoke in calming tones as they brought him chalky drinks and adjusted the shade umbrellas while he read his father's Bible.

Newspapers, business correspondence, and steel reports were considered too stressful and had been banned, but the nurses approved of the Bible. They probably thought it was a soothing, spiritual read, but Liam searched for the epic struggles in Egypt and Babylon. He read about men who girded their loins and stormed battlements. Fighting for a cause seemed natural to him, and he wanted to join a battle of his own.

The health clinic's ban on visitors was lifted after ten days, and Liam pounced on the chance to visit with his cousin Natalia. They sat on the patio facing the lake, where Natalia seemed more interested in admiring the wildflowers bordering the garden than carrying on a conversation.

"Why can't your music company make a record of that song about Gadsen Street?" he pressed.

She leaned over to inhale the fragrant purple flowers in a

planter beside their bench. "Our business promotes Russian music," she said. "We don't do popular songs."

"Publicizing 'The Ballad of Gadsen Street' will stoke resentment against Charles Morse," he began, but Natalia quickly interrupted.

"We're not supposed to discuss stressful topics. I'm not going to authorize a popular song, and that's the end of it. Oh, look, a chipmunk. Isn't it darling?"

The chipmunk was kind of cute as it scurried around, gathering nuts for the winter, a sign that summer was drawing to a close and the September vote was near. Instead of languishing in a health clinic, Liam ought to be gaining the upper hand to best Morse.

"The song will help people remember Gadsen Street and how they're still being railroaded by Morse's ice trust." He had additional arguments he wanted to make, but the nurse appeared with his morning glass of cabbage juice.

"You have another visitor up at the main lodge," the nurse said in her perpetually serene tone. "We told him you are permitted only a single visitor today, but he won't leave."

Liam shuddered as he swallowed the bitter, syrupy drink. "Who is it?" he asked after slamming the glass down.

"You don't need to worry about that," the nurse said as she shook a thermometer down. "We've sent for security to escort him away. Now, open your mouth and lift your tongue."

The nurse held the thermometer out expectantly, but Liam pushed it away. He got to his feet and started trudging up the grassy slope. Natalia followed, and he ignored her urging him to sit down and relax. If someone came all this way to see him, it might be important.

He rounded the bend and headed into the main lodge of the clinic, where a rugged man was arguing with the nurses at the reception desk. It was Antonio Gabelli, and the expression on his face did not bode well.

"Antonio! What's going on?"

"Trouble at the ice cream factory," Antonio said. "Someone vandalized the place in the middle of the night. The guy attacked Maggie. He locked her up in the freezer overnight, hoping she'd die."

Liam stood mutely, poleaxed by the implications. A nurse approached and started fussing again about stressful topics, but Natalia overruled her.

Antonio kept talking. "Maggie's appointment with the attorney general is today, and she's been getting a lot of threats from people trying to scare her out of testifying. She survived the freezer, but she's angry and still wants to testify."

Liam hung his head as Antonio recounted the events of the past few hours. He spoke of Maggie's blue lips and icy fingers after Dino carried her out of the freezer. If Maggie hadn't been able to dismantle the pipe, she would have died last night. Maggie was taking the 12:15 tramway to the attorney general's office, with Dino and the Lieberman brothers going along to keep her safe.

Liam would go too. Ignoring the nurses and Natalia's protestations, he barged through the clinic doors to bound up the stairs, taking them two at a time as his temper seethed. He'd change back into street clothes, grab his father's Bible, and be out of here in five minutes.

Natalia and the nurse hurried after him. "Don't leave," Natalia urged. "Your recovery is too important."

"So is Maggie's life!" He whirled to glare at Natalia. "*Now* do you see why I need to keep fighting Morse? Are you going to record Philip Altman's song about Gadsen Street or am I going to have to buy my own blasted record company to get it done?"

Natalia instantly agreed.

A doctor arrived and tried to stop him from leaving, but if Liam reverted to being an invalid while people were trying to kill Maggie, he would have a stroke or a heart attack and bust his ulcer wide open. The war was back on.

He rode back to the city with Antonio and arrived outside the government building well ahead of Maggie's two o'clock appointment. He paced on the sidewalk at the streetcar stop, waiting for her to arrive and stewing about how quickly the world could turn. While Maggie had been fighting for her life in that freezer, he was getting tucked into bed by a nurse giving him a glass of warmed milk. That was over. The gloves were coming off, and he'd protect Maggie with his own life if need be.

The tramway arrived, and he stood. Sure enough, Maggie was well protected by Dino and the Lieberman brothers as she stepped onto the street in her spiffy blue suit and matching boater hat. She looked professional and resolute . . . but her expression crumpled when she saw him waiting for her.

"*You're here*," she said in an aching voice, and he closed the distance and wrapped her in an embrace.

"I'm here," he assured her.

"He threw me in the freezer," she said in a shattered voice. "He vandalized the factory and cut our fan belts—"

"Shhh," he murmured, rocking her gently. "You're safe now."

He was going to grind Charles Morse's face into the dirt if it was the last thing he did. Pedestrians on the street looked at them oddly, but he didn't care. He held her and rocked her from side to side, shaking at how close he'd come to losing her.

Then she pulled back. "What are you doing here? I thought you were at the clinic."

"Not after I heard what happened. Wild horses couldn't keep me away, Maggie."

She reached up to frame his face in her hands, staring into his eyes with great care. "But are you all right? Are you better?"

He wasn't, but maybe he'd never get better. He couldn't sit on the sidelines while the world rolled on without him.

He conferred with Maggie and the others in the lobby of the government building, hearing more details of what had happened overnight. Maggie alternated between trembling anxiety and righteous anger, but the attempt to intimidate her had clearly backfired. Now that Liam was here, Dino and the others headed back to Gadsen Street to start repairing the damage at the factory.

Twenty minutes later, Liam walked with Maggie into the

private office of New York's attorney general. The honorable Clarence Newton had been the state's chief legal officer for three years. Everything about him was cultured and elegant. Lean build, long nose, perfectly groomed brown hair with a sprinkling of gray at the temples.

"Please," he said with a courtly gesture, beckoning them both to sit in the fine upholstered chairs opposite his desk.

"Thank you for agreeing to meet with me, Miss Molinaro," the attorney general began after taking his own seat behind his desk. "You initially came to my attention after filing your report about potential ethical violations by Mr. Morse."

That word *potential* rubbed Liam the wrong way. His temper gathered while the attorney general droned on about legal technicalities and due process. Wasn't Maggie the one who should be talking? She hadn't said a single word yet, and when the attorney general began touting a list of his own accomplishments in combatting corruption, Liam couldn't take it anymore.

"Maggie is lucky to be alive," Liam interrupted. "Why don't you shut up for half a minute and let her tell you what's been going on? Last night, one of Morse's goons tried to kill her."

The surprise was evident on Mr. Newton's face. "Good heavens," he murmured, sounding almost dainty in his dismay. Liam didn't want a well-mannered response; he wanted someone to go after Morse with a sledgehammer.

"Tell him what you know," he said to Maggie, and she was finally allowed to speak without interruption.

At least the guy was finally listening to Maggie. She recounted her personal history with the ice trust and how Gadsen Street still lacked ice deliveries even after the crisis in the rest of the city had eased. What she described sounded like clear-cut cases of extortion, intimidation, and vandalism, but the attorney general remained annoyingly impassive.

Then Maggie said something Liam had not anticipated.

"A bank owned by Charles Morse holds the mortgage on my building and my factory. He's setting me up for failure."

Liam swiveled to gape at her. "What?"

She wouldn't even look at him. Maggie's face was white as she spoke directly to the attorney general. "The bank knows we haven't been able to run our factory because of the ice trust. Then someone vandalized the factory last night. Our loans are coming due, and I think they're doing this so I won't be able to pay."

She continued speaking, but Liam sagged back in his chair. Why hadn't she told him this? If she needed money, she should have come to him. Frustration mounted as he sat trapped in his chair, listening to Maggie outline everything that had happened to her since the day she walked into Charles Morse's house to demand $95.00.

What would her life have been like if he hadn't goaded her to attack Morse? He'd driven her to this precipice, and even now she was putting her faith in the government and the attorney general to hobble Charles Morse and restore justice.

Maggie finished speaking, but instead of telling them how he intended to solve her problem, the attorney general launched into another monologue.

"Mr. Morse hasn't broken any laws," he said. "It is possible that his ice trust will benefit consumers by streamlining operations and coordinating distribution. A few kinks during the early years are to be expected."

Liam had heard enough. He stood and gestured for Maggie to do the same. "Keep looking through those lawbooks to see if there are any rules about how to put a leash on bloodsuckers who want to drain the working people of this city of their dignity and livelihoods, but we've got better things to do."

He stormed out of the office without looking back.

~ ❧ ~

Maggie scurried after Liam. This was exactly the sort of stress he didn't need if his ulcer was ever going to heal. His face was a thundercloud, his jaw taut as he strode into the hallway.

"Liam, we passed the elevator," she called after him, but he kept walking.

"We're not using the elevator," he ground out, then pushed through a doorway at the end of the hall. She followed him into the dank and dim stairwell.

He turned to face her. "Why didn't you tell me about the problem with your loan?" he asked in a wounded tone.

She backed up, but there wasn't much room on the landing and her shoulders bumped against the cinder blocks. "I didn't want to worry you. You've already done so much and have been so sick."

He braced his hands on the railing, staring down at the concrete steps. He didn't look angry so much as hurt.

"What did you think I meant when I said you could come to me for anything? Tell me about this loan and how much you need."

She folded her arms across her chest, shoulders hunkered in. It was embarrassing to be caught skipping bill payments, and heat flooded her body. "I'm current on the building mortgage but didn't pay last month's installment on the factory equipment."

"How much do you need?" Liam asked again. "Just tell me and I'll pay it off."

She shook her head. "I don't want money to be an issue between us."

"You're making it one by refusing my help. Tell me how much you need."

Her strength fading, she plopped down onto a concrete step. She felt trapped in a maze where the system was rigged and every escape hatch closed. She hung her head. "I'm afraid that even if I pay, Morse is going to keep coming after me until he's driven me out of business."

He joined her on the step, folding her hand into his. "That's why I'm going to stand beside you and fight," he said. "Patrick O'Neill is the world's best lawyer. Taking on a fat cat like Morse is what he does best. And guess what? We can go after Morse in the court of public opinion too. Natalia has agreed to make a recording of that song about Gadsen Street."

Maggie gasped. If she wasn't already sitting down, she would have fallen. "Really?" she asked, her voice echoing through the stairwell. When he nodded, she couldn't help herself. She grabbed him in a fierce embrace, a laugh burbling up from the unexpected bit of good news. "Oh, Liam, you can't imagine what this means to me."

"Why don't you tell me." His tone was flat, his expression guarded. It felt as if something very precious hung in the balance. He couldn't really be jealous of Philip, could he? Her heart still raced with the thrill of knowing one of Philip's songs might get the prize of a recording contract, but Liam deserved an answer.

"It means that someone I once cared for will have a glimmer of hope. That's all."

Liam glanced away and braced his elbows on his bent knees, staring straight ahead. "Do you regret walking away from him?"

Beside her, Liam's entire body was tense as he awaited her answer. She and Philip shared three years of a splendid courtship when the world was young and filled with terrifying possibility. Their paths had gone in different directions, but she would forever wish him well. How could she boil that cauldron of emotion down to a simple answer?

"I won't be mad," Liam assured her. "Just tell me honestly. I need to know."

"I want Philip to succeed, but not because I still love him. I will always love the dreams he and I shared, because once-upon-a-time we were splendid together. Does that make sense?"

He put an arm around her shoulders. "Yeah. I wish it didn't, but I understand." His expression softened with remembered pain of his own. He was probably thinking of Darla, the clever, brilliant artist who once dazzled him, but he kept the topic squarely on Philip.

"Natalia wants that song recorded as soon as possible," Liam said. "That means signing a contract, and Philip should probably have a lawyer for that. Patrick can help."

Patrick again. She sighed and scooted back to her side of

the step. The last thing she wanted to discuss was the chilly reception Patrick gave her, but this was the second time Liam suggested going to see Patrick, and he needed to know.

"I already talked with Patrick," she said. "I don't think he can help."

"When was this?" Liam's brows lowered in concern, and she summarized her brief, dispiriting meeting with Patrick. She hadn't gotten very far when Liam abruptly stood.

"You've got a long day ahead, and I have business across town," he said.

She rose and shook out her skirts, concerned at the distracted tone in his voice. Liam escorted her all the way home but didn't answer any of her questions about his urgent business across town. Maggie feared it had something to do with Patrick's refusal to help her and cringed at the thought that she might be the cause of a fallout between them.

Liam needed to get to the bottom of why Patrick had given Maggie the cold shoulder. He got straight to the point after storming into Patrick's office.

"You know that woman who came to you for help over threats from Morse's thugs at the Police Department?"

Patrick straightened in his desk chair. "Miss Molinaro?"

"Yeah, Miss Molinaro. She came to you for advice, but you told her to leave me alone because I ought to fight for steel, not ice."

"Those weren't the precise words I used."

Liam jabbed a finger in Patrick's face. "What you *precisely* did was turn away a woman who was smart enough to know her life was in danger. She almost died last night because one of those dirty cops shoved her into a freezer and locked her in. A few more hours and she'd have been dead."

The color drained from Patrick's face, and he stood. "Is she all right?"

"She's scared, as well she should be. Right now, she's got

people looking out for her, and it's going to stay that way until this whole thing is over. I'm taking her with me to Maine when I go for more ice in a few days."

Patrick grimaced. "Liam, please don't. Your first trip had a certain amount of panache that showed you in a good light, but it's starting to look personal."

"Of course it's personal. Morse practically killed the woman I love." He caught himself. It was too early to think of himself as in love with Maggie, but it was coming. "A woman I care about," he amended.

"Liam, you're letting your anger run away with you. *Don't* go to Maine. Hire an ice barge to make the run and let it dock at Pier 19."

"I want to be the one to do it," he replied. The goal was a lot bigger than just getting ice to Gadsen Street. It was to show the world who was a daring, generous person and who was a bloodsucking parasite. Liam's goal was to grind Charles Morse's reputation into the muck, and he was going to enjoy every moment of it.

⁓ ❦ ⁓

After the incident in the freezer, Maggie was frightened enough to accept the protection of two crew members from the *Black Rose*, whom Liam wanted with her always. They came with her everywhere, even when she went to Philip's current address to get his signature on the recording contract.

Natalia accompanied her to Philip's neighborhood to answer any questions he might have. "It's a straightforward contract that will allow him control over picking the musicians," Natalia said during the carriage ride, but Maggie still worried about it. Philip needed money more than artistic control. It was a little awkward holding a frank conversation in front of bodyguards, but there was no privacy in the tightly packed carriage as it bumped along cobblestone streets to Philip's neighborhood.

"How quickly will he start earning royalties?" Maggie asked.

With a new baby, Philip would need quick cash, and the amount Natalia outlined probably wasn't going to be enough. Music simply wasn't a lucrative career.

"Let me see him alone at first," Maggie said as the carriage arrived at Philip's street. "He's very proud, and he might try to turn the contract down if he thinks it's an act of pity."

"The Ballad of Gadsen Street" had gained traction all on its own. The topic resonated with people, and Philip had managed to pen a likable tune with charming lyrics. Well, mostly charming. It would have been better without the Sweet Miss Maggie part, but "The Ballad of Gadsen Street" was a worthy song, and she would fight hard to get Philip's signature on the contract.

Natalia was kind as she moved aside to let Maggie out of the carriage. "I'll be right here if he has any questions."

Maggie stepped out onto Philip's street, glancing around in surprise. It was so nice! A few of the houses could have used a coat of paint, but this was nothing like the seedy tenement where he lived a few years ago. Poplar trees lined the avenue, and each house had its own little front porch.

It had been five years since she'd seen Philip, and she prayed he wouldn't let pride stand in the way of accepting this deal. She nervously rolled the contract into a tube, twisting it in her hands as she headed down the block. There was no need to consult the street address because she spotted him on the front stoop of a charming little house, his blond hair shorter than when she'd known him, but he still possessed the same lanky frame.

A flood of memories rose as she approached. "Hello, Philip."

Surprise transformed his face, the lopsided smile she remembered so well spreading wide. "Hey, Maggie!"

He bounded down the steps, his arms opening for an embrace before he remembered and pulled back. She blushed and took a step back too. How many hundreds of times had they greeted each other with a warmhearted embrace? It was off-limits now.

"Sorry," he said, swallowing back a laugh.

"No, no . . . I'm sorry," she said. "You're looking well. And such a fine house!"

He grinned. "You're missing the best part. Come on up." He led her to the top of the porch, where a baby's cradle was gently rocking. The baby had Philip's yellowy blond hair and bright blue eyes, casually gnawing on a rattle as he stared up at her.

"This is Malcolm," Philip said with pride. "He just turned five months old, and I am completely in love."

"As well you ought to be," she laughed. He picked up the baby and demanded Maggie agree that the boy was the handsomest child in the city and surely destined for greatness. He explained that his wife had a job at a fancy hat shop on Fifth Avenue, but he got home from work early enough to take over tending the baby until she returned each evening at seven o'clock.

"I finally gave up on music and joined a law firm a couple of years ago," he explained. "And you know what? It's not so bad! I'm specializing in patent law, and it's kind of interesting. Nothing like probate law, which is what my dad wanted for me. So everything is working out okay."

"But you're still writing music, right?" she asked.

He lowered the baby back into his crib, then gave her an embarrassed nod. "Yeah. You were right about that part. I compose in the evenings when everything is quiet. I still put out a couple of songs a year, and it's been really great."

"Has it? Because I think it's about to become greater." She smiled in anticipation, unrolling the prized contract and handing it to him. "I know of a company that wants to record 'The Ballad of Gadsen Street.'"

Philip looked dumbfounded. His eyes grew huge as he let out a whoop of joy. "I can't wait to show this to my parents," he said as he held up a copy of the contract. "Who could have dreamed I'd have people fighting over me someday."

"Oh?"

"Yeah. I already signed a contract last week from a company on West Twenty-eighth. They mainly wanted the Gadsen Street song, but they signed a couple others too."

The news took the wind out of her sails. "You've already got a contract?"

"Can you believe it? After all these years, it's finally starting to happen. Not that I'm going to quit practicing law or anything crazy like that. I've got a family to support now, but it's enough to know that one of my songs has finally made it. *Finally*."

A lump formed in her throat. Philip wasn't a penniless failure after all. He'd taken a lot of hard knocks over the years, but he had figured out a way to be happy all on his own. Though it wasn't what he once dreamed, maybe it was better. He looked happy, and it made her wistful for their long-ago memories.

"What about you?" Philip asked. "Is there anyone special for you?"

There was a strong, swashbuckling hero who was planning another trip to Maine on her behalf, but it was too early to start building castles in the air where Liam was concerned. She hoped but couldn't be sure.

"I don't know," she admitted. "Maybe."

Philip beamed, a hint of bittersweet nostalgia in his gentle smile. "I hope so, Maggie. A good marriage is the best thing in the world, and I want that for you."

They spent a few more minutes admiring his baby. He invited her to stay to meet his wife, but Natalia and the others were waiting in the carriage. And she had what she'd come for, the assurance that Philip was doing okay and she didn't need to worry about him anymore.

She was free to leave her first love behind with no regrets, only hope for the future.

⚬⚬⚬

Liam was giving his dog a bath in an old washtub on the deck of the *Black Rose* when she arrived later that afternoon.

"Did you get his signature on that contract?" he asked, continuing to rub soapy foam into Frankie's coat. She took a seat on the upended bucket beside the tub and recounted how another company had beaten them to the punch. If Liam was surprised, he didn't show it as he lathered the dog's coat, his face the picture of concentration. Several moments passed before he asked what was really on his mind.

"How did it go seeing Philip again?" He still hadn't looked at her, just reached for a pitcher of water to rinse the soap away. She hadn't realized he was so nervous about her meeting with Philip. He couldn't even meet her eyes.

"It went great," she said. "He adores his wife and his little baby. I'm happy for him."

Liam set the pitcher down, looking at her for the first time, a hint of relief in his gaze. "Are we okay then?"

A sense of well-being flooded her. Philip was truly in her past now, and she was ready to step forward with this amazing man. "Yeah . . . we're okay."

Liam was still hunkered down over the washtub, but he grinned and leaned across it to give her a long, deep kiss. Frankie yelped, and Liam pulled back, but she could live forever on the hearty grin he sent her before hauling Frankie from the tub, sloshing water everywhere. She reached for a towel and helped dry them both.

A multitude of problems still loomed on the horizon. Rent was due in a few weeks, and it would cost plenty to repair the vandalized equipment. The ice runs to Maine were only a temporary solution to her problem with Morse, but for the next two days, she and Liam would enjoy smooth sailing on their next adventure to Maine.

23

Maggie was amazed at how different her second trip to Maine felt as she basked with Liam in their newfound understanding. It had rained on the sail north, keeping them down in the cardroom, where Liam showed her his fascinating stamp collection. In the evening, she taught him how to make ice cream in the ship's galley kitchen, using an old wooden ice cream churn to mix up a simple gelato recipe, and the following morning it was ready to be served to the crew.

Once they arrived at the Norberg Icehouse, loading the ice proceeded with ease. It was the third time the crew had loaded the *Black Rose*, and it took only two hours to fill the deck up to eight feet high with blocks of ice. By late morning they were on their way back down the Kennebec River.

It was too glorious a day to spend belowdecks. Overhead, the sky was a shocking blue, and the breeze carried the fresh scent of pine from the forest blanketing the rocky shoreline. The ship followed a tugboat as it guided them down the river and toward the ocean.

Captain Macauley and his first mate were huddled in the wheelhouse as they navigated the difficult channel. He had been in a surly mood all morning, complaining that the low water level in the river made navigation even more challenging than usual. While most of the deck was filled with walls of ice, a narrow strip about three feet wide had been left along the railing of the ship to allow for the crew to move about the deck. The only other deck space was the triangular area at the bow, where she and Liam played with Frankie, teaching him to fetch. Liam warned that English bulldogs were notoriously lazy and that she shouldn't expect much progress, but she was determined to try.

She held a lime out for the dog to sniff. "Look at this pretty lime. Are you going to be the world's best dog and bring it back for me?"

She tossed the lime a few yards, where it hit the wall of ice and scattered some sawdust before falling to the deck. The dog watched with interest but didn't seem eager to bring it back.

"Go on, Frankie," Liam prodded. "You can do it. I know it's hard to get those stubby legs moving, but be a champion . . . Yes! That's it. Keep going!"

The dog lumbered over to the lime, snatched it up in his mouth, and slowly waddled back to drop it in Liam's lap. Maggie cheered, and Liam rewarded the dog with a vigorous whole-body rub and lavish praise. It was impossible not to laugh.

The ship's engine groaned from somewhere near the back of the ship, and faint sounds of men shouting from the tugboat carried up on the wind. Liam set the lime down.

"Wait here," he said and headed to the railing. Noise from the engine grew louder. So did the shouting.

She looked toward the source of the noise but couldn't see behind the wall of ice. All she could see was the captain and the first mate up in the wheelhouse, signaling madly.

A massive scraping sound came from beneath the ship. The lime rolled across the deck. Was the ship listing? It didn't feel like it, but that lime just moved all on its own.

Liam sprinted down the narrow passageway along the ice toward the wheelhouse. "What's going on?" he called up, but Captain Macauley's answer was carried away on the wind.

They were at Squirrel Point, the only dangerous bend in the

river. The captain had been grumbling at dinner last night about how the river was low this summer, and now it seemed the hull had just scraped against something. Had they run aground? Everyone was yelling—the men in the tugboat, Liam, and Captain Macauley in the wheelhouse, whose face was flushed with anger.

The engine roared even louder. At least it was still working. That had to be good, right?

The ship was definitely listing toward the center of the river. Meltwater from the ice flowed toward the starboard side, puddling against the bulwark. *A lot* of meltwater.

Then a crack and a groan came from the wall of ice beside her. It was moving!

"Liam!" she screamed. "The ice—get out of the way!"

A look of horror crossed his face. He was already running as the ice began closing in on him. The ice was an unstoppable force, sliding slowly toward the railing. He made it past the wall of ice only seconds before it smashed against the rail. The crack reverberated through the air as thirty tons of ice hit the bulwark, most of it toppling over into the river.

And with so much weight shifting to starboard, they were now listing steeply. Frankie's paws struggled to grip the decking as he ran toward Liam, who scooped him up in his arms.

An ear-piercing whistle let out a series of short blasts, followed by the captain's voice through a megaphone. "All hands on deck!"

Liam's panicked gaze met hers. "Can you swim?"

"No."

Was it really that bad? Time seemed to slow as the captain shouted, ordering the crew to off-load ice. The weight of the sliding ice on deck would capsize the ship if they couldn't get it off soon.

Liam shoved the dog into her arms. "Hold on to him," he said, then ran to join the crew. The men grunted as they fought with the heavy ice to dump it into the river.

Maggie hugged Frankie tight, watching in horror as the crew

rid the ship of the precious blocks of ice, sending them plunging into the water.

Once all the ice stacked above the railing had been off-loaded, the engine was cut, leaving behind an eerie silence. Plenty of ice remained stacked below the railing, and getting it off without a pulley would be a challenge.

The first mate came striding toward them from the port side, where the shifting ice had left a wide berth. "We need everyone's weight on the port side," he instructed. "It's not much, but it could stop the ship from listing. And the tide is going out— things are going to get worse."

Maggie didn't understand, but she didn't need to. She trudged up the incline, clutching Frankie to her chest. She joined a few other crew members at the center of the ship where their body weight would do the most good.

Liam soon joined her. "We ran aground." He frowned and shook his head. "The water level was too low and the ship too heavy. And as the tide goes out, it's likely the ship will capsize."

"We don't know that yet," she said, trying to reassure him, but they were already listing at a terrible angle.

A man from the tugboat crew climbed aboard and headed straight to the wheelhouse, his expression grim. Maybe they could figure out something to do, but for now the engine had been killed and they were stranded.

The low boom of a foghorn came from the lighthouse on Squirrel Point, probably sending a message to the local community, but all it did was frighten Maggie even more.

Captain Macauley arrived with the tugboat skipper. "I'd hoped to dump the rest of the ice overboard," the captain said, "but as the tide gets lower, the danger of capsizing is increasing. Low tide is in one hour, and I'm ordering everyone off the ship. There's nothing the crew can do. I'll stay aboard with Mr. Archer in case the worst happens, but I want the rest of you off."

⁓

Liam felt trapped in a nightmare as he descended the ladder, balancing Frankie against his shoulder and arriving in a wobbly dinghy from the local rescue crew. Maggie had already climbed into the dinghy, but there was no more room on her bench, so Liam headed to the row behind her, unable to meet her eyes. They were filled with sympathy, and he didn't deserve it.

The wreck was his fault. How many times had he ignored Captain Macauley's warnings, all so he'd have the satisfaction of being the hero and thumbing his nose at Charles Morse? Even Patrick had warned Liam against taking this trip. Pathetic, shameful arrogance had put him in this situation and endangered everyone aboard.

Guilt weighed heavily as he squeezed onto the end of the bench and set Frankie on the damp floor. Soon the dinghy was crammed shoulder to shoulder with crew members from the *Black Rose*. All were silent except for the four men from the rescue team, who seemed almost cheerful as they rowed them the twenty yards to the shore. They joked about how this was an easy rescue because it was daylight, and it wasn't during a storm. There was no fog or any other of the perilous conditions that caused vessels trouble at Squirrel Point.

They meant to be kind, but it only made Liam feel worse because it was a calm, beautiful day, and he should have known better than to risk his father's ship when the river was so low.

It didn't take long to reach land. Squirrel Point was a rocky promontory with a clapboard lighthouse rising up from its middle. The only other buildings were the two-story keeper's house with its faded red roof, a boathouse, and a shed. Citizens from the nearby town were well practiced in helping stranded sailors and had already arrived to offer their assistance. Half a dozen women were setting out baskets of food and pitchers of lemonade.

A couple of strapping young men waded through the shallow water to haul the dinghy onto the rocky shore. Liam got out first, ignoring the water filling his shoes as he helped pull the boat the final few yards onto dry land.

He got Frankie out and lugged him up to a grassy spot, where the dog happily snuffled in the scrub. Maggie was already out by the time he returned for her, and she seemed determined to cheer him up.

"Look," she said brightly, "all these people have set out a lunch for us. And there are chairs if you'd like to sit."

All he wanted was to get away. If he sat at one of those picnic tables, he'd have a clear view of the *Black Rose* listing at that horrible angle, crippled and near ruin.

"I'm going to take Frankie for a walk," he said. Anything to get away from all these people looking at him.

"I'll come with you," Maggie offered, not waiting for a reply as she took his arm. With Frankie waddling beside them, they headed away from the picnic tables already crowded with people.

"Yoo-hoo," a woman chortled after him. He turned out of politeness to see a grandmotherly lady holding up a platter. "We've got cookies and milk if you'd like to join us."

Maggie gave the lady a friendly wave. "We'll be okay," she called back, but the grandmother recited all the other offerings.

"We've also got ham-and-cheese sandwiches and Mrs. Mueller's famous three-bean salad." A couple of guys made some rude comments about Mrs. Mueller's cooking, and then another woman added that in a few minutes Mrs. Cuthbertson would arrive with a carrot cake.

Liam kept walking while Maggie called out excuses before hurrying to his side. He took her hand, grateful she had the presence of mind to be kind to these people who only wanted to help.

"Am I a horrible person for not wanting to join them?"

She squeezed his arm. "If so, we're both horrible."

They continued walking, neither of them saying anything for a while. This was what he liked about Maggie. He didn't feel obligated to keep talking.

Frank's lumbering gate slowed to a stagger. Bulldogs weren't good for long distances, and Liam glanced around for somewhere to sit. A few slabs of granite jutted up from the ground, and they faced north so he wouldn't have to see his crippled ship. He scooped Frankie up to lug him the few yards to the boulders.

It took some doing to find a portion smooth enough to sit, but soon he had Maggie beside him and an unobstructed view of green splendor and the river straight ahead.

"I'm such a failure," he choked out, and Maggie mercifully didn't say anything. Everything hurt. His ulcer hurt, a headache pounded, and grief made it hard to even draw a full breath, but he needed to keep talking. "I've been trying so hard to make myself into somebody my father would have been proud of. He was good and kind and smart. A college president. He saved thousands of lives with the medicines he helped invent. He never got arrested or lost his temper or ran his ship aground."

"Liam, your father wouldn't blame you for trying to do something good," Maggie said, her voice aching with tenderness, but he didn't want to hear it.

"I hate my life," he said. "Every instinct in me wants to run back to Philly and be a welder again, but I can't. I need to shake it off, and tomorrow I'll swing back into action. My dad would expect it of me. But for today, it hurts pretty bad."

He looked up at the cloudless sky, wondering if Theodore Blackstone was looking down on him from heaven and could see the *Black Rose* lying mangled in the river. He cringed at the thought.

"I'm going to do better," he vowed. "I still need to defeat Charles Morse, but I'm going to do it honorably. In a way that would have made my dad proud."

"Liam, I'm sure he's proud of you right now. Of course, you're going to make some mistakes because you're human. A man as fine as Theodore Blackstone would understand that."

His father died three years before Liam returned to New York. Theodore mourned the loss of his son until his dying day, and they never got a chance to meet again. Liam would give anything if he could have a few hours with his father to assure him that he'd survived and turned out okay. To tell Theodore how much he admired him. He gazed up at the immensity of the sky, its beauty awakening his grief all over again.

"Sometimes I d-dream about . . ." The lump in his throat choked him up. Thinking of his dad always hurt, but he swallowed the grief back and tried again. "Sometimes I dream about being able to meet my dad in h-heaven. That's why I try so hard to be good, because I want that to happen, you know?"

"Liam, I know. I understand."

A tear rolled down his cheek to splat on his leg, and he swiped at his face. Normally he'd be horrified to be caught bawling in front of a woman, but Maggie understood, and he didn't mind letting her see it.

"Yoo-hoo!" It was that voice again, and he sagged because the cookie lady was heading toward them, wading through the tall grass with a cheerful smile. He drew a steadying breath and wiped his face once more.

"You folks will want to watch out," the older lady said breathlessly as she drew near, "because there are ticks all over this area. Are you sure you don't want to join us for cookies and milk?"

Liam sagged. What else could make this day any more horrible? Maggie sprang off the rock to shake her skirts. Liam picked up Frank and swiped at his fur—he didn't spot any ticks—and then they followed the cookie lady back to the shorter grass, where Liam got a glimpse of the ship. No matter how much he dreaded the next few minutes, it was time to go see how the *Black Rose* fared.

Low tide was coming in three minutes, and at that point the ship would either capsize or hold steady. Most of the rescue crew were optimistic.

"The angle of the ship looks okay," one of them said. "If it was going to tip, it probably would have happened already."

Liam closed his eyes, sending up a silent prayer to keep the ship safe.

The three minutes came and went, and the ship hadn't moved one iota. It took another hour for Liam to draw a full breath.

He was finally beginning to believe his ship might not tip over. Yet this was no time to celebrate because the next huge challenge loomed. Tides shifted twice a day, and an attempt to refloat the ship would happen in six hours at high tide. The best-case scenario would be to refloat the ship and then tow her somewhere they could repair the damaged hull.

But if the refloating failed? The lift and fall of four daily tide shifts would destroy the screw-driven propulsion system on the ship's bottom. The *Black Rose* would block river traffic for weeks or even months, rendering thousands of people unable to use the river and ruining their businesses. That wouldn't be allowed to happen. If Liam couldn't quickly refloat the ship, he would order it to be scuttled. Welders with blowtorches would arrive to dismantle the *Black Rose* section by section and haul it away to be melted down for scrap.

High tide wouldn't be for another six hours, and they were going to be the longest six hours of his life.

☙

Liam didn't have the strength to watch the refloating attempt, even though he understood the procedure. Chains were already attached to the *Black Rose*, and at high tide they would be pulled taut by tugboats. In combination with the rising tide, they hoped it would be enough to refloat the ship.

At least a hundred people from the local community had gathered at the lighthouse to witness the spectacle, but Liam retreated with Maggie to a grassy patch behind the shed where he wouldn't have to watch. High tide was at 6:24, so he'd learn in the next few minutes if he was responsible for destroying Theodore Blackstone's yacht.

"Okay, the chains are up, and the tugboat is drawing back," Maggie said. "I suppose that means they'll be starting soon."

He kept his back to the river, looking north toward the pine trees in the distance. But he could still hear the dull sound of the *Black Rose*'s engines gathering steam. His headache intensified, and he clenched his fists.

"Of all the stupid things I've done in my life, this is the worst," he said.

"You're not stupid, Liam."

Little did she know. "Crocket pulled me out of school in the eighth grade because I was failing. I'm as dumb as Crocket was, and I'm not worthy of my real father."

"Your real Father is God in heaven," Maggie said. "Your earthly father was Theodore Blackstone, and they both know your heart was in the right place when you sailed that ship up here. And whatever happens in the next ten minutes, if the ship rights itself or sinks to the bottom of the riverbed . . . it's all part of God's plan."

He glanced at his pocket watch: 6:24. Captain Macauley must have given the signal because steam hissed and the engines of the ship rumbled. He bowed his head and tried to pray, but all he could think to say was *please, please, please* . . .

"The tugboat's chains are taut," Maggie said. "That must mean they're pulling on the ship."

He closed his eyes but couldn't block out the gravelly sound of the tugboat's engine. It growled and chugged and stuttered. Chains clanked, and water sloshed from the underwater propulsion system. It was impossible to tell if the noises were from the tugboat or the *Black Rose*.

"I think the ship is beginning to straighten," Maggie said, but there was no letup in the growling engines. "Yes, it's definitely getting straighter."

He still couldn't look. Maggie's voice was tense, but shouts from the crowd at the lighthouse were growing louder. Some were yelling words of caution, others shouting encouragement. All of it sounded awful.

"The tugboat just dropped its chains," Maggie said. "It's backing away."

That meant the *Black Rose* was either going to be able to right itself or not. He would probably know in the next few—

A roar of cheers sounded from the lighthouse. Maggie's breath caught. "It's upright. *It's upright!*"

He spun around to look. Waves sloshed in the river as the *Black Rose* began to move on its own power. He dropped to his knees. "Thank you, God," he murmured over and over. Today was a painful and humiliating lesson, but now it was time to make good on his promises to become a better man.

24

The *Black Rose* was too crippled to risk the journey home. Instead, she was towed to the nearby city of Bath for repairs. Liam would stay in Maine to oversee the repairs and hire an ordinary barge to deliver a load of ice exclusively to Gadsen Street.

"It's what I should have done from the beginning," he acknowledged as he waited with Maggie at the train station. "Are you sure you can't stay? They say Maine has the best lobster in the whole country."

She gazed up at him, loving the way his eyes crinkled at the corners as he smiled down at her. Everything in her wanted to linger here, but Dino needed help getting the factory back in gear, and rent was coming due.

"I need to get back home to help Dino repair the fan belts, but someday I promise we'll have lobster in Maine, because I would love that too." She dug deep and reached for the courage to reveal her heart. "Almost as much as I love you, Liam."

He blinked in surprise. "You do? I only ask because it's kind of important. I can be a dumb idiot—"

"Stop," she said. "You're not dumb. You're the man I love. I know exactly who you are, with your big, generous heart and your bottomless goodwill." Emotion swirled with exhaustion, but she meant every word. "I love you and—"

He cut her off with a kiss. "Go home and fix those fan belts, Maggie. And know that I love you too."

She rode the train home on a cloud of euphoria. There were so many things she loved about Liam. He was a man she could lean on for help and inspiration, but perhaps the most exciting thing was knowing that he needed her too.

It was nine o'clock in the evening when Maggie arrived back at Gadsen Street. Business was lively with late-night diners crowding into O'Donnell's Pub and a few lingering at the tables outside Lieberman's Deli. The streetlamps cast a warm glow, laughter mingled with mandolin music from Enzo's Ristorante, and it seemed as if life was finally returning to normal. Dino must not have gotten the new mixing belts installed because the ice cream parlor was closed.

To her surprise, Dino sat in the front parlor with Spider, sipping cups of coffee at one of the tables. Mr. Prescott from the Porterhouse was with them too. She wiggled the locked door handle to get their attention, and Dino promptly rose to disengage the locks and let her inside. All three men looked at her with a somber expression.

"What's going on?" she asked Dino. "Did you have trouble with the new belts?"

"No trouble, but I sent the employees home," Dino replied. "Maggie, I don't think we can afford to pay them."

"What do you mean?" she asked. Instead of answering her, Dino handed her a letter from their bank. Her fingers trembled as she unfolded the pages and scanned them, a sickening feeling of dread growing with each line she read.

The bank had demanded full payment on the loan for the factory equipment. Unless they made good on the entire loan amount, the equipment would be repossessed on Friday. The amount stated at the bottom of the page was $13,651.

"Can they do this?" she asked, horrified.

Mr. Prescott nodded. "I've been looking over your loan documents all evening," he said. "Normally banks would rather grant an extension instead of repossessing the collateral, but they are within their rights to do so."

And the collateral on the loan was the factory equipment. The industrial mixing machines, the freezing equipment, the motors, the belts, and vat-sized churns. All of it would be repossessed. She felt like throwing up and covered her face with her hands.

"Now, don't you go getting sick too," Dino said in a kindly voice, which made her look up.

"Where's Aunt Julie?"

Dino sagged, his face troubled. "She was the one who got served with the papers when a bank officer showed up this afternoon, banging his fist on the counter and demanding payment. She fainted."

Maggie shot to her feet. "Is she all right?"

"She's fine," Dino said. "The doctor paid a house call and ordered bed rest. I don't want her worrying about this. I've tried to assure her that everything is going to be okay, but—"

Mr. Prescott held up the repossession notice. "If you pay off the entire loan before Friday, the equipment is yours. The bank is legally bound to honor this document. So . . . somehow you need to come up with thirteen thousand dollars, and soon."

"I think we can do it," Dino said. "Julie and I have about five thousand saved, and I know you have about the same. The pearl brooch I gave Julie for her birthday is worth something . . ."

Her shoulders sagged as the implications crashed down on her. "Paying off the loan would take away our safety net."

"But you'd own the equipment," Mr. Prescott pointed out.

True, but Charles Morse would still be lurking, waiting for another chance to pounce and grind her into the dirt. He'd come after her again and again. This was personal for him. A splitting headache made it hard to think clearly as she scrambled for a solution.

"Maggie, I hate to ask it, but . . ." Dino's voice trailed off, and she straightened to look at him. The shadows beneath his eyes made him look even more haggard than usual. "Liam is a very rich man . . ."

Dino didn't need to finish his sentence. They all knew where his train of thought was leading. It would be so easy to ask Liam for the money; he'd already said he would help her. But taking his money wouldn't solve her real problem. Even if they managed to survive this crisis, Morse wouldn't stop until he defeated her. Likely she would end up like Rupert Pine's father or old Mr. Gabelli, who quietly gave up after Morse cost them everything.

She wouldn't lose quietly. She would lose in a way so spectacular that she might be able to win in the end.

"I don't think we should fight this," she said.

"What do you mean we don't fight?" Dino roared.

"Shhh. Don't wake Aunt Julie."

Dino sat back down, but his voice remained earnest. "We worked too hard to lose it all now. Do you remember the Christmas when the rest of the world was celebrating, but you and I worked to build this front counter? Neither one of us knew what we were doing, but we sawed and sanded and painted. We cut the glass three times until we had it right, but on December twenty-sixth we were open for business with a beautiful front counter as good as any carpenter could have built. Do you remember, Maggie?"

She traced the scars on her knuckles from that long-ago Christmas Day when they built the counter. She loved that counter all the more for having built it herself.

Now Spider was mad too. "We've all worked too hard to let him win this easy."

"Trust me, Spider, nothing about this is easy." Her voice shook and she crossed her arms, glaring outside and wondering how to get out of this mess. Charles Morse had rigged the system to crush his rivals, and he'd been successful because he operated in the shadows behind corporations. What if she dragged all that into the light? Her idea was terrible and frightening, but it just might work. She gathered her resolve and looked at Dino.

"Let the bank take our assets," she said. "Let Morse win this battle, but we can still win the war."

Spider rocked back in his seat. "What are you talking about?"

"Let the entire city watch as his minions repossess our equipment. First they squeezed us on the ice to bring us to our knees, and then they struck when we were down by demanding full payment on their loan. Everyone in this city knows Molinaro Ice Cream. They know we run a good business, and if one vengeful man can drive us into ruin, who in this city is safe? Someone needs to expose Morse for who he is."

Dino flushed in anger. "You want us to become a sacrificial lamb, to lose everything to prove a point."

Did she? Her gaze strayed out the window to watch the owner of the cheese shop polish the glass in his bow-fronted window. David Lieberman was carrying a tray of sandwiches to late-night customers. This street was full of hardworking people who had gambled everything to start their businesses, but sometimes the rules were rigged. It was time for that to change.

"Yes," she said. "There needs to be a sacrificial lamb willing to take the hit. Our reputation will help us weather the storm. We invite every newspaper reporter in the city to witness what can happen if there is no law to stop the banks from colluding with a group like the ice trust to drive someone out of business."

Mr. Prescott watched her with a brooding expression. "It's a risk," he warned. "It might work, but it's a risk I wouldn't take."

Maggie didn't want to either, but she was going to roll the dice and do it anyway.

25

*L*iam spent the next week overseeing repairs of the *Black Rose*. The ship had been safely dry-docked, revealing the ugly scrape along her hull. It was strange to see the entire ship exposed to the light of day, propped up by stabilizing blocks and girders in a concrete basin. Liam borrowed a pair of dark glasses and a blowtorch to work alongside the other welders, who were installing the new alloy he'd been testing for U.S. Steel. The biggest damage was to the ship's screw-propulsion system, which would require skilled engineers and months to complete. In the end, however, the ship would be better than ever.

A smile curved his lips as the flame from his blowtorch cut away a damaged section of the hull. This was what he'd done for years in the shipyards, and it felt good to get his hands dirty again from an honest day's labor. Some of the local shipwrights had taken to calling him "Low-Tide Liam," which was an embarrassment but not unwarranted. He deserved the ribbing for his reckless act in running the ship aground, but the *Black Rose* was going to sail again.

"Hey, Blackstone," someone bellowed from the top of the harbor wall. Liam pushed up his glasses to see a clerk from the design office waving a slip of paper over his head.

"Hang on," Liam called out. "I'm coming up."

He climbed the ladder bolted to the side of the dry dock, his boots clanging on metal rungs the entire way up. The clerk met him at the top.

"A wire came in for you, sir."

Liam thanked the man and scanned the note. It was from Patrick.

Trouble at Molinaro factory. Debts being called in. Get home.

Confused, Liam read the note three times. Why hadn't Maggie contacted him for help? It didn't matter. He hurried to the engineers' office, which was equipped with a telegraph and telephone system. It took a few minutes for the local operator to patch him through to New York, but Patrick soon answered his telephone.

"What's going on?" he demanded, and Patrick quickly relayed the details of a report he'd seen in the newspapers about how all the restaurants on Gadsen Street had gone back into business, but the Molinaro Ice Cream factory was closing because their loan had been called in.

Patrick sounded grim. "I went to Gadsen Street to speak with Maggie, and she isn't fighting the bank. I even suggested that you would loan her the funds to bail her out, but she wasn't interested. I thought you'd want to know."

"Where's Charles Morse in all of this?"

"Nowhere to be found, but you can bet he's at the bottom of it. She told me the bank is planning on seizing the factory equipment tomorrow morning. That's not normal. Banks would rather grant an extension on a loan than repossess secondhand equipment. It smacks of a personal vendetta."

A rush of acid soured Liam's stomach at the prospect of Maggie facing Morse and his stable of minions on her own. That wouldn't happen as long as he had breath in his body.

"Thanks, Patrick, I owe you one," he said tersely before hanging up.

He needed to get back to New York. It would mean abandoning the *Black Rose*, but the ship could wait, and he feared Maggie could not.

⬿

Liam arrived in New York nine hours later—tired, hungry, and kicking himself for overlooking the danger that still loomed around Maggie. After leaving the train station, a private carriage took him straight to Gadsen Street. It was late, and the banks were closed for the night, but as soon as they opened in the morning he'd pay off whatever she owed before they seized her equipment.

Anger and apprehension gathered as he strode down Gadsen Street. All the other businesses seemed to be prospering. Most of the outdoor café tables were filled with diners, and music poured from the Irish pub. He walked faster, bracing himself for the likelihood of tears. Women's tears were his downfall. He hated it when they cried. He could be tough and aggressive, but when a woman cried, he lost all his defenses. But maybe she wouldn't be crying. Maybe she'd be furious or despondent or weepy, all of which would be understandable, maybe even expected . . .

What he hadn't expected to see was a party.

The ice cream parlor was lit up like a Christmas tree. Every table was filled, and tiny lights had been strung through the olive tree. Laughter mingled with the boisterous song being played by a fiddler. Molinaro pushcarts were scattered among the crowd, the vendors handing out ice cream for free. Maggie stood beside her aunt and uncle outside the parlor's door, listening to old Mr. Lindquist pay homage to the best ice cream in the city.

Had there been a reprieve? Given Maggie's nostalgic expression, it didn't appear to be so, especially when the pharmacist lifted his glass in a toast and said he would miss the Molinaros and wished them Godspeed wherever their next venture carried them.

233

Hearty applause greeted the toast as Liam shouldered his way through the crowd until he reached Maggie. "What's happening?"

Her face looked radiant in the lamplight. "Liam! This is our last night," she said, her eyes a little watery. "We want to go out with a party. One last glorious night to celebrate what we had here."

"It doesn't have to be this way," he insisted. "Let me help you."

She shook her head. "I know what I'm doing. It's for the best."

What? He didn't understand. He could *fix this* if only she'd let him, but someone else was giving a toast now and there were too many onlookers here. Frustrated, Liam glanced around. He'd prefer to have this conversation with Maggie somewhere private. Next, Mrs. Lieberman launched into a speech, prompting another round of applause.

Liam tugged on her elbow to draw Maggie into the parlor. It was quieter inside the shop. He cupped both her shoulders in his hands and looked down into her face. "Why won't you let me help you? Maggie, just say the word and I'll make this problem go away."

"I don't want you to," she replied. "Charles Morse's bank colluded with his ice trust to drive me out of business. It's not illegal, but it's wrong. Tomorrow morning, the bank is coming for our equipment. I want the whole city to see it, and then maybe the laws can be changed so he can't ever do this to anyone else."

It sounded too farfetched to risk her entire business. "What if it doesn't work? And even if it does, it might take years before you'll be compensated."

"We still have our pushcarts. We own those outright. Dino and I can buy ice cream from someone else and go back to operating a pushcart business. We'll be okay." Her face brightened. "I have a little good news," she added with a smile. "Officer Cardello has been arrested and charged by the district attorney for attacking me. And because he's terrified of prison, he's confessed to everything in hopes of getting a lighter sentence."

Liam was relieved and outraged at the same time. "*He's* afraid? How would he feel about being locked in a freezer and left to die?"

"Yeah, well, he's claiming ignorance on that front," Maggie said. "He says that when I stabbed him with the ice pick, he panicked and thought he was locking me in a storage closet."

It was hard to mistake a freezer for a storage closet, but not many places had a walk-in freezer room, so a jury might buy it. Either way, it was a relief to know at least one corrupt cop was off the streets.

"Tomorrow the real war begins," she continued. "It will be awful, but we refuse to mourn tonight. We had a good run here. We were happy. We gave work to dozens of people, and the Porterhouse said our ice cream was the best they ever served." Her bottom lip began to wobble, but she regained control and managed a smile. "We're proud of what we accomplished, even if it's going to end badly."

Her strength was humbling. Every instinct in Liam's body wanted to stand in front of her to shield her from what was coming. He wasn't the sort to stand by quietly while a woman he loved was stripped of her dreams and livelihood, but this was her decision, not his. She was too smart to have arrived at it lightly.

"Look at me," he said, tipping her chin up so he could peer directly into her eyes. She did so proudly, the lights from the party outside emphasizing the silvery scar splitting her brow. She was tough and beautiful and glorious.

"Are you sure this is what you want?" he asked, hoping she might still change her mind, but the confidence in her eyes gathered strength.

"It is."

"Then I'll stand beside you the whole way."

26

Maggie rose before dawn to take a final walk through the darkened factory as she braced herself for the day ahead.

Everything was quiet. Yesterday they fired up the equipment to make a final batch of ice cream to treat everyone on the street, but now the machines had been cleaned and dried, the steel vats gleaming as she walked among the equipment, setting a hand on the cold metal. One last goodbye.

These machines weren't alive and wouldn't be hurt by having their components taken apart and hoisted away by uncaring hands. Those were only *her* emotions running wild because she loved this equipment. She'd loved this job. Her ice cream helped to make people happy while providing work to good people.

Today she'd be saying goodbye to the machinery that made it all happen. She headed to the back room to unplug the equipment from the electrical boxes. She wound the cords and stored them beside each piece of machinery.

By eight o'clock, Dino and Julie were dressed and downstairs, and Maggie worried that this would be too much for Julie's fragile state.

"Are you going to be okay?" she asked Julie.

"It would be more stressful to stay upstairs and let the two of you face this alone," she replied, the spray of wrinkles deepening beside her gentle eyes. "The three of us have been in this together since the beginning. We will go out the same way."

David Lieberman came by, wearing a white apron and ready to open his deli. "Is there anything we can do for you, Maggie? Can I bring you something to eat?"

She declined, and he seemed sad but resigned as he nodded and returned to the deli. Mr. Alfonso arrived to commiserate with Dino, and even a few men from the pushcart crew came out in support. Rupert Pine arrived with a photographer, and he wasn't the only one. Soon journalists and photographers from all three New York newspapers were on hand to document everything, exactly as she'd hoped. Plenty of people resented bankers, and the stories that would flood tomorrow's newspapers might stoke enough anger to force a change in the laws.

Liam arrived not long after. He brought his dog and Caleb, who was tasked with minding Frankie for the day because things were about to get hectic.

"You haven't changed your mind?" he asked as he handed Frankie's leash to Caleb.

"No," she said. "We're ready."

"Okay then." He opened his arms, and she stepped into his comforting embrace. His heart thudded as hard as her own. The clip-clopping of horse-drawn wagons sounded, and she stepped out of Liam's arms to face them. Her stomach clenched at the sight of the wagons drawing closer. It was about to begin.

A dozen mounted police officers rode alongside the wagons, triggering a chill of instinctive fear. Officer Cardello was locked up, but the sight of a police uniform still set her on edge.

The lead officer cantered ahead of the others and dismounted in front of her. He respectfully tipped his cap. "Ma'am," he said. "We've been asked to accompany the work crew to ensure there's no trouble while they carry out their duties. Is that understood?"

All she could do was nod. The procession of wagons approached with three or four men atop each driver's bench. They didn't look like bad people; they looked like workhands who needed a paycheck.

"Go back where you belong!" someone from across the street shouted at the convoy, but none of the hired men paid any attention as they arrived at the ice cream parlor.

"What's the easiest way to get inside the factory?" the leader asked Liam. Why did men naturally defer to each other? Liam simply looked down at her, pity in his eyes.

"There's a double warehouse door in the alley behind the shop," she answered, feeling sick for cooperating, but she still owned this building and didn't want it damaged.

The lead driver spat a wad of tobacco juice onto the street before turning to her. "How do we get there?"

A smear of tobacco spittle clung to the driver's lip, and she covered her face. This man was about to have his dirty hands on her pristine equipment.

"I'll show them the way," Liam offered, and she nodded gratefully. Liam gestured to the man to follow him, and the convoy lumbered toward the alley that led around the block. She stared at them as they rolled past. Most of the men riding in the wagons seemed perfectly harmless, and a few looked at her with sympathy.

"Sorry about this, ma'am," one of them said as his wagon rolled by, and she dipped her chin in acknowledgment. Why was it harder to deal with kindness rather than the tobacco spitter? She reached a shaking hand out for a patio chair and sank into it, again covering her face with her hands. But she couldn't block out the noise of the wagons rumbling over the cobblestones or the musky scent of horses.

Everything about this morning was horrible, yet it was time to stand up and get on with things. She stood and entered the parlor, heading toward the factory to slide the warehouse doors open.

Liam was waiting on the other side. Some of the workers were rolling up their sleeves and unloading tools. It was hard to look at them.

Liam stepped in close and said in a low voice, "Maggie, it doesn't have to be this way. Just say the word and I'll put a stop to this."

It would be easier if he didn't keep reminding her. At least the lead driver had wiped the tobacco juice from his lip. She ignored Liam's plea and locked gazes with the driver.

"I've already disconnected the electricity," she said. "Do what you need to do."

The men needed no further instructions as they streamed into the factory. One of them flipped a toolbox open and distributed wrenches and crowbars. The men swarmed the equipment. It took only minutes for them to fill a cart with refrigerator coils and wheel it out the door. The ladder belonged to her, but she didn't fuss when someone moved it beneath the motor box to begin dismantling it.

Noise filled the factory. Clanging metal, tromping feet, and the scrape of equipment being dragged across the concrete floor. Every clatter and bang hurt her spirit, but she couldn't look away.

"Hey, be careful of that compressor," Gary barked at a worker, who was dismantling the component from the inside of the refrigerated room. How ironic that the surliest of all her pushcart vendors was here to stand up for her.

"The ladder is ours," Dino shouted when someone folded it up and began carrying it toward the door.

Maggie got the attention of one of the police officers. "The ladder is ours," she confirmed, and since no one wanted to fight for it, the officer instructed the worker to leave the ladder alone.

An hour later it was all over. The machines had been broken down to their component parts and hauled away, the compressors and evaporator coils taken out of the cold rooms. Without the haphazard maze of belts crisscrossing the air, the space looked cavernous. Bare spots on the concrete floor were all that was left to mark where her three mixing machines had been.

She headed out to Gadsen Street to watch the wagons leave.

It was ten o'clock and most of the restaurants hadn't opened yet, but the owners and staff were outside, lining both sides of the street to watch the solemn procession.

"Vultures!" someone shouted from one of the apartments above the pharmacy.

A chorus of boos and catcalls rose up from people lining the streets. Someone threw a tomato at the lead driver, who ducked to avoid it in the nick of time. A couple of mounted police officers trotted toward the troublemaker, but no more flying objects followed the tomato.

Flashbulbs went off and sulfur tinged the air as the photographers took pictures of the heavily laden wagons. The Lieberman brothers stood before the deli, arms crossed as they glowered at the departing work crew.

She watched as the last wagon rounded the street corner and disappeared. This wasn't the end. It would be a few weeks or months before she knew if the sacrifice would pay off, but today it felt like a terrible end to a bright dream.

⁂

Exhaustion clobbered Maggie after it was all over. Wasn't that odd? She hadn't done a lick of work during the repossession, yet she barely had the strength to make it back into the parlor and plop down at a table. It even took effort to lean over to pet Frankie's wrinkly fur when he looked up at her with mournful eyes.

Caleb noticed. He'd been minding the dog all morning, but now scooped Frankie up and deposited him on her lap. "Liam always says the dog is the best medicine to help cheer you up," Caleb said. The heavy dog was surprisingly comforting, and she gave Liam a tired smile, who stood in the corner watching her through pained eyes.

"Is that right?" she asked him.

"Dogs are simple creatures," he replied. "They remind us that all we really need to be happy is a bowl of water, a little food, and some companionship."

Maybe, but as her gaze trailed around the sad ice cream parlor, her heart wanted so much more.

"When was the last time you ate?" Liam asked. "I'm not talking about a little bit of ice cream at the party last night. I'm talking about a proper meal."

It must have been days. She'd been too anxious to eat much of anything since seeing the bank's letter. "I don't know," she said.

"Come on. I'm taking you to the Porterhouse."

A smidgeon of light pierced the gloom. The prospect of finally having her date with Liam at the Porterhouse beckoned, and she eagerly accepted his invitation. It had been almost three months since their first date collapsed after Liam overheard her gushing about him to Frieda as they cracked eggs at the worktable. At the time, she'd been thrilled at the prospect of a handsome man treating her to a meal at the Porterhouse. Now things were so different. Liam wasn't just a handsome man—he was a friend, a leader, a rock she could depend on.

Her businesswoman's eye assessed the gold-leaf stenciling on the steakhouse's front doors. Inside, white linen graced the tables set with crystal and china, and the scent of baking bread was heavenly. Mr. Prescott, already dressed in a three-piece suit, came out to seat them.

"How are you doing, Maggie?" Mr. Prescott asked.

"I'm okay."

He must have noticed her despondent tone because his face warmed with rare sympathy. "Only the best table in the house for you," he said and walked them both to a cozy booth beside a stained-glass window. She sank into an upholstered leather bench with deep squabs. The single bench probably cost more than every table and chair in her ice cream parlor. Mr. Prescott handed them menus, then lit a votive candle in the center of the table before disappearing into the kitchen.

A waiter, dressed almost as elegantly as Mr. Prescott, arrived to ask what they'd like to drink. Liam offered to buy her the best bottle of wine in the place, wanting only a tall glass of milk for himself. She declined the wine and asked for water instead.

"Is your stomach bothering you?" she asked after the waiter left.

Liam shrugged. "It's pretty bad today," he admitted. "My sister has been nagging me to go back to that health clinic, but the big vote trying to oust me from the board is coming up, so I'll stick around until that's over."

The waiter soon returned with their drinks and asked if they'd like to order. Liam gave him an apologetic smile. "We haven't even looked at the menu yet. Can you give us a few minutes?"

"Of course, sir," he said before quietly retreating. How much did it cost to hire a man like that to wait tables? His shoes had been polished to a high shine, and the formal attire likely cost a pretty penny. The pushcart vendors would scream bloody murder if she asked them to dress so nicely. She let out a heavy breath. All her vendors were out of work now.

Liam must have heard the sigh because he reached across the table and took her hands in his. "Look, Maggie, I know this has been a rotten day for you, but I don't think I've ever seen a woman be as brave as you were this morning. You're one tough cookie. I knew it from the moment you sashayed into Morse's house. You're going to get through this, and I'll be right there beside you every step of the way."

Liam continued offering words of comfort, but the waiter was soon back and they still hadn't even glanced at the menu.

"Just bring us two of your best filet mignons," Liam said, handing back the menus.

"A half or full order, sir?"

"Full, for both of us," he said.

She snatched her menu back from the waiter and skimmed the prices. Filet mignon was shockingly expensive and a ridiculous waste on a day like today when she probably wouldn't taste a thing.

"I don't need a full order of anything," she corrected. "The roast beef looks fine." As she handed the menu back, Liam gave a knowing smile to the waiter.

"She's never been here before and doesn't understand the magnificence of a perfectly seared filet mignon at the best steakhouse in town. Two of your best, Sam."

A headache began to pound. Who did he think he was to order on her behalf? Besides, frittering away money was a sin, even if someone as rich as Liam was paying.

"Truly, roast beef is fine," she repeated for the waiter.

Clearly annoyed, Liam's eyes glinted. "Two filets mignons *and* a roast beef," he said tersely. The waiter quickly nodded and retreated into the kitchen.

"That defeats the purpose," she said, but Liam remained intransigent.

"Anything you don't eat I can take home for Frank."

Her jaw dropped. "You would feed filet mignon to a dog?"

"It wouldn't be the first time."

It wasn't too late to cancel the order. She slid off the bench to do so, but Liam grabbed her elbow. "For pity's sake, why won't you let me do something nice for you?"

Her patience boiled over and she jerked her arm away. "This is a horrible day, and you're making it worse by throwing away perfectly good money."

All she wanted was to be alone. If she stayed in this oppressively dim restaurant another minute, she might start crying. She couldn't look at Liam as she fled from the steakhouse.

27

*L*iam climbed into a carriage with Caleb and Frankie for the ride home. The scent of the filet mignon in the sack now made him feel physically ill. How could he have piled on Maggie during the worst day of her life? Caleb sat on the bench opposite him, watching as Liam rubbed Frankie's fur while staring out the window at the passing city.

"We'll make it up to her, won't we, boy?"

"How will we make it up to her?" Caleb asked.

Caleb always took things so literally, but Liam didn't have it in him to describe the complicated swirl of emotions twisting inside. All his life he assumed he would someday marry a woman he could protect and pamper, but oddly that wasn't really what he wanted. He wanted a woman who could stand beside him as his ship went down, who could stick up for the people on her street and fight against bullies no matter how strong and powerful they were.

"I need to be more sympathetic," he told Caleb. "Maggie had a rough day, and I made it worse by ordering her around."

"Is it because she's a red herring?"

Liam cocked his head at Caleb's strange comment. "Why would you say that?"

"I heard the men loading the equipment say that she is a red herring to lead you astray."

Liam leaned forward, staring at Caleb intently. "Where did you hear this? And who said it?"

"I heard it when I was with Frankie outside the storage room. One of the younger workers felt bad because he dented a mixing bowl, but the older man said it didn't matter. He said that Morse doesn't care what happens to the equipment because the ice cream lady is just a red herring to lead Blackstone astray."

A red herring was the classic diversionary trick to get a bloodhound off the real scent. Liam wasn't sure what Morse was driving at, but he'd been distracted by the troubles at Molinaro Ice Cream since the day Maggie came to him for help.

"Back up and tell me what you heard from the beginning."

Caleb's extraordinary quirk for remembering exactly what people said often caused trouble because he didn't seem to understand sarcasm or humor, but the message behind the words Caleb repeated was chilling. He asked the boy to repeat it three times, and Caleb never once deviated from the statement.

"Morse doesn't care what happens to the equipment because the ice cream lady is just a red herring to lead Blackstone astray. Morse can crush whomever he wants, and Liam Blackstone needs to learn that the hard way."

A rush of acid filled his gut as understanding dawned. Morse wasn't ruining Maggie's business because she'd embarrassed him. He was ruining her because it kept Liam off the real scent of something far more important.

Anger bloomed and spread. He punched the side of the carriage, injuring his hand, but he didn't care. Everything Maggie was enduring had been his fault. She'd been a pawn in the vicious battle between him and Morse, and she'd lost everything because of it.

No more! He needed Patrick's help to get to the bottom of this because, heaven help him, if he had to lay eyes on Morse right now, there was no telling what would happen.

He pounded against the panel at the top of the carriage, ordering an abrupt change of plans to go to Gwen's house. It was her birthday and Patrick would probably be home.

It took twenty minutes to get to Patrick's house. Liam vaulted from the carriage the moment the wheels stopped rolling, and he stormed inside without knocking.

"Where have you been?" Gwen screeched the moment he crossed the threshold. She came rushing down the front hall toward him like a banshee with her hair on fire. Something was wrong.

"Why?" he asked, lowering Frankie to the parquet floor and quickly straightening. "What's going on?"

"Patrick has been trying to find you all day. Charles Morse filed the paperwork to hold the vote today. The board is going to vote within the hour."

The news hit him like a slap. "How can that be?" he demanded. "The board isn't even in session."

"Morse has pulled a fast one to trick us," Gwen said. "He's got a quorum, and that's all he needs to hold the vote. The meeting is taking place at Rudolph Keppler's office. Patrick thinks that's because if they tried to have it at the main office, you might have caught wind of it."

And Rudolph Keppler was no friend of Liam's. He was one of the fusty board members who had always disapproved of Liam's appointment to the board. Keppler was also chairman of the New York Stock Exchange, and the fact that he opened his office for a vote to hound Liam off the board couldn't be good. While Liam was distracted by red herrings, Morse was closing in for the kill.

"There's more," Gwen said, and her tone stopped him in his tracks. She had a sickened look on her face as she handed him a large envelope. It was addressed to Patrick, engraved with Charles Morse's letterhead, and it had been opened.

"Do you know what this is?" he asked Gwen, who nodded stiffly.

"You'd better look because you need to know. There are

photographs in there . . . scandalous photographs. Liam, I'm so sorry."

Dread began to gather, but he forced himself to open the envelope. Inside was a series of photographs of a nude woman. Darla Kingston.

He dropped them as if he'd been burned. Darla had told him about these photographs long ago. She always feared that her youthful act of rebellion might come back to haunt her. Now it had happened.

"Morse said that if you show up to contest the motion, he'll release those photographs to the press."

And ruin Darla. First Maggie, now Darla. Liam's hands curled into fists as rage began building inside him. Darla didn't deserve this, but he couldn't sacrifice his seat on the board to save her. He stared at the envelope where he'd dropped it on the floor, his breath coming hard and fast.

"What are you going to do?" Gwen asked.

He had loved Darla, yet he couldn't submit to blackmail even though this would ruin her. He clutched the banister and closed his eyes. "Oh, Darla, I'm so sorry," he muttered.

He was going to destroy Charles Morse if it was the last thing he did. He shoved away from the banister and stormed down the hall. The carriage was here and would be the fastest way to get to the New York Stock Exchange.

Gwen's footsteps scurried after him. "First you need to change into a decent suit. One of Patrick's will fit you."

"Not enough time," he said, then rushed out the back door and across the yard toward the carriage house.

Gwen caught up to him and grabbed his arm. "Liam, the rules at the stock exchange are very strict. You must wear a suit and tie. They even issue fines to people who curse on the trading floor."

"I'll pay it," he fumed.

She jabbed a finger in his face. "Slow down. For once in your life, get a handle on your temper. Calm down and think rationally."

"Too late. I'm going to fight fire with fire."

Five minutes later, they were in the carriage and heading toward the New York Stock Exchange. Gwen insisted on coming with him, scolding him throughout the entire ride.

"Let Patrick do most of the talking," she warned. "At all costs, you need to act calm and civilized. Don't hand Charles Morse any ammunition to convince the board that you don't belong in their midst."

He swallowed back the bile rising in his throat and tried to concentrate on Gwen's words. She was right about the formality at the stock exchange. He'd been inside the Baroque monstrosity the day U.S. Steel became a publicly traded company. A newer stock exchange building was to open next year, but for now all business was conducted at the elaborately gilded old stock exchange building on Broad Street.

"He ruined Maggie," he said through clenched teeth. "He ground her business into the dirt. He squeezed everyone on Gadsen Street, all to keep me distracted."

"Don't dwell on it," Gwen said. She continued jabbering about rules and behaving with decorum, which went against every instinct in his body.

The carriage rolled up to the fancy building on Broad Street, and he darted out, too impatient to wait for Gwen. He stormed through the front doors and headed toward the trading floor, where a wall of noise rose from traders shouting orders as they crowded around the trading columns. The open space overhead soared two stories high, where a stained-glass ceiling cast the room in elegant splendor. He scanned the crowd of men, looking for Patrick.

Gwen drew up beside him. "Do you see him anywhere?"

He shook his head. "They're probably meeting upstairs." Liam nodded toward the staircase and galleries circling the two stories above. He sprang up the first flight, then strode down the hall. Many of the doors were open to reveal empty meeting rooms, while others were closed. Liam twisted the doorknob of the first closed room, interrupting a group of accountants poring over ticker tape.

"Sorry," he said and marched toward the next closed door. Once again, only a few accountants busy at work. He closed the door and went on to the next. Gwen caught up to him.

"You can't do this," she hissed. "Why can't you at least knock?"

He rapped on the next closed door but didn't wait for a response before opening it. A bunch of gray-haired business-men, hunched over maps and accounting ledgers, looked up at him in surprise.

"I'm looking for Charles Morse," he announced. "He's hold-ing a meeting with Rudolph Keppler and the board of U.S. Steel."

"Upstairs. Last door on the right," a man replied. Liam sent a terse nod of thanks, then dashed down the hallway and vaulted up the stairs. He found the meeting room and gave two hard raps before entering.

The conference room was full, a dozen men sitting around a large oval table. Cigar smoke clouded the air. Patrick was among them, looking appalled at Liam's disheveled appear-ance. Charles Morse stood in front of a blackboard filled with tiny cursive writing Liam couldn't make out. When he was this nervous, it was always hard to read, and cursive was almost impossible.

"Ah, the man of the hour," Morse said in an oily tone. "And dressed like you've been working in a barnyard. How typical."

Liam raised his chin. "Somehow I missed the invitation you sent to the rest of the board."

Patrick stood. "Thanks for joining us. Mr. Morse has been attempting to declare this quorum sufficient to vote on your removal from the board, and I've been presenting our case that this meeting is in violation of the company's operating agree-ment."

Rudolph Keppler stood next. He wore a starched collar so high that it almost met the waxed ends of his massive walrus mustache. "Yes, you should have been invited to the meeting," Mr. Keppler said. "We didn't fully understand Mr. Morse's intent when he summoned an emergency meeting. Mr. Morse? Would you care to repeat your concerns?"

"With pleasure." Acid soured Liam's gut as Morse slithered to the blackboard and began ticking off the offenses.

"While Theodore Blackstone was universally acknowledged as a great man, his son has failed to live up to his father's wise and humanitarian instincts. Liam has consistently betrayed the board of U.S. Steel by siding with the workers instead of the shareholders."

"As if they aren't part of the company," Liam interjected.

"Read the first paragraph of the duties outlined for board members," Morse said. "If you can, that is. Your reliance on your attorney to read your reports has always been an embarrassment to the board. Perhaps that's to be expected of a man who cavorts with smutty women who pose for lewd photographs—"

"Shut up, you putrid little worm," Liam spat. Patrick stepped forward, trying to block his view of Morse, but Liam sidestepped him to challenge Morse.

"Let's take this outside and settle things once and for all," he demanded. "Or are you too cowardly without your bodyguard to protect you?"

"Not here, Liam," Patrick warned.

"Don't stop him," Morse said smugly. "By all means, let Mr. Blackstone have his say so everyone can witness what sort of man he really is. You're pathetic, Liam. After tiring of your smutty nude model, you've taken up with a woman who can't pay her debts. Now that she's lost her factory, maybe your tawdry pushcart vendor can take up nude modeling too. Or perhaps walking the streets. I hear there's demand for Italian streetwalkers."

Liam rushed forward, hauled back, and punched Morse on the jaw. The force knocked Morse against the wall, and Liam was drawing back for another blow when Patrick grabbed him from behind, locking his arms down. Liam kicked at Morse but only succeeded in knocking over a chair.

"He's drawn blood!" Morse shrieked, touching the trickle at the corner of his mouth. "That man has assaulted me. He's a back-alley thug."

Liam twisted out of Patrick's restraint and charged again, but Morse fled from the room. A couple of board members moved to block Liam from following. They stood shoulder to shoulder in front of the door, but he barreled through them. Morse was already down the first staircase and heading for the second.

Liam braced his hands on the railing and vaulted over it, dropping onto the landing of the staircase below. The force of it knocked him to his knees, but he scrambled upright and grabbed the next railing to hop over it. He landed only a few yards behind Morse, who scurried toward the trading floor to hide among the hundreds of brokers crowding the room.

Liam plowed through the hordes of dark suits, homing in on Morse, who sought cover behind a trading column. Men scrambled out of Liam's way as he charged toward the column. He grabbed Morse by the back of his jacket and hurled him against the chairman's rostrum. The wooden pedestal toppled over as Morse smashed into it, then tried to crawl away.

"Get up and fight me like a man," he demanded. Most of the traders pulled back, opening a ring on the trading floor. Morse scrambled to his feet and tried to hide behind them. It didn't work. A few men called out admonishments to Liam, but most had no interest in stopping the fight.

Morse darted up the stairs to a staging area where the trading board displayed hundreds of placards. Liam followed and planted a foot in the middle of Morse's back, sending him sprawling into the placards and knocking him down. He grabbed Morse's collar, hauled him up, then punched him on the jaw again.

A pair of arms like steel bands locked around him. "Liam, stop!" Patrick ordered. "Stop it right now."

"That man is a barbarian," Morse panted as someone helped him to his feet. "He belongs in jail. Someone send for the police!"

Bile rose in Liam's throat, but he swallowed it back. The pain in his gut was savage. The leap over the banister had torn something in his stomach, and rolling waves of nausea rose from his belly.

"Let's get out of here," Patrick urged, and Liam nodded. Heat cascaded through his body. Every instinct in him longed to keep up the fight until Morse begged for mercy, but then another surge of nausea came.

"I need a bathroom," he told Patrick, then staggered down a hallway. His heart pounded, making him dizzy and overheated, but he made it to the washroom and into a stall just before he lost the battle. He leaned over the toilet and threw up.

There was blood in the vomit. He braced his hands on his knees, unable to stand upright. Shaking. On the verge of passing out.

This was it. This was what all the doctors had warned him about. A ripped open, bleeding ulcer. Sweat poured off his skin, making him hot and cold at the same time.

"We need to get you out of here," Patrick said. "The police have grounds to arrest you."

"Let's take him to the nearest hospital." It was Gwen's voice, and he swiveled to peer at her through the open stall door. His elegant sister looked out of place in the men's washroom, but she wasn't condemning him. If anything, there was compassion in her eyes.

Rudolph Keppler stormed into the washroom, his face a thundercloud. "You should know that Morse is out in the lobby, telling everyone within earshot that you assaulted him without provocation. He says you tried to kill him."

"If I wanted to kill him, he'd be dead," Liam spat out.

Patrick shoved him back into the stall and followed him in, slamming the door to block Keppler from seeing them. His face was taut with anger.

"Shut up," Patrick quietly warned. "Don't say another word. Morse is going to milk this for everything he can, including attempted murder, so don't mouth off again in front of a potential witness. In fact, don't say another word at all. Do you understand?"

Liam nodded.

Patrick opened the stall door, his face devoid of anger as he faced Mr. Keppler. "My client is ill and not speaking in his right mind. I'm taking Liam to the hospital."

"The police can still arrest him at the hospital," Mr. Keppler said.

"Not without a warrant signed by a judge," Patrick replied. "And judges don't work this late on a Friday afternoon."

Mr. Keppler stepped around Patrick to be in Liam's line of sight. "I will expect your letter of resignation on Fletcher's desk before the start of business Monday morning."

Keppler left the washroom, and the weight of what Liam had done penetrated the fog of pain. The only treatment for a torn ulcer was surgery. He could die from it. Another wave of dizziness struck, and he leaned against the stall so he wouldn't crash to the floor. The battle with Morse was about to get even uglier, but he'd be half dead in a hospital bed because he couldn't control his temper.

Regrets crashed down on him. So many things had been left unfinished. He should have been kinder to Gwen. And Maggie . . . they could have been great together. But he had wasted so much time, and now he might die . . .

He struggled to draw a breath without puking again. "Get me to the hospital," he gasped, "and please send for Maggie."

28

Maggie couldn't endure any more sympathetic looks from people offering comfort after losing her equipment. Dino and Julie went to Lieberman's Deli to commiserate, but the place was crammed with people wanting to talk about this morning and Maggie didn't have the heart for it. Her ability to put on a brave face had run out of steam and she needed to be alone.

The apartment was blessedly quiet and housework a welcome diversion. She swept and mopped the apartment's kitchen floor, then decided it needed waxing as well. Getting down on hands and knees was good for the soul. She attacked the floor with wide, circular motions, all the while wondering what happened to her equipment. Had it been dumped on a scrap heap? Was it being readied for the auction block?

She flipped the rag to a clean spot to continue buffing, working harder to bring out the shine, while still worrying about her factory equipment. Which was absurd. Her machinery wasn't alive and didn't have feelings, but that equipment had served her well and she cared about it.

She was halfway through buffing the kitchen floor when the tears started, but she refused to let them slow her down. Sniveling over lost equipment was ridiculous. No one had died. As soon as the newspaper articles started to appear, she could begin advocating for a better banking system that would prevent the sort of manipulation Morse carried out with such ruthless efficiency. She furiously swiped the tears away and kept on buffing.

A knock on the front door interrupted her thoughts. She didn't want to talk to anyone, but it might be important. So she stood, wiped her face, and blew her nose before answering.

"Caleb?" she said.

Caleb swept his cap off as he nodded to her. "Liam is in the hospital and wants you to come right away."

Liam was hale and hearty only a few hours ago at the Porterhouse, but she sagged against the doorframe as Caleb described a vicious fight that ended with a ruptured ulcer. She didn't know anything about the implications of a ruptured ulcer, but it must be bad if Liam agreed to go to a hospital. She followed Caleb down the staircase without question, to where a Blackstone carriage waited for them, sent specifically to speed her to the hospital.

Caleb filled her in on what triggered Liam's attack on Morse as the carriage rolled toward the hospital. Her dismay mounted with each new detail. Charles Morse hadn't driven her into ruin out of personal animosity; he'd done it because she was a pawn to keep Liam angry and distracted. When Liam put the pieces together, he had punched, kicked, and hurled Morse across the floor in front of hundreds of witnesses. Morse didn't land a single punch, and Liam was probably facing criminal charges.

"Are the police going to arrest him?"

Caleb shook his head. "I was at the hospital when the doctor explained the surgery to Patrick. He said it's a tough procedure, and Liam could be dead by this time tomorrow, so there was no need to involve the police yet."

Maggie blanched at the blunt language, but Caleb tended to report exactly what he heard, including the surgical procedure as the doctor had explained it to Patrick.

"The doctor said he'll slice open Liam's abdomen, snip out

the damaged bits of stomach wall, then close it up with a purse-string suture. Then he'll swipe up the neighboring viscera soiled by acidic leakage, close him up, and hope for the best."

Maggie didn't understand the procedure, and when she asked for clarification, Caleb simply repeated what he'd just said word for word. By the time the carriage arrived at the imposing granite edifice of the Washington Hospital, the clerk at the front desk informed Maggie that Liam was already undergoing surgery.

"The doctor says if he survives the surgery, he's got a fighting chance to recover," the nurse said.

"How many people die during the surgery?" she asked, her body starting to tremble.

The nurse's face softened. "Would you like to go to the chapel? I'm afraid it's going to be a challenging few hours for Mr. Blackstone."

Maggie knelt in the chapel until her knees were numb. She said the rosary and sent up prayers to Jesus and God the Father, to all the angels and saints, and then silently implored Liam to be strong, to hang on, to make it through the night.

In her heart, she knew that death was not the end. Even if Liam died on the operating table, it would only be the end of his body; his soul would go on to another place. Liam had been desperately trying to become a better man. He hadn't always succeeded, but he fully and humbly acknowledged his shortcomings, and God didn't expect perfection.

She closed with a prayer for herself as she left the chapel and headed toward the waiting room outside the surgical wing. It was a crowded room furnished mostly with wooden benches and a few ladder-back chairs. Ordinary people filled the benches, but it wasn't hard to spot the Blackstones. While regular people wore clothes of broadcloth cotton in shades of blue, brown, and black, a cluster of women in the far corner wore tailored gowns of peach, turquoise, and canary-yellow satin. The gentlemen wore stylish waistcoats with gold watch chains and carried dapper walking sticks.

She would have preferred to slip in unnoticed, but Patrick recognized her and gestured her over. It would be rude to ignore him, and he might know more about Liam. She trembled so badly that it was a struggle to speak calmly.

"Is there any news?" she asked, clenching her fists until the nails cut into her palms.

"He's still in surgery, which means he's still alive," Patrick said, his face drawn and sober. His hand closed around her elbow, and he led her to the imposing group of rich people. "Miss Molinaro, this is Liam's family."

How different they seemed. Maggie still had on the grubby blouse she'd worn while waxing the floor. It was damp with perspiration stains and splotched with dirty wash water. She covered the worst of the stains on her cuffs while Patrick introduced her to a willowy-looking woman in a floaty green silk dress.

"This is my wife, Gwen. She's Liam's younger sister. And this is his uncle Oscar, and Oscar's wife, Poppy."

Uncle Oscar looked as hard as a piece of flint, but his wife gleamed in a spectacular orchid walking suit that showed off her slim, athletic figure. Poppy's amethyst earrings matched her gown, and her golden hair was artfully upswept with a spray of violets nestled to the side.

Poppy scanned Maggie's sweat-stained cotton blouse before she spoke. "You *cannot* be the woman he sailed to Maine for."

How should Maggie respond to such rudeness? Before she could draw a breath, Patrick came to her defense.

"Indeed, she is," Patrick said. "Liam launched the *Black Rose* for her. He braved Charles Morse's wrath for her. And Maggie has made Liam happier than I've ever seen him, so sit down and shut up, Poppy."

There was some growling from Poppy's husband and a little more squabbling from the rest of them. Maggie walked a few yards away to find an unoccupied corner of a bench among normal people. She didn't belong with the fancy Blackstones, but didn't care because Liam was fighting for his life at this very moment and she had bigger things to worry about.

She stared at the pale-green tiles on the floor. The last time she'd seen Liam was at the Porterhouse during their stupid spat. Would it be the last time they ever spoke to each other? Liam was only trying to be kind by treating her to a steak dinner, and she should have let him. She'd give anything to turn the clock back and relive that interaction to make it a joyous meal with a man she loved. Liam's strong, courageous heart had been her biggest ally throughout this terrible summer, and now his health was failing all because of her.

Another hour passed. Poppy ordered sandwiches from the hospital cafeteria and complained when they arrived wrapped in paper instead of being presented properly on a plate. When Poppy criticized the hard benches and cramped waiting room, her husband promised a hefty donation to fund a private waiting room for well-heeled customers.

"And what sort of criteria shall you demand for access to your exclusive waiting room?" Patrick asked.

"I think we all know what sort of people would belong," Poppy said, taking a moment to cast a surreptitious glance at a shabby-looking family with six restless children. "We can have upholstered furniture and regular delivery of fresh flowers to help improve the air."

Maggie rolled her eyes and turned away to block out Poppy's ramblings about how much better the waiting experience would be without having to rub shoulders with people like her or the large Italian family in the corner. Poppy didn't use those words, but it was clearly what she meant.

She sighed. Patrick was the only person in the Blackstone clan gathered here whom she could relate to, though they hadn't gotten off to a good start. As if sensing her watching him, he caught her eye, then closed the distance between them. Her bench was already too crowded to make room for him, so he hunkered down before her.

"I understand your factory equipment was taken this morning," he said.

She nodded and looked away. It was quite possibly the last thing on earth she wished to discuss.

"Why didn't you accept Liam's help? Or mine, for that matter?"

Why indeed. Dino still didn't understand her plan to become a sacrificial lamb, and she could only pray that it would work. "I think the world needs to see what can happen when a powerful bank colludes with monopolies and trusts to ruin a successful business. I have friends in the press. They can help me get the word out." She wanted to add more, but the lump in her throat stopped her.

"A lawyer or a politician would be of more help," Patrick said. "Stirring up the masses will get you sympathy. Stirring up elected officials will get you action."

She sighed. "I don't know how to do that."

"I do."

She considered his words. Could she and Patrick work together even though they'd gotten off to a bumpy start? Liam swore that Patrick was smart and could be relied on. She listened as Patrick explained his experience writing petitions to get the attention of elected officials. He could expedite her case and set the ball in motion. What happened to Maggie, along with Antonio Gabelli's testimony about the Department of Docks, was powerful evidence of collusion that could result in changing things for the better.

It might work. Hope began to take root, but from the corner of her eye she noticed a man with his shirtsleeves rolled up entering the room. He rubbed his hands on a handkerchief spotted with blood.

Maggie rose on legs that barely had the strength to stand. "Do you have news of Liam Blackstone?"

"Yes, ma'am," he said. "I'm Dr. Petrosino. The patient has survived the surgery and is being moved to a recovery room."

She collapsed back onto the bench. The doctor kept talking.

He said the next twenty-four hours would be crucial. Hemorrhages, infections, or, most chillingly, "general system collapse" could all strike within the next few days. The Blackstones all crowded around the doctor, asking him questions, while Maggie crossed herself and started praying.

⁂

It was three days after Liam's surgery that Maggie was allowed in to see him. Thankfully none of the doctor's dire warnings of physical setbacks had come to pass. Liam roused twelve hours following surgery, and the nurses reported that his recovery was proving unexpectedly strong, but his mood was low. At this point, the doctor feared that the biggest danger to Liam's recovery was a broken spirit.

"Bouts of melancholy are not uncommon following a life-threatening event. Still, they can be dangerous," the doctor cautioned. "At this point the best remedy is having someone he knows and trusts to lean on. He asked for you."

Maggie nodded and followed the doctor down a maze of corridors to the private room where Liam had been ever since the surgery. She finally arrived at the narrow room with white tiles on the walls and a familiar antiseptic tinge in the air. She expected Liam to look bad, but the sight of him was still a shock. He lay still on the mattress supported by an iron bed frame, his skin as pale as parchment with purple smudges beneath his eyes. Bottles of medicine cluttered the bedside table, and there was a sick bowl on the mattress beside him. His shirt was open, revealing a large white bandage covering the upper portion of his abdomen. The knuckles on both his hands were scabbed and bruised, a stark reminder of the beating he delivered to Morse three days earlier.

He didn't look up when she entered, and she hovered in the doorway, uncertain if she should proceed.

"Liam?" she whispered. "Can I come in?"

He spoke in a voice that sounded as weak as tissue paper. "Can you leave us alone?" he asked Dr. Petrosino.

The doctor nodded but left Maggie with a stern warning not to help Liam sit or stand. He then departed, the door clicking shut behind him. Maggie sat in the chair next to Liam's bed.

"Does it hurt?" she asked with a tentative glance at the bandage.

"They've shot me up with enough morphine that I don't feel much pain," he said, but he looked wretched. "I've lost everything because of this," he said, holding up one of his bruised hands. "Morse is going to press charges. If I get convicted of a felony, I won't be able to serve on the board—"

"Shhh, darling. There's no need to worry about that right now."

"It's the *only* thing I've been worrying about."

Maggie tried to steer the conversation to something else. She joked about Poppy's plan for a rich person's private waiting room and reports of the Pittsburgh Pirates winning baseball season. Nothing worked. Liam was utterly consumed with the incident at the New York Stock Exchange.

"Morse will say that I tried to kill him. He'll bring charges, and he'll win. I'm such a miserable, stupid failure."

She cradled his hand on her lap, gently tracing his bruised fingers. "Everybody fails sometimes," she said as gently as she could. "It isn't a permanent condition. You're going to get over this. I'll do whatever it takes to help you get healthy again and save your seat on the board."

If possible, Liam seemed to wilt even further. "I don't think either one of those things can ever happen."

She looked away. He was probably right. They'd be lucky if they could keep him out of prison, but no matter what, she'd stand beside him. Maybe they would both end up ruined by Charles Morse. Even so, she'd stand in the breach alongside Liam to the very end.

A worn copy of the Bible lay amid the bottles of medicine on the bedside table. Liam had told her he'd been reading it, but the messages obviously hadn't sunk in yet.

"You need to stop thinking of yourself as a bad person,"

she said. "God loves you. He's been calling you. Ever since we met, I've watched how you've been trying to do the right thing, even though you weren't brought up that way. You're a good man, Liam."

He gave a short, bitter laugh. "No, I'm not." He tilted his face away to stare at the wall as if he couldn't bear for her to look at him. "When I went after Morse, I became Crocket Malone, the man who raised me with his fists. The man who smacked me in the face with an atlas because I was getting too big for my britches."

The anguish in his voice was hard to hear, and she tried to soothe him. "You're not perfect, and everyone can see that you're sorry."

"But that's just it," he said, turning his head on the pillow to look at her again. "Maggie, it felt good. I *liked* hurling Morse across the floor. I *liked* punching him and hearing him whimper like a baby. In those few minutes, everything good and decent in me was stripped away and I was back to being Crocket Malone's son. No matter how hard I try to make myself into something better, I'm still just a thug from the streets."

Maggie got off the chair and knelt at his bedside, gently cradling his hand but raising her voice to match his. "Don't you know that I love you, flaws and all? I love that you're trying to be a better man. Sometimes you will stumble, but you always pick yourself up and try again, and that's all God asks of you. Don't lose heart. Don't give up."

He pulled his hand away and shielded his face with it. "Just stop, Maggie. All I want to do is get out of town and start over someplace else. Somewhere people won't know me as the miserable wreck of a man I am, a man who ruins everything he touches."

"Quit dwelling on your failures," she said. "I don't know what force is urging you to give up, but I don't think it's a godly one. Stop wallowing in your failures and try searching for what God is calling you to do."

He had no answer. He lay on the mattress, his breathing

ragged as he continued shielding his face from her. Had anything she said gotten through to him? Maybe she pushed him too hard when he wasn't ready to hear it. Sometimes a person could get kicked in the teeth only so many times before he was ready to surrender, but Liam would regret it for the rest of his life if he did.

That meant it was time to come alongside Liam and help him stand up to fight another day.

Maggie got permission from the hospital staff to sleep in the nurses' dormitory so she could be back at Liam's side at the crack of dawn and stay with him until he closed his eyes at night. His scary uncle Oscar probably had something to do with the hospital's leniency regarding her around-the-clock access to a patient.

Maggie didn't have much experience with sick people, but she learned quickly. She held the straw as Liam drank thin gruel and held a bowl when he threw up. She pretended not to notice his groans while helping him out of soiled shirts and into clean ones. She gave Liam sponge baths, helped him brush his teeth, and read to him since he wasn't allowed to sit up yet.

For six days, it felt as if they were the only two people in the world. Maggie read Liam passages from the Bible and short adventure stories from the hospital reading room. For a while he'd pay full attention, but inevitably he disengaged when a haunting expression of despair came over him. When she asked what he was thinking about, he always said the same thing: "The vote."

There was no need to elaborate. Day by day, Liam was becoming more convinced that he was a failure and didn't belong on the board. The vote was ten days away, but instead of rallying, he seemed to get a little weaker with each passing day.

That stopped one morning when she arrived to see the tension on his face gone and a spark of liveliness back in his eyes.

"I've made my decision," he said. "I'm going to lean on

Uncle Oscar to get Patrick appointed in my place. Oscar would rather have my grandfather, but that's no good. Frederick will side with the shareholders over the workers every time. Patrick won't. I'm done with U.S. Steel and ready to go back to being an ordinary welder. The shipyards are always looking for skilled men."

It wasn't what Maggie hoped for Liam, but she couldn't deny that as soon as he became resigned to being ousted from the board, he began to rally. He smiled more. He paid attention when she read to him. Soon he was well enough to sit up in bed. Each day she silently cheered as he got a little stronger. Eventually he was ready to stand and transfer into a wheelchair. Maggie pushed the chair as she led him on an impromptu tour of the hospital. Liam still wasn't well enough to get properly dressed, but it didn't matter. He buttoned his shirt, covered his bare legs with a blanket, and wore a spiffy bowler hat that he lifted to the ladies at the nursing station and the cafeteria counter. He was slowly regaining his humor and his spirit.

Once again, Liam flirted and joked and laughed. He pestered her for deliveries of ice cream, which the doctor agreed could be added to his diet now. As Liam emerged from beneath the smothering blanket of dejection, she started catching glimpses of the man with whom she fell in love.

But late in the evenings, as she helped him settle in for the night, his gaze would inevitably stray toward the window and regret haunted his face. Though she never spoke of it, Maggie feared that if Liam quit the board of U.S. Steel without a fight, he would regret his decision for the rest of his life.

Liam didn't want Maggie in his sickroom when he confronted Patrick about his plan to swap places with him on the board. She tried to hide it, but he knew she was disappointed in him. He was disappointed too, yet he couldn't win the vote and it was best to concede defeat now rather than endure the humiliation in the boardroom.

It had been nine days since his surgery, and he was well enough to sit in a wheelchair when Patrick and Gwen arrived at his hospital room. Aside from the bed, there was a single metal chair for visitors and a glass cabinet filled with medicines and spine-chilling medical equipment. Gwen took the metal chair while Patrick sat on the rumpled hospital bed.

Liam was proud of his ability to meet with them while sitting in a wheelchair instead of lying in bed like an invalid. A tug of pain pulled in his abdomen as he reached out to shake Patrick's hand, but the doctor said that was to be expected for a few more weeks.

Liam got down to business quickly. He told Patrick of his decision to resign from the board, which didn't go over very well.

"You're giving up too easily," Patrick cautioned. "If we play our cards right, you can save your seat. I ignored Keppler's demand for your resignation and notified the board of your intention to fight for your seat on September thirtieth."

Gwen perched on the chair, nodding in agreement with Patrick. Light from the window cast her in a sunny glow that made her look feminine and angelic. They were brother and sister but couldn't be more different.

"I'm a goner," Liam said. "We've only got a week left before the vote. We should focus on getting you appointed in my place rather than fight a losing battle to save my seat." Resigning was the sort of honorable, selfless act that would have made his father proud of him, but Patrick still wasn't convinced.

"Quitting is the easy way out," Patrick said. "You've worked too hard and climbed too high to be happy as an observer in the steel industry."

"I'm a welder. It's the only job I'm fully competent to do. I was in over my head from the day I stepped onto the board of U.S. Steel, and that hasn't changed."

Gwen gazed at him with a little smile hovering on her mouth. "I remember when you first came to New York and learned you had a chance to be appointed to the board. You fought for it like a gladiator. It was inspiring, like watching David gear up to

265

battle Goliath. No one thought you could do it, but you studied and planned and fought until you dragged yourself across the finish line and won that seat."

It was exhausting then, and it was killing him now. Being a failure made it hard to even draw a breath to reply to Gwen. "I've accomplished a few things on the board, but there was so much more I should have done. Every day I worry about how much more I could have done."

"Oh, Liam," Gwen said in an aching voice, "you sound just like our father. He used to say the *exact same thing*. He worried and fretted about setbacks as he fought to build the college. He lost more battles than he won and always regretted that he couldn't do more. It is in the nature of good men to think such things." A sheen of tears appeared in her eyes. "If I ever doubted you are Theodore Blackstone's son, you just put it to rest."

Liam met her eyes, uncertain but intrigued. It was hard to believe that a man of Theodore Blackstone's accomplishments ever wrestled with doubt or failure. The ache of never being reunited with his real father bloomed once again.

"I wish I could have known him," he choked out.

"He lives in you," Gwen said. "You have the grit he sometimes lacked, but the same fire to fight for a worthy cause. I see him a little more clearly in you every day."

Could it be true? Could Liam's harsh early years have somehow been part of God's plan to lead him to this spot all along? He marveled at the faint sensation of bonding with the father he'd never known. Theodore was a kind and humble man who always led with integrity, even if he lost more battles than he won.

If Liam kept up the fight for his seat, he was probably going to lose, but he'd survived worse. The vote was in one week. He owed it to his father to carry out the Blackstone legacy with dignity and honor. There was no shame in losing a battle, but running away from one was a regret he'd carry forever. If Theodore had the strength to keep fighting battles after a string of losses, so could Liam. A smile curved his lips. Like father, like son?

"Okay, I'll fight," Liam said, and Gwen beamed at him.

He was probably going to lose the vote, but he wouldn't go down easily, and before this was all over, he'd see Charles Morse voted off the board.

29

After ten days in the hospital, Liam rode in the back of a hospital ambulance to his uncle's mansion. It was the best place to hide out until the vote because it was more like a fortress than a house, and the police would have a hard time getting to him here. He immediately began meeting with Patrick and Uncle Oscar to overcome his biggest liability in the coming vote: a looming criminal conviction.

The trip home had been tiring, and Liam remained in bed, propped up on a mound of pillows and wearing only a nightshirt, while the other two men were formally dressed for a day at the office. Uncle Oscar sat in a throne-like chair in the corner of the room, smoking a cigar and looking mildly sinister while Patrick paced the floor.

"Morse is demanding a charge of attempted murder," Patrick said. "That alone is going to make it impossible for both men to sit on the board, and Morse has all the momentum in his favor."

"So?" Oscar asked. "Liam hasn't been charged with anything yet, so he needs to waltz into the board meeting asserting his innocence. He should display the justifiable rage of a man wrongly accused."

"Except that half the board witnessed the assault," Patrick pointed out.

Uncle Oscar shrugged. "That same half also saw Morse hurl slurs and deliberately provoke Liam's temper. What man wouldn't have defended the woman in his life?"

Oscar certainly had a track record of defending Poppy. When Morse slipped and insulted Poppy earlier this summer, Oscar retaliated by cutting Morse out of all Blackstone alliances.

"What Liam did was still a crime," Patrick said. "He'll be charged soon, and Morse has a track record of bribing judges and court officials, so we can't risk this going to a trial. I can help Liam to plea-bargain down to a lesser charge. So long as he escapes a felony conviction, he can still sit on the board."

Oscar shook his head. "I say he should gamble on a jury trial. People hate Morse and will applaud Liam for attacking him."

A knock on the door interrupted the conversation and a footman entered. "Begging your pardon, but there is a woman here to see the younger Mr. Blackstone. She gave her name as Mrs. Clemence Morse."

The name echoed in the room like a shot. This was the mysterious Mrs. Morse whose marriage to Charles Morse was collapsing after less than a year. Liam struggled to rise, but Patrick rushed to his side.

"This is the *last* thing you need," he said. "The doctor ordered bed rest and avoiding stress. That woman is here to disturb both."

"But sometimes the enemy of your enemy will prove to be a friend," Oscar said. Apparently he had heard the rumors of the disastrous Morse marriage as well.

"Have you ever met her?" Liam asked.

Oscar blew out a stream of cigar smoke. "No, but according to my wife, Clemence ran a boardinghouse where Charles once lived. They carried on a tawdry affair for ages before finally getting married last year."

And her husband was already cheating on her. Liam had seen proof of that the morning he barged into Morse's office to find the lovely Katherine Gelshenen on his lap. Perhaps Oscar was right and it might be useful to meet the enemy of his enemy.

"Show her in," he said, overruling Patrick. Liam was in no condition to get dressed to receive visitors downstairs, but he wanted to meet the enigmatic Mrs. Morse. Patrick warned him not to apologize or discuss the fight lest he hand Mrs. Morse damaging information that could be used against him in a trial. He only stopped the warnings when the butler led Mrs. Morse into the room.

She was a gaunt woman with chestnut hair and fine gray eyes, but mostly Liam noticed her jewels. A string of huge emeralds circled her neck and matched her gown of forest-green silk. Her boxy valise was covered in matching silk.

Despite her formidable appearance, she seemed hesitant as she stepped into the room, clutching the valise before her like a shield. "Mr. Blackstone?"

Liam nodded. "Yes, ma'am. How's your husband?"

The corners of her mouth turned down. "He's doing fine as far as I can tell, but he has been claiming lingering injuries from the incident at the stock exchange." She fidgeted with the handle of the valise, glancing around the room in discomfort. Liam fought the compulsion to apologize. She deserved an apology, but he would follow Patrick's advice and keep his mouth shut.

"May I have a seat?" Mrs. Morse asked.

"Yes, of course." Liam gestured to the pair of delicate chairs on either side of a tea table. Silk rustled as she lowered herself. Ever the gentleman, Patrick introduced himself, then offered to send for refreshment, which she accepted. Oscar kept smoking his cigar as he silently watched from the corner.

Mrs. Morse opened her valise and withdrew a stack of papers as she glanced at Patrick. "As Liam's attorney, I thought you'd like to see the list of judges my husband is in the process of bribing."

Liam blanched, but Patrick remained calm. "What is he bribing judges for?"

"At the moment, he is trying to annul our marriage," Mrs. Morse said. "If that fails, he will attempt to convict me of bigamy and see me imprisoned. So you can understand why I am interested in undermining his efforts. You can be sure Charlie will try to get his money's worth by steering Liam's assault case to one of these judges."

Mrs. Morse went on to explain the rocky history of her marriage. She and Charles had a long-term relationship when he lived in the boardinghouse she operated. They would have married had she been free, but her youthful marriage to a man who abandoned her made that impossible. It took years to track down her errant husband in Atlanta. A series of lawyers had been found to offer her husband a hefty settlement to sign off on a divorce, which occurred early last year. Charles and Clemence married, but he began cheating on her almost immediately.

"He is besotted with a woman named Katherine Gelshenen," Mrs. Morse said. "They want to get married, and Charlie has been treating me disgracefully. I was willing to grant him a divorce, but Katherine is a devout Catholic. Only an annulment will do for her, and the only grounds Charlie has for an annulment is to accuse me of bigamy." Her smile was thin, and she looked frightened. "It appears the official court records of my divorce have mysteriously vanished. My first husband is now claiming he never divorced me. I suspect he's taken another bribe from Charlie, this time to claim we are still married."

Her voice had begun to shake, and she dove back into the valise, hauling out more papers. "While Charlie has been off with his mistress, I've been monitoring his mail. These are copies of the officials at the Department of Docks he bribed to attain his monopoly of ice. And this one is from a congressman he bribed for favorable banking regulations. This is the receipt from Tiffany's for a diamond-and-ruby choker he bought for Katherine."

She balled up the receipt and threw it across the room. "All of those documents can be verified. I've been a good wife to Charlie. The servants can testify to that. I've done nothing to deserve this sort of treatment, but if I don't fight back, he is going to see me convicted of bigamy, which is a felony . . . and I will go to jail, all so he can marry *that woman*."

She fastened the straps of the valise and stood. She drew a steadying breath, and when she spoke again, her voice was calm. "Do you have any questions?"

Liam was so stunned by this reversal of fortune that he could barely draw a breath, but Uncle Oscar was a model of deportment as he stood to address Mrs. Morse. "If we bring this information into the light of day, may we say where it originated?"

"Of course," she said. "All of it is proof of my innocence. When you have finished perusing the documents, you may return them to the Morse summer home in the Adirondacks, where I am retreating for a well-deserved vacation. Good day, gentlemen."

Liam was speechless as she left the room, the rustle of silk fading into the distance. He'd always known Morse was a greedy scoundrel, but he never expected his villainy could stoop this low.

Oscar clapped his hands together and let out a shout of triumph. "This is our key to victory! It's proof of how deep Morse's corruption runs. If we publicize this scandal, we won't be discussing how to keep Liam out of prison; we'll be escorting Morse off the board of directors and into a jail cell of his own."

"Is it true?" he asked Patrick. "Could this sort of bribery land Morse in prison?"

Patrick nodded. "The only question would be how many years he would serve." Patrick continued paging through the documents left by Mrs. Morse. "It looks as though her first husband moved around a lot, so Morse had to bribe court officials in Atlanta, San Francisco, and here in New York. That makes this a federal offense. We're not talking about a sentence of a few years—Morse is looking at decades in prison."

Oscar leaned heavily on his cane as he limped across the room, his face radiant with excitement. "Those papers aren't just a smoking gun, they're a *smoking arsenal*. How ironic that it won't be his nefarious banking practices that bring Morse down, but a simple case of lust."

Liam tried to follow the legal discussion as Oscar and Patrick batted around terms like collusion, suborning witnesses, and criminal conversation, and yet something didn't feel right. He couldn't be proud of bringing down Morse because of this. Once, he would have gleefully led the charge to destroy Morse with whatever ammunition he could find. Not anymore.

"If Morse gets convicted of trying to frame his wife for bigamy, will it help Maggie and the other people hurt by the ice trust?"

Oscar scoffed. "No, but we've got bigger concerns than worrying about an ice cream parlor."

"What about the hospitals and orphanages and morgues that didn't get ice?" Liam asked. "The breweries and the canneries, and yes . . . the ice cream parlors? I don't want to bring Charles Morse down because of his lust. I want the business laws changed to protect those people."

"Forget the laws," Oscar said. "Once we see Morse in chains, we can break up his trusts and buy his companies at a rock bottom price."

"And the laws won't change?" Liam asked.

"The laws won't change," Patrick confirmed.

Liam sagged against the pillow. His father wouldn't have used those papers. They had a stink on them, and Theodore Blackstone would have concentrated his efforts on the campaign to reform the banking and corporate monopoly laws. It was the only way to ensure people like Maggie wouldn't be punished for failing to sign a contract with a corrupt trust or lose her equipment because the banks colluded against her. Liam could write a check and put the Molinaro Ice Cream Company back in business tomorrow, but it wouldn't change the laws.

"I think we need to stay the course," he said quietly. "I want Charles Morse to be the public face of the ice trust so people can see what a rotten business it is. Getting him thrown in jail for his sleazy personal behavior will rob us of the momentum to change the laws."

Oscar was not moved. "While you wait years for the laws to be changed, are you willing to let Morse usurp your position on the board? Without those papers, they'll never know the depth of Morse's corruption. They'll be concentrating on how you chased the man all over the New York Stock Exchange to give him a good drubbing. You will be the villain, not Morse."

"He's right," Patrick said. "Those papers will sweep Morse off the board of directors in a heartbeat."

But there were other considerations. If the fight got ugly, Morse might go after Maggie again. Or release the photographs of Darla. Those photographs hadn't been released yet and were still a weapon Morse had on his side. It was hard to win an honorable battle with an opponent who was prepared to play dirty, but Liam wouldn't back down now.

30

Maggie once thought she would never see a more grandiose building than the home belonging to Charles Morse. That was before she saw the gilded splendor of the Blackstone mansion. After living for two weeks in the spartan nurses' dormitory at the hospital, she moved to the Blackstone mansion to continue assisting Liam with his recovery.

Her first moments at the Blackstone mansion were embarrassing. She'd been awestruck and a little intimidated by the white granite fortress that looked like a castle from the outside and was even more impressive on the inside. A bright atrium painted in white and trimmed in gold leaf rendered her speechless. She had to crane her neck to look up and admire the stained-glass skylight three stories overhead.

An old man in formal black tails and white gloves beckoned her to step farther into the foyer. "I hope your journey was comfortable, ma'am."

Was this Liam's grandfather, the famed Frederick Blackstone? She didn't know how to greet a man like him and dipped into a clumsy curtsy. "I'm Maggie Molinaro," she said. "I came to see Liam, sir."

"Of course. Would you like a chance to freshen up?"

Never had she felt more out of place. Freshening up wouldn't

275

do much to improve her plain cotton walking suit or straw boater hat. "I'd really just like to see Liam. Would that be too much trouble, sir?"

The older man's face softened as he leaned in close. "I'm the butler," he whispered into her ear before straightening back into his regal demeanor. "Of course not, ma'am. The young Mr. Blackstone will be pleased to see you."

That was two days ago. Since then, she'd only seen Liam in the afternoons since he spent the morning and evenings holed up with Patrick, strategizing how to win the vote and overcome the pending criminal charges against him. That left Maggie in the unnerving company of Poppy Blackstone, the lady of the manor.

Poppy was a voracious snob who was only a year older than Maggie, but who seemed so much more sophisticated as she ruled over a household staff of eighteen, including a servant whose chief duty was to drive to the bank each morning and evening to retrieve Poppy's jewelry for the day. What kind of woman was so rich that she needed an actual bank vault to safeguard her jewels?

Poppy fancied herself an expert on style and had been relentlessly badgering Maggie to modernize the Molinaro Ice Cream designs. The conversation happened in the courtyard garden where Poppy was tagging the roses that would be clipped for the dinner table later in the afternoon. Poppy carried the basket of tags and directed where she wanted Maggie to tie them to a bloom.

"I've seen those blue-and-white-striped umbrellas on your pushcarts," Poppy said with a wrinkle in her nose. "They are hopelessly outdated."

The blue-and-white stripes had been with them all the way back to their pushcart days. They used them for the awning over their shop window, the umbrellas on the pushcarts, and the spiffy uniforms their employees wore.

"We like pinstripes," Maggie said, trying not to sound defensive as she tied a tag on another rose stem.

"There's nothing wrong with pinstripes, but they're very nineteenth century," Poppy said.

Considering it was only two years into the new century, Maggie didn't see that as a problem, but it wasn't worth arguing over. At this very moment Molinaro Ice Cream teetered on the edge of ruin. It would be another few weeks before Patrick would submit his petition to the government to prohibit collusion between banks and corporations like the ice trust, so it was impossible to know if she could ever expect compensation.

Poppy continued identifying roses while babbling about how pinstripes were lowbrow, but Maggie didn't care because Liam had suddenly arrived. He was in a wheelchair, but for the first time in weeks he was fully dressed and shaved.

"You're out of bed," she enthused as a servant pushed his wheelchair toward the rose garden.

"Yeah, I wanted to ask you something. Can you spare her, Pops?"

Poppy threw down her basket of tags. "You know I hate it when you call me Pops."

Liam dipped his head in acknowledgment. "My apologies, Mrs. Blackstone. I need to steal Maggie for a while. It's important."

With Poppy mollified, Maggie grasped the handles of his wheelchair to roll him across the garden path. Liam seemed ill at ease and upset about something. She followed his terse directions as he pointed to the carriage house behind the mansion, then parked his chair beside a bench beneath a poplar tree.

"What's going on?" she asked once she was seated and at eye level with him. He shifted, looking even more uncomfortable.

"You remember how I once had a fling with a lady named Darla?"

It sounded like it had been far more than a fling. "I remember."

"Morse is getting ready to turn his firepower on her if I won't resign from the board. He's got photographs." Liam cleared his throat and met her gaze. "Nude pictures."

Maggie choked, coughed a little, then listened while Liam

explained Darla's youthful folly posing for a sculptor and how she always feared the photographs might someday resurface. That day was here.

"I got another note from Morse this morning. He said that if I don't submit my resignation before the vote on September thirtieth, he's going to release the pictures to the press on the first day of October."

Maggie gasped. Everyone made youthful mistakes, but few people had to endure witnessing them printed and circulated for the whole world to see.

"Are you going to resign?" she asked, holding her breath.

"I can't," Liam said. "But I don't want this to catch her by surprise. I need to warn her about what's happening, and I'd like you to come with me."

She blinked. "That's not necessary. I trust you."

"You and I are a team now, and I don't know how Darla's going to take it. I'd feel better if you were there."

How could she deny him with an appeal like that? The fact that Liam wanted her support was flattering, even though she'd rather be on the other side of the universe than witness the awkward encounter with his old flame. "Then of course I'll go," she said, hoping her reluctance didn't show.

It took a while for the coach driver to strap Liam's wheelchair onto the back of the carriage, and Liam had to move gingerly to climb inside, but soon they were on their way to West 57th Street. Darla's studio was on the sixth floor of a redbrick building, and thankfully there was an elevator.

What sort of person was this woman who once held Liam's heart? Maggie took a fortifying breath as they arrived at the sixth floor, which was filled with artists' studios. The scent of oil paint and turpentine tinged the air. Maggie followed Liam's direction as she wheeled him to a room at the end of the hall. The door was wide open.

Light flooded the spacious studio, and a redheaded woman with a profusion of corkscrew curls wore a smock covered in plaster dust.

"Liam!" Darla gasped, dropping a chisel with a clatter onto the hardwood floor. She hurried to his wheelchair. "Did you hurt yourself?"

Liam flashed a smile and gave a single shake of his head. "Nah, just the old problem."

Darla nodded in sympathy. How easily these two communicated, but why should that be a surprise? They once were in love.

"Darla, this is my friend Maggie Molinaro," Liam said as he tugged her forward. "Molinaro Ice Cream, you know? That's Maggie's company."

Darla's expression was cool but polite as she welcomed them both into the studio. What a big, glorious mess it was, filled with easels, tables, and half-formed figures wrestling to emerge from stone. Liam gestured to a life-sized sculpture of a woman with a serene expression, her figure swathed in robes.

"That's pretty," Liam said, his expression reverent as he admired the sculpture. Darla straightened in pride.

"She's a Madonna I was commissioned to sculpt for the garden outside the new St. Jude's Foundling Home," Darla said. "They wanted me to show her holding a baby, but instead I'll have her holding a basin to collect rainwater for the birds. I like the idea of giving city children the chance to admire something of nature."

Liam said a few more words of praise, but the conversation quickly stumbled to an awkward pause. Liam shifted in discomfort, regret already starting to shadow his expression while Darla looked at them both with confusion.

Darla spoke first. "Why did you come?"

Liam sighed. "Well, there's no easy way to talk about this, so I'll just spit it out," he finally said. "You remember those pictures you did in the buff for that Frenchie?"

Darla's eyes widened a fraction, but she maintained flawless poise and didn't break eye contact with Liam. "It's not something I'm likely to forget."

"Yeah, well, Charles Morse got his hands on those pictures,"

Liam said. "He's threatening to release them if I don't leave the board of U.S. Steel."

For the first time, Darla was knocked off-kilter. She flinched and turned away, hiding her face. Several moments passed as she paced in the studio. She drifted to the half-finished sculpture of the Madonna and placed a hand on the statue's shoulder. She was trembling.

"Well," she said shakily, "the adage about not being able to outrun your past seems to be coming into play. Quite tragically, as it seems. I can't imagine the children's home will want me or my sculpture anywhere near them if those pictures get out."

"Morse is a real slime," Liam said. "He'll probably make good on his threat unless I resign."

A range of emotions flashed across Darla's face. Surprise, anger, and then a spark of fighting spirit. Her spine straightened, and she looked straight at Liam.

"Don't you dare resign," she said. "Not on my behalf. I'll survive, but I refuse to let him ruin you. The list of people that man has ruined is longer than my arm. I'll run those photographs up a flagpole before I let Charles Morse kick you off the board."

Liam rocked back in his chair almost as if he'd been struck. He looked at her with pure admiration in his expression. "You're a fine woman, Darla Kingston."

A sheen of tears filled her brown eyes. "Right back at you, Liam."

It was exquisitely uncomfortable for Maggie. What was she supposed to say or do as the magnetism flared to life between these two? Liam finally broke the tension, saying he needed to get back home to meet with Patrick about the coming vote. Darla walked them to the elevator and pulled a lever to summon the car. Then Darla put her hand on Liam's shoulder.

"Liam, I want you to know . . . I'm sorry about the things you overheard me say that day at the museum. I didn't mean them. Someday when I'm old and gray, I think that losing you will be the biggest regret of my life."

Maggie suspected that if Liam hadn't already been sitting down, he'd have been knocked off his feet by the openhearted sadness in Darla's voice. But all he did was swallow hard, nod his head, and start wheeling himself into the elevator without looking back.

A tangle of emotions plagued Maggie as they rode the elevator down in silence. The way Liam had gazed at Darla with a blend of affection and admiration had scorched. Maggie escaped from the elevator the instant the attendant cranked the doors open. All she wanted was to flee outside and disappear into the crowd of pedestrians, but she needed to push Liam's wheelchair through the lobby, out the door, and around the corner to the carriage waiting for them in the alley.

Mercifully, the coach driver was at the ready and could take over getting Liam aboard.

"I think I'll take a streetcar home," she said, glancing around the bustling intersection. There had to be a streetcar stop nearby somewhere. She started heading toward the closest intersection.

"Wait!" Liam called out, the panic in his voice making her pause.

"Yes?"

"Aren't you coming with me? If there's somewhere you need to go, I'll take you wherever you want."

She managed a smile as though the past fifteen minutes hadn't been awful. "No, I'd like a little fresh air. I'll be fine." Why should he look so wounded? She was the one who had to patiently stand by like a potted plant while he wallowed in the company of his first love.

"Why are you mad?" he asked, rolling the wheels of his chair to draw closer.

"Stop," she said in a rush. "Don't hurt yourself."

"Well, I can't let you walk away. Tell me what's wrong."

She glanced at the coachman, who pretended to be looking

281

at the wall of the apartment building next door, but surely he heard every word of this mortifying conversation. Running away was foolish, and Liam probably would try to chase her down. She wished Darla hadn't been so admirable. Maybe if Darla had been weak or cowardly, Maggie wouldn't feel so heartsick right now.

She looked at Liam and told the truth. "I wish she had been frumpy and mean."

That caused a spurt of laughter from Liam, whose gaze warmed in sympathy. "You don't have anything to fear from Darla. She was always beautiful and fun, but she let me down. We collapsed at our first real test. You and I have been tested since the beginning. Maggie, you're the woman I want beside me in any storm. Rain or shine. For better or for worse. In sickness or in health . . . it's *you*, Maggie."

Her heart started pounding at his moving words. The coach driver wasn't even pretending to ignore them anymore, and she ought to be embarrassed, but she wasn't. She beamed at Liam as he reached out for her hand.

"You're Miss Maggie of Gadsen Street," he teased. "Don't you know how proud I am of you? You fought hard for everything you've got. With class and grit and steel. No matter what happens with Charles Morse, you and I are going to get through this together, Maggie."

He spoke with such confidence that it was easy to believe him, even though Morse was likely to crush them both in the coming days.

"The list of people that man has ruined is longer than my arm," Darla had said, and Maggie knew what it was like to be on that list. So did Antonio Gabelli and the rest of his family.

She paused, myriad ideas flitting through her mind. Maybe they could capitalize on that metaphorical list of people. Patrick was going to submit a petition to the state government to make the ice trust collusion illegal, but it would be more effective if it was signed by the actual people and businesses who'd been damaged by the ice trust.

"Liam," she said, "what if you went into next week's vote with a formal declaration from the people who have been victimized by Charles Morse? It would show the board the real Charles Morse and why you snapped and attacked him. It wouldn't be to justify what you did, but it would force the board to see you as a man with a beating heart who won't quietly tolerate corruption, and that's worth something." .

Based on his reaction, Liam liked what he was hearing, so she continued outlining her idea. "Patrick is already working on something about all the shady business tricks Morse used in creating the ice trust. Let's round up a bunch of his victims to testify how he stomped on them. Patrick plans on using it to force the attorney general to act, and those names will give power to it."

It was going to take the combined efforts of a lot of people to pull off this plan, and they only had five more days before the vote.

<hr>

The irony of organizing a workingmen's revolt from the splendor of a robber baron's mansion was not lost on Maggie. She spent the week gathering signatures from tradesmen and small business owners who had been swindled, bullied, or extorted by Charles Morse during his creation and implementation of the ice trust. People from all over Manhattan arrived in a steady stream at the Blackstone mansion to put their names on the document Patrick had written.

It took courage to risk the wrath of the city's most vengeful tycoon by signing the declaration. Maggie and Antonio Gabelli were the first two signatories, but she soon had forty-three additional people endorsing the statement. Liam and Patrick were busy preparing for tomorrow's vote, leaving Maggie to collect the signatures.

She had not anticipated how awkward the job would be while sitting alongside Poppy Blackstone, who didn't appreciate having tradesmen tromping through her house. She allowed them no farther than the breakfast room, located only a few yards into the house.

Poppy and Maggie sat at the delicate table with the forms spread out for signing. The oval room featured white walls, white table linens, and a white tile floor. The only hint of color in the stark room was the lavishly painted pastel ceiling overhead. The artist had painted a pale-blue sky with wispy clouds, all framed by plump cherubs dribbling rose petals.

"It's called *trompe l'oeil*," Poppy explained to Captain Daniel Solis, an ice barge operator who had just signed the document and stared at the ceiling with ill-concealed amusement. "It is designed to fool the eye into thinking you are looking at the real thing."

Captain Solis had his thumbs tucked into his suspenders and his spine arched backward to gape at the cherubs. "They're fat little porkers," he said. "It must be hard for them to float on air when they're so tubby."

Poppy's smile was tight as she gestured to the table. "Would you care to take a raspberry scone as you leave?"

It was Poppy's technique for prompting people to finish their business and get out. So far, Poppy had ushered out dozens of restaurant owners, packinghouse operators, three fishmongers, and five morticians with the same offer of a raspberry scone and a gesture toward the door.

Mr. Solis didn't get the message. "How many signatures do you think we can drum up for this thing?" he asked Maggie while munching on a second scone. Captain Solis didn't have the cleanest of fingernails, but his bravery standing up to the Department of Docks and Charles Morse by signing the declaration made him a hero in Maggie's eyes.

"Mr. Whalen from the Brooklyn brewery came to sign it this morning, and he promised to spread the word on the other side of the river," she said. "I think we'll have plenty more people arriving this afternoon."

"Yes, and we must make room for those additional visitors," Poppy said, motioning Mr. Solis to the door. She looked so coolly elegant in her willowy ivory gown as she stood framed in the glass doorway. The topiaries on either side of the arched doorway were decked with white orchids in white marble planters.

Before Mr. Solis could leave, the butler approached the breakfast room with another visitor in tow, probably here to sign the document. The tough-looking man sported wiry chestnut hair and a battered leather jacket, but she couldn't tear her eyes from the extraordinary bouquet he carried. A dozen black roses.

"I'm looking for Liam Blackstone," the man said, barely able to suppress his grin.

"And you are?" Poppy asked, her voice like icicles.

"Jake Cannon from the Philly Shipyard," he said. "I took over union duties after Liam left and came all this way to see my favorite rabble-rouser on the East Coast."

The man's enthusiasm was contagious, but Poppy remained unmoved. "Unless you are here to sign the complaint against Mr. Morse, we are not receiving visitors today."

Maggie had been deferring to Poppy for days, but Liam deserved to see his old friend. She stepped around Poppy to speak to the butler.

"Mr. Tyson, will you see if Liam can come down to join us? If not, we'll go upstairs to his room."

"Absolutely not," Poppy said. "I am not opening my home to any riffraff who trickles in off the street. And I definitely have no need of *those*," she said with a pointed look at the black flowers.

Mr. Cannon held the black bouquet aloft. "I came all the way from Philly to deliver these, and trust me, Liam wants to know about them."

Five minutes later, the butler pushed Liam in his wheelchair into the breakfast room. Liam wore a bathrobe and a broad grin. "Cannonball! I couldn't believe it when I heard you were here."

Mr. Cannon grinned and leaned over to give Liam a hearty handshake. "Heard you were sick, boss."

Liam batted his concern away. "You're the boss now. How's everything in Philly? And where did you get those creepy-looking roses?"

Mr. Cannon handed them to Liam. "You ought to know that the managers at steel mills across the country are getting deliveries of black roses just like these to their offices today. We heard the rumors about you getting booted off the board, and we want to be sure the managers get the message about where the unions stand."

"That's simply foul," Poppy said with a wrinkled nose. "How on earth did you grow black roses?"

"Not that hard," Mr. Cannon said. "All you do is take white roses and put them in a glass of water that's been dyed black. Within a day you'll have black roses. And those roses will carry a powerful message. The managers are smart enough to know exactly what they mean without us having to say a single word. It won't be long before the guys on the board know what the unions think about what's happening to you."

Liam bowed his head, blinking suspiciously fast. "Thanks, Cannonball. This means more to me than you can know."

"You're the best," Mr. Cannon said. "You always had our backs, and now we've got yours."

Pride filled Maggie's heart. Nothing about Liam's journey through life had been easy, but he hadn't given up despite blows to his health or to his dignity. Most of the board's accusations against him were true. He was an uneducated man with little experience in the world of business, but he also had a heart of steel that was strong enough to do what was right, and tomorrow everyone was going to find out if it was enough for him to survive the vote.

31

The morning of September 30 dawned with the first chill of autumn and the city newspapers brimming with bad press about Liam. Word of the coming vote of no confidence had been leaked, and Liam had no doubts as to who had spread it. Most of the articles were respectful and simply reported that Liam had but an eighth-grade education, limited experience in business, and the board members doubted his ability to provide meaningful leadership.

The lead article in the *New-York Tribune,* however, was the most hurtful. It featured a surprisingly lifelike drawing of the *Black Rose* tilted at an angle as it lay stranded in the Kennebec River. The article labeled him "Low-Tide Liam" and excoriated him for risking the life of his crew in a vainglorious quest to paint himself a hero.

"Pay no attention to it," Patrick advised as he tossed the newspaper into the wastebin. Liam tried, but his hands were unsteady as he tacked a high stand collar onto his neckband. He combed a thin sheen of macassar oil into his hair. He might be a wheelchair-riding thug from the wrong side of town, but he would arrive at the meeting looking like a gentleman.

Today they would launch their three-pronged attack against

Charles Morse. The first stage had been successfully accomplished an hour ago, though Morse knew nothing about it yet. The second would take place in the boardroom as they fought to salvage Liam's seat on the board while striking a blow against Morse's continuing membership. The third prong would use Maggie's list of businesses damaged by Morse to launch a crusade to finally change American business law.

His nerves were strung tight as the Blackstone carriage rolled toward the U.S. Steel building. Patrick rattled out last-minute instructions about the importance of maintaining a dignified tone throughout the meeting while Maggie and Antonio Gabelli listened in nervous anticipation. Liam intended to bring both Antonio and Maggie into the meeting with him. It was a slight breach in decorum, but they were an important part of the plan about to unfold.

The only way to get Liam's wheelchair into the building was by using a ramp at the back entrance on Rector Street. Getting out of the carriage without stressing the muscles across his abdomen was challenging, but between leaning on Patrick's shoulder and the box a footman placed beneath the carriage door, he managed his descent with only a twinge across his middle. Antonio Gabelli already had the wheelchair in place for him to sit.

Antonio grasped the handles of the chair and began wheeling him toward the rear entrance of the building. For most of his life, Liam had been taller than the people around him, but now he was eye level with the buttons on Patrick's vest and Maggie's shoulder.

"Hold on," he said as another horse-drawn carriage rolled to a halt behind the U.S. Steel building. A wheelchair was strapped to the back of that carriage too. Normally the only people using the back entrance were deliverymen unloading wagons, but this was a gentleman's carriage, and Liam suspected whose it might be.

Sure enough, when the carriage door opened, Charles Morse jauntily hopped down to the street, a cigar clamped in his teeth. He looked hale and hearty as he adjusted his waistcoat and casually strolled a few paces down the block. Meanwhile, the footmen hurried to unstrap the wheelchair.

"He's still milking his injuries," Patrick said in disbelief. As anticipated, once the wheelchair was on the ground, Morse settled into it and let a footman roll him toward the ramp outside the loading door.

"Wheel me toward him, please," Liam instructed Antonio.

"Liam, don't," Patrick warned. "Don't talk to him. Don't even look at him. He'll do everything in his power to provoke you."

But Antonio was already wheeling him to intercept Morse at the base of the ramp. "I'm glad you're well enough to join us for the meeting," Liam said once he was face-to-face with Morse.

"I wouldn't miss it for the world," Morse said. "Today's meeting is going to be nothing but a pleasure." His attention slid to Maggie, his gaze tracking up and down her figure before recognition dawned. He smirked at Liam. "Still cavorting with Sweet Miss Maggie of Gadsen Street? You should know it's considered tacky to bring your floozy to a business gathering, but no one ever accused you of good manners." He smiled up at Maggie. "When you tire of slumming with Low-Tide Liam, you know where I live. Perhaps we can come to a mutual agreement."

Morse snapped his fingers, and his footman began pushing him up the ramp. It required all of Liam's patience not to shout an insult after Morse. Instead, he held his tongue and drew a deep breath. Maggie's face was white with mortification, but they both knew better than to let Morse goad them this early in the game.

"Let's wait here," Patrick cautioned. "We don't want to share an elevator with him."

Liam nodded and slid to the end of the seat, bracing himself to stand. "I don't want to use the wheelchair," he said.

"What? Don't be a fool," Patrick said.

"I won't flaunt my illness like Morse. I've got the strength to walk into the meeting on my own two feet."

Patrick urged caution. "Liam, don't let your pride throw you off track. We can't afford your getting sick again."

Liam paused. He needed all his strength today and wouldn't let pride be his undoing. He lowered himself back down in the chair. "Let's go," he said.

It was a tight fit, but all of them were able to squeeze inside the elevator. A trickle of sweat rolled down his back as the attendant closed the gate, pulled the lever, and began the ascent. His starched collar itched, and the worsted wool suitcoat was insufferably hot, but by the time he arrived at the seventeenth floor, he assumed a mask of calm he didn't feel in order to face the board members, most of whom resented him from the day he forced his way into their gilded world.

He was the last board member to arrive, and conversation among the men and their clerks, secretaries, and lawyers abruptly stopped as he entered the room. Antonio pulled a chair away from the conference table to make room for the wheelchair. Patrick took the seat to his right while Maggie and Antonio retreated to a row of seats in the gallery. On the far wall were floor-to-ceiling windows overlooking the city's Financial District.

His fellow board members sitting around the table perused papers and whispered last-minute instructions among their staff. Not one of them looked at Liam. Waiters brought in carts with carafes of coffee, tea, and ice water. A pitcher of milk had been added at Liam's request last year, and he was the only one who ever drank from it. Clerks shuffled papers, the stenographer settling a roll of paper into the stenotype machine.

Then a clerk wheeled in a cart with a huge vase of roses, and Liam smiled. The vase contained forty-two black roses, one for each steel mill in the company.

"Where shall I put this, sir?" the clerk asked Fletcher, who sat at the end of the conference table.

Fletcher frowned at the roses. News of the unusual arrangements arriving at the offices of steel mill managers all over the country had already been communicated to the board, and everyone in the room knew exactly what the black roses meant. The men in the mills were being heard today.

"Set them outside," Fletcher said. "Mr. Blackstone may take them at the conclusion of the meeting if he wishes. It's time to proceed to the matter at hand."

His fellow eleven board members had poker faces as the servants cleared from the room. Morse glared at him with savage excitement, but a few others looked at him with pity. He didn't know which was worse. In all likelihood he was about to be voted off the board, but he wouldn't go quietly, and with some luck he'd take Morse down with him.

The door clicked behind the last servant, and Fletcher opened his file. "Let's proceed," he said with no joy in his voice. "Mr. Morse, you are the individual who called for the vote of no confidence, so you have ten minutes to outline your concerns before Mr. Blackstone will be given a chance to reply."

Morse sat at a twisted angle in his wheelchair, his shoulders lopsided. His voice seemed just as sickly as he began speaking.

"Many of you witnessed Liam assault me earlier this month," he said. "While I still hope for a full recovery, it is a long way in the future."

"You had a full recovery within a couple of hours," Liam said. Patrick kicked him beneath the table, and Morse continued.

"Everyone on this board, except the man in question, has worked hard to secure our positions here. We are men of integrity, breeding, and education, but a chain is only as strong as its weakest link. Mr. Blackstone has been an embarrassment by failing to carry his weight on the board. He acts in the interest of low-level workers rather than our shareholders. Even today he flaunts the black roses, which are a subtle threat to all of us. Just last night my wife received a bouquet of black roses at our home."

Liam blanched. If true, such a delivery was a serious misstep and could be seen as menacing. Several men around the table scowled.

"Outrageous," Fletcher said. "Has anyone else had black roses sent to their home?"

Liam held his breath, but a quick survey showed no one else had gotten such a delivery. Liam suspected it was just another of Morse's lies, but a damaging one. Morse didn't back off.

"I want justice," he proclaimed. "My wife nearly fainted when she saw that bouquet."

His wife was in the Adirondacks because she couldn't stomach watching Morse carry on with his mistress any longer. Liam itched to shout it out loud but instead kept quiet.

"I have always been reluctant to press for this vote," Morse went on. "Liam's assault gives me no recourse, and since he will soon be a convicted felon, he will be ineligible to continue sitting on the board. I suggest he resign his seat now and spare himself the embarrassment of a unanimous vote for his ouster."

Every board member in the room swiveled to look at him, the weight of their eyes heavy in the stuffy room's atmosphere.

Liam cleared his throat before speaking clearly and without shame. "I have already pled guilty to assaulting Mr. Morse," he admitted. "My lawyer submitted my guilty plea to a misdemeanor assault charge this morning, and the judge has already accepted it. There will be no felony conviction, and I will not resign."

Liam would do community service for the next three months at the orphanage on Hester Street, but his success in evading a felony conviction meant there was no legal impediment to his remaining a board member.

Morse appeared stunned by having his trump card yanked away. He smacked his hands on the table in exasperation. "Then let's proceed to a vote immediately. Everyone here knows this man's character. Half of you saw him assault me, and all of us have witnessed two years of incompetence and disloyalty. I am ready to proceed to a vote."

"I'm not," Liam said. "You opened the door to reassessing the board's composition, and I want to put your name up for no confidence as well."

"Ridiculous," Morse spat. "I have rendered outstanding financial advice to this company. I daresay I am the most valuable contributor to this board."

"You have a track record of corruption and illegal intimidation," Liam said. Patrick began distributing packets of paper. "My attorney is distributing the sworn testimony of fifty-six business owners outlining the threats, extortion, or deprivation of services they received at the hands of Mr. Morse or members of his ice trust."

Papers crinkled as men around the table began paging through the document. Morse skimmed it quickly, but other board members gave it greater scrutiny.

"Hearsay," Morse spat. "You could have drummed up these witnesses and paid for their signatures, then like rats they've scattered back into the woodwork."

Liam turned to Antonio. "Antonio? Would you care to comment?"

Antonio stood, holding his hat in his hands a little awkwardly, but his head was held high and he spoke with clarity. "Charles Morse and his ice trust drove my family out of business. We had operated Gabelli Ice for thirty-five years when one of Morse's thugs showed up and said that unless my grandfather joined his trust, he'd drive us out of business. That's exactly what he did. I'm here as a witness to everything he did to my family, and my name is the first one on the list."

Maggie stood. "My name is the second. My uncle and I founded the Molinaro Ice Cream Company nine years ago and—"

"This woman is Liam Blackstone's floozy," Morse interrupted. Liam clenched the arms of the wheelchair. Morse was only trying to provoke him, but it wouldn't happen today. "Liam takes his tramp with him on overnight voyages on his ship. She's nothing but a two-bit ice cream peddler."

"That's right, she *is* an ice cream peddler," Liam said, struggling to keep the anger from his voice. He rose from the wheelchair to stand upright. "Maggie Molinaro left school at fifteen to work a pushcart so people like you could have something to eat. That doesn't make her testimony any less valid. She's a decent person whose honest work helps keep this city afloat."

Morse rolled his eyes, but the other men on the board were listening.

"Look out that window," Liam continued. From their lofty position on the seventeenth floor, they could see all the way to the Bowery. "Down on those streets are the people who drive the streetcars and collect the city's trash. People who get up before dawn to cook your breakfast and iron your shirts. You see people who shove pushcarts all over the city and mop floors in hospitals and dig out the subways. During the heat wave, they were the people Morse denied a drink of cold water. And he thinks they don't deserve a wage that will buy their children a new pair of shoes each year."

"Spare us your radical blathering," Morse said. "We are a steel company, not a charity to cure the ills of society."

"That's right, we're a steel company," Liam snapped. "And who do you think risks their lives underground to mine the iron ore? Who smelts the steel and sweats in the foundries? Who builds the ships and the railroads and the skyscrapers? *Who do you think built America?*"

He braced his hands on the table, overwhelmed and weak. Sweat beaded on his forehead, and it was hard to breathe with the stiff collar choking him. He swiped the perspiration from his face and met Fletcher's gaze at the end of the table.

"I may not be worthy to sit at this table," he admitted, "but I wanted you to meet Antonio Gabelli and Maggie Molinaro—two people Charles Morse drove out of business just so he could earn a few extra dollars. *They* built America, and I am proud to call them my friends." He drew a breath to calm himself. "And Morse is a lazy pig who can't pull up his own trousers without servants to help him."

He slumped back into his wheelchair, trying to ignore the way Patrick winced at that last insult, but Morse deserved it.

"Put us both up for a vote," Liam said. "For the past two years I've done my best to watch and listen and learn. I'm grateful for the help I've received from the people around this table, but it turns out I *do* have something to offer the board other than just union support. I figured out who Charles Morse is and showed it to the world. So, as long as you're cleaning house, his name belongs on the ballot right next to mine."

"This is outrageous," Morse said. "It is a violation of the corporate operating agreement and another example of Blackstone's reckless disregard for procedural order."

Fletcher tossed the list of names down on the table, his face grave. "Charles, the suggestion is not unwarranted," he said. "I could crack open any newspaper from last July and read about how you manipulated the ice market for your own personal gain. We never paid much attention to your private banking or ice industry concerns, but perhaps that was a mistake."

"I have already loosened the rules regarding ice distribution," Morse sputtered.

"Only because the press shamed you into it," Antonio called out.

Morse pounded the table. "Excuse me, sir! You are not a member of this board and have no right to speak."

"Shutting Antonio up won't make your problem go away," Liam said. "I'm not the smartest or most educated person here—I never pretended to be—but I have a moral compass that is generally pointed in the right direction. I want this company to thrive. I want it to develop new steel alloys to build skyscrapers taller than ever before. To build safer ships and longer-lasting railroads. I want the men on the line to be paid a fair wage. I want this to be done in an open, aboveboard manner."

He turned his attention to Fletcher. "I wish you'd invited the press to this meeting. This vote is the biggest humiliation of my life, but I've never tried to hide who I am. I've never cheated anyone. The thing that bugs me the most about this vote is that it was initiated by Charles Morse, possibly the biggest scoundrel to ever operate in this city."

To his surprise, support came from an unlikely source. Rudolph Keppler, the president of the New York Stock Exchange and the fustiest man on the board, leaned forward to speak.

"I agree with Mr. Blackstone," he said. "I move that Mr. Morse should also be subject to a vote of no confidence."

"Seconded," another board member immediately said.

Fletcher tapped his gavel. "So moved," he announced. "Charles, you shall be given time to prepare a defense against the charges—"

"This is ridiculous!" Morse said, standing so abruptly, the wheelchair rolled out behind him. "I was doing you a favor by agreeing to serve on this board. There's no need to hold a vote about my competence. Gentlemen, I hereby resign."

He picked up his briefcase and strode toward the door with the vigor of an enraged tiger.

A tiger that had been exposed and run off. Liam glanced at Maggie sitting in the front row of the gallery. Her eyes shone with pride, and he locked gazes with her. *They'd done it!* Morse still ruled over his corrupt banking and ice empire, but he would no longer be a part of U.S. Steel, and that was a victory.

Patrick cleared his throat and stood. "May I be recognized to speak?" he asked Fletcher, who nodded.

"I believe Mr. Morse was responsible for most of the hostility directed against my client," Patrick said. "Now that he is gone, I would like to request that you withdraw the motion for a vote of no confidence against Mr. Blackstone."

Liam held his breath. Every head in the room turned to Fletcher, who looked ill at ease. "Charles's departure does not obviate the legitimacy of his motion, and we should probably—"

One of the senior board members interrupted him. "Mr. Chairman, I suggest there is no need to proceed to a vote and move to endorse Mr. Blackstone's continued service on the board."

"Seconded," Mr. Keppler was quick to add. "We misjudged you, Liam. We do indeed have much to learn from you. Losing you from the board would hurt the entire company."

Liam glanced at Patrick. Could this be legal? Given the look of satisfaction on Patrick's face, it probably was. Someone moved for a simple voice vote, and the chorus of "ayes" to keep Liam on the board was unanimous.

He didn't understand what just happened. It moved too quickly to grasp, but the upshot was that he'd managed to hang on to a job he still wasn't qualified to hold. He looked at the agenda, printed on engraved stock paper and filled with topics he didn't understand. The rest of the afternoon was a discussion about recertifying the debenture accounts. It triggered an instant headache and a rush of pain in his stomach.

"Wait a second," he said. The stiff collar around his neck became unbearable. He tugged at it, causing the studs to pop free. He yanked the collar off his neckband and threw it onto the table. The platinum studs bounced across the polished surface, pinging as they rolled to a stop. The conversation halted, and every eye was on him now.

"I'll consider staying on the board, but on my own terms," he announced. Beside him, Patrick silently groaned while Maggie clamped a hand over her mouth, but he refused to keep pretending to be someone he wasn't. "I'm done with the starched collars and spending weeks before each meeting cramming so I can pretend to understand finance and capital markets. I don't. I know labor issues, and I know steel. When those items are on the agenda, I'll show up and provide my rock-solid support. I want to abstain from everything else."

Everyone looked at him in shock, and he leaned down to whisper a question to Patrick. "Am I allowed do that?"

"We're about to find out," Patrick whispered back. At the end of the table, Fletcher huddled with a couple of his lawyers.

It appeared they didn't know either, and it was reassuring to learn he wasn't the only man fumbling in the dark.

Fletcher stood, a look of relief on his patrician face. "Deal," he said simply.

Liam tossed the agenda on the table. He'd rather eat nails than sit through the next eight hours of this tedious meeting, and he had better things to do . . . like launching the third prong of their plan to make sure Charles Morse would no longer trample on the businesspeople of America.

New York's attorney general had already let them down. It was time to take this issue to Washington, D.C.

32

There was a time when Liam would have loved to have gone to Washington with Patrick to personally deliver their petition to the U.S. Capitol. It would be an important part of dismantling Charles Morse's ice trust, but now wasn't the time. Maggie's business was gasping for air, and Liam needed to return to the health clinic so his ulcer might finally heal. That meant the best he could do was accompany Patrick to the train station to see him off.

It was the day after Liam's triumph in the boardroom, and Maggie came with them to Grand Central Station. Liam had become accustomed to feeling dwarfed while out in public. Yet rolling through the main concourse with its immense ceiling soaring twelve stories overhead made him feel especially small. Much of the station was being torn down to accommodate an expansion that would transform Grand Central into the largest train station in the world. Traffic continued during the renovation, and construction workers swarmed over the site that was part Baroque masterpiece and part exposed steel skeleton.

They passed through the grand concourse and arrived at the outdoor platform where Patrick would depart. Massive ironwork arches expanded across six railway lanes. Trains rumbled in and out with hissing steam and rattling gears. Patrick's train had already arrived, and passengers were boarding. Maggie rolled Liam as close to the embarkation point as possible.

"Good luck, Patrick," Liam said as he extended his hand. "You're carrying the hopes of Gadsen Street and fifty-six other businesses with you."

Patrick's handshake was firm and confident. "I'll get the petition to the relevant folks in Congress and pray it plants a seed. We're in for a long battle, but Rome wasn't built in a day." Patrick turned to Maggie. "And *thank you* for taking the initiative on this petition. Liam got lucky when he found you, and I never should have suggested otherwise. I was wrong, and I apologize."

Liam tensed. It was a heartfelt apology, but would Maggie accept it? To his relief, her good-natured practicality came to the fore.

She gave Patrick a smile and said, "Bring back good news from Congress and you can have free ice cream for life."

Liam stifled a snort of laughter. Maggie was a woman who could roll with the punches and didn't carry a grudge. He thanked God for that or she would have given him his walking papers long ago. They remained on the platform to watch the train pull out of the station on its way to Washington—with their long-shot hope of shining a spotlight on the need for business reform.

"Do you think it will do any good?" Maggie asked after the rumble of Patrick's train faded into the distance.

"I don't know," he admitted. In the past, he would have banged his fist and stormed the battlements with all the righteous anger he could muster. In the last few weeks, however, he'd come to appreciate the value of patience. It could take years for the laws to be reformed, but their petition might lay the foundation and possibly shame the Morses of the country into cleaning up their act.

He looked up at the patches of blustery sky through the open framework of steel arches overhead. It would probably take another two years before this wing of the station would be completed, but for now he admired the cathedral of iron and steel as trains came and went.

Maggie sat on a bench next to him. "It's rather beautiful, isn't it?" she asked, and he knew she spoke of more than just the architecture. There was a pageantry to the hundreds of trains rumbling in and out of the station. A slow-moving cargo train approached a platform with dozens of boxcars behind it. Those boxcars probably carried wheat and corn from the faraway plains of the Midwest. Then came flatcars loaded with timber and gondola cars carrying iron ore, copper, and coal. The tank cars brought oil and refrigerated cars fresh milk and meat to the masses. Most of the other trains consisted of passenger cars, bringing thousands of people in and out of New York City every day, moving through the station in a magnificently choreographed dance that made modern life possible.

A vendor from a rival ice cream company rolled his pushcart onto the platform, and Maggie watched it pass with a hint of envy.

"You don't miss working a pushcart, do you?" It was what she and Dino were going to do if she couldn't get her equipment back in short order. A faint smile hovered as Maggie watched the vendor greet a mother and her eager boy.

"It's a lot harder than it looks," she said, but there was a note of wistfulness in her tone. It seemed to him it was the hardest things in life that left people feeling proud.

As if shaking off the memories, Maggie leaned in close. "That company makes lousy ice cream," she whispered. "They skip the custard stage so they can sell it cheap."

He hid a smile. Thanks to Maggie, he now understood how much extra time it took to prepare a rich, yolk-based custard, which was the secret to Molinaro's extraordinary ice cream. Her new egg-breaking machine had been repossessed along with the rest of her factory equipment, and she probably couldn't replace it anytime soon. Her sacrifice had garnered plenty of outrage and sympathy from the public, but that didn't pay the bills. And Liam didn't want her to go back to working a pushcart.

"Maggie, I know you don't want money to come between us, but will you let me do something nice for you?"

She looked at him with caution. "Like you tried to do at the Porterhouse?"

"Yeah, but this is a lot more important." He glanced back at the pushcart vendor, envious of the man's ability to put in a full day of manual labor. Liam wouldn't trade places with the vendor, but he didn't want to be incapacitated in a wheelchair for the rest of his life either. "I need to return to the health clinic for a longer stay, but I don't want to leave when you're broke. Will you let me buy you new equipment for your factory? Top of the line stuff, free and clear of debt. You never would have lost your equipment if I hadn't nudged you toward taking on Morse in the first place."

He held his breath, hoping she wouldn't get all prickly again like she had at the Porterhouse. Instead, she looked pensive.

"I hadn't thought of it that way," she said. "If we'd never met, I'd still have my factory. I'd probably still be waiting to go to court over that ninety-five dollars."

"Which Morse never would have paid," he pointed out.

She nodded. "I know that now. But I got so much more after joining forces with you. I got to see the icehouses of Maine and the inside of a Wall Street boardroom. And what it's like to sail on the ocean with a man I love. It's all been worth it."

"Will you let me buy you the equipment? It will make it easier for me to head off to the clinic knowing you aren't struggling with a pushcart."

It went against Maggie's nature to accept a gift without doing anything to earn it. The tension knotting her brow made that clear, yet it soon eased. She took his hand and pressed a kiss into his palm.

"Yes, I'll let you buy the equipment. And thank you, Liam. Dino and I will be very grateful for your help."

He squeezed her hand. Another train entered the station, filling the structure with noise and vibration, and they watched it slow and then come to a stop at the platform. Porters and linemen arrived to open the doors. Soon hundreds of passengers disembarked—businessmen in suits, couples holding hands, families, immigrants, and schoolchildren.

"I like this," Maggie said, mesmerized by the multitudes of people.

"I do too." Sometimes everything felt right in the world, and this was one of those times. There was nothing extraordinary about it. The weather was iffy, his stomach hurt, and they still had miles to go in ensuring Charles Morse and his like couldn't keep trampling on decent people. While the world was far from perfect, there was still satisfaction to be had in the struggle.

A sense of well-being that felt almost holy descended on him. It came out of nowhere and blanketed him with the assurance that he was on the right track. He had found a woman with the ambition to take on the world, but who could also sit beside him and appreciate the simple joy of watching trains roll in and out of the station. This day was a gift from God.

"I feel very grateful right now," he said, "even though there's still so much that's wrong with the world. And I'm glad you're here beside me, Maggie."

They spent a lazy afternoon watching the trains come and go. It was a brief hiatus with a woman he adored. Next week he would head off to the health clinic for three months in hopes of a full recovery, making these moments of companionship more precious than ever . . . because there were no guarantees he would have more days like this. His health remained uncertain, Maggie struggled fitting in with the Blackstone clan, and Charles Morse still roamed free in the world.

33

Maggie dreaded the formal dinner to celebrate Liam's triumph in the boardroom. It would take place at the Blackstone mansion but was delayed until Friday so Patrick could attend after his trip to Washington. While Maggie thought it was sweet that Liam wanted Dino and Julie to attend so that their families could get to know one another, it was going to be awkward.

Dino, Julie, and Maggie all wore their Sunday best, which were fine store-bought outfits, but they still seemed terribly homespun inside the gilded splendor of the Blackstone mansion. Liam looked particularly dashing in his formal tuxedo as he led them into the dining room glittering with gold and crystal. Grim sculptures of Roman busts atop marble plinths surrounded the dining table, and Maggie had the disconcerting feeling the Romans disapproved of the three interlopers who didn't belong at the opulent feast.

Oscar and Poppy were as chilly as ever, while Frederick Blackstone, Liam's grandfather who had built the family's fortune, was gentlemanly. He asked Dino about the restaurant business and complimented Julie on their ice cream recipes. But making conversation down the length of the twenty-foot table made it hard to be heard, and everything seemed so stilted. Dino and Julie sat to her left, Liam on her right. Natalia and her Russian husband, Count Dimitri Sokolov, sat opposite them, but there were two empty places where Gwen and Patrick should be.

It annoyed Poppy, who summoned the butler. "Please make a telephone call to Patrick and find out why he's late," she instructed. "His train arrived back from Washington hours ago, so there's no excuse for his absence."

Uncle Dino shook out a linen napkin and tucked it into his shirt collar. "If Patrick is making progress stopping men like Charles Morse from trampling on small businesses, I think we ought to let him keep plugging away."

Maggie glanced at the other men around the table. Everyone else spread their napkins on their laps, but Liam noticed Dino's faux pas and obligingly worked his napkin into his collar as well.

"Thank you," she whispered to him, and he flashed her a wink. He'd been feeling better now that the stress of the vote was behind them, but still he kept to a bland diet.

The eight-course meal began with a molded rectangle of gelatinous aspic with five dots of caviar geometrically arranged around the gold rim of the plate. Silver clinking on china seemed unnaturally loud in the marble room as she timidly sampled a bit of the salty aspic that tasted like beef broth and strange spices. Liam had a bowl of oatmeal with cream.

"Want to trade?" she whispered, and he suppressed a grin. Beneath the table his foot toyed with hers. She slipped out of her pump to let her toes return the caress. Footmen in formal tailcoats with white gloves circulated, pouring glasses of wine and clearing away plates. At last, Oscar was ready with a toast. He stood and raised his glass.

"Liam, you have been a thorn in my side from the moment you returned to New York, but you've surprised us all with your determination and competence. Congratulations on saving your seat on the board, and good luck at the Woodlands Clinic."

Oscar raised his glass in a dignified gesture. It had been faint praise, but Liam still looked flushed with pleasure and raised his glass of milk in a return salute. Oscar Blackstone was the toughest, flintiest businessman on Wall Street, and any sort of compliment from him was a hard-won prize.

The ongoing courtship beneath the table continued as she slipped her toe up Liam's ankle.

The footmen cleared away the aspic and delivered pickled quail eggs on a bed of watercress. Liam was allowed to continue working on his bowl of oatmeal, but his left hand was now tracing patterns on her wrist, and it was the most divine sensation this side of paradise.

Then came the soup course, and Dino didn't realize that cucumber soup was supposed to be cold and asked the footman to warm it up. The footman glanced at Poppy for guidance, who nodded her consent. When the bowl of warmed soup was returned, Dino dove in with gusto and seemed to enjoy every drop.

Soon a disturbance at the far end of the dining hall drew everyone's attention. Patrick burst through the double doors, dressed only in his rolled-up shirtsleeves and suspenders. Gwen followed close behind.

"Charles Morse has fled the country," Patrick abruptly announced.

"He did what?" Liam dropped her wrist and shot to his feet. He bumped the table, sloshing the soup course, and Poppy glared at the disturbance.

Patrick nodded. "The attorney general issued a warrant for Morse's arrest, but he must have gotten word of it. Apparently, he and his wife fled to Paris just ahead of the police."

Maggie's jaw dropped, unsure what to make of this baffling development. Uncle Oscar, however, was coolly speculative. "What are the charges against him?"

"It looks like New York's attorney general has a spine after all. He found evidence that Morse was bribing judges in his wife's bigamy case. They had enough to put him away for years, so he's hightailing it out of the country."

Poppy brightened with delight. "Bigamy? Do tell!"

Oscar gamely filled his wife in on the scandalous Morse marriage, but perhaps the most amazing facet of the story was that Mrs. Morse was willing to leave the country with her unfaithful husband. The same woman Morse had been trying to convict of bigamy was now standing by her man in his flight to escape prosecution.

Maggie sagged back in her chair. If Morse was gone, what did that mean for the case against his seedy business practices? Had her sacrifice of the factory been for nothing? Poppy and Oscar were both giddy, talking about the scandal, batting around stories of Morse's lurid personal life, but all Maggie could think of was her empty factory.

"What does this mean for our petition?" she asked.

Patrick met her gaze with sad resignation. "It's going to lose momentum now that Morse is gone. He was the main catalyst driving it. I'm sorry, Maggie."

The news infuriated Liam. "We shouldn't let this end here," he said. "The police need to go after him. Haul him back to America in handcuffs so he can be tried in a court of law."

"Let him stay in France," Uncle Oscar said with a shrug. "Without him here to crack the whip, his ice trust is now headless. It will die soon. And since he won't be able to keep greasing palms, his army of corrupt judges and government officials will obey the laws or go to jail. The city can breathe freely again."

"Not good enough," Liam snapped. "Charles Morse extorted his way into a fortune. He drove decent people into bankruptcy. He ruined Maggie's company. He should be made to pay."

Did he ruin her company? Morse had dealt them a body blow, but they still had their building, their reputation, and their freedom. Charles Morse didn't have any of those things. Likely he would live the rest of his life exiled in some fancy French resort hotel, but he'd lost his freedom to come home again.

"He's a cheat and a scoundrel," Liam ranted, yanking the napkin from his collar and throwing it down. "As soon as the

Black Rose is seaworthy, I'll hire my own private army and drag him back to New York to face justice."

"Liam," Maggie said, her voice echoing in the marble chamber. "Liam, we won."

"How did we win?" he demanded. "He cheated you and everyone else on Gadsen Street. He still has his freedom. None of that sounds like a win to me, Maggie."

It was all a matter of perspective. She could win without punishing Charles Morse. Perhaps robber barons like Morse would always find a way to save their skins, but it wasn't a life she envied. She wouldn't trade her workaday life on Gadsen Street for a castle with no soul.

Patrick tried to calm Liam by saying that in the coming months, the government would be bringing to light the trusts, schemes, and alliances Morse had built over the years. He pointed out that in time, Maggie might even get compensation for what she'd lost. But Liam was still annoyed. He was a swashbuckler ready to strike out for the horizon on a hopeless quest for justice.

Big, strong, generous Liam, who looked as handsome in a tuxedo as he did brandishing a blowtorch. They'd met because of their mutual antagonism against Charles Morse, but that part of their life had just come to a swift and definitive end.

"Liam, you're not striking out for France; you're going to the Woodlands Clinic to heal. This isn't worth stressing your ulcer. Sit down and join us for this fine meal. Look . . . the cheese course is on its way."

"Camel milk cheese," Poppy said triumphantly. Footmen delivered china plates featuring white wedges of bizarre cheese artfully presented, along with a selection of olives, dates, and threads of saffron.

Who could have imagined that cheese could be made from camel milk? Maggie seized the opportunity and tugged on Liam's hand. "The cheese looks delicious. And I'll bet your diet will allow you to have some. Please sit. It's time to relax and stop worrying about Charles Morse."

It was an order, not a request. Maybe it was presumptuous of her to issue commands in another woman's house, but Liam was leaving tomorrow, and their final few hours together were too precious to waste ranting about a man who couldn't hurt them anymore. Could he?

The only way Charles Morse could hurt them now was if Liam couldn't accept this partial victory and find the peace of mind to cure himself at the health clinic.

34

Maggie kept careful watch on the daily newspapers during the first week of October, anxious to see if Charles Morse would make good on his threat to release the racy photographs of Darla Kingston, but nothing appeared. He probably had other priorities as he fled from the country. The only time Maggie spotted Darla's name in the newspapers was later in the month in an article celebrating the opening of a new orphanage, which boasted of an original Darla Kingston statue in their garden.

Life on Gadsen Street returned to normal as October turned into November. The new equipment Liam bought was delivered, and Maggie's factory went back into production making two thousand gallons of ice cream each week. The parlor re-opened, her pushcarts were fully stocked, and she was back to delivering ice cream to all her restaurant and hotel contracts.

The only glitch was that Dino disapproved of Liam paying for the new factory equipment. "Men don't give gifts like that unless they want something in return," he warned.

"Liam has always been a perfect gentleman," she said. If anything, it was she who had encouraged more kissing and chances to cuddle in shadowy corners. Though Liam was a healthy red-blooded man, he still insisted on restraining himself in his quest to prove he was a reformed man. Even so, it wasn't enough to reassure Dino.

"It's bad luck to do business with someone outside the family," he insisted. "When things get tough, they can turn and stab you in the back."

It was nonsense, but Liam wasn't here to defend himself because he wouldn't return from the health clinic until the end of December. She missed him terribly, even though he wrote to her every day. Though his handwriting wasn't the best, she treasured his letters all the more because she knew how he struggled with the written word.

And yet, as the weeks went by, Dino's warnings began tainting Maggie's delight in the new factory. Taking a handout didn't feel right, even if it came from someone she loved.

Mr. Prescott from the Porterhouse agreed with Dino. "Friends should never enter into a business arrangement without terms of the financial obligations spelled out in a legally binding agreement," he said one evening as they sat outside at a café table. She often traded an ice cream sundae for Mr. Prescott's business advice, but tonight the sundae sat melting in its bowl as he described the dire consequences that could result if the friendship soured. The equipment could be repossessed if she couldn't prove it was a gift. Liam could even come after her for accumulated profits.

"He wouldn't ever do that," she protested, but Mr. Prescott was ready with counterarguments.

"Fine, but what if Liam dies? Whoever inherits his estate could assert ownership. Without the protection of a formal agreement, you are completely vulnerable. So are Dino and Julie."

Maggie fidgeted, glancing inside where Dino stood behind the service counter, chatting with a customer and once again content with his life. Dino and Julie shouldn't be at the mercy of her relationship with Liam.

Her worries took root and grew heavier day after day. When she fired up the mixing machines each morning, the whir of the fan belts didn't sound quite as satisfying. The ice cream didn't taste quite as velvety. Everything seemed a little less special because she hadn't earned it all on her own.

December finally arrived, and her apprehension eased only after she decided to reimburse Liam. She didn't *think* he would ever double-cross her, but a legal document outlining the terms of a loan would benefit them all. She could once again take pride in her ownership of the factory. She hired Mr. Prescott's accountant to draft a formal repayment plan. It included eight percent interest, which was the going rate for a loan like this one.

On the fifth day of December, she got the thrilling news that Liam was being released from the health clinic two weeks early. It coincided with the repair of his ship too. When Liam heard that the *Black Rose* was ready to sail home, the doctor concluded it would be more stressful to keep him locked away than to let him swing back into the normal pattern of his life. He would probably always need to be mindful of his diet and control his stress, yet the ulcer was now manageable and he was ready to rejoin the world.

The *Black Rose* sailed back into port on December 16, and Maggie met the restored yacht at the pier with a pushcart filled with every flavor of ice cream her factory could make. She drew her woolen wrap closer, her heart bursting with pride as the ship approached the dock. The sun was beginning to set, turning the men on deck into dark silhouettes against the blaze of the amber twilight.

Docking seemed to take forever as the ship inched closer to the pier. Liam finally appeared on deck, and she waved up at him, her laughter carried away on the breeze.

"Is that ice cream for me?" he bellowed down as she wheeled the pushcart closer to the ship.

"I brought enough for the whole crew," she called out. "Free of charge!"

Soon the gangway was lowered, and Liam bounded down the ramp, his arms outstretched. She ran into them, and her feet left the ground. He was strong and vibrant and healthy as he twirled her around, his laughter coming from deep in his chest.

"Welcome home," she choked out against his shoulder. She wanted to say more, but he was kissing her, and she could barely draw a breath. Then he pulled away to inspect the offerings in the pushcart, marveling over his old favorites plus a new toffee flavor. He lowered his face into the compartment, breathing deeply of the cold vanilla-scented cream.

"How's the new factory equipment?" he asked once he straightened.

"It's great," she said, even though the envelope with the loan agreement in her satchel suddenly weighed heavily on her.

"Then why did you grimace?"

"Did I grimace? It must be the sun in my eyes."

He drew her against him with a grin. "Come aboard. I have a surprise waiting for you. I'll have someone from my crew take care of your pushcart."

Her heart squeezed when she arrived on deck and saw a table at the bow of the ship with two place settings, a basket of fragrant corn bread, and two plates loaded with lobster straight from Maine. His goblet was filled with milk, but hers was empty. A nearby table had pitchers of milk, tea, and an assortment of wine bottles.

"What would you like to drink?" he asked as he pulled out a chair for her.

"Milk," she replied. There was no need for fancy champagne to make this night special. She would share this evening with Liam on an equal footing, and that meant she would enjoy a glass of milk as if it were the finest wine in the world.

They toasted their reunion, then shared a delicious meal that tasted even better because they ate it with their hands. They made plans to have dinner with Dino and Julie the following night at Lieberman's Deli, which they both enjoyed more than the gourmet meals served at the Blackstone mansion.

For dessert they had her new toffee ice cream, and Liam proclaimed it to be the best flavor she'd ever made. They watched the sun sink below the horizon and then the moon rise. She stayed until midnight, gazing at the stars as Liam enfolded her against him and closed the flaps of his overcoat around her. Everything was perfect . . . except that in the back of her mind she worried about the financial arrangement she wanted put in place.

When a cab arrived to take her home, she slipped the envelope with the repayment plan into his pocket just before leaving. "Open this when you are alone," she said.

He yanked out the envelope, looking at it in confusion. "What's this?" He slid a thumb beneath the flap to open it, but she clasped both hands around it to stop him.

"Read it later. We can discuss it tomorrow when we meet for dinner at Lieberman's Deli, but please give it careful consideration, okay?"

He pocketed the envelope, cupped the back of her head in his palm, and pulled her in for a kiss. "You got it, Sweet Miss Maggie."

The love radiating from him stayed with her all the way home. It felt as if she were living in a fairy tale as she gazed out the window of the carriage at the store windows already draped with Christmas decorations. She was quite certain this was going to be the best year of her life.

⟶ ∞ ⟵

The fairy tale ended abruptly the following afternoon when the legal demand from Liam arrived by special delivery. The hefty envelope contained a simple cover letter followed by a fat contract filled with tiny print and scary language. The letter made it abundantly clear that Liam declined her repayment plan but had a counter proposal, and it knocked the wind out of her.

"This is what I feared," Dino moaned as he scanned the contract in the quiet of their cramped business office on the second floor. It had been drafted by Patrick and used lots of formal terms she didn't fully comprehend, but the upshot was clear.

Liam wanted half the Molinaro Ice Cream Company!

She fanned herself with the empty envelope. It wasn't even hot in here, but she was sweating from every pore in her body. Had Patrick put Liam up to this?

"I can't believe he's really serious," she said, but Dino's face looked like a thundercloud.

"We accepted his equipment. Maybe he has the right to demand partial ownership. We need to get a lawyer to find out."

Maggie shook her head. "No more lawyers, no more accountants," she said. "I'll go see Liam face-to-face and ask who put him up to this."

Last night, Liam told her he planned to spend the day installing new brass lanterns outside the wheelhouse of the *Black Rose*. She loved the way he babied his ship and took care of its maintenance with his own two hands, but she didn't think it fair that he wanted to get his hands on her factory too.

She took the streetcar to Pier 19 and nodded to the vendor at the Molinaro pushcart, which was now permanently stationed here. Caleb saw her coming and lowered the gangway. Her nerves ratcheted tighter with each step she took up the steep incline. What kind of mood was Liam going to be in? It was hard to guess, but Caleb said he was over at the wheelhouse, where the screws, sockets, and canopy of a brass wall lantern lay disassembled on the deck.

Liam glanced her way as she approached but didn't break the rhythm of his work. He screwed a brass mounting plate to the wall with methodical precision and didn't seem at all angry or annoyed. Instead, he seemed entirely calm. A little grease stained his fingers, and his sleeves were rolled up, revealing strong forearms as he worked the screwdriver. She didn't want to fight with him, but she didn't want to sign half her factory over to him either.

"Watch out for the socket cover," he warned as she drew near.

She stepped back from the hardware scattered on the deck and held up the envelope without a word.

A slow, fiendish smile spread across his face. "I figured that would bring you running."

"You can't seriously believe I'll accept these terms," she said, and he merely shrugged and went back to screwing another brass plate to the wall.

"You were the one who changed the terms of the deal," he said. "I just proposed one I like better."

"Liam, half the company is way too much."

"Why?" His tone was casual as he reached for another screw to continue anchoring the brass plate. "The most valuable thing in your entire factory is the equipment, and I paid for it all."

"I think you're forgetting that Dino and I own the pushcarts outright. Those were very expensive. And I'll be taking a hit by parking one of them at Pier 19 instead of a more profitable location."

"Don't be so cheap, Maggie. Think of all the benefits I bring to the table if I own half the business." Now it looked like he was battling a smile.

She suspected the only reason he had Patrick draw up this contract was to get a rise out of her, and he'd succeeded. She would play along and outline the benefits of having him as a business partner.

"It's true that you would be a good partner," she admitted. "If anything breaks down at the factory, you might fix it for free."

"Yup," he confirmed. "I've also got my own tools."

"And you have a lot of connections in the New York business world and at the harbor. All those things might come in handy. You're usually in a good mood, which is a bonus, plus you're a good kisser."

The corner of his mouth quirked into a smile, but he kept working on the light fixture without breaking pace. "Keep going."

"You're very handsome. I never tire of looking at you. But that's still not worth half my company, Liam."

He carefully set the screwdriver on the deck and picked up

a rag to wipe the grease from his hands. His humor had vanished, replaced with a cautious, hopeful expression with just a tinge of fear.

"In exchange for half your company, I was thinking about offering you half of the *Black Rose*," he said.

She gaped at him. What had she done to deserve half the *Black Rose*? She could barely grasp the concept, but Liam hadn't stopped talking.

"I'll also throw in half my stake in U.S. Steel. Half of everything I own. Half of my future, and all my somewhat battered and bruised heart. Maggie, I want us to be real partners in all things. I love you. I don't want you to sign that document—I want to stand in front of a priest with you."

He closed the distance between them and touched the scar that split her eyebrow. For years the scar had itched and annoyed her, but not anymore.

"We're alike, Maggie. We've both survived a lot of hard knocks, but we always spring back to face a new day. Never bitter. Never giving up. I love you to bits, Sweet Miss Maggie of Gadsen Street. Will you marry me?"

She tossed the legal paperwork over the side of the ship. "Yes, I'll marry you," she said, loving the warmhearted happiness in Liam's eyes as he smiled down at her.

She had found the business partner of a lifetime, and a man who would stand beside her through any storm. Their life wouldn't always be smooth sailing, but over the past year she had learned to value something more than safety and security. She wanted the crusade, the adventure, and the rollicking good cheer of a man who lost more battles than he won, but who still had the strength to wake up to a new day with faith, hope, and optimism.

Together, with God's love and a little hard work, the adventure ahead would be a good one.

Epilogue

At long last, the granite memorial Liam commissioned for his father was ready to be dedicated on the campus at the college Theodore Blackstone founded. The life-sized statue captured Theodore in later life, his strong features a little haggard by age and exhaustion, but still reflecting the kindness for which he had been universally beloved. Liam and Gwen chose the perfect place for the statue in a memorial garden right outside the Chemistry Building. Two hundred chairs had been set out on the lawn and a speaker's podium placed beside the monument. Students, professors, and dignitaries were already starting to gather to hear Liam's speech dedicating the statue.

Public speaking was always a chore, but Liam wanted to be the one to dedicate the statue. He'd been practicing his speech for weeks and wanted to run through it one final time for Gwen, who was busy gossiping with Natalia and Dimitri over by the fountain.

"Hey, Gwen, can you help me out for a sec?"

Gwen didn't look at him but instead listened with openmouthed amazement to whatever Natalia was nattering on about behind her hand. Natalia's kids were running amok in the garden, trampling through the recently planted herbs, and

319

neither woman was paying them any mind. Natalia and Dimitri now had seven kids. Seven! One of them was only an infant draped over Natalia's shoulder, the others ranging in age from two to ten, all of them adopted from the orphanage on Hester Street. One was busily ripping out the newly planted marigolds at the base of his father's statue.

Liam bolted over to scoop up the toddler before she could do any more damage and started carrying the girl over to Natalia. Maggie and Patrick had also joined in to listen to Natalia. Patrick was scowling, Maggie looked mildly amused, and Natalia abruptly stopped talking when she saw him approach.

"What's going on?" he asked, passing the toddler to Dimitri.

"It's nothing," Natalia said with an artificially bright smile. "Are you ready for your big speech?"

"Not really, and your kids were destroying Gwen's herb garden. So spill it . . . what were you talking about?"

Patrick put an arm around his shoulder. "How about one more practice run of your speech?" he asked, pulling on Liam's arm and drawing him toward the Chemistry Building.

"How about you tell me what everyone is gossiping about? You're making me nervous."

Patrick managed his own artificially bright smile. "Not now. Today is meant to celebrate your father, not wallow in the muck of the past."

Now he was more intrigued than ever. In a few minutes, hundreds of people would be gathering to honor his father, and here his own family was distracting him, gossiping and holding out on him. For pity's sake, even Poppy had joined the little group. Poppy was still the most vain, self-centered woman he'd ever met, but she was entranced by whatever Natalia just whispered in her ear. Poppy's blue eyes widened, and her squeal of delight echoed across the garden.

"Tell me what's going on," he demanded. "I won't be able to concentrate on the speech unless I know."

Patrick's frown deepened. "It's about Charles Morse. The judge finally handed down his sentence this morning."

That *was* a surprise. A few years after fleeing the country in disgrace, Morse returned to America and went straight back to his old tricks. Instead of targeting the ice industry, this time he cornered the copper market, which sent the steel industry into a crisis and caused the national stock market to crash. Morse's scheme helped to plunge the entire country into an economic depression from which they were still emerging, but at least it removed the blinders from everyone's eyes. Morse had been tried and convicted of fraud. His army of lawyers was attempting to avoid a jail sentence, but it looked as though the judge was made of stern stuff.

"He's been sentenced to fifteen years in the federal penitentiary in Atlanta," Patrick announced. "He was carted off in chains a few hours ago. There'll be no escape for him this time."

Liam stared into the distance, waiting for a surge of triumphant satisfaction, but it never came. Whatever happened to Charles Morse paled in comparison to the fulfillment Liam had found in his work and family. He and Maggie had a three-year-old son now, and their second child was due in a month. Revenge against Charles Morse no longer mattered.

"Do you want to go inside and run through your speech one more time?" Patrick asked.

Liam glanced down at the wilted pages. He'd practiced it so many times in the past few weeks that it was engraved on his mind. He could recite the speech backward if necessary.

"No, I'm okay," he said, watching as his son walked over to gape at the granite monolith of Theodore Blackstone. Teddy was the same age Liam had been when he was kidnapped. It wasn't until Liam became a father himself that he appreciated the magnitude of what Theodore must have suffered in the years and decades after Liam disappeared.

Liam hoisted Teddy into his arms. Good heavens, this boy was getting heavy. He turned so that they could both be eye level with the statue.

"That's the man we named you after, Teddy," he said. "He was your grandpa."

Teddy's childish fingers explored the statue's careworn features. A renewed ache from never having been reunited with his father bloomed in his chest, but at least Liam now had faith they would meet again someday. It would be a joyous reunion when all the toil and sorrow of a fallen world became only a memory.

For now, Liam looked reverently at the father he lost decades ago. While neither of them had an easy life, Theodore had funneled his grief into building the college, and Liam's tough upbringing had left him with certain gifts as well. It had forged him into a man of compassion who wouldn't ever give up, no matter how hard the battle. He still served on the board of U.S. Steel, and still lost more battles than he won, but he had helped shape the company for the better.

A sting of tears prickled as he gazed at the statue. Liam would give anything for the chance to tell his father that he'd survived, that he made something of himself and grew up to be a good man. The coming years would be filled with challenge and he would strive to keep his eyes pointed true north, guided by the invisible thread of energy that pulled him toward God's will. Patrick would call that thread the Holy Spirit. His father would have called it basic Christian compassion, and that was good enough for Liam.

Life was good. God had guided him back to New York to be reunited with his family and given Liam a purpose. Maggie came into his life to walk beside him on that journey. Life had come full circle, and now he gazed at the face of his father forever carved in stone—the gentle expression of a man who never quit mourning the loss of his son.

"I'm okay, Dad," he said.

A cool breeze floated across his face. It was only a few seconds of comfort that descended from heaven and then it was gone, but the memory remained. He hoisted Ted a little higher in his arms and smiled. "We're all okay, Dad."

It was time to deliver his speech and rejoin the living.

Historical Note

*M*ost of the people in this novel are fictional, but Charles W. Morse was real. He was born in Bath, Maine, in 1856. His first job was managing the books for his father's tugboat company, for which he was paid a salary of $1,500. Morse found an accountant willing to do it for $500, speculated with the balance, and made a fortune before he graduated from school at eighteen.

For the purposes of the story, I condensed the events of his life from 1899–1903 into a single year, and I included Morse on the board of directors for U.S. Steel. When Morse cornered the ice industry in 1899, it attracted little attention until a massive heat wave in the summer of 1900 drove the price of ice too high for poor people to afford. Reports of children in orphanages and other sick people passing away from heatstroke filled the newspapers, shining a spotlight on the unfair monopoly of the ice trust. Large consumers of ice such as morgues, factories, and restaurants were forced to close. Although Morse quickly lowered prices, crusading journalists uncovered a network of extortion, bribery, and threats that had been used to drive competitors out of business and create his ice trust.

None of the attempts to hold Morse legally accountable succeeded, and his marital problems were what caused him to flee the country to avoid criminal charges involving his wife's

divorce. Ironically, the only person to go to jail over the bigamy scandal was Morse's own attorney, the clever Abraham
Hummel, who was found guilty of suborning perjury. He was
suspended from the practice of law and sent to jail for a year.
Morse and his wife reconciled and sailed for France, proclaim-
ing the trip "a second honeymoon."

The good times did not last. In 1907, Morse cornered the
copper market, which caused panic on Wall Street and a run
on the banks, which could not make good on their deposits.
This triggered more panic as banks all over the country started
to fail. The Panic of 1907 laid the foundation for the creation
of the Federal Reserve Act of 1913, which put new regulations
in place to curb speculation and guarantee bank deposits, and
they're still in force today.

Morse was sentenced to fifteen years in prison for violating
federal banking laws. Clemence Morse remained loyal to her
husband, ardently working to reduce his prison sentence. He
succeeded in faking an illness to win a presidential pardon in
1912, and once again he returned to various moneymaking
schemes. In later life he was indicted for mail fraud and war
profiteering, but a series of strokes rendered him incapable of
defending himself in court. His wife cared for him until she died
in 1926, after which he was placed under the guardianship of a
court, having lost his ability to speak or reason. He died in 1933.

Questions for Discussion

1. Liam preferred his job as a welder over life as a businessman, but he ends up sticking with the job that isn't easy or enjoyable for him. Was this the right decision? How important is it to enjoy a job?

2. When Liam is in despair and ready to give up, Maggie tells him, "Quit dwelling on your failures. I don't know what force is urging you to give up, but I don't think it's a godly one." What does she mean by this?

3. Liam and Maggie both experienced trauma in their lives but became more resilient for having survived it. What qualities can help people become resilient after trauma instead of having it break their spirits?

4. Maggie's old flame, Philip, walked away from a law career to chase an improbable dream in the music industry. Was she wrong to break up with him for this? How would you counsel someone who wants to pursue a dream with a high likelihood of failure?

5. Both Liam and Maggie had a serious relationship with someone else before they met. What benefits or challenges does a significant prior relationship bring to a person who ultimately marries someone else?

6. Maggie holds a huge party the night before she loses her factory because she refuses to mourn before

absolutely necessary. While admirable, is this really possible? What advantages accrue from refusing to mourn until the end officially occurs?

7. Liam thinks his string of failures make him unworthy, and he isn't inspired to keep up the fight until he learns how often his father also failed. What are the advantages of failure? Why do so many people hide their failures?

8. Maggie struggles with accepting gifts she didn't earn. Why do you think this is? Why do we tend to value something we bought from our own earnings more than something that was easily acquired?

9. Near the end, Maggie concludes she doesn't need to see Morse punished to consider herself a winner in keeping her business afloat. How important is it to see wrongdoers punished?

Elizabeth Camden is best known for her historical novels set in Gilded Age America, featuring clever heroines and richly layered story lines. Before she was a writer, she was an academic librarian at some of the largest and smallest libraries in America, but her favorite is the continually growing library in her own home. Her novels have won the RITA and Christy Awards and have appeared on the CBA bestsellers list. She lives in Orlando, Florida, with her husband, who graciously tolerates her intimidating stockpile of books. Learn more online at elizabethcamden.com.

Sign Up for Elizabeth's Newsletter

Keep up to date with Elizabeth's news on book releases and events by signing up for her email list at elizabethcamden.com.

More from Elizabeth Camden

Natalia Blackstone relies on Count Dimitri Sokolov to oversee the construction of the Trans-Siberian Railway. Dimitri loses everything after witnessing a deadly tragedy and its cover-up, but he has an asset the czar knows nothing about: Natalia. Together they fight to save the railroad while exposing the truth, but can their love survive the ordeal?

Written on the Wind
THE BLACKSTONE LEGACY #2

You May Also Like . . .

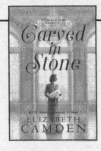

When lawyer Patrick O'Neill agrees to resurrect an old mystery and challenge the Blackstones' legacy of greed and corruption, he doesn't expect to be derailed by the kindhearted family heiress, Gwen Kellerman. She is tasked with getting him to drop the case, but when the mystery takes a shocking twist, he is the only ally she has.

Carved in Stone by Elizabeth Camden
THE BLACKSTONE LEGACY #1
elizabethcamden.com

Luke Delacroix's hidden past as a spy has him carrying out an ambitious agenda—thwarting the reelection of his only real enemy. But trouble begins when he falls for Marianne Magruder, the congressman's daughter. Can their newfound love survive a political firestorm, or will three generations of family rivalry drive them apart forever?

The Prince of Spies by Elizabeth Camden
HOPE AND GLORY #3
elizabethcamden.com

With a notorious forger preying on New York's high society, Metropolitan Museum of Art curator Lauren Westlake is just the expert needed to track down the criminal. As she and Detective Joe Caravello search for the truth, the closer they get to discovering the forger's identity, the more entangled they become in a web of deception and crime.

The Metropolitan Affair by Jocelyn Green
ON CENTRAL PARK #1
jocelyngreen.com

⬥ BETHANYHOUSE

More from Bethany House

During WWII, when special agent Sterling Bertrand is washed ashore at Evie Farrow's inn, her life is turned upside down. As Evie and Sterling work together to track down a German agent, they unravel mysteries that go back to WWI. The ripples from the past are still rocking their lives, and it seems yesterday's tides may sweep them into danger today.

Yesterday's Tides by Roseanna M. White
roseannamwhite.com

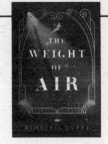

In 1911, Europe's strongest woman Mabel MacGinnis loses everything she's ever known and sets off for America in hopes of finding the mother she's just discovered is still alive. When circus aerialist Isabella Moreau's daughter suddenly appears, she is forced to face the truth of where, and in what, she derives her worth.

The Weight of Air by Kimberly Duffy
kimberlyduffy.com

When Mennonite woman Ivy Zimmerman's parents are killed in a tragic accident, her way of life is upended. As she grows suspicious that her parents' death wasn't an accident, she gains courage from her Amish great-grandmother's time in World War II Germany. With the inspiration of her great-grandmother, Ivy seeks justice for her parents, her sisters, and herself.

A Brighter Dawn by Leslie Gould
Amish Memories #1
lesliegould.com

BETHANYHOUSE